Faithfully Entangled
The Fallen Guardians Series:
Book 3

Written By:
E.F. Rose

Faithfully Entangled
The Fallen Guardians Series, Book 3

Written by E.F. Rose
www.facebook.com/DarkestRose13

ISBN: 978-0-9898906-7-0

Edited by: Kim Young

Cover Design by: Diana M. Photography
www.facebook.com/DianaMuniz.Photography

Warning

This book is intended for mature audiences only (18+). This book contains some explicit language, sexual content, and paranormal mischief

Dedication

This book is dedicated to everyone who has been waiting patiently, and sometimes not so patiently (hehe), for Nicky's book. I couldn't have gotten through this without all of your support.

Previously in The Fallen Guardians Series...

Hayley paced around the kitchen. The guys had been gone a couple hours, but ever since they left, she had felt an uneasiness growing within her.

At first, she had chalked it up to nerves. The thought of Manuel going out there after the incident in the Indigo parking lot had left her feeling ill. She'd been physically shaken after her encounter with the demons, drained from the effort she had used to keep them at bay. Then finding out the one who had come to her and Ella's rescue had been one of Manuel's brothers, one all the boys had thought was lost to them, had been an emotional blow.

So it wasn't too surprising that she wanted Manuel close. Wanted to be wrapped up in his strong arms as she attempted to wish away the day.

But he'd gone out. She understood his need to be with his brothers, to get answers concerning Dev and the demons at the bar, but the selfish side of her had wanted him to stay. Knowing that wouldn't happen, Hayley had tried the next best thing. She'd demanded to go with them. She knew she could help. At least that was what she told herself, even as the

voice in her head said she would end up being more of a distraction than anything.
    Shit.
    She hadn't even tried to do anything with her magic since the bar. If all she could do in this state was muster up a small gust of wind, she could end up getting Manuel or one of his brothers injured. So, yeah, she had put up a fight to go with them, but as soon as Ella said she would stay with her, realizing Nicholas would also stay behind, she had given in.
    It was after they had been gone a half-hour that the images of her dream started flashing through her mind. What was wrong with her? She had been so wrapped up in her own needs, she hadn't even stopped to think about what going out to hunt some demons could mean for them. She had warned them about the dream again, even sobbed as the emotions of the day and her fears for their future had collided. But she'd still let them go because, in the back of her mind, she hadn't really thought it could happen tonight. God, she was stupid. Even after she had realized her fears could be coming true, she'd still talked herself out of it. She would know if her dream were going to turn into reality tonight, right?
    So, trying to get it out of her head, Hayley had gone upstairs and taken a bath, hoping the soothing warm water and

relaxing bath oils would calm her nerves. However, it had been anything but relaxing. With each minute that passed, her mind kept drifting back to her dream. To the smell of the rain, the details of the fight, the feeling of helplessness.

It hadn't been long after that she found herself in the kitchen, Ella and Nicholas wandering in. Ella hadn't said a word, just walked over and sat down, watching her with worried eyes as she paced. Nicholas, for all his mixed feelings toward her, had tried to calm her down. He even fixed her a cup of tea in an attempt to get her to sit. That mug was all but forgotten on the counter, only a tiny bit gone before she had set it down to continue her pacing.

Now, almost an hour-and-a-half later, she found herself more anxious than ever. Rubbing her sweaty palms on her jeans, Hayley glanced over at the kitchen table where Ella and Nicholas sat.

Sighing, she stopped and turned to them. "Something's wrong," she stated with a shaky breath. "I can feel it."

"Hayley, I'm sure everything is fine. It hasn't been that long, and the guys will be home-" Nicholas started.

"No, Nicholas," Hayley said, walking up to the table. "Please. I... I know you don't think much of me, believing I made up the dream I had of Manuel to get

him to listen to me, but I didn't. It's real and it's happening now. I know it is. We need to do something."

Nicholas took a deep breath and stared at her, his red eyes flashing as he tapped his fingers on the table. Finally, he gave a sharp nod. "Okay, let's say that your dream, vision, whatever was real. Let's say that something is happening. What do we do? Do you have any idea where this fight is supposed to take place?"

Thinking hard, she shook her head. Tears of frustration threatened to fall as she looked between him and Ella. "All I know is it happens in an alley."

"Of course it's an alley," he mumbled.

"What?"

He waved one of his hands. "Nothing. Do you remember anything else?"

Glancing out one of the windows, she watched as the rain beat against it, drop after drop running down the glass until it disappeared from sight. "No. I just remember running in the rain through the streets and finding them in an alley. What if we can't find them?"

"We'll find them," Ella spoke up, her voice filled with confidence. "I have an idea."

Both Hayley and Nicholas looked at her. "What are you thinking?" he asked.

"Well, one of my powers is dowsing, the ability to find missing things, right?" At their nod, she continued. "What if, while she is focusing on her dream, I use Hayley as a focal point and see if I can find them?"

Hayley felt a spark of excitement as she thought about it. "That might just work. Hold on." Rushing out of the kitchen, she ran up to Manuel's room. Digging into her bag, she found her little black pouch tucked beneath her shirts. Reaching in, she felt the tingle in her fingertips as the object she was in need of answered her silent call. Pulling out the shiny black obsidian stone, she sent out a thank you. This was exactly what she needed.

Skipping steps as she ran back toward the kitchen, she entered to find Ella and Nicholas looking at her questioningly. "I got it."

"Got what?" Nicholas asked skeptically.

"It's an obsidian gemstone. It's used for many different things, from knife blades to jewelry. But..." She said with a smile, setting the stone in the center of the table, "it can also be used to help clear any unconscious blocks, sharpening internal and external vision." Seeing that they still seemed a bit confused, she rushed on. "I'm hoping that with the help of this stone, I'll be able to see details in my dream more clearly, helping Ella have a better focal

point." Pleased with herself, she sat down and faced Ella. "How do you want to do this?"

"Just try and relax," she instructed. Nodding, Hayley shifted slightly in her chair. Reaching out, she palmed the cool stone before closing her eyes. Taking a deep breath, she held it for a second, then let the air leave past her lips on a soft sigh. Within seconds, she was focused on her breathing, her anxiety settled. "Okay," she heard Ella say softly. "Now, try to bring up your dream. You said you were running through the street, right?"

"Yes. The street is wet from the rain. It's so quiet."

"What do you see?"

Hayley felt the slightest pressure on her hand as Ella reached out and grasped it. "I see...lots of buildings and parked cars."

As the dream rushed back to her, she found herself on the street, her shoes slapping against the pavement as she ran. Building after building flew by her. This time, unlike before, she focused on her senses. What she felt, smelled. It wasn't long before she found herself at the opening of an alley.

She heard yelling, the voices deep and angry. She knew what she would find if she went into the alley, just as she knew the outcome. Glancing around, she spotted *a street sign, its name obscured. Taking a deep breath, she reminded herself that she was back at the house, in the kitchen with Ella and Nicholas. She reminded herself that she needed to focus. Feeling a coldness in her hand, she looked down at it. Although she was in her dream, she knew that she was tightening her grip around the stone back at the house.*

"Help me to see," she whispered, instantly feeling the cold stone grow warm within her palm. The heat flew through her as she looked around. It was more than the stone, though. It was Ella, her power flowing through her as she glanced at the buildings. Even though she still couldn't make out the street sign, Hayley felt a sudden certainty that they would find them. The feeling washed through her as she gave a slight shudder, blinking until she focused on the kitchen table once again.

Looking up, she saw that Ella was now looking straight ahead, her eyes glowing white, her power whipping around her. Goosebumps rose across Hayley's arms as she tightened her fingers around Ella's hand. Please find them. *Her mind screamed for her to hurry, but she knew she needed to be patient. Ella would find them. She had to.*

Seeing movement out of the corner of her eye, she watched as Nicholas stood and made his way to Ella's side. Bracing one of his hands on the table, he leaned down. She saw a faint flash of light and tore her eyes from Ella, gasping in shock as a bolt of light streaked from beneath the sleeve of Nicholas' shirt, traveling quickly down his arm, then disappearing. Like lightning, *she thought in awe as her eyes flew up and found Nicholas staring at her. The red in his eyes wavered as a grayness flew through them.* Like a cloud in a storm.

With a slow blink, he looked away, focusing on Ella. "What do you see, Ella?" His voice, though quiet, held a faint growl.

"I see...," she started, pausing briefly as her head tilted to the side, "brick buildings. One has a large window... Maybe a salon? No. A barber shop with red lettering in the window."

"Crews," Nicholas said, standing up. "It's the only barber shop in town. Down on Central Avenue." He looked at Hayley. She watched the storm building in his eyes until none of the red could be seen. "It's on the corner with an alley leading behind the building."

They were there.

She knew it instantly, but before she could utter a word, Nicholas was on the move, his back rigid as he left the kitchen. Looking back at Ella, Hayley noticed her eyes were back to normal, a tired look upon her face. "Go with him," she said softly. "I'll be no good to you guys in this state." Ella reached up and gripped Hayley's arm. "I felt the darkness in that alley. Something horrible is happening there. You must hurry. Go. Find the boys and bring them home. Bring them all home."

She could see Ella's fear for Christian's safety in her eyes. Feel it in the air around them. Jumping from her seat, she gave Ella a quick hug. Yelling a promise to her that they would find them in time, she ran to find Nicholas.

Following the power rolling off him like a beacon, she found him in his room, extracting an intimidating black compound bow from a case. "I'm going with you and I don't want any argument about it," she blurted out, standing in the doorway.

He glanced up at her, slinging a case across his shoulder, arrows protruding from its top. "I figured you would," he said slowly. "After all, this is your show, princess."

"Right. Then...we should go." Glancing down the hall, she took a step away from the door. "I'll go grab my keys. Unless you want to drive." Looking back at Nicholas, she watched as his lips twitched into a small smile. "What?"

"We're not driving."

"We're not?"

"No." He shook his head. Walking toward her, he grabbed her arm and led her back downstairs and out the front door.

Feeling the cold rain hit her face, she looked up at Nicholas, unsure of what they were doing. "Well, if we're not going to drive, how do you suggest we get there?"

She watched as he took a step away from her, his eyes holding hers. "I know I have given you no reason to trust me. For that, I apologize."

"Nicholas, there's no need-"

"I'll make it up to you later, though. I promise." His face was serious as he watched her. "But I need you to trust me right now."

"Okay," she said immediately. Hayley had no reason not to trust him. No matter what he thought, she understood. She knew his reaction to her was from something he had dealt with, something in his past that had made him feel the way he did about witches. Sure, he had been a little short with her, kept himself at a distance, but at no time had she truly felt threatened. He had never made her feel like he would hurt her.

He seemed to look at her for a moment, deciding whether to believe her or not. Finally, he must have seen that she meant it because he gave her a quick nod.

Taking another small step back, she watched as his body tensed. With a growl, his shoulders curled forward as his back hunched. She was just about to ask what was wrong when a flash of light shot through the dark behind him. It was so bright, she closed her eyes, seeing spots begin to appear behind her eyelids.

"I hope you're not afraid of heights," she heard him say.

Blinking her eyes a few times, she felt her breath hitch. Never in her wildest dreams did she think she would see what she was seeing now. Sure, Manuel had told her he and his brothers were angels, but to have Nicholas standing before her now, his wings proudly spread out behind him, was something else. His wings were huge. The light from the house cast a faint glow upon them, lighting the edges so she could see the top of them towering high above his head, the bottom brushing the ground. They were black, but there was something more. Stepping closer, she smiled as she began to make out the red edges lining some of the feathers, like streaks done by a salon or brushstrokes done on a canvas.

Red, like his eyes, she mused, finally meeting his steady gaze.

Noticing his right hand stretched out to her, she reached out and grasped it. Nicholas immediately pulled her to him, wrapping his arm around her. "Now, hold on," he said calmly. "And do me a favor."

"What's that?" she asked, wrapping her arms tightly around him, barely holding back her gasp as he lifted into the air.

"When you tell Manuel how we got downtown, make sure I'm not in the room."

"Why is that?" she gasped, trying not to pay attention to how high they were or how fast they were flying. Her hair whipped around her, causing her to turn her face into his chest to keep it from stinging her eyes.

She felt his chest rumble with laughter before he answered. "Something tells me that when he finds out I held you to me and flew you across town, no matter how grateful he is, he's going to want my head." She joined in his laughter, knowing that he was probably right. "So let me get a head start before you let that cat out of the bag. Deal?"

"Deal," she laughed.

What felt like mere moments later, Nicholas set them down. She looked

*around, spotting a building with red
lettering less than a block away.
Wondering why he didn't get them closer,
she turned to ask him just as another flash
of light streaked through the air.*

*"You need to warn me when you're
going to do that," she grumbled, blinking
to try and get her eyes to readjust.*

"Sorry," he chuckled.

*"Why did you put us down here?"
she asked quietly, pushing her wet hair
behind her shoulders.*

*"Any closer and the demons might
have seen us coming," he said with a
shrug. "Now, stay behind me." With that,
Nicholas began to move down the street.
She noticed how he kept himself close to
the buildings, so she did the same, moving
behind him like his shadow until they came
to a brief stop by the edge of the barber
shop. She watched him peer around the
corner before turning to her. "Okay. It
looks like they're around the bend at the
end of the alley. Stay quiet as we make our
way down there. I want to see what's
going on before we rush into the fight."*

*Giving him a nod, she moved when
he did. The need to hurry rushed over her
with each step they took. She could hear
them now. Voices filled with anger, grunts
of pain, and the power... Oh god, the
power swirling around her was like*

nothing she had ever felt before. As they neared another corner, she braced herself.

She felt Nicholas reach back and rest his hand against her arm. With a quick shake of his head, Hayley knew that he wanted her to wait. Standing as still as she could, she noticed that the rain had stopped. The air was now cold, the moisture still clinging to the hairs on her arm making her shiver.

As time ticked by, she began to wonder what they were waiting for. It wasn't until the tingle of his power along her skin began to grow that she looked around in wonder, noticing a light fog had begun to build along the ground. It swirled around them, growing thicker as she watched. Looking up, she saw Nicholas watching her. Raising her eyebrow in a silent question, he winked at her, causing her to shake her head as he turned back.

She could feel some confusion in the air as the fog began to reach the ongoing fight. As a snarl echoed against the walls, she blinked, practically missing when Nicholas ran around the corner.

Moving quickly, she ran after him, coming to a sudden halt as she gazed at the fight before her. Nicholas had slammed into one of the two demons that had been trying to corner Christian. Jumping back just as quickly, Nicholas reached for one of his arrows and let it fly into the demon's chest. A screech from the creature was the only sound he made before he crumbled to the ground.

Christian, in the meantime, traded blows with another demon. His dagger glowed in his right hand as he twisted it around, his arm flying through the air in a sudden move, slicing right through the demon. Blood sprayed into the air as the demon fell into the fog, his form nothing but a shadow within the gray.

Darren battled yet another, his broadsword swinging low, just missing the demon as he jumped back. As he started to run at Darren, she watched as the angel threw his hand into the air, sending the demon crashing into the wall down the alley.

Her eyes darted around quickly, noting that there were at least three demons down, leaving the one Darren had just tossed and the other... Her eyes widened when she spotted Manuel facing off with a much larger demon, their movements slow as they stared at each other, moving around much like the fight within her dream.

"Castigo," she whispered. The sudden movement of Manuel's head swinging around to face her had Hayley covering her mouth.

His eyes glowed when they met hers. She could feel the anger and *confusion rolling off him. Then, just as she had feared, she saw the demon behind him lunge forward. Before she could scream, Castigo had knocked Manuel to the ground.*

"No!" she yelled, fear tightening her chest.

The two began to roll around beneath the fog. Moving closer, she could see Castigo snarling as he landed on top of Manuel, wrapping his hands around his neck. A darkness had begun to grow around Castigo then, its thickness slowly blocking out the boys behind him as his power intensified.

She could feel Manuel's power, too, but it was weaker. They had been fighting a long time, and with Castigo's grip around his throat, Manuel seemed to be losing steam. Hayley felt the ground shudder beneath her as Manuel attempted to call the Earth to him.

With a screech, she ran toward them, feeling tears burning her eyes as Castigo looked up at her, his silver gaze laughing as he pushed more of his power out around him. She stumbled as it hit her. Its darkness threatened to crush her, but she wouldn't stop. She would get to them, to Manuel, and prove her dream wrong. Hayley refused to believe that fate would put her on this path to find Manuel, to give her the man she loved, only to take him away. It wouldn't happen. She wouldn't allow it.

Calling on the light, the wind, and the air, she swirled her power around her, making Castigo's power shudder. "Give me strength to fight this evil," she whispered as she pushed forward. "Give me light to fight this darkness." She felt her skin warm, a glow beginning to work its way around her. A look of uncertainty filled Castigo's eyes as she got closer. "Give me power to save this life." Meeting Castigo's gaze, she pulled her power tight within her, mentally molding it into a ball of burning white light. Its heat warmed her as she stopped before them. Hearing Manuel's gasp, she watched as Castigo rose up, taking a step to the side as he growled at her.

Manuel will be okay, *she thought with relief.* They all will be.

"You are playing with fire, little girl," Castigo said, his voice growling through the building wind. Watching him take several more steps back, she smirked.

"That may be, demon," she responded, her own voice unrecognizable to her as she stepped up until she was standing protectively over Manuel. The darkness around Castigo had now dissipated, leaving him standing there in Nicholas' fog, a look of anger upon his face. "But, then again, I've never had a

problem with fire. In fact, it is you who should be worried about getting burned."

Swirling her power within her, she felt the demon begin to call his own once again. *Oh, I don't think so.* Smiling, she felt her skin start to tingle as the power within her sought release. *"And give me what I need to end this."* With those last words, she felt her body tense as the energy within her erupted. In a ball of white light, it spread out around her, burning through the demon's power as it lit up the alley. She heard Castigo's howl when her power slammed into him. Then, just as quickly as she sensed him, he was gone.

As the power around her began to dim, she knelt down beside Manuel, his eyes blinking against the brightness. *"Hey,"* she whispered, running her hand against his chest. The feel of his heart beating within him almost made her cry.

"Hey," he said back, his voice coming out rough as he pushed himself up. Bracing against his left hand, he reached up with his right, pulling her hand tightly to his chest. They stared at each other for a moment before movement around them drew their attention. She watched as Christian and Darren made their way over to them, gasping when she noticed Darren's cheek had been cut badly, the blood from it running down his face.

Seeing the worry in her eyes, he smiled. "I'll be fine," he said, absently wiping at the cut. "The little shit surprised me with a pocketknife. It'll be healed before we get home."

"Well, that's useful," she laughed, moving slightly as Manuel rose to his feet. He reached down and pulled her up, holding her snug against his side. "Where's Cyrus?" she asked, glancing at Christian.

"He took off right before we found the demons," he responded with a snarl. As she started to ask what happened, he raised his hand. "It's a long story. Something that would be better to get into later over a bottle of Crown."

With a smile, she nodded. She found there were certain topics that were better discussed over a strong drink, and she had a feeling anything having to do with Cyrus would definitely fall into that category. Looking up at Manuel, she blinked. "Sorry. I think Castigo got away."

"Yeah. He's kind of like a cockroach," Christian growled. "Don't worry, though. We'll get him one of these days."

"Maybe if we had gotten here sooner-" she started.

"As grateful as I am that you were here, you shouldn't have been," Manuel said with a huff. The others nodded their agreement.

"Yeah. That ball of light was no joke." Christian smirked.

Blushing slightly, Hayley just shook her head. "Thanks."

"Hey," Manuel said loudly, drawing all of their attention to him. "Where's Nicholas?"

"Nicholas!" Darren immediately called out.

"I thought he was over with Christian," Hayley said, looking around wildly.

"He was, but then he ran over to help Darren." Christian looked at Darren, who had already stepped away from them, concern building in the air around him.

"He did," Darren said, walking several steps away. "The demon I was fighting was trying to go after that gun." Glancing around, he looked up. "Nicholas!" he yelled again, his voice echoing through the alley.

"What gun?" Hayley asked in confusion.

"One of the demons was waving around a gun," Christian said absently.

Looking up at Manuel, she shook her head. "But... Can a gun even hurt you guys?"

"No. I mean, if we get shot, it'll hurt like hell, but that's about it," Manuel said, frowning. Looking from her to Darren, he *shook his head. "Which a demon would know."*

"True," Christian hummed. "But I don't think that was a normal gun. There must have been something special about it for the demons to have put so much faith in using it against us." Manuel and Darren both murmured their agreement as everyone got lost in their own thoughts.

Darren spun and looked at them, his eyes glowing. "In the midst of the fight, I thought I saw the demon get his hands on it. If I saw it, so did Nicholas."

"And if the demon took off to try and get away with that gun...," Christian started.

"Then Nicholas would have gone after him," Manuel finished with a growl.

"But," Hayley said, looking quickly between them. "Nicholas wouldn't have known that you guys thought there was something special with that gun. He showed up well after the fighting started."

"He would have noticed the way I reacted to seeing the demon grab it, though," Darren remarked, a look of unease crossing his face. "He would have known something was up."

"He would have gone after the demon regardless, but if he thinks that gun's important, he won't stop until he gets it back." Manuel sighed.

"Fuck!" Christian exclaimed.

Hayley watched as Darren walked past Christian and squeezed his shoulder, making his way over to the far wall. He skimmed his hand against the brick.

"Darren? What are you looking for?" Hayley asked, taking Manuel's hand in hers as they walked over to him.

"It should be...," Darren mumbled, his fingers searching over the cracked and chipped wall. He glanced over his shoulder, then back at the wall. He stepped back for a second, moved a few steps to the side, then walked back up to the wall. "If I were a stray bullet, where would I be?"

By now, Christian was standing at her other side as they watched Darren, his movements slow.

"Gotcha," he exclaimed. Reaching back, he wiggled his fingers. "Christian, let me see your dagger."

"What?" Christian asked. With a sideways glare from Darren, he shook his head and reached behind his back, pulling out his black dagger. The blade's edge glowed softly as he flipped it around in his hand, holding the hilt out to his brother.

"Thanks," he mumbled, putting the tip into a crack in the wall. With a little wiggling, Hayley watched a small piece of metal fall out, landing in his palm. Holding what remained of the bullet between his fingers, he raised it for them all to see. "This will tell us what was so special about the fucking gun."

"What do we do about Nicholas?" Hayley asked softly.

Darren looked at her, his dark blue eyes soft as he let his concern for his brother show through. "Right now, we head home. If he catches the demon, he'll show up there."

"And if he doesn't?" She hated to ask, prayed that he would be there waiting for them, but she needed to know the answer.

"If he doesn't..." Manuel paused, his fingers wrapping tightly around hers. Clearing his throat, he tried again. "If he doesn't, we go find him."

As Christian and Darren agreed, Hayley looked between them. A tightness in her chest began to grow as she thought about Nicholas. She saw the way they loved each other. Even when they were angry, the love radiated through them all.

They were truly a family, and she hoped nothing would happen to him. Looking up at the sky, she sent out a silent thank you for the help in saving Manuel, then a prayer that Nicholas would come home. This group needed to remain strong and whole, and that wouldn't happen without Nicholas by their side.

Chapter 1

Nicholas sensed the power rolling from the alley below him. It was an overpowering mix of his brothers as they warred with the demons, causing Nicholas' skin to pull tight from the pressure. The fight was already in full swing when he showed up with his brother's girlfriend, Hayley. She was a witch who, even put up against them, was definitely a powerhouse herself. Hell, he was sure a good portion of that power beating against his back as he flew above the rooftop radiated from her. He'd felt it the minute they'd burst around the corner, recognized the waves coming off her the second she'd seen Manuel.

Damn, he hoped they'd shown up in time. The knowledge she'd dreamed she'd arrived too late to save his brother sent a lick of fear down his spine.

He couldn't think about that now, though, and as much as he'd wanted to stay with his brothers, he'd seen the look that had flashed across Darren's face when the demon he'd been fighting took off with the gun.

Nicholas wasn't sure what about this particular gun had Darren looking so worried. Whatever it was, he knew it was bad. He'd just have to find out once he got it.

Moving quickly over the rooftops, he just barely kept the demon in sight. Thrusting his wings out behind him, he pushed himself to go faster.

The demon headed away from downtown, weaving through the alleys and empty streets at a pace that made Nicholas wonder if he'd been injured. Yet he moved just fast enough, dodging behind cars and dumpsters, giving Nicholas whiplash.

Fucking demons.

He needed to catch him before he got to the quiet suburbs that lay beyond the shops and bars. If the demon made it into the housing development, he could easily disappear. Nicholas couldn't let that happen.

Shoving his power out, he felt the wind around him begin to build. It curled around the edges of his feathers, giving an extra boost to each flap of his wings. Chuckling in satisfaction, he watched the demon ahead of him falter as the wind hit him. It slowed him down just enough that as the demon ran out into the street, mere steps away from the first group of houses, Nicholas was on him.

Calling the Shade, he collided into the back of the demon just as he felt the shiver run through the air when the Shade slammed to the ground. He hit the demon so hard, it felt like he'd run into a brick wall, the force sending them both tumbling across the wet pavement. The roughness of the ground bit into Nicholas' skin as they both rolled.

Finally coming to a stop near the center of the street, Nicholas released a groan as he shoved himself up. His muscles protesting, he pushed himself to move.

With a flash, his wings disappeared, causing the demon to look away as Nicholas was finally able to get to his feet.

Towering over him, Nicholas growled. "Where's the gun?"

"What gun?" At Nicholas' snarl, the demon smirked. Slowly getting to his feet, the demon kept his eyes fixed on him. "Oh, you mean this gun?" He laughed, his red eyes glowing as he pulled the gun from behind his back and held it at his side.

Reaching to his own back, Nicholas unhooked his bow from its clip. The weight of it in his hand comforted him as he tightened his grip. With a sharp flick of his wrist, the bow snapped open, its corners jetting out as the cable between them pulled tight. He felt his tattoo tingling in response to his growing agitation.

Seeming to find the whole situation amusing, the demon's smirk turned into a smile. "You want this gun, angel? Why not just come get it?" He raised the gun slightly, it's barrel now focused squarely on Nicholas' chest. "Or are you afraid?"

That's laughable.

There were many things in this world Nicholas felt uncertain or even uneasy about, but the possibility of losing his family was the only thing that would cause him to feel any true sense of fear. However, some demon? No. And he was especially not afraid of some two-bit demon with a little gun.

Pulling out one of his arrows, he watched from the corner of his eye as the cross etched into its head flared to life. "Yeah, I'm afraid of you like I'm afraid of the ice cream man," he snarled, leveling his bow at the demon's chest.

The air around them crackled as he widened his stance, turning ever so slightly as he prepared to take his shot. His fingers itched to release the arrow.

"Maybe you are not afraid of me. But this..." The demon waved the gun. "This you should be afraid of."

"Really? And why's that?"

The demon sighed dramatically. "Because this gun is special. Or, more specifically, the bullets within it are. Yes. These bullets are very special."

Nicholas frowned, glancing at the gun, then back at the demon. His mind ran through all the possibilities of what the demon's statement could mean. One thing he knew for sure was he needed to get the weapon away from him...now. He saw the demon's finger hover over the trigger, the gun steady. Nicholas needed to somehow get him to shift his aim. Last thing he needed was for it to go off while the business end was still pointed his way.

"You demons sure like to talk," he murmured, shifting slightly, the tip of his arrow now angled slightly to the side. If he could just-

A loud snarl ripping through the demon's throat was the only warning Nicholas had before the deafening sound of a gunshot echoed around them. A searing pain in his left side barely registered in his mind as he aimed at the demon's chest again. With a swift twitch of his fingertips, he released his arrow, hearing the demon howl in pain as it sliced through his skin, burying within the bastard's chest.

Quickly, Nicholas had another arrow lined up and aimed at the demon's head. He felt the pain in his side slowly spread through him, causing his aim to waver slightly. "What are the bullets made of?" he ground out, stepping closer to the downed figure. Spotting the gun lying next to the demon, he swiftly kicked it a few feet away.

"It is too late for you, Guardian," the demon laughed. The blood coating his teeth and mouth was more visible as he smiled up at him.

"What are you talking about? What are the fucking bullets made of?"

The demon tried to laugh again, coughing as his lungs filled with blood. "Stupid angel. Those bullets are made from the melted steel of one of Andras' cursed daggers."

Feeling his blood run cold, Nicholas sent a quick glance to the gun, then back to the demon. *Fuck.* He'd really hoped the dagger he'd taken from Castigo had been the only one.

He felt the wound throb. The bullet hadn't gone completely through. He could sense it twisting and burning within him as he shifted. If the cold sweat starting to coat his skin was any sign, he didn't have a lot of time left before he passed out.

Deciding to end the demon and send him to the Nether Realms while he still could, Nicholas pulled in a steadying breath through his teeth.

The demon, who started coughing and spitting blood onto the street, stared up at him. His eyes filled with humor as he watched the different emotions cross Nicholas' face.

Seeing the look in his eyes only made Nicholas' anger intensify.

The pain from his wound traveled up his back and down his left leg. It was getting to the point that he could hardly put weight on it. Grinding his teeth, he felt sweat running down his body as he pulled back the arrow. The muscles in his arms quivered under the tension.

"You don't look so good, Guardian." The demon tried to laugh in between ragged coughs. "My, my, my..." *Cough.* "That bullet sure is working fast." *Cough.* "Maybe you should go lie down." *Cough.* "Because, by the looks of it..." *Cough.* "I don't think you have much longer." *Cough, cough, cough.*

"Yeah, well, I still look better than you." Before the demon could come back with a snarky remark, Nicholas released the arrow. The demon's head slammed back onto the ground, the arrow embedded between his eyes. Taking a painful breath, Nicholas collapsed his bow and clipped it onto his back with agonizing slowness. "And you still talk too much."

Feeling a wave of dizziness, Nicholas gave his head a quick shake.

Almost done.

Leaning over the prone body, he felt his power tingle through him as he softly spoke the words that would send the demon's oily soul on a one-way ticket to the Nether Realms.

As the body smoked and slowly dissolved into the ground, Nicholas reached down to grab his two arrows, as well as the gun, which he tucked into the back waistband of his pants. He felt a wave a dizziness as his mind began to fog. It was an odd sensation. He stumbled away from the smoking tar, which was all that was left of the demon. The Shade fell down around him as the last hint of smoke evaporated.

The pain racing through his body doubled as he stumbled off the street. "Fuck," he groaned. Reaching into his pocket, he discovered his phone was missing.

No, no, no.

He continued to search through his pockets as he stumbled over a curb, barely keeping his balance. He felt the muscles in his side cramp as his body attempted to fight the effects of the bullet. His vision becoming worse by the minute, Nicholas shuffled his feet and shook his head, trying to clear his muddled mind.

He needed his brothers. Needed to call out to them, let them know he needed help. But without his phone or any way of getting home, he felt his despair beginning to consume him.

This feeling, along with the pain, only intensified as the adrenaline began to wear off.

Suddenly stumbling up against a fence, he leaned heavily upon it. Using its sturdy frame, he forced himself to continue moving. He didn't know how long he walked, his hands traveling blindly over wood fences and prickly shrubs. The need to get off the street warred with his need to lay down. God, the pain was excruciating, but he felt his body beginning to go numb. Shock maybe? He didn't know. All Nicholas did know was he couldn't feel his power anymore, and with every second that passed, he practically sensed himself fading.

He was going to die, he was sure of that, but what hurt him most was his brothers would never know. Never know how much they meant to him, how much he loved them. And Manuel would never know how sorry he was about the way he'd been acting. The fact that one of them thought he didn't trust his judgment, didn't care about his happiness, caused his heart to clench in despair.

If only he could call out to them.

Not realizing he had come to a partially open gate, he fell through it, landing on his knees painfully. Groaning, he rolled onto his back, ignoring the pinch of his bow biting into him, and pushed the gate closed with his foot. The cool cement beneath him made him shudder as the cold seeped through his clothes.

Nicholas couldn't remember the last time he'd been so cold.

With great effort, he turned over, crawling down the side of the house and around the corner. The scent of flowers and wet grass caressed his senses as he pulled himself onto the back porch and rolled onto his back. His vision blurry, he watched as a soft light began to build in the sky. The rays from the rising sun caused the edges of the remaining clouds from last night's storm to glow.

Shit, as beautiful as this sight is, I can't die like this. Lying on the ground in some stranger's back yard. There has to be a way, something I can do.

Sending out his mental thoughts, he prayed for a miracle. Blinking rapidly, he tried to think of a way to get out of this mess, but the more he did, the more sluggish his mind became. He tried to move, finding himself too weak.

"No," he mumbled.

"Oh, my god."

A soft gasp reached his ears as he struggled to keep his eyes open. A light touch to his face and hands caused his body to hum as he fought to stay awake.

"Oh god. I need... You need a doctor. I'll call for help. Just hold on."

"No," Nicholas groaned. "No hospitals... Please... I just need..." His voice was barely above a whisper.

"But," the soft, feminine voice started. Slight air flowing across his face told Nicholas that the mystery woman leaned over him. The scent of lavender curled around him, causing his tense muscles to immediately relax. "If I don't

take you to the hospital, you could…
There's so much blood."

"I-I need…," he tried again as his mind filled with more darkness. He needed her to help him. She was his only chance at survival. If he could get her to trust him, he knew he'd be okay. She was the answer to his prayers, but he needed to talk to her, tell her that he needed her help. If only…

"What? What do you need?" Her muffled voice broke through his muddled thoughts. It almost sounded like he was under water.

"The bullet…," Nicholas forced out in a rush. "I need you to remove the bullet… Please…" Just as the last word left his lips, the world around him went black.

Chapter 2

Amy watched as the stranger's body went limp. Her surprise at finding him in her back yard had been quickly smothered by her sudden need to help him. But what could she do? There was so much blood. It pooled beneath him, spreading toward her as she knelt on the ground.

No hospitals... Please...

His plea echoed through her mind as she desperately felt for a pulse beneath his cooling skin. Finding one, although faint, caused the pressure within her chest to loosen. Amy wasn't sure what it was about this man, but as soon as she saw him, she felt an instant connection.

And his eyes... Those amazing, deep red eyes had taken her breath away. They should have startled her, their unnatural glow giving her pause, but all she saw in them was warmth. Yes, she had seen pain, even a small amount of fear flashing through their depths, but they also held trust. For some reason, this gorgeous stranger trusted her.

But how could she help him?

Looking over his body, it didn't take long for her to realize there was no way she'd be able to wrestle him into the house.

At least not yet. She needed to stop the bleeding first.

Reaching down to his blood-soaked shirt, she pulled it up and gasped.

The wound was jagged and looked angry. Blood flowed from its opening, streaming down his side to the ever-growing puddle beneath him.

Yet that wasn't what had her gasping in horror.

She had seen horrible injuries before. Growing up with a father who, even on his best day, was accident prone subjected her to a wide variety of memorable wounds. What she saw now was different.

Spreading from the ragged edges of the wound was a spider web of black lines. These vein-like lines completely covered his lower torso and had started climbing up his chest. Blinking, it took Amy a moment to process the fact that the lines were moving. She wasn't sure what they were, but the sight of them getting closer to his heart had her running into the house.

I need tweezers...towels...a knife...

Her mind frantically listed off everything she'd seen people on TV use when extracting a bullet. Was she a doctor? Nope. She was a blogger, book reviewer extraordinaire, and this was so far out of her comfort zone, it wasn't even funny.

"Aha!" She pulled her favorite tweezers from her bathroom drawer and sprinted out to the kitchen, grabbing a knife.

Knife and tweezers in hand, as well as an armful of towels she had snatched from the linen closet and the sewing kit her mom had pushed on her - *Every woman needs to have a sewing kit* - Amy threw open the door to find her patient still lying on her concrete porch, his breathing shallow.

Kneeling beside him, Amy dumped her supplies onto the ground and took a deep breath. "Okay, I don't know who you are, but I'm going to do the best I can to save you." She thanked her lucky stars that the sun had risen enough to give her light. With knife in hand, she took a deep breath and got to work.

Though her mind tried to make her doubt herself, she pushed it back. She could do this. She had to. There was something about this man that awakened her nerves, something no other guy had been able to do. Not that there had been many. But the lack of connection with any of her past boyfriends was definitely the leading cause to her still very intact virginity. It wasn't as if she were holding out for marriage or for *the one*. It was the fact none of them had done it for her. None of them had given Amy that I-gotta-have-him feeling. She figured she'd never experience that sensation...until she had looked into the mysterious, pain-filled eyes of this stranger.

One look at this gorgeous male lying unconscious on her pack porch, sweating profusely, had made her want to shimmy out of her clothes. Of course, now really wasn't the time for that, but the idea had definitely been there.

Making as even a cut through the wound as she could, Amy paused, her tweezers hovering as she attempted to calm her racing heart. She could do this. She leaned closer, then pulled back several times before releasing a rush of air. The black lines were spreading quickly, and she didn't have time to continue second-guessing herself. *I can do this.* With renewed determination, Amy slipped the tweezers in and began to feel around.

Please, let me find the bullet without causing more damage.

Even in the cold morning air, she felt her body heating up, sweat beading across her forehead. With a steady hand, she continued to feel around, pausing when she felt the tip of the tweezers touch something hard.

Pulling her bottom lip between her teeth, Amy prayed she was grasping the bullet. Her pulse increased as she watched the oily black lines zigzagging beneath his skin.

"Come on," she ground out. Puffs of breath left her lips as she inhaled and exhaled cold air in quick gasps. After what felt like hours, but was probably mere seconds, her tweezers grasped the hardened item. She took a deep breath and began to slowly pull her hand back. With a steadiness that would make top surgeons jealous, she released the breath she'd been holding as the tip came into view...a shiny, blood-covered bullet secure in their grasp.

"Who said TV wasn't educational?" Amy laughed, placing the offending object on the ground next to her.

Wiping away the blood on his side, she quickly threaded a needle and got to work stitching the wound. While she did, she stared in awe. The black lines that had been making their way up his body started to recede as she sewed up his tattered flesh. Which, if she were being honest with herself, already looked less...woundy.

Huh, was woundy even a word? Well, I'm still running with it.

Finished stitching, she tied a quick knot and cut the thread.

Ten points for accuracy and precision, she thought with a smirk as she looked over her handiwork.

With a sigh of relief and a mental pat on the back for a job well done, she once again looked over the stranger's body. His skin was already beginning to look healthier, his wound losing the redness around it.

Amazing, she thought as she ran her hands over his side, finding his skin warming beneath her touch.

"Now, I need to figure out how to get you inside," Amy murmured, eyeing her back door, which still stood wide open. Shaking her head, she eyed her cat's orange head as he peered out at her. "Any suggestions?" she asked Charlie. He just looked at her curiously, offering no helpful insight, obviously anxious to see what she came up with. With a huff, Amy smirked. "Didn't think so."

Looking back down at the stranger, She sighed. She really didn't want to drag him in. Not having an overabundance of upper body strength, the thought of pulling this massive male across the ground had her frowning. Mind racing, Amy contemplated making some sort of a gurney or stretcher. She just needed some wood or metal poles, a tarp or thick blanket, and rope. Glancing through her door, she sighed. All she had was a blanket.

"Looks like I'm going to have to drag you."

Stepping up to his head, she reached down and grasped under his arms. That was a task in and of itself, seeing as his shoulders were so much wider than hers. With a grunt, she straightened her legs and lifted his upper body off the ground, instantly falling backwards.

"Geez. What do you do? Lift weights for a living?" That must be it. He must be a bodybuilder on steroids. She was happy to see no veins raised along his arms, and he had a neck. So, if that were his profession, he didn't seem to be too far involved with it. "Not that there's anything wrong with being a bodybuilder," she huffed out. She didn't want him to unconsciously hear her and think she was already judging him.

She took a deep breath and grasped his body again. Using all her strength, she moved him across the ground slowly, stopping when she heard the scraping of metal on concrete. "What in the world?"

Leaning down slightly, she saw the end of some metal contraption hanging from his back, along with what looked like a thin case. He had been lying partially on her porch and partially in the grass, so she thought the slight bend of his body was from that. She realized he had several things slung across his back. Looking at his chest, she noted the thin, yet sturdy leather strap running across it. In her rush to save his life, she must have missed that.

Point deducted for lack of observation, she mused.

"Hope whatever that is on your back can handle some rough terrain," she mumbled as she once again began the effort to pull him into her house. The metal object screamed at her the entire way. Her arms had begun to shake by the time she stepped through her doorway.

Must be how those musclemen on TV feel flipping those ridiculously large tires.

As much as watching those types of sports had always fascinated her, Amy now had a newfound respect for what they went through.

With a lot of huffing and puffing, she finally pulled the stranger through her back door. She glanced over her shoulder at the long hallway, a quizzical Charlie standing there, that led to one of her two spare rooms. Yes, she was a single woman in a house made for a family. Mostly thanks to her mom, who insisted she have plenty of room to grow. *Just in case the need for more room arises.* Right now, as much as she would love to get Mr. Hot and Hunky into one of those rooms, the thought of dragging him that far left her feeling less than inspired.

Looking to her left, she saw the couch, her favorite place in the whole house and where she did her blogging. With a mental nod, Amy began to pull the unconscious man toward the couch. Each successful step was followed by a silent *yippee* for not falling. If she fell and he landed on top of her, she may never get out.

Not that the thought of him lying on her was a bad thing, but she would like him to be conscious when it happened.

When? she thought with a laugh. She, Miss Never Wanted A Physical Connection With A Man, was already making plans with this stranger. *I don't even know his name?*

With a loud sigh of relief, grateful that she'd fallen asleep on the couch the previous night so there was a blanket to lay him down on, she heaved the man's upper body onto the couch, taking care to support him as she moved to lift his legs up, as well.

Arching her back to relieve the strain, she felt a warmth of satisfaction run through her as she looked down at him. *Take that mean gym dude who said I lacked any upper body strength,* she thought with a smirk.

Eyeing the leather strap, she noted his body was again bent at an uncomfortable angle from whatever was strapped to his back. She really needed to take that off so he'd be more comfortable. Kneeling, she ran her fingers over the soft leather. Moving his left arm, she found the buckle of the strap. With a little effort, and some more lip chewing, Amy finally felt the leather release and slide off his chest.

Grunting, she rolled him partially to his side. Using her shoulder, she held him up as she pulled the case and metal contraption free from his body. Placing them on the floor, Amy eased the man back down, moving his left arm so it now lay comfortably across his chest. Her eyes absently took note of the tattoo along his arm, disappearing beneath his sleeve. She trailed her fingers over it, yanking her hand back when a spark jumped from his skin to hers.

Must be from dragging him across the carpet.

Knowing that he was inside and no longer in danger of dying, she hoped, Amy leaned back on her heels and let her eyes wander from his deliciously tattooed arm to his face. Smiling, she eyed his dark, shaggy hair. It wasn't long enough to reach his shoulders, but it curled around his head just the same. The soft look of it was too enticing. Before she knew it, she reached out and ran her fingers along the edge of his face, moving the soft wisps of hair off it. His face looked strong, but not sharp or angled. Just strong enough that, even in sleep, he looked manly.

Then there were his lips. Full and firm, Amy was sure he could pull off a good pout if he wanted to. *Trouble*, she smirked. To her, his bottom lip was especially nibbleable. An image of those lips descending on her own had Amy's breath hitching. Allowing her eyes to linger on them a moment longer, she shook her head.

Her eyes traveled down his neck to his chest, watching as it rose and fell with each breath. There was a calmness that overtook her as she watched him. Amy felt a slight flutter of annoyance at having the rest of his body hidden from view by his clothing. The idea of ripping the shirt away from him to reveal what she could only guess was a well-toned body made her fingers tingle.

After an inner battle with her suddenly awake sexual side, Amy decided stripping the unconscious man down so she could see him, all of him, was probably not the best idea. If she did, what would she say when he woke up?

Hey, glad I was able to save your life. By the way, sorry about your clothes. I needed to take them off to make sure you were okay. Couldn't help but notice you must work out. We should exercise together...in my bed.

Yeah, that just didn't seem like the kind of conversation she wanted to have. His boots, though... She could take those off him. Not only for his comfort, but, well...they were on her couch. Making quick work of the laces, she braced her feet and yanked the bulky boots off with a grunt. Each one had to weigh at least five pounds.

Walking over, Amy set them by the back door, their soles hardly making a sound as they hit the floor. With only a passing thought of how right they looked sitting there, she walked down the hall to get another blanket. It wasn't cold in her house. Even with the back door open while she was outside, her furnace had kept the temperature inside at a steady seventy-five. Still, he'd just been on the brink of death. She wouldn't be wrong in making sure he didn't get chilled, right?

Covering him up with the blanket she had since high school, Amy looked at him for a moment longer. Questions of who he was and where he came from swam through her mind. All questions that would have to wait until he woke up. Which could be moments or days. Either way, she planned to keep him as comfortable as possible until then.

Seeing the glint of metal out of the corner of her eye, Amy looked over at the man's leather case and metal contraption on the floor.

Leaning down to pick up the items, Amy puzzled over them as she made her way into the kitchen. The leather case was long and cylindrical with a cap at one end. Placing it on the table, she glanced between it and the metal item in her hand. There was something familiar about it, but it looked off. Like it was broken or...folded up maybe?

With a little fidgeting, she released it from the leather strap and held it out before her. It was heavy. At least to her. She imagined her mystery man could probably hold it up with little to no problem. Turning it over, twisting it around, Amy couldn't make sense of what she was seeing. The more she looked at it, though, the more it definitely looked folded up. Like maybe it had collapsed in on itself.

As she started to set it down, she felt her grip loosen. Moving quickly to grab it in the hopes of not having to explain how she had broken his...whatever it was, she grasped it just before it hit the table. The sudden movement must have triggered something because the next thing she knew, the contraption bounced in her hand and sprang out into a huge bow.

Releasing a very unladylike squeak, Amy quickly set it on the table and took a step back, almost as if she thought it would jump at her.

She'd seen compound bows when she watched *The Walking Dead*. This one seemed larger, more intimidating. As she walked around her table, eyeing it, she looked over at the cylindrical case. Its length started to make more sense.

Reaching over and pulling the cap off, she was not surprised to find the case filled with multiple arrows, their ends lined with black feathers. As she slowly removed one of them, she noted how the thin metal was cool to the touch. It felt like it vibrated in her hand, which she wrote off as it just sliding against the others, the silver gleam of the arrowhead catching the soft morning light filtering through her shades.

With a sigh, she stared at the weapon on the table. It looked extremely deadly and not just for show. Yet it was almost beautiful in its deadliness.

Holding the arrow up to the light, she could almost swear she saw it shake and vibrate, yet her hand was absolutely still. Just as that observation crossed her mind, Amy felt a sudden warmth spread through her. It traveled up her body, down her arm, and into her hand. Seeming to increase, the vibration became a low hum she could actually hear. It was as if a switch had been flipped on and the arrow was coming to life in her hands.

As her breath caught in her throat, Amy watched as a cross etched within the center of the arrowhead began to glow. *This isn't possible.* She couldn't look away as details in the golden cross became more distinct. She'd seen that cross before...but where?

With a shake of her head, she quickly, yet gently, set the arrow down on the table. The glow instantly dimmed and the cross faded.

Amy stared at the man lying on her couch. The questions she had now numbered in the hundreds, perhaps thousands.

Mr. Yummy definitely has some explaining to do.

Chapter 3

"This is starting to become a recurring problem where you are concerned." Andras stepped around the desk in Dev's office, his fingers trailing along the smooth wooden surface. Castigo's eyes followed the demon, his breath frozen in his lungs from the fear coursing through his veins. "I had really hoped your last incident would have taught you a lesson, made you more careful."

"I *was* careful, Andras," Castigo spoke slowly. "Pret and the others wanted to go downtown to look for souls. I told them we should stay on the outskirts, that there was less chance of us running into the Guardians, but Pret did not want to hear it. He showed me the gun you gave him. Said the Guardians would not be a problem and he hoped we saw them." His voice lowered as the final words left his mouth. He could tell Andras wasn't happy, and he knew it didn't matter what he told him.

Andras walked up to him. Castigo felt the demon's power simmering just under the surface, a low growl rumbling through the air. "And who has my gun now?"

Clearing his throat, Castigo glanced down. "The last time I saw it, Pret had grabbed it off the ground and ran from the fight. Maybe he got away."

"I would say that is pretty unlikely," Agalon growled from where he leaned against the wall.

"Why is that unlikely?" Castigo hissed, still keeping his eyes on the floor, respectably. He knew he shouldn't question Andras' second, but dammit, the demon really pissed him off sometimes. Agalon always had it out for him. For as long as he could remember, the demon had tried to make him look bad. *Not that I needed any help with that lately*, Castigo mentally growled. With how his luck had been running, he might as well just tell Andras to end him now. Even as the thought crossed his mind, Castigo recoiled from it. That wasn't an option.

"Because," Agalon said, stepping away from the wall and moving closer to Castigo. "If he *had*, he would have immediately contacted us, like a good little soldier. Not that you would know anything about being a good soldier, Castigo. Maybe you need a little reminder."

Castigo felt the demon's power roll across him aggressively. Unlike Andras, who didn't have to follow his threats with a show of power, Agalon seemed to feel the need to throw his around like a personal calling card. Tensing his muscles in order to stop himself from buckling beneath the pressure, he felt his jaw twitch.

"Well?" Agalon asked. His breath hot against Castigo's face as he leaned into him.

"I came here like a good soldier, didn't I?" he growled, titling his head away from him.

"Yeah, after you saved yourself, losing Andras' gun in the process."

"Like I said, I did not-"

"Enough," Andras snapped, making Castigo flinch. "I am not in the mood to listen to you two bicker. Now, Castigo, where do you think my gun is?"

Castigo's mind raced back to last night. Pret being a little ass, the Guardians showing up, then that feisty, extremely dangerous witch of theirs popping up out of nowhere. He hadn't seen that coming, but now that he thought about it, he wasn't entirely surprised. The rush of power that had flown off the little minx had definitely caught him off guard, though.

Man, what a fight it'd been. Just thinking about it made him want to break out into a huge grin, stopping himself when the heaviness in the air quickly reminded him of where he was. As far as Andras' question went, he had no idea where the fucking gun was. Castigo figured one of the Guardian's had it by now...hopefully after prying it out of Pret's cold, dead hands. He couldn't very well tell Andras that, though, especially not with his guard dog literally breathing down his neck.

Fucking Agalon!

If he could figure out a way to get that demon out of the picture, maybe he'd be able to finally get some power, some respect. The more Castigo thought about that, the more he wasn't sure he wanted anything else from Andras or the other demons in this fucked-up group. With a mental sigh, he suddenly felt tired. The time he spent just snooping around the town on his own, even his run-in with that human homeowner, had been the highlight of his miserable existence for the last... Shit, who knew how long. Though getting Braktis out of the way, and hopefully Pret, sure came in at a close second. Unfortunately, all his high moments always seemed to be followed by a confrontation with his boss and his boss' second.

Feeling the air around him start to thicken with Andras' impatience, Castigo shifted his feet. He didn't know what to tell him. Nothing that came to mind ended with him walking out of here without any loss of blood. Memories of the last time, when Agalon needed to drag him away after Andras had shown his displeasure about the loss of his sword, echoed through his mind. A cold chill slithered down his spine. What he wouldn't give to get out of having to go through that again. Or something worse.

"Well?"

Andras' voice hissed through the quiet office. Castigo swallowed roughly as he frantically thought of something to say. But nothing came to mind. Nothing at all. Just as he was about to accept defeat and let Andras take out his anger on him, there was a soft knock on the door.

Castigo felt Andras and Agalon shift as they looked toward the door. Agalon growled low as he strode over and opened it. "Now is not a good time, Dev."

At hearing the fallen angel's name, Castigo held his breath.

"I understand, but..." Even though Dev's voice was steady, Castigo felt the light tremor in the air from the angel's unease. "There is a Mr. Brighton here to see Andras. He said it was important."

"Well, tell him he will just have to-"

"No," Andras cut him off. "I will see him." He leaned closer to Castigo, his voice dropping to a harsh whisper. "We are not done here. You *will* find my weapons, just as you promised you would the last time, but this time, Castigo, there will be no more chances should you fail me again."

Without waiting for a response, Andras turned on his heel and walked out of the office, Agalon trailing not far behind.

As the pressure in the air eased, Castigo took a deep breath. He felt his heartbeat begin to slow and his muscles relax. He had been given a reprieve from Andras' anger. Even if it was only a temporary one, he would take it. It wasn't until he felt his tattered nerves start to calm that he realized he wasn't alone.

Glancing up, he saw Dev standing by the door. The angel leaned against the wall, watching him closely. His bright blue eyes flashed with both understanding at what Castigo was feeling and uncertainty the angel always had when they were around each other. Castigo couldn't blame him for that. Their last encounter, which Andras had demanded, had not ended well for Dev. Although Castigo didn't feel bad for what he'd said or the way he'd treated the angel...he needed to get his point across at how dangerous it would be for him to go up against Andras...he felt a certain level of kinship with him. A kinship he would quickly deny if ever asked about it

Looking at the angel now, he shook his head and sighed. "What do you want, Dev."

"Rough night?"

Castigo rolled his eyes as he sat down heavily on the couch. "What do you care?"

"I don't." At Castigo's raised eyebrow, Dev shook his head. "I felt

Andras' anger out in the bar. Figured you must have had a really bad night to piss him off that much."

"You could say that," he growled.

Eyeing the angel, Castigo felt his anger rise over the way he always got treated by Andras and even Agalon. He was just tired of it. After every decision he made, those two just laid into him. He felt like he couldn't do anything right and, dammit, he was fucking tired of it. The worst part? He couldn't even blame all his troubles on the Guardians. That really pissed him off. He felt the unease rolling off Dev as he remained leaning against the wall.

"Your brothers really know how to put a wrench in Andras' plans."

He smirked as Dev's whole body tensed. His eyes took on a light glow, his power rolling through the air briefly before he pulled it back. *Interesting*. Castigo knew Dev was a power to be reckoned with, but he'd figured Andras had bled it out of him by now. Seemed the angel was just really good at keeping that side of him under control. At least he *had* been...

"What do you mean?" Dev's voice came out low, the barely controlled anger evident in every word.

"Every time Andras sends one of his fancy weapons out into the world, your brothers have a habit of showing up and taking it. I believe they took the one Pret had last night."

"Weapons?"

Castigo just smiled. "Do not worry about that. As I said, your brothers now have them."

"Are there more?"

"That, I don't know." Castigo shook his head. "You're not really in a position to do anything about it if there are, though, are you?" He watched Dev take a deep breath.

Neither wavered as they stared at each other, seemingly trying to figure out the other as they let the silence stretch between them. Castigo could practically see Dev's wheels spinning. He seemed to be waging a silent battle with himself, his emotions coming off him in waves. Castigo wasn't sure what the angel was thinking, what inner battle he struggled with, but he could practically feel the minute he reached a decision.

Dev took a step farther into the room, his eyes trained on Castigo as he moved. "You're right, Castigo. I wouldn't be able to do anything about what Andras may have planned, what weapons he may have stashed away somewhere."

Castigo remained silent as Dev moved closer. The angel's body tensed more and more with every step. He didn't know where Dev was going with this, but he suddenly had a feeling he didn't want to hear it. Judging by the look on Dev's face, he was going to hear it anyway.

"What are you getting at, Dev?" he growled softly.

"Just that you're right. I mean, even if I found out there is another weapon out there that Andras could use against my brothers, I'm not in a position to do anything." Dev stopped a few steps away, his power pulsing as his eyes seemed to plead with him. Their depths searched his face for a sign that he could trust him. In that moment, his anger toward Andras and Agalon still simmering, he suddenly wanted to know what the angel was thinking. Holding himself still, he watched Dev nod, letting out a soft breath. "But, Castigo, you are."

A smirk started to slowly lift the edges of Castigo's lips. He could practically taste his freedom from under Andras' thumb, from Agalon's constant threats, from this sinking ship. And he knew it would sink if the Guardians continued their fight against Andras. But if he could put a wrench into his boss' plans, the destruction of his little group happening that much faster, he could be free of it all. Hell, he was starting to get bored anyway.

Seeing Dev's eyebrow lift slightly, he couldn't help but release a dark chuckle. Oh yes, this was going to be fun.

Chapter 4

The first thought Nicholas had as his mind began to wake was that his whole body felt like it had been hit by a semi. His second thought... He was freaking starving. When he forced his eyes open, pain flashed behind them and pulsed through his head, making him slam his eyelids closed.

What the hell?

Reaching up, he squeezed the bridge of his nose. Damn, he hadn't had a headache this bad in months. Not since Ella had been practicing controlling her powers and had sent him flying through the door to the garage, head first into the wall.

This felt worse. The pounding behind his eyes made his cheek twitch.

Yeah, this is much worse.

Keeping his eyes closed, he let out a sigh when he felt the pain start to subside. Once it receded enough that Nicholas could breathe, he slowly reopened his eyes...staring at a very unfamiliar cream-colored ceiling. Allowing his gaze to wander, he followed the ceiling until he came to the wall farthest from where he lay. The blinds covering the window allowed soft light into the room, its glow giving off a faint purple hue as it filtered through some sheer purple curtains.

Which were obviously more for decoration than to keep out the light.

He took in the rest of the room around him. With nothing strange standing out and no sense of unease, Nicholas used his arms to push himself up, only to stop when he felt something behind him. Glancing over his shoulder, he was surprised to find a large tabby, staring intently at him, perched on the arm of the couch.

"And I thought Holly was a big cat," he mumbled as he stared into the green eyes. The feline gazed, unblinkingly, back at him. His head tilted slightly to the side, as if trying to figure out how this stranger had landed on his couch. It was a question Nicholas also pondered. He couldn't remember how he had ended up in some stranger's house...let alone on their couch.

Thinking back, he remembered he and Hayley showing up near the alley where his brothers were fighting some demons. As he rushed in to help them, he spotted the one who had been fighting Darren grab a gun off the ground. Nicholas remembered chasing after the demon, confronting him in the street, and ultimately killing him.

Images of the gun flashed through his mind and he blinked rapidly. A fleeting sense of pain skittered across his brain as he was suddenly taken back to the sound of the gun going off, the feeling of the bullet ripping into his side.

Reaching down, Nicholas ran his fingers under the hem of his shirt. He frowned as he touched some thread sticking out of his skin. Twisting his head so he could see, he pulled up his ripped shirt to inspect his side.

"Huh," he breathed out, pulling gently at the thread. His skin, which was only slightly pink and swollen, lifted at the tug. "Going to have to cut the string out," he mumbled absently as he pulled his shirt back down. Grimacing at the material's stiffness from the dried blood, he sighed. "Going to need a new shirt, too." Pushing his arms against the cushion beneath him, Nicholas forced himself into a sitting position, stifling a groan as his muscles protested.

How long have I been lying here?

Reaching tentatively behind his back, Nicholas found the demon's gun still secure in his waistband. *That would account for this excruciating pain in my lower back*, he thought with a groan. While he was relieved the gun was still there, he did notice that his bow and arrows were not.

Glancing around, he absently noted the orange tabby still staring at him as he scanned the rest of the room. Noticing his bow and arrows lying on the table in the kitchen, Nicholas felt a sudden sense of unease. But surely, whoever had brought him into the house didn't mean him any harm. Not that he was easy to hurt, but he'd been out cold. If they wanted to hurt him, wouldn't they have tried something already? Not sown him up and taken care of him.

Unless they're waiting until I'm all better before they come in and torture me. Bleed me until I give up all my secrets. Not that I really have any to give.

Narrowing his eyes, he looked again at the décor of the room. From the looks of it, this house was mainly inhabited by a female...a single one, judging by the lack of anything remotely manly. So, unless the mystery female planned on torturing him by forcing him to watch reruns of *Gilmore Girls* and *Friends*, which he noticed sitting by the TV, he would be okay. Although he wouldn't argue with being subjected to hours upon hours of *Friends* because, well, then he'd get to stare at Rachel. Something about the feisty brunette always got to him. Not that he'd ever say anything about it out loud, or the fact that he'd seen every episode.

Chuckling silently at his own thoughts, Nicholas glanced back over at the tabby. The cat had now shifted to rest upon his right hip as he watched him. Nicholas let out a low groan as he forced his legs over the side of the couch. His eyes still focused on the tabby, he was just about to say something about how staring wasn't very nice when the sweetest smell he'd ever encountered washed over him.

Sitting straighter, he inhaled deeply as the delicious scent of lavender flooded the air.

The cat suddenly turned his head toward the hallway, his ears perking up. Sure enough, as soon as Nicholas opened himself up and listened, he heard the soft padding of bare feet on plush carpet. The sudden sound of the cat purring told him the owner of the house was about to make an appearance. If the warmth spreading though his veins wasn't clue enough as to how eager he was to lay eyes on her, his sudden desire to start purring was.

Not that an angel can purr, he thought with a huff.

Even as his brain wanted to analyze what was going on, Nicholas' heart told him to just go with it. Seeing he was all for following his heart, that was exactly what he planned to do. And thank God he did, too. Even if he had allowed his brain to try and figure out what he was feeling right then, it wouldn't have lasted long. The minute the adorable five-foot-nothing female cautiously stepped around the corner, all his thoughts just stopped. Hell, the world could have split open at that moment, the walls of the house crumbling around him. It wouldn't have mattered. All that mattered was the instant she looked at him, the second her chocolate brown eyes collided with his deep red ones, the world suddenly felt...better. All of a sudden, his life up until this point, everything he'd gone through since his fall from Heaven, made sense. It had led him here, to this woman. He was sure of it.

At the sight of him sitting there, her eyes grew wide and she stopped abruptly. He was certain she probably thought he'd still been asleep because the sudden feeling of nervousness flowing off her was staggering. Wanting to reassure her that he wasn't a danger, Nicholas scooted back on the couch.

Shit, I must look like a giant to her, he thought, attempting to make himself look smaller. He quickly found this was not a simple thing for a male over six feet tall to do.

"You're looking better."

He watched her sweep her brown hair behind her shoulders. His focus was so caught up with the way the light reflected off her hair, it took him a moment to realize she'd spoken.

Clearing his throat, Nicholas met her gaze. "What?"

"It's just... You were so pale for so long." She shrugged, moving closer to the couch. "It's nice to see that you're looking a lot better today."

"For so long...," Nicholas mumbled, his eyes trained on her lips. The corners of them lifted as she gave him a shy smile. And her voice...

It matched the rich color of her eyes. Its warmth brushed across him with every word. Then there was her sweet scent wafting in the air around him. It caressed his skin, as if she had reached out and touched him. And god, he wished she would. A vision of her hands roaming across his body caused his pulse to quicken. Of course, this was quickly followed by a vision of him exploring her body...with his tongue.

Licking his lips, Nicholas glanced down at the carpet, attempting to rein in his thoughts. What the hell was wrong with him? He didn't even know her name. He should really find that out before he started daydreaming about making her scream his.

After counting slowly from ten to zero, Nicholas raised his eyes to see her still staring intently at him. Before he could utter a sound, he watched her bite down on her bottom lip.

What am I going to say? he thought, watching her pull her bottom lip between her teeth and slowly release it.

"Um... How are you feeling? Are you hungry? Or thirsty? Or-"

"Who are you?" he asked abruptly. He had to cut in because her questions made his head spin.

"What?"

Nicholas leaned over, resting his arms against his thighs. He felt his power stir slightly within him as his eyes lingered on her lips before moving up to her eyes. His need to know everything about this mysterious woman was insistent, but to start, he would settle for knowing her name.

With a smile, he tilted his head, studying her as he did so. "Who are you?" he asked again, his voice rumbling through the suddenly quiet room. "And how long have I been here?"

"Oh, um…" She laughed lightly, pushing her hair behind her ears. "I'm sorry. I probably should have led with that. My name is Amy. You've been unconscious for almost ten days now."

Chapter 5

Amy watched a multitude of emotions fly across the man's handsome face right before he looked away. She imagined this was what it felt like to watch a book addict's expression when they found out the next book in a series they loved had been out for months without them knowing. Confusion and denial, maybe a bit of betrayal. Even though you knew it was unrealistic that anyone would have known to tell you about it, you still felt like someone should have.

In this man's case, it seemed more like he was mad at himself for being unconscious for so long. Not that he had any control over that. In fact, she thought it amazing he was up now.

She'd seen his eyes flash a deep red when she told him her name, then darkened to almost black when she told him how long he'd been out. Not knowing much about him...other than his interesting choice of weapon, his larger-than-life presence, his red eyes...she really should have been wary of him, of what he could possibly do to her. But she didn't feel that way at all. Even standing here now, watching him come to grips with the fact that he'd lost the last ten days, she only felt a need to go to him, to comfort him.

The man started rubbing his hands together. Amy could tell he was trying to calm himself, figure out what had happened. Maybe he couldn't remember how he got here, or even asking her to help him.

She must have gasped or made some kind of sound because his head suddenly jerked up and he looked at her.

"Amy?" he sighed.

Walking around the small end table by the couch, she took a few steps closer to the center of the room. "Yes?" she asked slowly, reaching down to absently run her hands over Charlie's fur. His sudden purring filled the silence as she waited for the man to continue.

"It's just... Ten days? I don't..." He shook his head.

"Well, honestly, I'm surprised you're awake already," she said. "The way you were when I found you... It was bad."

He frowned. "I don't really remember much. I mean... Was I lying on your back porch when you found me?"

She nodded. "Do you remember being shot? Asking me to not take you to the hospital?" She watched as one of his hands trailed down to his side. He grimaced as he dropped his eyes to the floor.

"Yes," he faintly mumbled.

Amy immediately felt a twinge of concern run through her. "I stitched you up, though. Got the bullet out and everything. And you seem to have healed...exceptionally fast," she said softly, smiling as she watched a smirk tug at the corner of his mouth. "So your side should be as good as new now."

His red eyes flashed as he gazed up at her. She felt her pulse quicken at the intensity of his stare before he cleared his throat.

"So you've been watching over me this whole time?"

Amy felt a blush spread across her face at the wonder in his voice. He sounded surprised someone would do what she did. Though she knew many wouldn't have, it was in her nature to help. It always had been. Amy could only smile as she nodded. "It's not like I was just going to leave you on my back porch. After all, what would the neighbors say?"

At that, he released a soft laugh. The warmth in it breathed across her soul like a warm wind. It quickly became her new favorite sound.

"I don't know how to thank you," he said after a minute.

Amy smiled. "How about your name?"

He laughed again. "Yeah. That would probably be good."

"Yeah. I mean, I could just call you stud muffin, but-" Realizing what she'd just said, Amy felt her eyes widen. "I mean..." She watched his lips pull back into a huge smile, exposing his perfect white teeth.

"You can call me stud muffin if you want to," he said, his voice a sexy rumble. At her answering smirk, he laughed. "Or you can call me Nicholas."

"Nicholas." She smiled, reaching out her hand. "Well, it's nice to meet you, Nicholas."

He grasped her hand. "It's nice to meet you, Amy."

Sparks flew up her arm. The tingling caused a warmth inside of her. A warmth that made her feel a sudden sense of safety and rightness. She suddenly wanted him to wrap his arms around her so she could bury herself against him. She slowly extracted her hand from his. The loss of his touch hit her in the chest. And, judging from the sudden frown that spread across his face, Nicholas felt it, too. At least a part of her hoped this sudden rush of feelings wasn't one-sided.

"So, how are you feeling?"

"I'm good actually," he said with a grin. She watched as he began to stand, his jaw clenched slightly as he straightened his legs.

Damn!

She felt like she had to keep tilting her head back just to keep her eyes on his. By the time he stood straight, Amy figured he had to be well over a foot taller than her. It wasn't until this moment that she realized just how short she really was compared to him. If there were any other questions concerning their height difference, the sudden kink in her neck wiped them right out.

Crap on a cracker, she thought, taking a step back to get a better look at him. How in the heck had she dragged him inside?

Nicholas laughed. "Crap on a cracker? Who says that?"

Amy's mouth fell open. "Shit. Did I say that out loud?" At his smirk, she felt her face heat up. What was it about this guy? Just being around him seemed to make her crazy. Whatever it was, she was going to have to get over it. Straightening her shoulders, she gazed up at him. "That is a very real statement. I'll have you know, there are a lot of people who use it."

"Well, I've met a lot of people and have never heard it before. Ever."

"Yeah... Well... Maybe you have only met snooty people."

"Snooty?"

"That's right. People who only say stuff like 'my word' and 'golly gee'."

"What?" His eyes widened. "Honey, do I look like the kind of guy who would hang out with people who talk like that? Shit. Do *I* look like I talk like that?"

Amy glanced over him. No, he definitely looked more like a body builder, but... She put her hands on her hips in a huff. "Well, I don't know you, do I?" She stared up at him. "For all I know, you could be a tea drinking, crumpet eating, golfing kind of guy."

And to think she was worried about him thinking she was judging him while he was unconscious. She hated being like that, but if she were being honest with herself, this was kind of fun.

She watched in amusement as he shook his head, his sexy lips twisting as he attempted to not laugh. "For your information, I like coffee, not tea. I have no idea what in the hell a crumpet even-"

"It's a griddle cake," Amy cut in. At his raised eyebrow, she stifled a laugh and waved for him to continue.

"A *griddle cake*? Well, now I can say I know what they are." With a smile, he took a deep breath and sighed. "I don't watch, participate in, or follow golf. I'm more of a football, hockey, MMA kind of guy." His red eyes flashed as he smirked. "And I sure as fuck don't say 'golly gee'. Hell, I don't think I've ever heard any of my brothers say that, either." He smirked.

"Now that I think about it, though, I'll be sure to say it around Cyrus. I'm sure he'll love it."

"You have brothers?" Her mind instantly latched onto that bit of information. Just the thought of there being more like him seemed overwhelming.

"Four..." His gaze dropped to the floor as a frown spread across his face. "I mean, five."

"You forgot about one?"

"It's a long story," he said, refusing to meet her gaze.

Amy felt the shift in the air as his body tensed. Realizing it might be a sore subject, she tried to lighten the mood. "So, do they all look like you?"

She couldn't hide her smile as his gaze jerked back up to hers. His eyebrows arched in surprise.

"Look like me?"

"Yeah, you know... Like you're one of the Chippendales or something?"

She watched as he tried to remain serious, which failed miserably because he couldn't hide the amusement in his eyes. "You mean those little chipmunks? Why would you say I look like one of those cartoon characters?"

Amy waved one of her hands in the air in mock frustration. "No, not the cartoon. That's Chip and Dale. I'm talking about the strippers." As soon as the word stripper passed her lips, Amy slapped her hand over her mouth.

I can't believe I just said that.

"A stripper..." He gave her a lazy smile. "Well, knowing that's how you see me, the fact you wanted to call me stud muffin makes a lot more sense." He winked.

Amy sucked in a sharp breath. "Well... I just... You know what? I'm going to make some coffee. You want some?"

She'd already turned toward the kitchen before she'd finished her question. Her mind started going a hundred miles an hour with how silly she was acting and how she needed to get her head on straight. It didn't help that he was like *all* her favorite book boyfriends rolled into one. Well, at least in the looks and humor department. As for the other areas...

Shaking her head, she turned to ask him again, slamming into his hard chest. "Oof."

"Whoa there." He placed his hands on her arms to steady her.

The warmth from his hands seeped into her arms as she gazed up into his eyes. Her heart slammed against her chest from the sparks running through her. "I, um..."

"I would love some coffee." He smiled as he slowly released her and took a small step back.

"Coffee. Right," she said in a rush, smiling as she turned back around. Her smile kept growing because with every step, she felt the warmth of his stare on her back. Maybe after coffee, she'd be able to learn more about this sexy, handsome man...then she'd try to talk him into staying for lunch.

Chapter 6

Sitting across from Amy, Nicholas watched as she made a sandwich for each of them. It was lunchtime, and though he'd started to tell her he needed to go several times, he just couldn't seem to get the words out. Not yet.

Maybe after lunch.

Amy hummed softly as she turned back to the fridge. Her fingers pushed her soft brown hair behind her ears as she made her way back toward the counter, a jar of mayo in hand.

"I hope you like mayo. I haven't been to the store, so..." She shrugged.

"Mayo's perfect," Nicholas said quickly. He didn't want her to be upset or think she hadn't done enough for him. Truthfully, she'd done so much already, he couldn't wrap his head around it.

After she set a plate in front of him, Nicholas looked at her as she took a bite of her sandwich. She moaned softly as she chewed, her eyes closing slightly.

Momentarily lost, Nicholas cleared his throat and took a huge bite out of his own sandwich. He chewed almost mechanically as he attempted to rein in his suddenly very horny thoughts. For the hundredth time since he woke up, Nicholas wondered what it was about this female that had him acting this way.

If my brothers could see me now, they'd surely have a good laugh over this.

Females were not his area of expertise. Just ask any of them. After falling to Earth, it hadn't taken long for Nicholas to figure that out. Hell, he'd known what it felt like to be put in the *friend zone* before there was even a term for it. It wasn't that women weren't attracted to him. Like his brothers, he was taller than the average human male, with more defined muscles and a way about him that just screamed of him being *more*. It was just a feeling people had when they were around him and his brothers for any given amount of time, even though none could put their finger on what it meant. It was... What did Ella call it? Aura. Yes, it was that same aura that screamed of them being more than what they appeared to be that also drew women to them.

So it wasn't his looks that made him fall into that dreaded friend zone. No. It was him. Truthfully, a relationship with a woman, any woman, was usually the last thing he wanted. Then there were one-night stands... He'd been involved in his fair share of those, his need for closeness winning out over his need for self-preservation. Some of those connections had been amazing, fulfilling, and sexually enticing.

But, even so, he tried to avoid those like the plague. To messy. To complicated.

The one and only woman who had ever called to him, made him want more, had turned on him so quickly, his head still spun.

So this sudden need to know everything he could about Amy, to take her and possess her, was not only extremely out of character for him, but also, if he were being honest with himself, downright terrifying. He just wasn't sure he wanted to open himself up like that.

"So..." Amy's soft voice broke through his thoughts. "Where do you live?"

Nicholas looked down at his half-eaten sandwich and frowned. He and his brothers weren't really big on telling people where they lived...for several reasons. The main one was they never really knew whom they could trust. Throw in all the demons they'd prefer to not find out where they slept, and handing out that kind of information was not even a question. But here he was, wondering if he should. Something in him said he could trust Amy. Hell, she'd saved his life. But a part of him, the part that was protective of his brothers, screamed not to.

Deciding to play it safe, Nicholas glanced back up at her. "I live here, in Fhallon Heights."

Her eyes widened. "Really? For how long?"

He frowned again. "Eight years."

"That's crazy. I've lived here my whole life and don't remember seeing you around. I mean, this town isn't that small, but it's small enough that I've seen everyone who lives in it at least once. I've never seen you before." She waved her hand at him. "Trust me, I would have remembered. Do you not go out much?"

"Actually, my brothers and I go out quite a bit. You've probably just missed us." He didn't want to explain that when they're out, they're usually not driving and, more often than not, have the Shade wrapped around them. He could just imagine how that conversation would go over. "I mean, I've never seen you around, either. Like you said, this isn't really a small town."

"Right," she said slowly, obviously not buying into his flimsy explanation.

They finished the remainder of their lunch in silence. Both seemed to quietly observe the other, trying to figure out what to make of the person sitting across from them. Nicholas wasn't sure what Amy was thinking, but part of him really hoped she felt the same type of pull toward him that he did toward her. If she did, he also hoped she was just as confused by it. He'd hate to be the only one teetering on the balance beam.

With their sandwiches finished, he stood to take their plates to the sink, only to have her shoo him away. Raising his hands in mock surrender, he took a step back and watched her clean up. His thoughts went back and forth on what he should do next. Damn, he'd never felt this indecisive. Ever.

Looking down at the counter, he splayed his fingers against the cool tile as his thoughts warred with themselves. A part of him really wanted to stay here and try to understand this female and what she meant to him. There was just something about her. He couldn't quite put his finger on it, but she had his attention. Unfortunately, he had responsibilities he needed to see to. Family matters he'd been away from for far too long.

That was what the other part of him called for. He needed to get home. Needed to see his brothers, make sure they all made it out of that alley in one piece. As much as it pained him, it was time for him to go home.

"You know... If you were a cartoon, there would be smoke coming out of your ears right about now." Nicholas glanced up to see Amy leaning her hip against the counter. Her eyebrows raised as she watched him, her eyes filled with curiosity. "Penny for your thoughts?"

"It's nothing. I just…" He paused, watching her smile start to falter. "I was just thinking I should probably let my brothers know I'm okay."

Her eyes widened. "Oh, my god. Of course. Do you have a phone?" Before he could answer, she walked past him toward the hallway. "Of course you don't. You would have used if by now if you did. Here… Let me get my phone for you."

He listened to her move down the hall and into what he assumed was her room. The sound of things being moved around reached his ears as she rummaged through something. Actually, she was going through several things because the shuffling got louder. Frowning, he turned toward the hallway. As he was just about to ask if she needed help, he heard her let out a soft "aha" before her footsteps started heading his way.

"Here it is," she said breathlessly as she emerged from the hall. "I always lose it in the office." She laughed. "After all this time, you'd think I'd have figured out a place to put it where it won't get hidden beneath a ton of books and papers."

Taking the cell phone from her outstretched hand, he hit the button and swiped the screen to open it up. "You work from home?"

"Yeah. I'm a blogger."

Glancing up, he tilted his head at her. "A what?"

"I run a blog for independent authors. I do reviews of their books, offer bundles for cover reveals and release days. Sometimes I even do interviews." He was sure his face showed his confusion because she paused and chuckled. "I help authors spread the word about their work, and help readers find their next book to fall in love with."

Her love for what she did was obvious as her smile continued to grow. Words like social media events, internet parties, and live chats fell from her pretty lips. Her eyes sparkled, and he felt the happiness flowing off her.

Nicholas grinned as she paused to take a breath. "How interesting. Truly. It all sounds really rewarding, Amy."

"It really is. I love books, and the people I've met since I started doing this are just amazing. Do you read?"

He thought over how hectic his life had been lately. Between rescuing Ella, moving, Andres, Castigo, Manuel's girl...Dev, he really hadn't had a lot of downtime. With what spare time he had, Nicholas either found himself having a drink with Cyrus or trying to pass out... Okay, it was more like having a drink with Cyrus so he *could* pass out.

"I haven't really had the time," he said slowly.

"Well, you should try to make time." Amy grinned. "Reading can be a good escape."

He returned her smile with a lazy one of his own. "I'll keep that in mind."

Turning his gaze back to the phone, he suddenly realized he didn't know who to call. What should he say? He'd been gone for almost two weeks. His brothers must be a wreck. And Ella. Even Hayley. He wanted to call them all. His fingers hovering over the screen, he threw one name after another around in his head before finally starting to dial.

Glancing up at Amy, his breath caught as she gave him the most beautiful smile. With her nod of encouragement, almost as if she sensed his dilemma, he hit call.

He counted the rings until his brother answered the phone.

Chapter 7

"I said I'm fine."

Slamming his bedroom door in the hopes of stopping any further questions, Cyrus snarled into the empty room. They just wouldn't stop. He knew it was because they were worried about him, but hell. There were plenty of other things to worry about than his state of mind, like the fact that Nicholas was still missing. And they still hadn't found out anything new concerning Dev.

To him, that was way more important. But whatever. If they wanted to concentrate on him, they could do that while he looked for their missing brothers. And Nicholas was missing. He wouldn't allow himself to think otherwise.

Taking a couple deep breaths, he walked toward his bed and plugged in his cell phone, watching as the little red light blinked to life. He hated to have his battery run too low. *Not that anyone ever called me.* He frowned. His phone used to go off a lot more. Nicholas liked to send him stupid pictures and jokes at random times of the day. God, it drove him crazy. He kept telling him to stop, but the little shit would just laugh and tell him it was good for him. That he was too serious.

Cyrus knew he could be hard to deal with sometimes. Oh, who was he kidding? He'd been a mess for a long time now. Saying he was hard to deal with was putting it nicely. He understood that. It just couldn't be helped.

Sitting down with a sigh, he felt the mattress dip beneath his weight. He'd never admit it to anyone, but he missed those stupid messages.

He and Nicholas were probably as close as they could be, given his need for space, but Cyrus had always felt protective over him. Even though he rarely showed it. And the fact that he hadn't been there that night, hadn't been around when Nicholas decided to go all *Lone* fucking *Ranger* and chase down a demon on his own, ate at him. He just couldn't let it go. What if he could have gotten to that gun before it became an issue? Stopped Nicholas from going after that demon? Or at least gone with him so he didn't have to fight that POS alone?

He controlled the fucking shadows, for fuck's sake! Cyrus was sure he could have done something. But no. He'd let his anger get the better of him. Let his mind conjure up some bullshit scenario where his brothers were the enemy. He'd bailed, just fucking left.

And for what? He hadn't found a damn thing. No sign of Dev. No way to get into the club without being detected. Nothing.

He'd tried, too. For hours, he'd paced around the block, getting as close to the club as he dared. His need to find Dev, to not abandon him again, overpowered anything else. He'd even tried to mask his presence with the shadows surrounding the club, but with the storm clouds in the sky, there hadn't been many shadows to work with. Plus, as he'd moved closer to the building, the smell of sulfur surrounding its perimeter had been almost nauseating.

Two hours into his search, he'd spotted his first demon. The fiend had stepped out of the side door, its red eyes glinting in the darkness as it looked around. The demon had been big, like Hulk big, and was probably some kind of security. He had felt pretty confident he could take the demon, should the need arise, but after the fourth one exited the building, Cyrus decided to let things be for the night.

He'd hated to admit it, but he needed his brothers.

It had been foolish of him to run off on his own that night. He should have remembered how nothing good ever came from trying to take on a problem alone.

Reaching up, he ran a finger down the scar on his face and felt his chest tighten. Yes, that was definitely a lesson he'd learned the hard way.

To top it off, his reckless need to go after Dev alone had brought more trouble to his family than even he was ready to handle. In the act of trying to save one brother, he'd abandoned another.

He didn't know why Darren and the rest of them even kept him around.

Lying back on his bed, he stared up at the ceiling. His hands rested on his stomach as he tried to concentrate on his breathing. He heard, and felt, his stomach growl in protest.

Damn, when was the last time I ate anything?

Rolling to his side, he closed his eyes. It'd probably been at least two days. He just hadn't been hungry. In the past ten days, he'd probably only eaten a handful of times. And those meals had been forced on him by one of his brothers or one of the girls.

Thinking of Ella and Hayley caused him to curl in on himself. They hadn't come out and said Nicholas' disappearance was his fault...but did they really need to? He could tell by the way they looked at him, especially when they didn't think he'd notice. He didn't fault them. As far as he was concerned, they were pointing, though probably unconsciously, in the right direction.

Rolling to his other side, Cyrus squinted at the clock.

Two o'clock.

He'd give it another seven hours or so, then he'd head back to the alley to retrace Nicholas' steps...at least to the street where Manuel had last picked up his trail. Not that he thought tonight would be any different. But every night since his brother had vanished, he'd gone out looking, and would continue to do so until he was found.

Every night, Christian, Manuel, or Darren would go with him. Sometimes all of them. A part of him knew they all felt guilty for Nicholas running off. Each one wondered if they could have done something different, been a little quicker, and stopped him. The knowledge each of them felt equally responsible didn't make him feel like it was any less his fault.

His stomach churned as he went over the events of that night again. Fuck, if only he had-

The ringing of his cell yanked Cyrus from his thoughts. Glancing toward the phone where it sat on the mattress next to him, he frowned. "Don't Worry, Be Happy" blared throughout his quiet room. Its sickeningly sappy lyrics and upbeat tune had him frantically reaching for the phone. But not with the intention of answering. He wasn't in the mood to make small talk with some wrong number. No, his mind was solely focused on making the ridiculous song stop.

He wanted to be angry, pissed that Nicholas had obviously gone into his phone and changed his ringtone, but he couldn't be. Instead, he just felt his mood darken even more.

Glancing at the screen, he scowled at the unknown number. Nobody outside his brothers had his number. Shit, he didn't even think Ella had it and she was the closest thing to a sister he had. As his finger hovered over the ignore button, he paused.

"Probably some telemarketing bullshit," he muttered, taking his phone off the charger and sitting up. Nicholas' idea of a joke repeated again as the unknown number stared unblinkingly up at him. "Could be the wrong number." His finger moved toward the answer button. Cyrus didn't normally answer random phone calls. He hated telemarketers almost as much as he hated wasting his time.

And anyone on the other end of an unknown number usually landed under both categories.

Yet something made him answer. As the ringing stopped, he stared at the phone for a heartbeat before raising it to his ear.

"Yeah?" he growled.

"Cyrus?"

The sound of Nicholas' voice almost made him fall out of his bed. Cyrus was on his feet instantly and spun around, searching, as if expecting Nicholas to just suddenly be in his room. "Nicholas? Where...? What...?" He could hardly get the questions out as his brain attempted to wrap itself around the fact that Nicholas was calling him. Running a hand through his hair, he finally took a deep breath, his eyes focusing on his bedroom door as his grip tightened on his phone.

"Hey, brother," Nicholas' voice drawled through the phone. "Miss me?"

Chapter 8

Dev stood in the corner of the room, watching the humans sway their bodies in time to the fast rhythm the DJ set. The club had been open for four days now. So far, everything was going smoothly. He had been worried it wasn't going to be ready in time. It always came down to last-minute problems, and even with Sy's help, those last few days before they opened had been rough.

Between the outside sign not lighting, the waitresses whining about every*fucking*thing, and the DJ they'd originally hired disappearing - he had a feeling one, if not both, of the twins was involved - Dev just couldn't seem to catch a break.

Damn Lakmi and Vhin.

Out of all the demons lurking around, those two were the worst. And he had thought Kanibal was going to be the hardest to be around. Yet K had made himself scarce since that first meeting in Dev's office.

Thank fuck.

On top of those small, yet teeth-grinding headaches, he also had Andras and Agalon breathing down his neck, just waiting for him to mess up.

But he hadn't, and the club had opened up on time.

Not that him working his ass off to make it happen had received even a nod from anyone, but then again, the less attention he got from any of them was probably for the best.

Opening night had been insane. Two hours beforehand, Dev had stepped out the side door to find the line stretching to the alley. As shocked as he was, the type of people standing in line hadn't surprised him one bit. They were young, dressed like they were going into a sex club. Exactly what Andras was looking for. Rich kids with family issues. And from the moment the front doors opened and the music started, the crowd had gone wild.

It was the same last night and today...even though it was still early and a Tuesday. Andras couldn't be more pleased. At least that was the impression Dev got from the few conversations they had since Saturday.

After the first day, Andras had decided the club should be open around the clock, at least to start. The demon had latched onto the idea of having the local business scums coming by on their lunch breaks, making deals with the demons at all hours of the day. This had caused a rush in hiring and, though he wouldn't show it, made for a very tired Dev. Of course, it didn't help that Andras, or any of the other demons, seemed to be around every fucking corner that Dev turned.

Except Castigo. Walking in on him, seeing him being confronted by Andras and Agalon, was still seared into his mind. He hadn't gone into the room with the intent of helping the demon. Actually, he hadn't planned on going in there at all. But that ass-hat, Mr. Brighton, had insisted he go tell Andras that he was there. Dev had been sweating the whole walk to the office. He'd known Andras was in there with Agalon, but he hadn't any idea what he was going to see when he opened the door. The sight of Castigo looking so...broken in front of the two demons still caused his shoulders to tense. And he didn't even like the guy.

Which led Dev to his most recent conundrum. Why did he ask Castigo to help him and his brothers? Regardless of the fact that he agreed to get involved, it had been one of the riskiest moves he'd made to date. And that was saying a lot given Dev's interference with the, thanks to him, botched plan to kidnap Ella and Red. If Castigo had decided to go the other way, to deny his request and use it against him instead, well... He really didn't want to delve too deeply into the *what ifs*.

Shuddering, Dev shifted his weight against the bartop. He hadn't seen Castigo since that conversation, and seeing as he was still topside, not chained in Andras' dungeon, he knew Castigo hadn't turned him in...yet.

Today, both Andras and Agalon hadn't been around. Dev had been on the floor most of the day, making sure everything was all set for that night's crowd and that the VIP rooms were ready for any surprise guests. Those rooms still creeped him out, so he never stayed in them long. Saturday night, he saw a man disappear into one with who Dev assumed was his date, though the age difference between the two had been hard to ignore.

He could only hazard a guess as to what they did in that room. All Dev knew was that when they exited the room, three hours later, the girl had seemed confused and not quite sober. At Dev's questioning look, Andras, who had appeared out of nowhere, had informed him that what happened in the VIP rooms was of no concern to him.

At Andras' tone, Dev had only nodded and gone back to watching the bar. The look on the girl's face haunted him, now being the only thing he saw when he looked toward those rooms. Part of him didn't want to know what went on back there. Didn't want to think about the leather, chains, and various other dungeon-like items. Nope, it was probably best if he left that alone.

Yet another part of him, the part that wanted to yell for all these people to leave so he could save their souls from the club's black cloud, wanted to find out what happened in those rooms so he could put a stop to it. What could he really do, though?

After the fight in the parking lot of Indigo, and the short talk he had with Ella and Red, Dev had silently hoped to see his brothers come storming through the front door. As one day had bled into the next, that hope had dwindled down to just an occasional thought.

Why would they come?

There was a very real chance once his brothers had talked to the girls, they'd been indifferent, maybe even angry he'd been there. Sure, they were probably grateful he'd been able to stop those demons from getting to the girls, but after all this time, his attempt at reaching out to them had probably come too little, too late. He didn't blame them. Not really.

"Dev?"

Hearing Trix call his name, Dev turned to find her standing behind the bar, staring at him. Her mouth turned down into a deep frown, a look she'd been sporting ever since Andras' *security* had shown up.

"Yeah?" Dev asked, silently hoping she wasn't about to ask him to deal with something that he knew he couldn't, like the demons.

"I know I've mentioned this to you before, but could you tell that jackass, Lakmi, to stay the hell away from my bar?" Her eyes flashing, she swept them toward the end of the bar.

Dev's eyes followed her gaze, seeing Lakmi standing at the far end, rapping his knuckles against the dark wooden top. As the demon's eyes met Dev's, he gave a knowing smirk. The ass was trying to make Trix angry, and he knew there was nothing anyone could do to stop him. Dev was just glad that angering her was all he was trying to do. One of Lakmi's skills was bringing out a person's greed. He could make them so greedy, so self-centered, that a person would do *anything* to get what they wanted. What they felt they were owed.

The last time he'd been allowed to, as Andras put it, *play with the humans*, Lakmi had single-handedly started a riot. In the end, thirty-five humans had been killed, almost a hundred injured. When asked, nobody could say what started the riot, let alone why they were involved.

The demon keeping that nasty little skill in check was probably a demand of Andras. Wouldn't want this little pet project of his to go down in flames. At least not before the boss wanted it to.

Eyeing the demon, Dev could only sigh. Looking back at Trix, he found her watching him expectantly. "Listen, Trix-"

"You know what? Never mind." She slapped a towel down on the counter and began to aggressively wipe it off. "Just forget I said anything."

Before he could respond, she had moved on to a customer who waved his money in the air to get her attention.

With a mental growl, Dev pushed away from the bar and walked steadily through the crowd. Even if he were to say something to Lakmi, the demon would just laugh it off and tell him to mind his own fucking business. That was exactly what happened the last time he'd tried to get him to leave Trix alone. The less he had to deal with him or his twin brother, the better.

Walking around the edge of the dance floor, Dev watched the humans grind against each other. The club had really only begun to fill up about two hours ago, but the party was already in full swing. Drinks flowed, drugs were being passed around, and the music was as sexually charged as it could get. All in all, it felt like the makings of a huge orgy.

Wouldn't surprise him if that was the goal.

Curling his lips in disgust, he looked away from the dance floor toward the many tables scattered around the outer edge of the room. It was amongst the empty glass-covered tables and randomly placed chairs that he saw a woman who truly didn't belong.

Her blue eyes were wide as she looked around, huddling into her chair in an obvious attempt to not be noticed. His watched as her fingers curled around the corners of the napkin on the table. An untouched drink sat at the side.

She was nervous. He could tell.

With a slight shift, Dev changed direction and began to head her way.

The closer he got, he saw the way she had swept her blonde hair into a clip behind her head. Only a few curls had fallen free and now framed her heart-shaped face. She was even dressed modestly.

What is she doing here?

Once he was a few steps away, she suddenly looked up at him. Her eyes grew wider as a tendril of fear curled through the air. Moving slowly, Dev walked up to her, being sure to keep the table between them in an attempt to put her at ease.

"Is everything going okay?" he asked. What he really wanted to know was why she was sitting there when she obviously wanted to be anywhere else.

"Yeah, um... I'm just waiting for someone." Her voice shook slightly.

"Well, I hope whoever you're waiting for gets here soon."

"Me, too," she laughed. "This really isn't my scene."

"I can tell," he said, biting the inside of his cheek as he made out the light blush spreading across her face. "I mean, you just don't seem comfortable. If you don't mind me asking, who are you waiting for?"

Dev suppressed a frown as the question left his mouth. Not only should he not get too chatty with any of the club's customers, but the sudden desire for her to not say she was waiting for a date caught him completely off guard. He'd never had this feeling...ever! Swallowing, he watched her pretty blue eyes scan the room behind him before settling back on his.

"I'm supposed to be meeting a potential boss here." At Dev's raised eyebrows, she shook her head. "I know. I thought this was a weird place to meet up, too. He said he was friends with the owner and there was a back room that could be used for interviews and meetings."

Flashes of the young girl from Saturday flickered through Dev's mind as he stared down at this innocent woman. Opening himself up to her, he watched as the white light within her pulsed. She didn't belong here...and she definitely didn't belong in one of those back rooms. The need to get her out of there was so strong, he felt his hands ache as the gripped the back of the chair before him.

Thinking fast, he looked around, then glanced back at the stunning female. "Are you sure you were supposed to meet him today?"

He watched a frown mar her forehead as she chewed her lip. "Yeah. I mean, this is the day he told me."

"Hmm... Well, I'm the manager here and don't remember hearing anything about a meeting, or interview, happening in one of our back rooms." As far as truths went, what he just fed her was a partial one...at best. But she didn't need to know that.

"Really?" Her shoulder's slumped slightly.

"Hey, listen... I don't know about this potential job you were going for, but do you really want to work for someone who wants to interview you at a club?"

"Well, not really, but-"

"You seem like a smart girl. I'm sure you can get a job anywhere."

At that, she released a snort. "Thank you, but I've been trying to get a job for months and have yet to land one."

So she was young, desperate, and innocent... Just what Andras and the bottom feeders surrounding him looked for. He needed to get her away from this club before they got their hooks into her.

"Anyway, this job is a good opportunity," she continued. "I'd be his personal assistant, get benefits, overtime, and the pay is wonderful. So what if the guy has odd interviewing habits. I need this job."

Realizing it wasn't going to be easy to convince her to go, Dev felt his chest tighten. Looking around again, he was relieved to see that their conversation hadn't drawn any unwanted attention, and he couldn't sense any demons nearby. If he was going to get her out of there, now was the time.

Focusing his gaze back on the woman, Dev leaned down. "Look, I really think you should just call it a day and head home." As her eyes narrowed, he forced some of his power to rise to the surface. Not a lot, but enough that she should feel something. When he heard her inhale sharply, he felt a small sense of relief. "Trust me... Whatever job you were offered isn't worth it." Reaching his hand out to her, he held his breath.

Dev could almost see her fighting with herself. The need for a job battled her need to leave. He knew a part of her sensed something wasn't right here. Any innocent who stepped through the door could feel it. The darkness in the air, the evil. Most would ignore it, but Dev hoped self-preservation won out, especially in this case. As a sigh of acceptance left her lips, she reached up and slid her delicate hand into his.

He felt the warmth of her touch immediately as he wrapped his hand around hers. Pulling her from her seat, Dev tried to not concentrate on the rightness of her hand in his, or the smell of flowers that suddenly surrounded him. Gritting his teeth, he practically dragged her toward the exit at the side of the club, which led to the parking lot.

Should have asked if she drove here.

It was too late now, though, as the exit came into view. Letting his power out before him, Dev opened the door with little fear of there being anyone, or anything, waiting for them on the other side.

Cool air blew gently across his face as he stepped over the threshold and led the woman past him and into the lot. With the early afternoon sun glaring down on them, Dev was finally able to get a good look at her.

Her dress was black and fit her curves in such a way that it looked sexy and professional at the same time. The bottom was slightly pleated, causing it to move gracefully around her as she turned to look at him. His eyes followed the smooth lines of her legs right down to the matching black heels that hugged her feet, straps wrapping delicately around her perfect ankles. Swallowing hard, he looked back up, once again struck by the blueness of her gaze.

"I feel like I should be thanking you," she said softly.

He smiled, only just realizing they still held hands. With a frown, he released her and clenched his fist at his side. "You should get going," he said, his voice coming out rough.

"Yes, right." She seemed at a loss for a moment before turning to make her way through the lot.

He watched her reach into her purse and pull out a set of keys as she stopped by a black car. As her hand slid over the handle, Dev willed her to look back. He knew he would never see her again, so the desire to look into her blue eyes one last time felt important.

As if sensing his gaze, she turned just as she pulled open her door. Her eyes held his gaze as they stood there, silently waiting. For what, he didn't know.

"My name's Maria," she said softly, her voice as clear to his ears as if she were standing right by him.

"Maria," he breathed.

Even the feeling of her name on his tongue felt right. He watched her lips curve up into a smile. Realizing she waited for him to give his name, he paused. He didn't give out his name to anyone. Ever. Hadn't even told Ella and Red, though he knew his brothers would know who the girls were talking about once they explained what happened. Even knowing that, he still hadn't said it. But now, to Maria, he felt like it was okay. That he could trust her enough to give her this. In truth, it was the only thing he could give her...but it was something.

Looking around to make sure they were still alone, Dev glanced back at Maria. "Devlin." He blinked quickly, not understanding why he'd given her his full name.

"Devlin?"

The sound of it on her lips felt so good, he couldn't help but smile. He tilted his head down a bit, still watching her. "Yeah, but you can just call me Dev."

"Well, Devlin," Maria said after a short pause, smiling, "thank you for walking me out."

"You're welcome, Maria."

"Maybe I'll see you around."

Without waiting for an answer, Maria got into her car and Dev watched her pull away. It was probably for the best. At any minute, one of the demons could come upon them. He really didn't know what he would have said to her in that instance. No matter how much he wanted to see her again, Dev knew that, for her sake, he couldn't. To keep her safe, he knew it would be best if he just forgot about her.

Dev shook his head as he walked back into the club, closing the door securely behind him. It wasn't like she was anything more than just another woman. At least that was what he told himself.

Chapter 9

The phone call with Cyrus had gone better than expected. Well, after Cyrus finished cussing up a storm and shooting out one question after another without giving Nicholas a chance to answer.

He'd gone on and on so much, Nicholas ended up having to hold the phone away from his ear, making faces at Amy the whole time. He needed to make sure she didn't take Cyrus' outburst too seriously. He'd seen the uncertainty in her face when his brother got over his shock and started acting like, well...like himself. Nicholas was used to his outbursts, even understood them to a certain degree, but he knew Amy wouldn't. So he lightened the mood by doing what he did best...joking around. And it worked. She'd laughed softly, shaking her head as they both listened to Cyrus.

Man, he missed his brothers and couldn't wait to see them. He had a feeling he wouldn't have to wait long. The whole crew would probably pull up at any minute.

Nicholas grinned as he sat at Amy's kitchen table, carefully removing the remaining bullets from the demon's gun. Cyrus had wanted him to just dematerialize and head home. Normally, he would have done just that, but Nicholas still didn't feel fully charged. He felt fine physically, but when he tapped into his power, the most he could muster up was a gentle breeze. He'd decided it would be best for his brothers to just come get him.

After a couple growly comments from Cyrus, he had said they'd be there soon.

As he'd hung up the phone and told her they were coming to get him, Nicholas had watched in amusement as Amy raced down the hall to clean up. For some unknown reason, she seemed to think she needed to get changed into something else before his brothers got there. Which was ridiculous. As far as Nicholas was concerned, she looked fucking gorgeous. He'd even voiced that, only to get an eye roll and a *you wouldn't understand.*

Listening to her flitter around in the back rooms, Nicholas had begun to inspect the gun he'd taken from the demon. It didn't look like anything special. In all his years here on Earth, he'd seen a lot of guns, and this one looked like any other Glock .45 that he'd seen. It wasn't until he'd released the magazine and gotten a good look at the bullets that his skin grew cold.

With the last of the bullets now sitting on Amy's table, he set the gun down and stared at them. Each one was a shiny silver, demonic symbols carved on the casings, a star encased in a circle etched onto the rounded ends. "Original," he muttered. He knew the etching on the end was done for looks more than anything, which caused him to mentally roll his eyes.

Looks like even demons seem to lean toward the dramatics.

Reaching down, Nicholas ran a hand over the spot on his side where the bullet had entered. Dramatics or not, those bullets where bad news. Shit, if the demon had aimed just a little higher or if he'd been just a little slower, he probably wouldn't have even made it off the street. No, he was certain he wouldn't have. It was a miracle he'd made it as far as he did even with the bullet going into his side. From what Amy had told him, the wound had been pretty bad. But it was the blackness that had started crawling its way across his body after he'd been shot that had him the most concerned. He needed to talk to his brothers, see if they'd come up with anything.

Hearing footsteps heading his way, Nicholas looked up and smiled as Amy walked toward him. She'd changed from her soft cotton sweatpants and t-shirt, which hugged her curves in the most mind-blowing way, for a pair of light blue jeans and a black tank top that left Nicholas' mouth watering. She'd pulled her hair back into a loose ponytail, only a few strands framing her face. Her cheeks were still slightly flushed from the effort.

Nicholas really didn't understand why she had felt the need to change, but seeing her standing there, looking so sexy and touchable, well... He wasn't exactly going to complain.

Giving her his best smile, he relished in the way her eyes immediately lit up when she looked at him. He briefly wondered if the warmth spreading though him was similar to what Christian and Manuel felt when they'd met their women. He immediately brushed that thought aside as he reminded himself that he really didn't have time for a relationship. Not that Amy was interested in having one with him anyway. Why would she? It wasn't like he was some prime catch. Not like his brothers.

As he felt his heart constrict with disappointment, he looked back at the table and busied himself with the demon's gun.

"What's with the gun?"

"Hmm?" He glanced up to see her looking between the gun in his hand and his face.

"The gun."

"Oh, yeah. I took this off the de...deviant who shot me."

"Are you going to turn it in? I don't know a whole lot about the law, but I'm pretty sure when a gun is used to shoot somebody, it should go to the cops."

Nicholas watched as she raised a single eyebrow, almost daring him to say otherwise. He couldn't help the smirk that pulled at the corners of his lips. Her sassiness was adorable.

"I actually know a few private investigators who will deal with this. The gun will end up right where it's supposed to. I promise."

Of course, that wasn't entirely a lie. He *did* know some PIs and *did* plan on getting the gun to the right person. Just not to Cindy or Ella. He thought Darren would be better.

Looking back down at the gun, he let out a soft sigh. He hated lying to her, even about something so small as to where this gun would end up. Hearing her hum softly, Nicholas figured she knew he wasn't being completely truthful, but he'd hoped she'd let it go.

"Are your brothers on their way?" she finally asked.

Without glancing up, Nicholas nodded. He kept his eyes on the table, hoping to keep Amy from seeing the warring emotions going on in his mind. With his thoughts bouncing back and forth between getting out of there as quickly as possible or following this unrealistic need to keep Amy close, Nicholas felt it was best to busy himself with getting ready for his brothers' arrival. All the while, he chided himself for acting the way he was.

"Are they all coming?" He heard the nervousness in her voice. "I mean, I'm sure they are, but..."

Finally looking up, he met her gaze. "I'm not sure if they will all be coming or if it will just be Cyrus. Either way, it's going to be okay."

"Okay." She walked over and sat across from him. "If you say it's going to be okay, I believe you."

"Just like that?" Nicholas asked with a smirk.

"Yeah." Amy grinned back. "Just like that. So... Tell me about your brothers."

For the next twenty minutes, Nicholas did just that...the human version anyway...while he placed the bullets into a shoebox Amy gave him. She listened quietly as he talked, laughed when he described their antics, frowning when he got to the recent arguments. He hadn't meant to get into that, but he couldn't seem to stop himself. Without going into details, Nicholas talked to her about the concerns he had with Manuel's girlfriend and how he now thought he'd been wrong.

"Why didn't you like Hayley?" Amy asked.

"She reminded me of a woman I used to know. Someone who wasn't a good person," he said slowly. "I was worried Hayley would hurt my brother the way that other woman had hurt me."

"She isn't that other woman, though."

"Yeah. I see that now." He paused as she reached across the table to place her hand on his arm. Feeling her warmth seep into him, he took a slow breath before going on. "It just took me a while to get used to the idea of Manuel being with someone like her. But now that I think about it, I believe they're really going to be good for each other."

"It sounds like Manuel and Christian are doing well in the relationship department."

"Yeah. They're a real-life David and Killian."

"David and Killian? Like the characters from *Once Upon A Time*?" She giggled. "Does that make you Robin?"

He smirked. "Hardly. I'm definitely more like Dean from *Supernatural*. That would make Cyrus my Sam." Nicholas laughed. "Don't tell him I said that, though... No, you know what? Tell him. I'd love to see the expression on his face."

Amy just shook her head and laughed. He loved the sound of it.

Nicholas opened his mouth to crack another joke...at Cyrus' expense, of course...but stopped when her doorbell rang.

She glanced over her shoulder, then looked back at him with wide eyes. "Your brothers?"

He nodded, standing up slowly. "I'll get it." He smiled. Walking by her, he trailed his hand along her shoulder. "I'll be right back."

Leaving her sitting quietly in the kitchen, Nicholas made his way toward her front door, his excitement growing with each step. Sensing his brothers on the other side, he reached for the handle as a huge grin spread across his face. Pulling the door open, he met his family's eager gazes.

"Hey," he sighed. "Boy, am I happy to see you guys."

Chapter 10

Amy tapped her fingers against her kitchen table. To say she was nervous about Nicholas' brothers showing up was putting it mildly. Not that she could figure out why she felt that way. It wasn't like they were coming to meet her, right? Amy figured they'd come in, maybe make some small talk, then whisk Nicholas out of here...leaving her alone, able to get back to her life.

A life that suddenly didn't seem as appealing as it had eleven days ago. Now it just felt empty. She'd deal with it, though. She didn't have a choice.

He was going to leave.

Of course he was going to leave, she chided herself. He had a life to get back to. Family to be with. But she was woman enough to admit feeling a certain level of disappointment about him taking off. It just couldn't be helped. After all, he may have only known her for a couple hours, but she'd been taking care of him for over a week.

She heard Nicholas open the front door. The heaviness of the wood scraping along the door frame as familiar to her as the sounds of Charlie's purring. Yet it was the loud burst of excitement that had her jumping in her seat. Turning toward the hallway leading to the front door, Amy listened.

The voices were muffled. Each man seemed to talk over the next, blending into each other until it was just an excited jumble of sounds rumbling through her house. She smiled at the noise. Even though she couldn't make out what they were saying, Amy recognized the happiness in their tone. As the voices started to lower, she made out Nicholas' deep tone.

He laughed. "I'll explain everything. First, let's stop hanging out in Amy's doorway and get inside."

"Who's Amy?" she heard a gravelly voice ask.

"Like I said," Nicholas remarked slowly. "I'll explain everything in a minute."

Mumbling was the only response as Amy heard her front door close, followed by the sounds of several pairs of boots walking across the floor. Standing slowly, she waited for what she could only assume would be a large group of males to come into her kitchen.

And to think, just weeks ago, I lectured myself on never going out to meet anyone, she mused. Now she had several strangers walking through her house. Well, not entirely strangers. After all, they were Nicholas' brothers. And if they were anything like him, she was definitely in trouble.

Nicholas walked into the kitchen first. His gorgeous red eyes lit up as they met hers. He gave her a quick wink, one that instantly had a blush crossing her face, before he moved to the side so four men could make their way in behind him. It took all the strength she had to stay standing and keep her jaw from dropping open as each turned his gaze on her.

My God, these men are gorgeous...and huge.

Amy was so mesmerized, she could only nod and smile slightly as Nicholas made the introductions. Christian and Manuel where first, each smiling at her as they said their hellos, then moved off to the side. They took up a spot along her counter and glanced around them. Their relaxed pose comforted her as Amy turned toward the remaining two.

Darren also smiled at her, but Amy sensed he was more guarded, more cautious as he looked her over. His eyes searched hers as he stood there. There was no judgment in his look, just a shielded curiosity that clouded his blue eyes. She had a sudden need for Nicholas' brothers to like her, so as she silently held Darren's gaze, she tried to will him to believe her desire to help his brother.

After what felt like forever, she finally released a soft sigh when Darren nodded at her and took a seat at the kitchen table. He didn't seem as tense as when he'd walked in, so she hoped that was because he didn't see her as a threat. Though she wasn't sure how she could be. For heaven's sake, he looked like he could flick someone the size of her with just a quick movement of his wrist. Not that she believed he would do that. Even though she could feel his uncertainty, there was no sense of danger coming off him.

In truth, all of Nicholas' brothers made her feel safe in their presence, except...

Turning from Darren, Amy was met with the blackest eyes she'd ever seen. They were unblinking and seemed to gaze right into her, as if to pull her entire world right out of her eyes. She felt her breath catch as she looked at him. Cyrus, the one Nicholas had talked to on the phone. The one who had demanded to know where he was and what happened to him. Nicholas had assured her his bark was far worse than his bite, but looking at him now, Amy wasn't quite sure his description of him was accurate.

Swallowing hard, she watched as Cyrus' eyes flickered over her, like he was trying to figure out if she was the enemy or not. She really hoped he'd decide she most definitely was anything but a threat to him, to Nicholas. That hope was quickly dashed.

"So, you're the one who's been keeping Nicholas from us," Cyrus growled, silencing all chatter around them.

Amy felt her mouth fall open as she rocked back slightly. "I-"

"Cyrus!" Nicholas exclaimed, his eyes narrowing.

His dark gaze focused on Nicholas. "What, Nicky? We have been looking for you for ten days. *Ten*! And you've been here doing what?" He looked back toward Amy before glaring back at Nicholas. "The way I see it, you either didn't think to let your family know you were okay, which I find hard to believe, or she was keeping you here somehow. You can stop shaking your head at me." As the other brothers began to speak up, Cyrus growled and pushed on. His voice dropped, eyes narrowing on Amy. "I demand to know who you are and what you've been doing with our brother for the past ten days."

As his gaze bored into Amy, she felt the need to cower beneath his anger. Her mind raced as she glanced around and noticed everyone looking at her. Well, everyone except Nicholas, whose eyes practically blazed as he stared at his brother. She looked back at Cyrus.

"I... I wasn't keeping him from you...from any of you. Nicholas just woke up today. He... He couldn't have contacted you sooner."

"Just woke up?" Darren asked, causing her head to swivel his way. His sapphire blue eyes stared intently at her. "What do you mean?"

"Just what she said, Darren." Nicholas took a step closer to Amy. The heat from his body seemed to reach out to her, calming her frazzled nerves almost immediately. "How about we stop with the interrogations..." He glanced pointedly at Cyrus before looking around at his other brothers, "and let me tell you guys what happened. Okay?"

When they all nodded, including Cyrus, Nicholas looked back at Amy. He smiled softly, her face warming. "Why don't you sit down next to Darren, love."

"Okay," she responded softly, moving toward the table. It didn't escape her that Nicholas sat her on the opposite side of where Cyrus still loomed, which she was fine with. The man seriously gave off some bad vibes.

Sitting, she ventured a glance at Darren. He'd leaned forward, resting his elbows comfortably on the table. His gaze locked on Nicholas as he waited for his brother to start filling them in. She had a feeling that even though he seemed to be focused one way, he was still very much aware of his surroundings. He suddenly shifted his gaze to hers. Amy's breath caught from the intensity, only to let it out in a soft chuckle as he gave her a slow wink before turning his attention back to Nicholas. If she didn't know any better, she'd swear he'd known exactly what she was thinking. But that was crazy. Right?

Feeling movement behind her, Amy glanced over her shoulder to see Christian and Manuel moving closer. Christian's gaze was focused completely on Nicholas. His concern and need to know what had happened to his brother was evident on his face.

Manuel, on the other hand, flicked his eyes curiously between her and Nicholas. She marveled at the deep purple of them when his gaze finally landed fully on her. Like Nicholas' red and Cyrus' black, Manuel's eyes were a shade she'd never seen before. They'd make the most natural amethyst pale in comparison and seemed to darken, then lighten again right before her eyes.

Hearing Nicholas clear his throat, she pulled her gaze from Manuel, but not before noticing the smirk that danced upon his lips from catching her staring.

Men.

She was amazed, though. With all these good-looking men in her kitchen...and yes, even if Cyrus was acting like a dick right now, she could still admit he was rather good looking...any other woman would probably swoon to have any of them look at her. However, it was only Nicholas who made her heart speed up. Looking at him now, she smiled as he met her stare.

With a tilt of his head, she watched him take a deep breath before he started talking. The tension in the room seemed to spike almost immediately when he began to speak of the man he'd chased. His eyes remained locked on hers, though. In that moment, as he spoke softly of the fight that took place, Amy could only feel for the man before her.

The man who was quickly becoming all she saw.

Chapter 11

Nicholas watched as Amy's body slowly relaxed. He could have punched Cyrus for the way he'd acted toward her. Treating her like she was the reason behind his disappearance...

The ass.

At least he'd gotten her to calm down. Plus, sitting her next to Darren, he figured he could at least count on her being safe should Cyrus go off the deep end. He just wished he knew where his brother's head was at lately. Nicholas knew there was a lot of darkness creeping around up there, but shit. He seemed to be getting worse each day.

Glancing over at the brother in question, Nicholas stared into his coal black eyes as he began to tell them about following the demon through the alley and onto the street. Of course, he didn't say it was a demon and left out the fact that he flew after him, not ran.

"After I caught up with him, he'd pulled the gun and pointed it my way." Nicholas shifted his feet, seeing the fight unfolding in his mind. "I was able to get the gun from him, but not before he managed to get a shot off."

He felt the tension in his brothers spike. Even Amy bit her lip as she listened. Sadness and worry rolled off her in waves, slamming into him with a force so strong, he had to pause and take a steadying breath.

"He shot you?" Darren growled, drawing Nicholas' attention. "How did... I mean, what..."

"After everything was over, I wanted to call you guys, but I couldn't find my phone," he went on softly, knowing Darren was so frustrated, he could hardly form his questions. "I have no idea how I ended up here. I remember fences and bushes. I think I may have even fallen a time or two. I don't really know." He looked from one concerned face to another, his gaze finally landing on Amy. "It was luck, fate... I'm not sure, but I somehow ended up on Amy's back porch."

He watched Amy give him a soft smile. Grinning back at her, he felt the warmth in his chest spread just a bit more.

"And that's where I found him," she said quietly. She kept her gaze on him as she continued the story. She told them how he'd asked her to not take him to a hospital and how she needed to get the bullet out. Amy talked about the black lines that climbed across his body and how nervous she'd been about removing the bullet on her own. She'd done it, though, then sewed him up.

Nicholas still couldn't wrap his mind around the fact that Amy had been able to get the bullet out herself, then somehow wrestled him inside and onto her couch. The courage, the strength it must have taken to do that for a stranger was unheard of to him. Sure, he and his brothers would jump in without a second thought if someone were in danger, it was what they did, but for another human to do that, to so willingly help out a stranger without stopping to question it, was a strength Nicholas hadn't seen before. With each word that fell from her lips, each soft smile she sent his way as she described how she'd watched over him as he'd slept, he wanted her more and more. The fight within himself to leave Amy behind slowly started dying.

Just listening to her talk about all she went through after finding him in her back yard made his heart race. How could he leave her after all she'd done for him?

"So, um..." The nervousness in her voice brought Nicholas out of his thoughts. He watched as Amy looked around before focusing on her kitchen table. "He only woke up a few hours ago. After having a bite to eat, he called Cyrus. That... That's it."

The room fell silent. Nicholas looked around and noticed the wide-eyed stare all his brothers gave her. Even Cyrus shook his head, his eyes flashing briefly with the pain he always tried to hide. Nicholas knew better than to point it out. His brother tried so hard to act as if nothing got to him. Ever since he was taken, he'd changed, gotten more angry, built up a wall around himself. Nicholas still felt hope that the old Cyrus would reemerge someday. Until then, though, he'd allow his brother to keep his false sense of indifference. Rare moments like this, when his true feelings seeped through, would remain unnoticed. It was the least Nicholas could do for him.

Looking back at Amy, he saw her fidgeting with a napkin. Her fingers curled the edges, twisting them slightly beneath her fingertips as her eyes lifted occasionally to glance around. Feeling an unexplainable pull to her, Nicholas decided to just give in to it. Before he knew it, his feet moved toward her. Her gaze snapped up to his as he got closer, a small smile tugging at the corners of her lips. He needed to see that smile, craved it. Ever since he'd woken up and seen her smile for the first time, he'd grown addicted to it.

Stopping at her side, he reached down and ran a hand over her shoulder, feeling her shiver slightly beneath his touch. "You okay?" he asked softly, watching her eyes light up.

She nodded, leaning into him. Her fingers stilled on the table as she visibly relaxed. It wasn't until a throat cleared that Nicholas looked up from her and noticed his brothers watching them intently.

As he frowned at the smirks on Christian's and Manuel's faces, he sensed Darren shifting in his chair.

"Amy," Darren said slowly, drawing everyone's attention to him. "You were able to remove *all* the bullet from Nicholas' side, right?"

"Yes." She got up and stepped around Nicholas as she retrieved a small baggie from a box on the counter. He watched her give Cyrus a wide berth as she headed back to the table, handing the baggie to Darren. "This is the bullet I pulled out of him. I held onto it because I wasn't sure if he would need it or not."

Nicholas tried to keep his attention on Darren as he studied the bullet, but Amy moved back to his side, the warmth from her body seeping through his shirt as she leaned against him, keeping his attention split between her and his brother.

"You did good, Amy," Darren said, looking up from the bag in his hand. "I don't think any of us can thank you enough for saving Nicholas."

Nicholas felt the happiness rolling off her at his praise. Her beautiful eyes flashed up at him before looking back at Darren. "I'm sure anyone would have done the same thing." Her voice was soft as she glanced around the room. "I'm just glad I was here to help him."

"I think we're all happy about that," Christian laughed as he walked around the table and took the bag from Darren. He held it up, squinting at the piece of metal inside. "So, you dug this little guy out of my brother, huh?"

Amy laughed softly. "I did."

"Hey. That bullet may be small, but it packed quite a punch. It's not like I had a splinter in me. I was *shot*."

"Maybe if you hadn't gone off on your own...," Cyrus grumbled, his voice just loud enough to draw everyone's attention. Nicholas watched his brother's coal black eyes take on a dark glow as he stared back at him. "What were you thinking, taking off after that de-" He snapped his mouth shut, giving Amy a glance, "that piece of shit by yourself?"

Nicholas felt his anger starting to rise. "I saw him pick up the gun Darren was trying to get to, then I saw him run. I did what any one of you would have."

"Wrong. You did what you always do." Cyrus' muscles tensed. "You took it upon yourself to go off alone, and..."

"And what?" Nicholas took a step toward his brother.

"And you shouldn't be so irresponsible! What? You think you're invincible? Like you can take on these...these assholes like they're the normal kind we usually face? They aren't, Nicholas." Cyrus' words rushed out as his temper grew.

"Cyrus," Darren warned, attempting to put a stop to the argument before it got out of hand.

Either choosing to ignore Darren or just not hearing him, Cyrus went on. "They're far worse than the ones we're used to. And I hate to break this to you, brother, but you're *not* invincible." He flicked his wrist toward the bag in Christian's hand. "But then, I guess you know that now, don't you?"

"You know what, Cyrus? Fuck you," Nicholas growled. "I was right where I was supposed to be, doing what I was supposed to be doing...helping our brothers. And calling me irresponsible? Actually, you know what? I'm not even mad about that." He snickered, ignoring Manuel and Christian as they both begged him to calm down. "I find *you* calling *me* that kind of funny. Downright hysterical."

Cyrus narrowed his eyes. "What the hell is that supposed to mean, brother?"

"Exactly how it sounds, *brother*," Nicholas bit out. "You are the last one who should point a finger about that. Like I said, I was right where I was supposed to be." He gave Cyrus a look of disdain.

"That's enough," Darren said, standing abruptly from his spot next to an obviously tense Amy.

Nicholas knew where his brother's concern and agitation stemmed from. If this argument, or whatever it was, between him and Cyrus continued to escalate, things could get out of hand quickly. If they came to blows, the damage to their relationship, as well as Amy's house, could be irreparable. He just wasn't sure he could stop this train wreck if he tried. The anger running through Nicholas' veins was too much.

Darren rested a comforting hand on Amy's shoulder as he continued. "It's been a long ten days. We're all stressed out and tired. So why don't we all sit down and-"

"No, Darren," Cyrus hissed. "Our long-lost brother here obviously has a point he's trying to make, so let's hear it."

"You know what? Yeah, I probably shouldn't have gone after that shithead on my own. I should have waited for someone to go with me, but everyone was a little busy at that exact moment and I just couldn't let him get away with that gun. So

I did what needed to be done. Not that you would know any of that."

"Nicholas, I don't think now's the time for-" Christian started as he took a couple steps to the side, only to have Cyrus cut him off.

"Just spit it out, Nicky. What's your fucking point?" Cyrus practically yelled in his face. His anger pushed against Nicholas, causing a noticeable shift in the shadows curling around them.

"My point, I would think, is pretty damn obvious," Nicholas growled, pulling himself to his full height so he was eye to eye with his brother. He sensed the air around them thickening from their combined anger. Both seemed to be barely holding onto any semblance of control. Nicholas felt his tattoo giving off a slight throb as a breeze lifted the bottom of his shirt.

He really should have pulled back, heed Darren's unsaid warning, and table this conversation for another day. Hell, the knowledge alone that any blowup would be right in front of Amy should have given him pause. He was sure she could probably already sense something. If not from him, the steadily growing shadows behind Cyrus would have caught anyone's attention.

As if to confirm his suspicions, he heard Amy release a strangled gasp.

However, even that couldn't stop the storm that had started building within him.

Staring at his brother, meeting his angry gaze with one of his own, Nicholas felt his muscles tense. "I was right where I was supposed to be, Cyrus. I was there, in that alley, fighting alongside our brothers. We all were there..." Cocking his head slightly, he felt his lips pull back into a snarl. "Except for you. Isn't that right? You... What? Just chose that moment to go off? Where in the fuck were you when your brothers needed you?"

The minute the last word left his mouth, he watched Cyrus jerk back like he'd been hit. The anger that had covered his face just seconds earlier now mingled with pain and uncertainty. The emotions flew over his features in waves before he visibly tensed, slamming down anything but his normal mask of irritation and disinterest.

Nicholas stood still as he watched his brother take several steps back, then move toward him with almost predator-like ease. He took a deep breath as Cyrus got back in his face, his eyes pools of black ink.

The added tension radiating off his other brothers caused the air in the kitchen to feel even thicker, making it almost hard to breathe.

He hated fighting with them. The last argument he had with Manuel had practically gutted him. And now, staring at Cyrus, he felt that familiar pain roll through him. They just all meant so much to him and he'd been looking forward to reuniting with them. This really wasn't going the way he wanted it to. But it was too late to stop.

Ever since he had woken up on Amy's couch, the questions of where Cyrus was during the fight had bounced around in his mind.

However, now had probably not been the right time to bring them up. He'd just been so angry. Still was, to a certain extent...though it had slowly started to dissolve. He really looked at Cyrus, not the wall he'd erected to hide behind. His words, his accusations, had hurt his brother deeply.

Which he regretted.

Cyrus seemed to glance over Nicholas' shoulder before looking back at him. "I think, *brother*..." His voice was a mere whisper, "that maybe you should handle your little human here and worry about yourself, not about what I'm doing or where I was. That's my business." Pulling back, Cyrus again looked over his shoulder. "See you at home." Without giving him another glance, Cyrus turned and quickly left the kitchen.

A sudden rush of power followed by utter silence meant Cyrus choose to dematerialize instead of going out the front door.

Taking a couple deep breaths, Nicholas slowly turned to find his brothers sharing a look between themselves, but it was Amy who drew his immediate attention. She stared at him as if she wanted to say something, not finding the words. Her mouth opened and closed a few times before she just shook her head, yet he could see her mind racing.

Worried about what she might be thinking, Nicholas took a cautious step toward her. "Amy..."

"Did he leave?" she asked quietly.

"Yes, um... He headed home." At her slight frown, Nicholas rushed on. "He drove himself here, so..." Glancing at his brothers, he quickly realized they weren't going to be any help. *Great.*

"Oh, well... Your brother, Cyrus, is, um..." She waved her hand in the air, glancing around at everyone else before blowing out a rush of air. "He's...intense."

Manuel gave a loud laugh. "That's one way to describe him."

Darren glared at Manuel. "He's just been having a hard time of it lately." Looking up at Nicholas, he nodded toward the door. "We should really be going." Glancing at Amy, he gave her a gentle smile. "It was very nice meeting you, Amy. Thank you again for watching over

Nicholas. I'd say farewell, but I have a feeling we'll be seeing you again." Nicholas watched him give her hand a light squeeze before walking out of the kitchen.

Before Darren turned the corner, he shot a knowing look at Nicholas. His gaze not only said to not take long, but was also questioning. Sure, Darren had told Amy that he'd see her again, but Nicholas knew he was ultimately leaving it up to him on whether he wanted to wipe her memories. A sentiment he was sure was shared by all of his brothers. They couldn't know the very thought of doing that caused Nicholas' skin to crawl. He may not be sure if he wanted to pursue whatever was going on between them, but he sure as hell didn't want her to forget about him. Call it selfish or unfair, but that was how he felt.

Standing back, he watched as both Christian and Manuel stepped up to Amy.

Christian gave her arm a light squeeze. He didn't say anything, but whatever she saw in his eyes must have said it all because her face lit up, her smile growing.

Manuel, on the other hand, pulled Amy out of her chair and into a hug. A gasp of surprised laughter burst from her. Nicholas smiled as he listened to Manuel murmur his thanks for all she did. Her eyes sparkled as he stepped back. With a nod at

Nicholas, he followed Christian from the room.

Finally finding himself alone with her, Nicholas watched as she turned to face him. "Sorry about all of that," he said as she met his gaze.

Her smile never faltering, she shook her head. "I'm just glad you're okay. They were obviously very worried about you. I mean, you all seem to be very close."

"Yeah, well, we've kind of had a few years to grow on each other."

"And you all live together?"

"Um, yeah. We actually just moved into a new house. It's pretty big, so we don't feel so cramped."

"And Christian's and Manuel's girlfriends live there, too?"

"Yup... Well, Ella does." Nicholas frowned. "Right before I, um...I ended up here, I think Manuel was just getting ready to ask Hayley to move in." He walked over and picked up his arrow case from the counter, sliding it over his head. "I guess I'll find out when I get home."

"Yeah," she said softly.

He turned and picked up his bow. The weight of it in his hands normally comforted him, but today, it couldn't help soothe the growing sadness he felt in his chest. Who had he been kidding? He'd almost convinced himself that he could just take Amy with him, like she was some kind of a stray he'd found. Laughing softly, he realized that in this scenario, *he* was the stray. It was rather fitting. Regardless, though, he couldn't just uproot her from her life, her home, and whisk her away to his.

Be realistic, you idiot, he chided himself as he clipped his bow onto his back. What he wanted to do was nothing short of some Disney fairy tale, and stuff like that just didn't happen to him.

Turning back, he found her watching him. He was so close, he could see the flecks of gold in her brown eyes as she stared into his. Nicholas wasn't sure what she was looking for.

Clearing his throat, he tore his gaze away and looked over the room. "I need to get going," he stated lamely. "I'm sure my brothers are waiting for me."

Without waiting for a reply, he turned to head out. Better to just leave rather than let this sudden awkwardness between them grow. He was just to the edge of the kitchen when he heard the shuffling of feet.

"Nicholas?" Amy's soft voice floated through the quiet.

Turning slowly, he looked at her, her eyes now sad as she stood there. "Yeah?"

"Will I see you again?" The hope in her voice was unmistakable. It made his pulse increase, his stomach tense.

Not allowing himself to consider what he was doing, Nicholas took several quick steps toward her, stopping right in front of Amy. Her eyes shimmered from the tears building just at the edges. The sight caused a gasp of pain to leave his lips as he reached down and pulled her face to his.

The kiss wasn't sweet or gentle. It wasn't anything Nicholas would have expected his first kiss with Amy to be. Yes, he had been thinking about it, wondering what it would feel like to have her gorgeous lips pressed against his. In a way, he'd known this moment would happen. What he hadn't been prepared for was the hunger in the kiss. The raw need that seemed to pour out of them the second their lips touched.

There was no gentleness. It was a claiming, a proclamation of their desire for each other.

As Nicholas deepened the kiss, he felt Amy moan as she pushed herself against him, her body molding to his. He could practically hear her blood rushing through her veins as she grasped onto his shirt, her fingers digging into the fabric. Whether to anchor herself to him or keep him from pulling back, he wasn't sure.

Tangling his fingers in her hair, he growled when he felt her tongue dip into his mouth, meeting his demands and needs with her own.

God, I wish I could just stay here. Even as the thought crossed his mind, he knew he needed to go.

Finally pulling himself away, he rested his forehead on hers, both of them gasping softly. Closing his eyes, he took a moment to breathe her in. Memorizing her scent as he fought to rein in his desire. Feeling her pull back, he opened his eyes, watching as she reached up and pushed a strand of his hair out of his face.

"Would you *like* to see me again?" he asked softly. Even though he thought he knew the answer, he couldn't help the feeling of doubt that wiggled around in the back of his mind.

"Yes."

"Okay," he sighed.

"Okay," she murmured, smiling at him as he slowly pulled away. His fingertips lightly running down her arm, he began to turn. "Here," she whispered, reaching over to grab a notepad off the counter. With a pen, she wrote across the top page before ripping it off, folding it, and placing it into his hand.

Without looking down, Nicholas curled his fingers around hers. He felt the edges of the paper digging into his palm as he held it tightly, then shoved it into his back pocket. Giving her one last kiss, he turned and made his way out of the house.

Nicholas tried to ignore the hurt from Cyrus' absence as he climbed into the Hummer next to Manuel. Glancing at his brother, he saw his amethyst eyes flash as he smiled at him.

The general mood in the car was one of relief and excitement. He let his brothers' energy wash over him as he unhooked the strap around his chest and set his bow and arrow case at his feet, sinking into the soft leather seat. His mind bounced between his brothers, home, and Amy. He'd just left her, but Nicholas already wondered how quickly he'd be able to sneak away so he could give her a call.

"Are you ready to go home, brother?"

Darren's voice drifted back to him from the driver's seat. Looking up, Nicholas met his gaze, along with Christian's, as they looked back at him. Taking a deep breath, he finally felt the tension he hadn't known he was carrying fall from his shoulders.

Home. The single best word he'd heard in a long time. The place he'd wanted to go since he'd woken up.

"Yeah. Let's go home."

Chapter 12

Looking down from the roof of the club, Dev tapped his fingers against the edge. He watched as group after group of stumbling humans made their way in and out of the building. Each time the door opened and the loud music confined within escaped, it thrummed through the air, vibrating along his spine. It was still light out, so he had no trouble making out the cars driving past, the humans walking leisurely along the street, and the freedom that seemed just out of reach as he gazed beyond the road before him.

God, he wished he could just leave.

Life didn't work that way for him, though, and the sooner he stopped with the foolish notion that he'd be free of it all, the sooner he could give in to the numbness that slowly consumed him. It would be better that way. Hope never did anything for him.

After he'd escorted Maria out of the club and she'd driven away, he'd found himself cornered by Kanibal and the twins. They'd complained to him about one thing or another. He wasn't sure because he'd blocked them out shortly after they started talking. He'd actually gotten pretty good at that. Their power display didn't faze him anymore and their words meant nothing.

Once he'd successfully gotten away from them, Dev had finished making his rounds through the club. Spending the next hour or so dealing with whiny humans and Trix's cold shoulder had taken what little energy he still had left. It was exhausting. So, the first chance he had, he'd slipped down the hall and into his office. The quiet in the room had felt so soothing, he'd finally been able to relax. He allowed his guard to slip, allowed his mind to wander. He'd imagined his brothers coming through the door, feeling the safety that could only come from being around those you loved. He'd imagined standing under the sun, soaking it up with little worry of who was around.

His moment of escape had been shattered by the opening of his office door. He'd thrown his mental wall up so quickly, it would have left him dizzy if it hadn't been for the shudder that jarred him back to reality as Andras and Agalon walked in.

The day had only gone downhill from there.

The mood the demons had been in, the anger simmering in the air around them, was frightening, to say the least. Dev had feared that they knew about his involvement with the failed attempt at grabbing Ella and Red. The news of that had flown through the club almost as quickly as the questions of where the six demons that Andras had sent after them had gone. It didn't take long for Dev to mentally sigh with relief. Within the first few seconds of Andras' growling his displeasure, it had been apparent Dev was not the cause.

Not that he had known at that point what Andras had been so angry about. The demon had growled and snarled like a wild animal before dismissing Dev from his own office, slamming the door loudly behind him before he'd even been a step past the threshold.

The temptation had been too great to stay there and linger by the closed door, to try and listen to the argument happening inside. It was just so rare to see Andras lose his composure, he couldn't squash the curiosity rolling through him. So, after a lot of internal arguing, he'd leaned against the wall next to the door, opening himself up slightly to hear what was happening.

The first voice he heard was Agalon. The second-in-command was equally agitated, his voice vibrating the walls as he talked rapidly about a dark witch and the trouble she could bring them. Dev's eyes narrowed. From what he gathered, Andras was in need of a black witch in order to track down Ella and Red. Agalon, for the first time that Dev could recall, strongly argued against Andras' idea.

He needed to figure out how to warn his brothers. Once he got back into his office, he'd see about tracking them down or, at the very least, finding someone he could trust to get a message to them. Feeling the power from the two demons building rapidly within the room, Dev briefly wondered if he was going to have an office to go back to.

Just as he started pulling himself away from the wall, he heard Andras' voice growl through the air. This time, his power pulsed, emphasizing each word.

"I will be meeting with the witch tomorrow night, Agalon. This is not up for discussion. And before you decide to argue your point further, I need you to stop and remember who the fuck you are talking to."

Dev heard some shuffling. He imagined Agalon moving a step back from Andras as the argument they'd been having really set in.

"Of course, Andras," he heard Agalon finally say, his voice a lot lower than it had been. "I just do not trust witches. No matter what you have over them, they cannot be trusted to do exactly what you want."

"You think I am not aware of how these individuals work?"

"No, of course not. You are right, Andras. We will meet with this witch tomorrow night, then you will finally have the females in your hands."

"Yes, and once I do, those pesky Guardians will fall to their knees before me."

He heard Andras release a soft chuckle. Dev's skin crawled. He felt the hatred behind his words as the demon spoke of his family.

With the knowledge that the meeting would happen tomorrow, Dev had stepped away from the wall and made a quick exit. He needed space, time to think.

Now here he was, finding solace in the one spot that, as of now, he'd claimed as his own. He liked to come up here to get away from everything, to catch his breath. Not that he was delusional about the demons below him not knowing exactly where he was, but so far, they'd let him be when he was up here.

Taking a deep breath, he gazed out at the slowly descending sun. It wouldn't be long until it was too low, hidden by the buildings of downtown, for him to see it. Until then, he'd soak in what little bit of warmth it gave him. He allowed his mind to wander as he leaned against the edge of the roof.

He needed to get his thoughts under control. Needed to stop looking around every corner in the hopes his brothers showed up. If he didn't, someone was bound to notice, start to question who he was looking for. He didn't want to think of what would happen if they did.

Add in the knowledge of the demons teaming up with a dark witch, and Dev suddenly found himself with a lot more than just his desire to find his brothers that he needed to keep under wraps.

Then there was his conversation with Castigo... His moment of pure madness when he'd asked the demon to aide him in protecting his brothers. He knew it probably wasn't his best idea, but damn. He was in real need of some help right about now.

On a positive note...not a huge plus, but he'd take what he could get...Sy hadn't been in touch with him since that day in Indigo's parking lot. Dev felt that was probably for the best. Especially seeing as Agalon had been following him around inside the club lately. The demon made him nervous. Dev knew he was just looking for a reason to drag him before Andras. Without Sy's surprise visit and calls to worry about, Dev had been pretty confident that he'd been able to stay off of Agalon's radar, much to the demon's dismay.

Chuckling, Dev closed his eyes briefly as a breeze swept over him, bringing with it the sweet smell of the bakery down the road. Thoughts of warm muffins and chocolate chip cookies reminded him that he hadn't eaten yet today. Not that he was trying to starve himself, but when you were constantly looking over your shoulder, eating wasn't always at the top of your to-do list. It was quiet right now, though. Maybe he could make his way down to grab something to eat before the night crowd started showing up. Slip away before anyone noticed he was missing.

Yeah, right. Add that to the list of wishful thoughts that will never happen.

But if he could...

With his mind wandering over the possibilities, Dev straightened from where he leaned against the ledge. Thoughts of ways to escape the club filled his head. He quickly decided that if he were to try to get out of here, it would probably be easier to just jump down into the alley in the back of the building.

I probably shouldn't just head down and walk out the front door. He released a soft laugh at the thought.

Damn, now I really want a muffin.

Just as he turned away, movement down on the street caught his attention.

Moving back toward the edge of the roof, he squinted at the alley across the street. It was an odd disturbance. A flicker in the shadows, a change in the air. He couldn't physically see anything. That didn't change the fact that he knew someone, or something, was down there.

Letting the air leave his lungs on a sigh, he allowed his power to rise to the surface and flow out before him. He felt the humans who walked on the sidewalk below, the cat that sat beneath the truck parked along the street, the hum of the power that always circled the club. All shivered against his power as it brushed against them.

It was the power pulsing within the alley that held his attention, though. It felt strong, familiar. Shaking his head, he leaned forward, focusing all his attention on that narrow opening between the buildings. Just as he felt his power come up against what he thought was a brick wall, the wall pushed back.

What the hell?

The power flared against his, causing Dev to grip the ledge. The shadows against the buildings grew before his eyes. They reached out across the walls, curling though the air. He thought they would completely overtake the building, spill out onto the street, and race his way. His pulse pounded in his ears as he braced himself, but then, just as suddenly as the area had flared to life, the shadows, as well as the power, simply disappeared. A sense of loss gripped him as he threw his own power out, searching wildly.

It had felt so familiar. His mind flooded with hope as his memory pulled up images of who that power could possibly belong to. It couldn't have been one of his brothers, though. Could it?

He'd ached to see them for so long, he was sure his mind had finally snapped. What took it so long to break was beyond him.

But... What if it hadn't been just in his mind?

Glancing around, he felt what little hope he had fade away. As he was about to give up, chalk it up to his stressed nerves playing tricks on him, he felt a rush of warmth hit his back.

"Dev?" a deep, familiar voice rumbled behind him.

Goosebumps rippled across his arms as he spun around, his lungs freezing. Fear mixed with happiness. Uncertainty mixed with excitement. All his emotions ran together until they were like a storm within his very core. His hands shook as he took a timid step away from the ledge.

At the same time, the owner of the deep voice took a step toward him, the moonlight seeming to give his onyx eyes a light glow as the male stared unblinkingly his way. The sight caused Dev to release a breath in a rush.

It couldn't be...

He blinked rapidly. His thoughts latched onto the necessity to believe what he was seeing. He felt the need to hit pause on this moment. To suspend these precious seconds for a lifetime. In the middle of the club's rooftop, the center of his personal darkness, stood the one person he hadn't planned on seeing again. The one who, for all intents and purposes, shouldn't be here...but was.

"C-Cyrus?" Dev finally choked out.

"Hello, brother," Cyrus responded with a deep sigh. He gazed at him as he took another step his way. "I've been looking for you."

Chapter 13

He still felt torn.

Part of Nicholas longed to have Darren turn around to head back to Amy's, while another part of him wanted to tell him to drive faster and get him home. He thought he'd been okay with leaving her when he'd settled into the Hummer, yet the farther they traveled from Amy's house, the more unsure he was that he'd made the right decision.

The silence in the car didn't help, either. He didn't like quiet. Never had. The need to start talking was overwhelming, but he could feel his brothers' contentment. Their relief was obvious in each breath they took. He understood how they felt. Hell, he remembered that feeling the day they found and brought Cyrus home.

He was supposed to have gone out with Cyrus that night. The knowledge that if he had, the Shadow Demons may not have gotten to him, taken him, still hurt. Even years later, he couldn't shake the feeling that he'd failed his brother.

The absence of Cyrus as they headed home only seemed to enhance the fact that he still was.

Shit.

If he hadn't gone after the demon that night, taken it upon himself to retrieve that gun on his own - no matter how much he felt it had been the right thing to do - he wouldn't have been shot. He wouldn't have been away from his brothers for the past ten days, and he wouldn't have added to their stress. And maybe, just maybe, Cyrus wouldn't be teetering on the edge now.

Of course, if things hadn't played out the way they did, he wouldn't have met Amy. The thought caused an ache to start in his chest.

Nicholas shifted slightly as he stared out the window. No, it was a good thing he was heading home. He'd been away too long.

When they finally pulled through the front gates, Nicholas felt a calmness wash over him as his eyes landed on the front door. It already stood open, Ella and Hayley standing there.

Stepping out of the Hummer, he had just enough time to clear the door and brace himself before Ella flew into his arms. A groan escaped his lips as he lifted her off the ground. Her laughter rang through the air.

"Thank God, you're home," she exclaimed, tightening her grip around his neck. "We were all so worried about you. Where were you? I tried to find you, we all did, but it was like you just vanished. *Poof.* What happened?"

Giving her a gentle squeeze, he set her back on the ground. "Hey. I'm okay."

"Yeah, if you call getting shot and being in a coma for ten days okay," Manuel said, walking up next to them.

Before Nicholas could tell his brother to shut up, an audible gasp sounded from not just Ella, but also Hayley, who walked their way.

"Oh, my god. You were shot?" Hayley asked, wringing her hands together.

They may not have been close, something he definitely wanted to fix now that he was back, but that didn't stop him as he reached out for her. Dragging her into a tight hug, he looked over her shoulder to see Manuel standing there, watching them. The look in his brother's eyes spoke volumes. They swam with multiple levels of warmth and concern. Warmth from the love that obviously rolled through him as he looked at Hayley. Concern as he seemed to be trying to figure out if he truly was okay.

With a slight tilt of his head, Nicholas sent Manuel a questioning look as he felt Hayley sigh against him. His amethyst gaze darkened slightly, then he nodded. Nicholas would have questioned it, but Christian's voice pulled his gaze his way.

"Don't worry, babe," Christian said, wrapping his arm tightly around Ella's shoulders, meeting Nicholas' gaze. "He may have been away from us, but he was not alone. Actually, it looked like he was well taken care of." He smirked.

"By whom?" Ella asked.

"What does that mean?" Hayley enquired at the same time, pulling back from his embrace. Her green eyes flashed up at him as an eyebrow rose.

"It's nothing, really," he started, Manuel interrupting.

"I'd hardly call the looks going back and forth between you and Amy nothing." He laughed, his arm wrapping around Hayley's waist, pulling her gently from Nicholas' arms. "And since you now have your own girl, I'll ask you to keep your hands off mine. Savvy?"

"Savvy? I see someone's been watching *Pirates of the Caribbean*," Nicholas joked. He watched as Hayley relaxed in Manuel's embrace. She rested her head back against his shoulder as she hugged his arms tightly around her. They truly were perfect for each other. Just as Christian and Ella seemed made for each other.

His gaze wandered to the couple. Christian unconsciously rubbed one of his hands in circles on Ella's shoulder as they smiled at each other. Both his brothers were so happy, so in love, he almost made a crack about how sickening it was. Almost. Instead, he just stood there, glancing from one happy couple to the other. Fuck. He felt a pang of jealousy shoot through him. It came on so quickly, he practically felt the air rush from his chest at the sudden pain.

Pushing it down, he schooled his features. There was no reason for him to be jealous of his brothers. They were happy. That was all that mattered.

With a mental shake, he forced a grin to spread across his face. "Next thing you know, you're going to be asking where the rum is?"

"Ha... Ha... Ha..." Even though Manuel acted put off, his eyes lit up with laughter. "It'd be no worse than you spitting out quote after quote from *Get Him to the Greek* every time I turned around."

"Oh shit. I almost forgot about that," Christian chimed in. "For a straight month, all Nicky kept talking about was *stroking the furry walls*."

"Yeah, and how people's brains are *filled with lollipops, rainbows, and cheese*." Manuel chuckled.

"Whatever, you guys," Nicholas rolled his eyes, trying to act annoyed, even as a soft laugh escaped his lips. "Anyway, I don't know what you are going on and on about. You two quoted that movie right along with me. Of course, neither of you quoted anything as much as you did after you saw *Ghostbusters* for the first time. I mean, really, if I had to hear one more time about being the *Gatekeeper*..." He smirked. At the grumbling from his brothers, Nicholas sent a wink to Ella and Hayley. "You know you missed me."

The girls' laughter curled around them before they all fell into a thoughtful silence. At least it was thoughtful on his part. Why couldn't he just turn off his brain? Stop the multiple questions that knocked against his mind like a battering ram? He wasn't sure what was on everyone else's mind. Possibly thoughts about him being home and Cyrus' absence. His mind, though, was a jumble of thoughts. Some tugged at the edges of his mind, but didn't come through clearer than static on a TV.

Now Nicholas felt the silence stretching between them like a physical thing. It pulled at his emotions and weighed down his shoulders. Just as he thought he'd snap, either laughing hysterically or crying over everything that had happened, he sensed movement behind him.

He didn't need to turn to know it was Darren, his brother stepping up to the group. His presence, as always, seemed to bring a calmness to him.

"Hey, where's Cyrus?" Ella asked, looking around.

"He, um-" Nicholas started, only to be interrupted by Manuel. Again.

"Cyrus decided to head out for a bit," he said smoothly. "I'm sure he'll be home in a while."

"Oh, well, he has seemed stressed lately," Ella conceded, then looked at Nicholas. "I just hope with you home, he can start to relax a bit."

"That would be a miracle in itself," Christian grumbled, letting out a soft groan when Ella elbowed him playfully in the ribs.

"He's been going through a lot," she said softly.

"Haven't we all," Christian said, sending a pointed look to Manuel that Nicholas couldn't help but notice.

How had Cyrus been while he was laid up at Amy's? Nicholas had just assumed he'd been his normal, surly self. Angry at the world, probably disappointed in Nicholas for running off. He started to get the feeling there was more to it than that. Actually, he got that impression while at Amy's house. Maybe he just hadn't wanted to look too deeply into it. Maybe he'd been afraid to.

Darren cleared his throat, gripping Nicholas' shoulder before moving a couple steps past him. "Why don't we head inside. I'm sure Nicky would like to relax for a bit now that he's home."

With a nod from everyone, they all started making their way toward the front door.

It wasn't until he'd taken a few steps to follow Darren that Nicholas felt a hand snake around his arm. Looking down, he saw Ella leaning against him.

"So... Are you going to tell me who Amy is?" she asked softly, her voice drifting up to him like a soft breeze.

Damn, he'd thought he'd avoided this conversation. Guess he should have known better. Smiling, he hugged her hand to his side. "There really isn't much to tell."

She smiled. "Oh, I doubt that."

Blowing out a breath, he stepped up to the front door, ushering in Ella before him. "How about we talk about this later? I could really use something to eat."

"How about I fix you a box of mac 'n' cheese while you fill us in on Amy and what happened?" Ella smirked at him, reaching out for Christian, who walked close by.

Nicholas' eyes drifted to his brother's before landing back on Ella's expectant face. "Well, when you offer up mac 'n' cheese in the mix, how can I say no?"

"That's the idea." Laughing, Ella shook her head as she walked away, disappearing into the kitchen. Following close behind, he paused as Christian nudged his side.

"Really glad you're home." Christian's voice cracked slightly with emotion, his eyes softening before he blinked rapidly and glanced toward the kitchen.

"Me, too, brother." Looking to the side, Nicholas saw Darren, Manuel, and Hayley all glancing his way. Smiles tugged at the edges of their lips, the happiness and love in their gazes causing warmth to spread through him as he watched them walk into the kitchen. Releasing a slow breath, he looked back at Christian and nodded. "Me, too."

Chapter 14

Trudging up the stairs, Nicholas let out a sigh of relief. What should have only been an hour-long conversation had turned into a four-hour interrogation. Most of the queries shooting from either side of the dining room table had been voiced by Hayley and Ella.

Who knew just one simple comment about waking up on Amy's couch could bring on such a barrage of questions?

He'd answered everything from what color her hair was to if he was going to see her again. Add in all the questions from his brothers concerning the demon he had hunted down, the gun with a magazine of cursed bullets, which may or may not still be sitting in the center of their dining room table, and the bullet taken from his side, which Nicholas last saw still in a baggy clutched tightly in Darren's hand, and he felt like his head was about to spin right off his shoulders.

The whole thing had left him exhausted.

Making his way down the hall, his steps slowed when he came to his bedroom door, completely stopping as he stepped in. Nicholas hadn't really put much thought into what he expected to find after two weeks. He'd left the room that night with boxes strewn everywhere and a partially made bed. The plan had been to unpack everything and get his room set up as quickly as possible, but one thing after another kept coming up. Then there had been the fight in the alley. So he'd figured his room would be the same as he'd left it.

What he actually found, though, left him speechless. His posters covered the walls, his bookcase had been set up and filled, and he could just make out the outline of his clothes through the slightly open closet door. Who had done this? Realistically, it could have been any one of his brothers. He shouldn't be so caught off guard, but he was surprised. Especially since taking care of little things like this usually fell to him.

So who did this?

Feeling a slight brush against his leg, Nicholas glanced down to find Holly looking up at him. Her bright yellow eyes seemed to see right through him as she waited for the attention she demanded.

"I know. I know," he murmured, lifting her into his arms. His fingers rubbed through her soft, black fur as she curled into his chest. "I missed you, too. Sorry I was away for so long, little one."

Stepping farther into the room, he noted his phone plugged in and sitting by his bed. The blue light blinked rapidly, letting him know he had some notifications. Probably all those social media sites his brothers didn't know he was a part of. Memories of the conversation he'd tried to have with Christian concerning Twitter caused him to bark out a laugh as he set Holly on the bed.

He watched as she went over and curled up against his pillow. Her eyes stayed on him as she laid her head against her front paws. Her unwavering stare reminded him of Amy's cat, Charlie. He had the same look in his eyes when he looked at him this morning.

Wow, had it only been this morning, less than twelve hours ago, that he'd woken up to find the mischievous tabby watching him from the arm of the couch?

Shaking his head, he ran a hand along his dark blue bedspread. Everything in his room was so neat, so put together. He'd never had a room look so tidy. Ever. Even his bed seemed to have been carefully made.

"He refused to leave your room, even to eat, until he was done in here," Manuel said, breaking through his thoughts.

Nicholas turned to see him leaning against the door frame. "Who?"

Manuel raised an eyebrow, his eyes drilling into his, almost as if he should know exactly who he was talking about. And he did.

"Cyrus?" Nicholas asked in surprise.

"He blames himself, you know."

"For what?"

"For not being there. For you disappearing and us not being able to find you for the last ten days."

Sighing, Nicholas sat on his bed. He sensed Holly shift slightly behind him before she settled back into her little ball. He watched Manuel make his way over to lean against his dresser, the wood groaning slightly as he rested his palms behind him.

"He took what happened to you very hard, probably the hardest out of all of us. That's saying a lot, seeing that Hayley cried herself to sleep on a nightly basis."

"Why? It wasn't her fault." Nicholas shook his head. "And as far as Cyrus goes, he sure didn't act like he'd missed me when he was biting my head off at Amy's."

Manuel gave him an odd look. "She knows it wasn't her fault, but she cares about your crazy ass. We all do. You see, Hayley was so sure there was something she should have done, she just couldn't seem to get past her guilt." He frowned. "We all took your disappearance hard, Nicky. As far as age goes, I know we're all technically the same, but I've always seen you as my little brother. And that feeling comes with a need to watch out for you. So how do you think I felt when the fighting ended and you were gone? Well, take that and multiply it by a hundred. That might be close to how Cyrus felt when he found out you were missing."

Stunned, Nicholas leaned forward, resting his elbows on his knees and his head in his hands. He felt the pressure building in his chest from the weight of Manuel's words. He looked up. "Hey, Manuel, listen... About all of the fighting between us and some of the things I said-"

He waved his hand through the air. "Hey, it's in the past. Yeah, it sucked to feel like we were constantly at odds with each other, but I knew you were only looking out for me. Even if you were wrong." He smirked, chuckling softly as Nicholas rolled his eyes. "But I don't want you to worry about it now. We're good. I mean it. As far as Cyrus goes... Sure, he's being a dick lately...hell, he's been a dick for the last several years...but he still cares. So, when he gets home, just cut him a little slack, yeah?"

Nicholas looked up at Manuel, his brother's eyes searching his as he waited for a response. He wanted to say something. To tell him he could look past Cyrus' anger and rage. That he could forgive him for the hateful words he so carelessly threw at Amy, just as Manuel had forgiven him for his, but he just wasn't sure if he could. At least not right now. So the only thing he could seem to do was nod.

His mind kept repeating everything Manuel had just said. How they'd all missed him, how they all cared. As warm as the words made him feel, they also brought about a strong feeling of unease.

That worried him the most. He couldn't explain why it was there, why he felt his stomach twist into a knot, why he suddenly had an overwhelming urge to leave.

But it was there.

Manuel walked over and squeezed his shoulder. "It's so good to have you home, brother." They held each other's gaze for a second before Manuel took a step back and headed for the door. Stepping out into the hall, he turned. "Oh, and Nicky?"

"Yeah?"

"No more playing with demons on your own," Manuel said with a smirk, wagging his finger in his direction. "Deal?" He waited for Nicholas to nod. "Great. Good. Next time you decide to have a little fun, feel like going a little wild, invite your brothers to come play, too."

"Will do," Nicholas laughed, giving him a sarcastic salute.

He listened to Manuel's laughter fade away as he walked down the hall. Lying back across his bed, Nicholas bent his arms and rested his hands under his head. Feeling a soft, furry warmth suddenly press into his arm, he looked over to find

Holly had rolled closer to him. Her soft purrs reached his ears as he took a steady breath.

"What's going on with me?" he asked softly. Shaking his head, he gazed up at the ceiling. He'd never felt so torn, so out of sorts. Maybe he needed to get over his desire to start something with Amy. What did he even know about her? Sure, there was the way her eyes lit up when she laughed. The way she bit her bottom lip when she was nervous. The fact that this feeling of being lost hadn't started until he had left her house. That had to be a huge coincidence. Right?

Shit, maybe he just needed to get some sleep. Work on getting his life back to normal before he started dissecting the short time he had with her.

Then again, maybe talking to her again was exactly what he needed.

Nicholas' mind ran in circles, one question leading into a slew of others, before he finally fell asleep. Only to dream about a beautiful woman reaching longingly for him and calling his name.

Chapter 15

Darren excused himself from dinner early that night. Making his way down to his office, he closed the door softly behind him. Standing still for several seconds, his eyes lingering on the plastic bag still gripped tightly in his hand, he felt his chest tighten.

It wasn't so much the bag itself that had Darren's lips pulling back into a snarl. It was the bullet within it. The bullet that was oddly shaped, disfigured. A reaction to being shot into a body. But that made it sound too clinical, too cold. Even though he usually tried to distance himself from any emotional connection when it came to these kinds of things, he just couldn't this time. This time, it was different. This time, the bullet he was studying had gone into his brother.

Rolling his shoulders, Darren unconsciously clenched and relaxed his empty hand at his side. The thought of his brother being shot, lying in some street, alone, as his body was consumed by pain made his gut churn. For the third time in so many hours, he found himself torn between wanting to throw up and wanting to go down to Hell to find the demon who had shot him...just so he could kill the fucker again.

The first time had been in Amy's house when he'd first found out that Nicholas had been shot. The second time was at the dining room table about an hour ago when Nicholas had gone over the whole event, in detail, during an impromptu family meeting. And again now as he stared at the offending bullet and truly allowed what could have happened to sink in.

If Nicholas hadn't made it to Amy's house...

If Amy hadn't been able to get the bullet out in time...

God, we could have lost him.

Running a hand down his face, he finally took the few steps to his desk. He sat heavily in his chair, never looking away from the plastic bag as he laid it on the desk before him. Reaching around to his back, he pulled out the gun Nicholas had taken from the demon, along with the bullets he'd placed within its magazine, and set it next to the bag.

Tapping his fingers on his desk, Darren tried to pull his thoughts back to the problem at hand. Or, if he was being accurate, problems. Groaning, he leaned back in his chair. There were too many issues that needed to be looked into, taken care of. With everyone's attention divided between them all, it was harder and harder to tell where one problem started and another began.

One puzzle at a time.

Opening the desk's top drawer, Darren pulled out a little plastic box, which contained the bullet he'd pulled from the brick wall the night of the fight. Setting each of the bullets side by side, he stared at them.

The fact Andras had more than just the one dagger worried him. The knowledge that he'd taken one of them, melted it down, and turned it into bullets was something else altogether.

How many did he make?

He knew of these two, the ones still in the gun, and the bullet that had been meant for Christian when they'd been down in Hell rescuing Ella. Thankfully, that one had ended up in one of Andras' men, which was exactly where the rest of them would go if Darren had his way. Seeing as these were made with the intention of them ending up lodged someplace within the Guardians, he could only assume there was a definite chance Andras got at least two cartridges worth out of the melted blade. But that was just a guess. Realistically, without hunting down the demon and asking, there was no way he could know for sure.

It was better they plan for the possibility he had more than he probably did. Last time, when Nicholas had brought the first dagger home after his fight with

Castigo, they'd assumed that had been the only one.

Obviously, they were mistaken. One Darren didn't plan on making again.

Thoughts of his battle with Andras that day in Hell teased the edges of his mind. It had been one of the toughest, most strenuous fights he had in a long time. Andras was as dangerous as he was mysterious.

Just one of the many mysteries Darren had been trying to solve ever since.

Andras' problem with them almost felt personal. The demon could have accomplished a lot of things quietly, without drawing his and his brothers' attention. At first, Darren had just shrugged this feeling off, but after finding out the demon had set up shop right here, where they lived... Sure, Ella had some of the demon's power trapped within her. That could definitely be a reason he'd want to be in their town, the need to get his power back causing him to risk it all to get it. But he could have tried to get to her while setting up his business elsewhere. Instead, he brought it to them. Hell, he may as well have just walked up to the front door and rang the fucking bell.

On top of that, they found out Andras had their brother, Dev.

Shit, he's had him since he was sent from Heaven, doing who knows what to him ever since.

If that knowledge alone wasn't enough to cause Darren and his brothers to lose their minds, the fact their missing brother was so close definitely did. After all this, and with a set of balls the likes of King Kong, Andras had brought Dev topside and was keeping him at his fucking club. Right under their fucking noses.

Darren knew Cyrus was right in assuming that was where he was. Somehow, he had known since the first time it had been mentioned.

But why?

Something Darren had been asking himself a lot lately.

At least we have Nicholas back, and if I have anything to say about it, we'll have Dev back soon, too.

Tapping his fingers along the armrest, Darren shifted restlessly in his chair. One problem solved. About a hundred more to go.

Not that Nicholas didn't come home with a whole new set of problems. It didn't take a genius to know that something was going on between him and Amy. The glances they shared, how quick they were to jump in to protect each other, the very feeling in the air that screamed of the sexual tension between them.

Was it a good time for Nicholas to have found a possible love interest? Probably not. But then again, that seemed to be going around.

Was Nicholas even ready for a relationship? Darren had no idea. His brother had never been one to play the field. He'd never even dated, at least not that Darren knew about. And if that were the case, how could he be ready for one? Especially with everything going on right now. Darren guessed he'd just have to wait and see. This question was one only Nicky would be able to answer.

Did he think Amy would be good for his brother? The answer to that was easy. Absolutely. He could see it in her. The goodness radiated off her like sunbeams, and he felt his brother could definitely use some light in his life right now.

He refused to play matchmaker, though. That wasn't his gig. So Darren just had to hope Nicholas would figure out what was going on between him and Amy on his own.

The sound of his phone ringing brought Darren out of his musings. Reaching into his pocket, he clicked to answer without even checking the caller ID.

"Hello." His voice sounded rough, even to his own ears.

"Darren?"

Darren felt his grip tighten on his phone. The sound of Cindy's voice always seemed to do that to him. It was soft and sexy with just the right amount of lift to it that left him yearning for more. Not that he'd ever tell her that. No. That would be asking for a level of trouble he just couldn't afford right now.

"Darren, I know you're there." Her voice took on an exasperated tone.

"Yeah, Cindy. Listen, now isn't-"

She sighed. "It isn't a good time. I know, Darren. It's *never* a good time. But I tried to call Ella just a bit ago and she didn't answer, so I was wondering if you knew where she was."

"Did you ever think that maybe she's busy?" he snapped. She was silent, and Darren had to fight to suppress a groan. Trying to rein in his irritation, he pushed on. "She's here. Nicholas came home and-"

"Wait! Did you just say Nicholas came home? When did that happen? Where has he been? Why didn't you call to tell me you found him?"

His irritation instantly melted away. As excited as she was, Darren felt a twinge in his heart at the hurt she was trying hard to hide. She would have been successful, too, had she been talking to anyone else, but he heard it loud and clear. And she was right. He should have called.

Even though she was Ella's best friend, and Ella was the one who should have called her, Darren still felt awful.

Cindy, as annoying as she was, had helped out tremendously around the house since Nicholas had disappeared. She never asked a lot of questions, never pushed for him to talk about it. She was just there, fixing meals, straightening up around the house, sitting by him when all he wanted was some time to think.

He should have called her.

Licking his lips, Darren leaned forward in his chair. "You're right, Cindy. I'm sorry. Everything just happened so fast today. Nicholas called out of the blue this afternoon, saying he was okay. The next thing I knew, hours had gone by and he's home now. I should have called to let you know."

"It's okay, Darren. I'm just glad he's back home. I know you all must feel relieved."

"Yeah. Yeah, we are." He was quiet as emotions he'd never felt before started to build inside him. Running a hand along his jaw, he stared at the dark wood of his desk. "Hey, um... I never did get a chance to thank you, you know, for all you did for us...for me. I know we haven't always gotten along, but I want you to know how much you being here meant to me. Having you around really-"

"Hey, Darren. Sorry, I, um... I have to go."

Darren frowned. Her tone was off and he practically felt a steel door slamming between them.

"Is everything okay?"

"Of course. It's just a case I'm helping out on. Something came up and I need to go. I'll give you a call later."

"Did you want me to let Ella know you're trying to get a hold of her?"

"What? Oh yeah. Just tell her I'll call her tomorrow."

"Okay, if you're sure nothing-"

"Thanks, Darren. I really am glad Nicholas is home. I'll.... I'll talk to you later."

"Yeah. I'll talk to you later."

"Bye, Darren."

"Bye."

Darren pulled the phone away from his ear, staring at it as the silence stretched. Frowning, he started going over what had just happened. Cindy had never rushed to get off the phone with him before. Hell, it was usually the other way around and he couldn't get her to say goodbye.

Something was up with her. He could feel it. Was it this new case? He didn't remember her mentioning taking on anything new. Maybe he'd find a way to ask Ella about it later. Shit, maybe it was him. Did he say something he shouldn't have?

He couldn't remember saying anything wrong. Sure, he should have called about Nicky, but he'd apologized for that. And she'd accepted his apology, hadn't she?

"Fuck," he hissed, tossing his phone onto the couch across the room. Cindy had always been a mystery to him. His feelings for her, how she acted around him, had always thrown him off. He couldn't do this right now. There was too much on his plate. He was just going to have to trust that, like Nicholas and Amy, this...whatever *this* was...would eventually work out on its own.

Until then, they had bigger concerns. He looked back at the two bullets. *Much bigger concerns.*

Cindy rested her phone on the arm of her couch. Well, that had been unexpected. Part of her had wanted to stay on the phone, call Darren out on his sudden show of emotion. Hell, she'd been trying to get some sort of reaction out of him for weeks. Well, besides the grief that had consumed him and his brothers since Nicholas vanished.

God, she felt her gut clench just thinking about the atmosphere in their house. The look on Darren's face when she'd shown up that next morning... You could tell the poor guy hadn't slept at all. While his eyes were guarded, his body practically shook from the emotion he was trying to keep in check. Everyone else was noticeably distraught, but not Darren. She could tell he was trying to stay strong for the rest of his family. Finding him sitting in the yard several nights later, staring aimlessly into the dark, had broken her heart. He hadn't allowed himself to break down as she'd sat quietly beside him, but she felt like her presence had helped. Even if they had just sat in silence the whole time.

Thank heavens Nicholas was home now. She wasn't sure what Darren and his brothers would have done if he'd disappeared forever.

Using her thumb to twist the band on her finger, Cindy's mind went back to what Darren had just said to her. Or, more importantly, what his voice had done to her. She'd wanted nothing more than to keep him talking, tell him she'd been happy to be there for him, to be the one he'd leaned on when his emotions had gotten to be too much.

Yet, as much as she'd wanted to figure out whether his sudden change of tone had meant anything, her need to keep some emotional distance between her and this confusing man had won out. She'd gotten attached to someone before. To leave herself vulnerable, thinking she was safe and cared for. She even allowed herself to think that William, her boyfriend, had loved her. Man, how wrong she'd been. That was a mistake she still dealt with. She couldn't permit herself to go down that road again. Especially not with William still on the loose and looking for her. The thought that she wouldn't get away from him next time...

Stopping her runaway thoughts, Cindy thought back to Darren. In her haste to put a halt to the conversation before her heart latched onto him any more than it already had, she'd made a hasty retreat.

Crap, she couldn't even remember her reason for hanging up.

With a sigh, she ran her hands through her blonde hair. She didn't know how this man had gotten under her skin so much in such a short amount of time. But since the minute she'd first laid eyes on him, seen the bright blue of his, the sexy dimples in his cheeks when he smiled, she hadn't been able to get him out of her mind.

If he weren't such a big question mark in her mind, maybe she would have been able to let it go. Probably not, but she could lie to herself from time to time.

Who was she kidding? She couldn't even lie to herself without rolling her eyes. She was screwed.

The sound of her phone buzzing brought her out of her thoughts.

Glancing over, she saw a text had come through, Ella's name flashing across the screen.

Hey, girl. Just wanted to let you know Nicky's back. I would have let you know sooner, but it has been crazy around the house.

Cindy smiled, her fingers flying across the screen as she shared in her best friend's happiness.

That's fantastic! I bet everyone's so relieved.

She was going to let Ella think she had no idea Nicholas was home. Cindy didn't think she was ready to tell her best friend about the strange conversation between her and Darren. There would just be too many questions she wasn't prepared to answer, let alone think about.

You'll have to come by for dinner one of these nights to see him.

Ella's message made Cindy's chest tighten. Her emotions twisted out of control as her finger hovered over her phone. As much as she wanted to put space between her and Darren, she wouldn't do that to her best friend. No matter what.

Absolutely. Just let me know when :)

She hit send before she let herself think about it too much. Maybe she could spend time with Ella, Hayley, and the boys without it getting too awkward.

Yeah. She chuckled. *And maybe I'll finally win the lottery.*

Hell, the chances of her winning the lottery were better than those of her avoiding any awkward moments with Darren. She knew he'd want to know the real reason she hung up. There was just no way her excuse had been believable, and she wasn't about to tell him the truth. No matter how much she knew he was nothing like William, there were just some levels of trust she wasn't willing to give. No matter how much she wanted to.

Wonderful. I'll let you know what night is good for everyone. Miss your face :)

Despite her uncertainty, Cindy had to smile. She'd missed Ella...and Hayley, too, who had become a good friend during these last few weeks. She just needed to get her head on straight between now and whatever night she went over there. Otherwise, she figured there wouldn't be enough wine in the world to get her through it.

Miss your face more :) Can't wait to see everyone.

As soon as she hit send, a pair of bright blue eyes flashed through her mind, causing her stomach to flip. Damn, if she was having this reaction from just imagining his eyes, she was in trouble.

Chapter 16

Feeling the sun's warmth spread across his face, Nicholas blinked at the still open blinds.

"Should have closed those," he mumbled, turning away from the blinding light. His legs felt tangled, stiff. It wasn't until he finally lifted his head that he realized he'd fallen asleep with his clothes on. Hell, it looked like he'd hardly moved from the spot he'd collapsed in after Manuel left his room last night.

The thought of getting out of bed to change didn't appeal to him, so he decided to just pop the button on his jeans and wiggle out of them. The shirt was easy to pull off without moving much. Reaching over his shoulder, he bunched his dirty t-shirt up and, with a slight tug, pulled it over his head. Twisting his torso, the shirt went flying off the side of the bed. However, removing his boots without sitting up proved to be a huge challenge, but in the end, and with a rather childish "whoop", he was victorious. Once his pants and socks followed his boots to the floor, Nicholas released a loud yawn.

Stretching out in nothing but his boxers, he decided to celebrate his victory with a nap. This idea, he found, was not shared with the other members of the house. Well, one member in particular.

"Dude, put some clothes on. My girl doesn't need to be walking by and seeing that," Christian said, walking into his room.

Nicholas peered over at him and smirked. "Afraid she might realize the grass really is greener on the other side and leave you for me?"

"Shit no. You got nothing on me," he said, shooting Nicholas a cocky grin. "I'm just trying to save your feelings, brother. Wouldn't want you getting embarrassed."

"Whatever. Why are you in my room?"

"Because I missed you," he responded with an exaggerated pout.

"And?" As he watched Christian tilt his head to the side, Nicholas sighed. Sitting up, he let out another yawn. "Christian, I missed you, too. But it's like..." He peered over his shoulder at the clock by his bed. "It's eight in the freaking morning."

"I know. It's late."

"Late?" Nicholas repeated, flopping back onto the bed. "I'm going back to sleep, Christian. I look forward to talking to you when I get up."

"Um, no."

"Wha-" Before he could get the whole word out, he flew up into the air as Christian jumped on the end of his bed.

With a huff, he landed back down and immediately shot a glare at his brother. "What are we? Five?"

"Oh, hush. Come on. I've let you sleep long enough."

"Have you now?"

"Yes. Anyway..." Christian smirked again, hopping back off of the bed and pointing to the doorway. "Manuel's downstairs with the girls making french toast."

At that, Nicholas' stomach decided it was a good time to let him know he needed to eat. Christian just laughed and shook his head.

"Come on, brother."

Groaning, he sat up and slid to the edge of the bed. "Okay, okay. You had me at french toast."

"Yeah, yeah." Christian turned to make his way out of the room. "Just don't take long. You know how I am. I can't promise to leave you any if you decide to take forever before you make your way downstairs."

"You'd better not eat it all." Christian glanced over his shoulder. Seeing the look on his face, Nicholas stood to show that he was indeed getting up. Give his brother too much time and he would eat everything. "I'm up. I'll be right down."

Nodding, Christian walked out of his room. "And, Nicky?" he yelled from down the hall.

"What?"

"Put some fucking pants on."

Shaking his head, Nicholas leaned down to grab the jeans he'd just discarded. The promise of a good breakfast had him moving quickly as he grabbed a clean shirt out of one of his drawers, throwing it over his shoulder as he ran into his bathroom to brush his teeth. It felt like ages had passed since he'd woken up at Amy's house yesterday.

Looking into the mirror, he paused. Setting his shirt and toothbrush onto the counter, he leaned forward.

He didn't look any different. Maybe his eyes were a little darker, his power still felt a little off. But, all in all, he looked okay.

Mentally flexing his power, Nicholas felt the familiar warmth spread through his back and down his arms. His fingers tingled with the itch to send it out around him, to call to the elements. Right as he was about to do just that, just to feel the breeze pick up in this otherwise still room, he felt it. It was slight, almost undetectable, but it was there.

A small hiccup in his power. A pause in its flow as it swirled within him.

Reining it back in, he kept his eyes glued to the mirror. His red eyes had darkened drastically from the force, his skin glowing with an almost moonlight hue. All of this was normal. But it was his tattoo that really drew his attention. The lightning bolt seemed to have grown, reaching down to his wrist where he could physically feel its heat burn his skin. He shifted slightly. The clouds on his back had now crawled over his shoulders. They were a mass of angry black swirls that, even though he'd pulled his power back, still twisted and rolled. It wasn't uncommon for his tattoo to literally have a life of its own, but this felt different.

He needed to talk to Darren about it. Nicholas knew his brother had a lot going on right now. It was written on his face, reflected in his eyes. But Darren was, well, Darren. If there was anyone in this house who might know what was going on with his power, it was him. Nicholas just felt it.

Making quick work of brushing his teeth, Nicholas sighed. The sooner he could get this weird glitch in his power figured out, the sooner he could start getting his life back to normal. Well, as normal as his life could be anyway.

Pulling his shirt over his head, he looked down to see the lightning bolt still pulsing down his arm. *Not much I can do about that*, he thought with a shrug. They'd all eventually figure out something was off with him. Maybe this was just a leftover side effect from that bullet. Yeah, he was sure that was it. Running his hands through his black hair, he smiled.

Grabbing his phone off the bed, Nicholas headed down the hall. The smell of french toast and maple syrup teased his senses as he got to the stairs. Glancing down, he paused when he noticed the light blinking on his phone.

Turning the screen on, he quickly made his way through most of the notifications. As he'd thought, most were from his social media pages. So-and-so checked in here. Another person shared a picture there. With a laugh as he quickly walked down the steps, he contemplated posting a picture of his breakfast. You know, just to fit in with everyone else. His laughter stopped as he came to the last step and noticed a text message.

Amy.

Pausing at the bottom of the stairs, his thumb hovered over the notification. Did he want to open it now? What did she say? Did she miss him like he missed her? Disgusted with himself for being chicken, he quickly clicked to open the text.

Hey. I was just thinking about you... Wanted to make sure you got home okay.

She'd been thinking about him? Glancing at the time stamp, he saw she'd sent it at eleven last night. Which meant she'd been lying in bed while he'd been on her mind. Yeah, he liked that. A lot. Hell, probably too much.

"Nicholas, you coming?" Manuel yelled from the kitchen.

Looking up from his phone, he nodded, realizing his brother couldn't see him. "Yeah. I'll be right there." Glancing back at his phone, he clicked to reply. His need to say something, anything, so she'd know he was thinking about her, too, was strong.

Sorry. I crashed early last night and just got your text. Everything is good here. Brothers are annoying as ever, but it's good to be home. I'm just about to have breakfast, but I wanted to let you know that I was thinking about you and I'll call you later. Hope you slept well. xx

Reading it over again, he smiled. It was a little long, but that was okay. Clicking send, he slid his phone into his pocket. He was sure Amy was still sleeping...he would be, too, if it hadn't been for Christian...so he figured he'd hear from her later.

Making his way into the kitchen, he stopped abruptly. It wasn't the sight of Manuel and Christian hovering over their girls as they cooked. Or Darren as he leaned

against the counter, nursing a cup of coffee.
No. It was Cyrus sitting at the table, staring
at him. Was he ready to talk about their
argument at Amy's? Was Nicholas ready to
forgive him for upsetting Amy the way he
had? That would be a big, resounding no.

Yet it looked like he wasn't going to
get a choice.

Stepping into the kitchen, he smiled
as everyone turned his way. There was
more hugging, more back slaps as he made
his way toward the coffee. Nicholas could
still feel Cyrus' eyes on him as he reached
for a mug and the creamer. Taking his time,
he glanced over at Darren.

His brother's normally bright blue
eyes seemed duller this morning. He looked
tired.

"Everything okay?" Nicholas quietly
asked.

Darren made a sound that
resembled a mix between a groan and a
sigh before taking another sip from his
mug. "Just tired," he finally said. As if he
sensed Nicholas wanted to push to find out
why, he gave him a sideways smile. "Don't
worry about me. How are you? Did you
sleep well? You know, finally being back in
your own bed and all."

Allowing his brother to change the
subject, for now, Nicholas grinned. "I feel
fantastic. Slept like a baby."

"I never understood that saying," Ella said offhandedly as she placed some more egg-laden bread into the pan. "From what I hear, babies are up crying most of the night. Tossing and turning as they try to tell everyone in the house that they're hungry or need to be changed." Nicholas watched a blush spread across her cheeks as she looked up and noticed everyone staring at her. "What? I just don't think saying that you slept like a baby is technically a good thing."

"You're right," Nicholas said with a laugh. "How about I say I slept like Holly does after, well...after pretty much anything she does."

Ella's laugh rang out. "She definitely knows how to sleep, doesn't she?"

"Yeah, she does," Christian chuckled.

"Anyway, I slept great. Really," Nicholas said, taking a healthy gulp of his coffee. He felt his muscles loosen the second the smooth, warm liquid hit the back of his throat. Closing his eyes, he savored the feeling as he took another sip. The conversation about baby sayings continued, but he tuned it out. Turning, he found Cyrus still watching him from his seat at the table, his gaze narrowed.

Slowly walking to the table, Nicholas slid into the chair across from him. "Morning." Tucking his left arm beneath him, Nicholas curled his right hand around his mug. He saw his brother glance briefly at his arm before meeting his eyes.

Cyrus, seeming to sense he didn't want to talk about the sudden extension of his tattoo, just nodded. His hands rested on the table by his untouched coffee mug as he glanced over Nicholas' shoulder before leveling his onyx eyes back on him.

Nicholas tilted his head as he studied his brother. He didn't seem as angry as he had the day before. Actually, he seemed almost...happy. Maybe even a little eager. Nicholas glanced around to see if anyone else noticed Cyrus' mood, but they were all still laughing as they got breakfast ready. All except for Darren, who glanced his way. Nicholas gave a slight nod of his head toward Cyrus before turning back to his brother.

"So," Nicholas said, watching a light shimmer within his brother's eyes. "Did you get in really late last night?"

"Not too late," Cyrus simply said, grabbing his mug to take his first drink of it.

Nicholas frowned. "Well, where did you go after you left Amy's house?"

Cyrus looked at him for a moment, seeming to think about how to answer as he took another sip of his coffee. The fact he was drinking coffee and not an alcoholic beverage further piqued Nicholas' curiosity.

Before that night ten days ago, he couldn't remember a time when he'd seen his brother drinking something other than alcohol. At least not since after they'd rescued Ella from Hell.

It felt like a lot had changed since then.

Seeing Cyrus still seemed unsure about what to say, Nicholas decided to try a different tactic. "I, um... I wanted to thank you for fixing up my room."

He seemed to tense, become as still as a statue before his very eyes. His brother looked at him over his coffee cup, unblinking. After what felt like hours, but was truly only a few seconds, Nicholas watched as his brother's shoulders relaxed, his onyx eyes softening.

"I couldn't let it sit like that. Couldn't let you come home to a room that was still boxed up."

Nicholas felt a wave of shock shoot through him as he tried to think of something to say. Of all the responses he'd expected to hear from his brother, what just came out of Cyrus' mouth was not one of them. Hell, he'd been fully expecting his brother to tell him to fuck off. But this... This told him the truth that Cyrus tried to hide behind a wall of aggression and sarcasm. This told him that his brother really did care. Sure, Manuel had said as much the night before, but to hear Cyrus admit it just seemed to mean more.

"Thank you," he finally said, his voice laced with all the emotions he was trying to swallow down.

Not wanting to freak his brother out, Nicholas looked away. Cyrus had never been able to deal with other people's emotions. In fact, he hated it. Something that had become more and more obvious since the day he'd been taken. Nicholas hadn't felt his brother this open in a long time. He'd be damned if he was the one who caused him to shut back down.

"So," Manuel said, taking a seat at the table, his amethyst eyes sliding from Nicholas to Cyrus and back. "It's been a while since we've all been able to sit down together for breakfast."

"Yeah," Darren chimed in, sitting at the head of the table. "This is nice."

Nicholas wanted to agree with them, but something nagged at him. Something, or someone, was missing.

Watching the girls and Christian walk over, he couldn't help but think of Amy. His mind wandered to the breakfast she had made him the day before. While they set plates of french toast on the table, he listened to them as they each took their seats. They were discussing Manuel's most recent addition to the downstairs gym and how it was going to help them train. Hayley mentioned how she wanted to start training with Ella so they could learn to fight. This was met with a lot of different responses. The main consensus was that none of his brothers wanted them to go up against demons.

Something he completely understood and felt the same about. While the girls were powerful in their own right, they were definitely not ready to go up against Andras. Which seemed like it was becoming more and more likely. Ella still worked on controlling her powers, and Hayley, while extremely powerful, still had a lot to learn. When she'd gone hunting with some of his brothers, it had come as a shock when she'd admitted to having only gone up against a Shadow or two. She'd held her own, though, and from what Nicholas had been told, the whole event had been quite a sight.

Cyrus remained quiet during breakfast, only nodding now and then when someone asked him a question. He picked at his food, not seeming that hungry. As the plates circled around the table again, Nicholas couldn't help but push some more toward him. With every pass, he tried to place another piece of french toast onto his brother's plate.

This earned him a few growls and a glare, but nothing more. Yup, something had definitely happened to put Cyrus in a better mood. As the seconds ticked by, Nicholas' curiosity continued to grow. Finally, as he swallowed the last bite of his breakfast, he couldn't hold his questions at bay any longer.

"So, Cyrus," Nicholas said, looking over at his brother. "You never did answer my question from earlier."

He let out a long sigh. "And what question was that?"

"I had asked where you went after you left Amy's yesterday."

"Out."

"Well, I figured that much. With you storming out and not being here when we got home and all, I kinda figured you were *out*."

Cyrus rolled his eyes, setting his fork down on his plate with a dull thud. "I went by the club."

By the silence that fell over the table, you would have thought he just said he decided he wanted to be a woman. Nicholas heard several forks hit plates, a couple cups hit the table as he stared at him.

"You went by The 9th Circle?" he asked slowly.

"I thought we decided nobody was going to go by there alone," Darren said, tapping his fingers on the table. "That *is* what we all decided, isn't it?"

Murmurs of agreement rolled around the table as they all stared at Cyrus.

His black eyes seemed fixated on his now empty coffee mug.

"Cyrus?" Darren asked.

He looked up and smirked. "You can't honestly be surprised that I went there."

"No. I just wanted to make sure you're aware we all had an agreement when it came to that club." Darren shook his head. Judging by the look on Cyrus' face, this said *agreement* hadn't really mattered. "Fine. So, what did you find out? Anything?"

"Actually...," Cyrus started, letting out a deep breath as he paused. Licking his lips, he gave them all a small smile. "I found him."

Nicholas heard Manuel let out a soft gasp as he leaned closer to Cyrus. "You found him? Dev?" His voice shook from the excitement threatening to burst out of him.

He nodded. "And I talked to him."

There was a sudden stillness in the air as his words soaked in. Then, like a floodgate had just been opened, everyone around the table started talking at once.

Question upon question were thrown out as Cyrus leaned back in his chair. Nicholas wasn't sure what to say. His brain kept going over the fact that he had not only found Dev, but he'd talked to him. It was more than he had hoped for. More than he could have dreamed. God, how he'd missed his brother.

"How could you not tell us right away?" Christian barked. His eyes narrowed as he stared Cyrus' way. "Were you going to even say anything?"

Cyrus released a harsh growl as he glared across the table. "Of course I was going to say something."

"Then why did you wait this long to bring up the fact that you found Dev?" The pain in Christian's eyes tore through Nicholas as his looked between his brothers. "I know you don't like to come to any of us for, well, anything. And I get it. I do. That's why I make sure to give you your space. But this... Dammit, Cyrus. This concerns all of us."

"I know. I just..." Cyrus' voice softened more and more with each word. Nicholas noticed that his brother's eyes were uncharacteristically cloudy as they moved around before landing on the table. "I've been searching for him for so long, I think I just needed a few hours to wrap my mind around the fact that I'd found him. After I got home, I sat on the bench in the back yard for hours. Just sitting there thinking about Dev, about what we should do next. I wasn't keeping this from any of you. Not on purpose."

Everyone began talking once again. Their voices became white noise to

Nicholas' ears as he watched Cyrus. He wasn't mad at his brother for keeping this from them. Ever since they'd brought him back all those years ago, his brother had pulled away from them. Kept his thoughts and feelings buried deep, seemed to need more time than the rest of them to dissect things. He imagined finding Dev had really thrown his brother for a loop.

God... Dev.

Reaching out, Nicholas grasped Cyrus' arm. He felt his brother tense, but he refused to pull back. Black eyes latched onto his. They glowed with an intensity that only his brother could conjure. Though he would never admit it, Cyrus' glare had always left him feeling uneasy, kind of freaked out. Right now, he didn't sense any of that. Instead, his brother's onyx stare called to him, silently telling him their family would soon be whole once again. And whatever his reasons were for not rushing in to tell them, the fact he'd told them now was all that mattered.

"Is he okay?" Nicholas asked. His voice, though quiet, seemed to carry over everyone else's. The rest of the table once again began to quiet down as they waited for Cyrus' answer.

The sad look in his brother's eyes should have been enough, but Nicholas wanted to hear it. He kept his gaze on Cyrus until he let out a sigh.

"You know Dev. Even after all this time, he hasn't changed. At least not when it comes to hiding what he's going through. I mean, he tried to play it off like he was good...after he got over the shock of seeing me standing behind him on the roof." Cyrus chuckled softly, his eyes still heavy with emotion. "But no, Nicholas. He's... He's not doing well."

Everyone got really quiet after that. Even Ella and Hayley seemed upset as they looked from Cyrus to the men by their side. Nicholas felt his stomach clench. If he hadn't been out of commission for over a week, maybe they would have been able to locate Dev sooner. Maybe they would already have him home where he belonged. Thoughts of what his brother must be going through flooded his mind as he stared down at the table.

"What do we do?" Hayley asked quietly. "Now that you know where he is, what's our next move?"

"We should go there," Manuel said. "We should get him out...tonight." His fist hit the table so hard, Nicholas heard the wood crack from the impact.

"I agree with Manuel. We should get in there and get him out. We can't wait any longer... I *won't* wait," Christian snarled.

Nicholas nodded, even as he looked over and saw a frown cross Darren's face. He could practically see the wheels in his brother's head turning as he stared intently at Cyrus.

"I agree that we should go to see Dev as soon as possible," Darren started, breaking though everyone's rising demands. "But I'd like to talk to him before we pull him out."

"Talk to him?" Nicholas frowned. "About what?"

"We don't really know what Andras has planned-" Darren started.

"Darren-" Cyrus cut in.

He held up a hand. "I just think having Dev be our eyes and ears inside the club would be a huge benefit."

Darren had hardly gotten the last word out before everyone started talking again, increasing in volume as the seconds ticked by. Everyone was angry. Why would Darren even consider leaving Dev in there a moment longer, let alone ask him to spy on Andras for them? And nobody was shy about letting their feelings be known.

Nicholas just kept looking between Darren and Cyrus. Cyrus' eyes glowed as he glared at Darren. The power rolling off him was suffocating. As it spread throughout the room, the arguing around the table began to fade. Before long, Nicholas realized he wasn't the only one starring Cyrus' way.

"Are you seriously thinking about leaving our brother, who has been in Hell for decades having who knows what done to him, in a club filled with his tormentors?" Cyrus snarled as he slowly stood from his seat. Pulling himself up to his full height, he curled his fists at his side.

The scraping of chair legs against the floor drew everyone's attention to the other side of the table where Darren now stood, his own blue eyes darkening as his power swept through the room. "Do you think I *want* to leave him there? Do you think I *want* to put him in any more danger than he already is?" Darren's eyes flashed black as he braced his hands on the table and leaned toward Cyrus.

"I don't know what to think," he growled. "Because I still haven't been able to wrap my mind around you even suggesting we leave him there."

"That's why I said we should go talk to him," Darren all but screamed, the table shuddering under the sudden rush of power blasting out around him. They all watched him close his eyes and take several deep breaths. "I don't want to leave him there. I want him here where he belongs. But let's be realistic. Andras and his demons pose a major threat to not just us, but everyone. Even so, if he doesn't feel comfortable staying there..." Darren raised his hand as everyone began to talk, "or if we don't feel comfortable leaving him there, we'll pull him out." He looked around the table, once again relaxing into his chair. "Tonight. We go see Dev tonight."

"Well, we can't all go," Ella said with a frown.

"Ella's right," Hayley chimed in, leaning into Manuel. "I think we may stick out a bit if we all head in there."

"We can't go in there anyway," Christian sighed. "I'm pretty sure they'll know who we are. It's not like we can just sneak into the club undetected. Shit, I bet if I step within three feet of that place Andras' spidey senses will go off."

"They don't know who I am," Hayley said quietly.

"No," Manuel growled.

"But they don't."

"No. Just no."

Nicholas looked between the two as Manuel and Hayley glared at each other. His brother's eyes blazed as he shook his head. He was obviously not happy. Not that Nicholas could blame him. If he had his way, the girls would be kept as far away from any and all demons as possible. However, the look on Hayley's face said she was going to help whether any of them liked it or not.

"Look, I can even cloak myself so they won't sense anything magical about me. I'll just be another human girl trying to get a drink."

"But Castigo has seen you," Darren pointed out.

"Yeah. What if he's there?" Manuel all but growled.

"I'll just change the way I look." Hayley glanced around the table, her eyebrows raised as she met everyone's concerned stare. "I can do this. I'll get in, find Dev, and tell him to meet you guys on the roof. Then I'll get a drink at the bar, just so it doesn't look like I was there for anything else, and leave. Or... I'll go up to the roof with him and we can all leave from there."

"I just-" Manuel started.

"I know, babe," Hayley said softly, reaching over and giving his hand a light squeeze. "But I won't be there alone." She reached up and touched his face. "You'll be nearby. I can do this. You guys can't get in there without being noticed, and like Darren said, you need to be able to talk to Dev tonight." She looked around the table again, her eyes lingering on Cyrus before traveling back to meet Manuel's amethyst stare. "Please. Let me help you."

They were all quiet as they mulled over whether what Hayley offered would actually work. At some point, Cyrus had sat back down and now looked at her, seeming to contemplate what she offered. His expression may have been blank, but his eyes showed his growing agreement.

Nicholas still wasn't sure if he approved of this, but one look at Darren and Cyrus told him that at least a few of his brothers were seriously considering sending her in.

"Manuel, I think sending Hayley in is the best chance we have at getting to Dev," Darren said slowly. "I know you're worried-"

He let out a humorless laugh. "Worried? Brother, I passed worried a long time ago." Manuel shook his head. "I'm sliding right into fucking panic." At Hayley's sigh, he looked over at her, his eyes pleading for her to understand. "It's not that I don't think you can do this, babe, because I do. I just..." He swallowed. "What if something happens and I can't get to you in time?"

"Come on, brother. I heard about what she did in that alley," Cyrus scoffed. "I'm sure she can handle a couple lower-level demons if she has to."

A deep growl resonated throughout the room. "And what if Andras realizes who she is? Huh? Or Castigo? Then what, Cyrus?"

"Then she gets the fuck out of there," Cyrus snapped. "We need to get to Dev, and Hayley is our best shot. Unless any of you have a better idea." The silence that followed only seemed to hammer his point home. He glanced over and met Nicholas' eyes. Nicholas could feel his brother's silent question.

Licking his lips, he realized Cyrus wasn't the only one looking his way. But what should he say? Was he comfortable sending Hayley into a club full of the most powerful, most fucked-up demons they'd ever come across? No. Could they figure out another way to get to Dev? Probably, but not quickly enough to get to him tonight. And that was the kicker. This needed to be done tonight, and Hayley was offering the fastest way to do it.

Sighing, he looked over at Hayley, her eyes pleading with him. She could do this. He knew she could. "I want to have it known that I'm not happy about this at all. But..." He sighed. "I think we should let Hayley go in. We need to talk to Dev and I can't see another way to get to him. Not by tonight anyway."

"I don't accept that." Manuel shook his head. "There *has* to be another way."

"Sure. I mean, we could always just forgo the cloak-and-dagger shtick. You know, just bust through the club walls like the fucking Kool-Aid man." Nicholas rolled his eyes. "Or maybe just *poof* ourselves into the middle of the dance floor, or whatever the hell they have going on in there, and start yelling for him."

"Come on, Nicholas-" Manuel started, only to be cut off with Nicholas doing his best *Wonder Dog* impersonation.

"'Here I come to save the day,'" he sang loudly, waving his hands through the air. Nicholas turned his head from left to right, eyes narrowing. "Dev? Oh, Dev?"

"Oh, shut up, Nicky," Manuel growled as everyone else just shook their heads, a few coughing behind their hands to hide their laugh. "Fine. So there isn't another way for this to happen by tonight. But, shit, do you really expect me to be okay with Hayley going in there alone?"

"Of course not," Nicholas responded quickly. "I doubt any of us is truly okay with this. But we need to do something, and Hayley's our best bet."

"Yeah, well, what about Amy?" Manuel raised his eyebrows. "Nobody knows her."

Nicholas' jaw dropped. "Are you out of your fucking mind?"

"All I'm saying is-"

"No," Nicholas cut him off, his voice a low growl as he shook his head. "I know exactly what you're saying, and the answer is a big fucking no. Not only am I not sending her in there blind...unless you want us to sit her down and go over the last several decades of demon shit in less than twelve hours...but I'm also not sending an innocent human into a building full of

demons who are looking for... Wait for it..."
Nicholas waved his hands in the air.
"*Fucking humans.*"

"Are you done?" Manuel asked,
tapping his fingers on the table.

"I am, and so is this conversation."

"I agree with Nicholas," Darren said,
pulling everyone's attention his way. "Even
if she were willing to help, the answer
would be no. This just isn't a situation I
would feel comfortable sending her, or any
human, into."

"Any human?" Manuel questioned
slowly. "So I guess me suggesting we ask
Cindy to help would be a no then?" At the
sudden flash of light within Darren's eyes,
Manuel gave a sharp nod. "Right. I'll take
that as a hell no."

"There really isn't any need for all of
this arguing," Hayley spoke up. "I said I'd
do this, and that's that. Now, we can spend
the rest of the day fighting with each other,
or we can come up with a plan and I can get
ready for tonight."

At that, the conversation shifted to
plan mode.

Manuel eventually came
around...after getting Hayley to agree to
several stipulations, including keeping a
hidden microphone on her so Manuel could
hear what was going on. Cyrus even stayed,
saying that since he'd already been on the

roof, he was the one who should figure out where they should be when Dev showed up.

Nobody could argue with that.

Cyrus also told them about some meeting that was supposed to happen tonight. Seemed Andras was trying to get a dark witch to aid him in finding Ella and Hayley. Hearing this brought a snarl from both Christian and Manuel and an even stronger sense of urgency from the rest of them to get to Dev. With the meeting happening at eight, they figured if they got there a little after that, Hayley could get in, find Dev, and get back out before the dark witch left the office. It all sounded good to Nicholas, and now that they had a time frame, they could move forward with the planning.

Five hours later, they had a solid strategy. It got a little heated at one point because, of course, everyone wanted to be there to see Dev. But they all eventually agreed that Darren would approach him first while the rest of them held back until they got the okay to step forward. It had been a long time since they'd seen their brother. They didn't want to overwhelm him.

At that point, it looked like everyone planned to do their own thing until it was time to go. Hayley said she needed to get her charms and spells ready, so Ella, deciding to give her a hand, would spend the afternoon with her. That meant Christian and Manuel would be with them. Darren and Cyrus both seemed eager to head off to wherever they were going, which left Nicholas on his own, something he was more than okay with.

So, with a promise to be ready by eight, Nicholas excused himself from the table. His feet felt heavy as he made his way upstairs. His mind was filled with all the ways tonight could go down, some of which left him feeling antsy.

Pulling his phone out of his pocket, Nicholas couldn't help but grin when he saw a message. Amy's name flashed across the screen as he swiped to unlock it.

So glad to hear things are good for you at home. I slept well. Passed out on the couch after I texted you. Lol. Anyway, call me when you can. Miss talking to you. xx

Nicholas smiled as he made his way into his room and sat down on the edge of his bed. Glancing around, he took in all the posters on the walls and movies stacked on his shelves. It felt so good to be home. Though he'd been asleep the last ten days and wasn't aware he'd been away, he must have known on some level. Sitting here now, taking in the comfort of his things, the sounds of his family moving throughout the house, he felt like he could finally breathe.

The knowledge they were going to see Dev tonight, hopefully bringing him home, made his body relax even more. He was finally going to see his brother.

God, he'd missed him.

He felt a chill as a sudden thought of what Dev may have been through since he'd been sent to Hell crept through his mind. Doubts of whether they'd be able to get him away from there spread, threatening to devour his hope. Gritting his teeth, Nicholas shook his head. They would get to Dev. And they would save him. There was no room for doubt when it came to the safety of his family. When it came to the ones he cared about.

Running his thumbs over the side of his phone, his mind was suddenly filled with chocolate brown eyes and a dazzling smile. His thoughts swam with images of Amy smiling as she wandered around his room, sitting around the table with his brothers, meeting Dev. They were desires, dreams of what he wanted. A life with her in it.

He quickly realized he didn't want to fight this pull he felt toward her. During breakfast, he'd watched the way Christian and Ella were with each other. Watched as their eyes lit up every time they looked at each other, how the very air around them seemed to crackle from their closeness. Then there were Manuel and Hayley. They couldn't seem to go more than a few seconds without unconsciously reaching toward each other. Their need to be close, to feel the warmth from the other person, seemed to come as natural to them as taking their next breath.

He wanted that connection, that closeness. He wanted to have someone to wake up next to, to eat with, to love. Nicholas didn't know if he would have those things with Amy. Or if she would even want that with him. What he did know was she wanted to see him again. For now, that would be enough.

Hovering his thumb over the call button, he hesitated for a brief moment. "Come on, Nicky," he mumbled. "You hunt demons for a living and have been to Hell...literally. You already know Amy. Were passed out on her couch for over a week. Just call her." He gave a mental nod and hit the button.

As the phone rang in his ear, he started to feel a sense of doubt creep in. It would have won, too, made him think this was a bad idea if it hadn't been for Amy answering her phone.

"Hello," her soft voice whispered. "Nicholas?"

"Hey," he said, smiling when he heard her release a soft sigh, practically feeling it caress his face.

"Hey," she responded.

And just like that, Nicholas knew his day was going to get better.

Chapter 17

Dev checked the time on his phone for probably the tenth time in the last fifteen minutes. Tapping his fingers against the wooden rail, he let out a frustrated sigh. In a few minutes, the mysterious dark witch was supposed to meet up with Andras, and Dev still had no idea what to do about it.

Should he do something to make sure the meeting didn't happen? Should he let it happen, somehow finding a way to listen in on what was being said? Maybe it would be best to not be there, then try to follow her afterward and get some information directly from the source.

Not that he'd be very intimidating right now. With his powers on the fritz from years of being broken down by the demons holding him, he was lucky he could count on them when he needed them at all. Sure, he was stronger than he let on. One positive thing about being topside was that the longer he was, the more he felt his strength slowly returning. Using large amounts in a short period of time, though, like the fight in the Indigo parking lot, still wiped him out. Something like that used to tire him out as much as lifting a piece of paper would. Now he felt more like he'd just run six blocks. Still, better was better.

He definitely wasn't strong enough to go up against a witch, though, especially one who used dark magic.

Shit, he didn't know what to do.

He'd told Cyrus about the meeting...

Damn, he still couldn't believe Cyrus had been here. Dev was pretty sure part of him was still in shock. But as far as their conversation went, he really hadn't been able to tell him much. Just that Andras was meeting with a dark witch around eight tonight and he planned to use her to find the girls, which Cyrus hadn't seemed too surprised about. What had shocked him was when Dev refused to leave with him. It wasn't like he didn't want to go. Shit, he'd been dreaming of getting away from these demons for longer than he cared to consider. But he couldn't just yet. After some growling on his brother's part, Dev had mentioned how he was going to try to find out any information he could about the witch. They needed to know exactly what Andras was up to. After a lot of back and forth, all his brother had said was to be careful not get himself hurt or sent away from the club before they could figure out how to get him out.

Yeah, that was definitely going to be easier said than done. Especially when every time he turned around, one of the demons in this place was trying to get him to fall into a bad way with Andras.

Snorting, he leaned over the rail on the second floor and looked out over the club. He watched as several drunken customers danced and stumbled around, not aware in the slightest of the danger lurking only steps away from them.

He could see the twins, Lakmi and Vhin, greedily taking in the crowd, no doubt trying to figure out which one would be their plaything for the night. Ever since they'd come topside, it had become a nightly thing for them. They'd find some poor, unsuspecting human - male or female, they weren't picky - and lure them in with the promise of a good time. From there, Dev could only imagine what happened once the door to their private room in the club closed for the remainder of the evening.

Sometimes he'd see the person leaving in a daze in the morning. Other times, he'd never see them again.

Shuddering, Dev pulled his mind from thoughts of the twins' extra-curricular activities. It did no good for him to stress over it. He'd tried to step in once, but hadn't made it very far. Castigo had shown up, seemingly out of nowhere, and blocked his path. The demon's silver eyes had glared down at him, their intensity making him feel the need to take a step back and look away. Yet he'd held his ground.

"It's wrong," Dev had said in a hushed tone.

"That may be, but there is nothing you can do about it," Castigo had responded, his voice gravely. He'd glanced over his shoulder in the direction the twins had gone with the human. "It would be best, for you, if you stayed out of their affairs." Seeming to sense his reaction, the demon's gaze had snapped back to his. His eyes narrowed briefly, as if daring him to argue. But Dev couldn't. As much as he'd hated to admit it, the demon had been right.

Dev's shoulders had deflated as he'd looked away from Castigo's piercing stare. "So I should... What? Just let it happen?"

"What choice do you have?" He'd shifted slightly. "Do not argue with me on this, Dev." His voice was hard, demanding. "As much as you wish me to help you with any possible problems, I also may ask you for a favor. If you get involved with this, with them, it will not end well. Then you will be in an even worse position than you are now. How will that help your brothers when the time comes?"

At that, Castigo had given him a knowing look and disappeared back to wherever he'd come from. Dev wrestled between his desire to save the human and the need to keep himself in one piece to help his brothers should the need arise.

The desire to be there for his family won out. He still wasn't sure if it had been the right decision.

So here he was, two days later, watching the twins move toward yet another human. They'd picked a young one this time, a boy really, who had to be no more than twenty-five. He sat alone at the bar, nursing a beer, staring off into the distance. Dev could already tell the boy wouldn't put up much of a fight. His posture screamed of loneliness, of a deep need for attention. Two things the twins fed off of.

Taking his eyes off the scene before it really began to unfold, Dev felt his gut clench. Fuck, he hated this. Hated knowing what was going on around him, loathed the fact that he wasn't able to do a damn thing about it.

Someday...

Someday he'd be able to help put a stop to all this. Be of use to someone and start feeling good about himself again.

For now, he'd try and hold up his promise to Cyrus to keep himself safe. Thoughts of his other brothers flittered through his mind. Dev had asked Cyrus about them, but there hadn't been much time to go through everything that had gone on over the past several decades. Really, would there ever be enough time for that?

Yet he'd asked anyway. Cyrus has just assured him that everyone was good. There had been a hint of something when his brother mentioned Nicholas, but when Dev had pushed to find out what had happened that put the tightness in his brother's face, Cyrus had changed the subject back to how Dev needed to look out for himself.

After watching his brother disappear back into the shadows, Dev had stood on the rooftop for another hour. He'd not only done that to digest what had just happened, but also to get his emotions in check.

Who knew what would have happened if he'd gone right in and someone saw him? Shit. Who was he kidding? He knew exactly what would have happened. It was that knowledge that had him keeping to himself, even after taking an hour to rebuild the walls around him. If he'd walked right in after Cyrus had left, he would have probably found himself face to face with at least one of the demons who roamed the club. And they would have known something had happened, that something was up with him. He would have quickly found himself in Andras' grip.

Running a hand over his face, Dev leaned forward and rested his arms on the rail. Taking a deep breath, he slowly blew out the air as he continued to look around at the growing crowd below him.

It was then that he caught sight of someone he thought he'd never seen again.

Maria.

Her hair was different, darker, but he'd know those blue eyes anywhere. He watched as she confidently made her way through the crowd. People parted before her, as if they could sense her coming. Dev's eyes narrowed. A slow realization came over him when he noticed more than the color of her hair was different. The very air surrounding her seemed off, wrong.

Her blue eyes flashed as they landed on someone in front of her. Leaning forward to see better, he felt his pulse spike when he watched her walk up to Andras, who had suddenly appeared by the bar. With the poise that only came from knowing she was a dangerous Being in her own right, Maria shook Andras' hand and nodded as he signaled for her to follow him.

No. It's not possible.

Dev's mind spun as it went over the details of meeting her the other night. Of the innocence, the light he'd sensed in her. How nervous she had seemed as she sat in the club. How grateful she'd looked when he'd led her outside.

This couldn't be the same girl. Because if she was, if the woman following Andras from the bar was Maria from the other night, that meant...

Shit.

That meant she was the black witch Andras had been expecting. Even worse, it meant she had played him.

Dev felt a stab of fear shoot through his core. She could tell Andras what he'd done, how he had gotten her out of the club. What would his boss do with the knowledge that he'd tried to save someone he thought of as an innocent? Someone he thought had been there for one of Andras' *clients*?

As the demon disappeared from sight, Dev felt a thin sheen of sweat beginning to build upon his skin. His breathing was loud, even to his own ears, as he tried to pull air into his tightening lungs. Eyes still glued to the top of Maria's head, he felt himself tense as her steps slowed to a stop.

He watched her slowly tilt her head and look up at him, her gaze landing right on his, as if she'd known he'd been there the whole time. And maybe she had.

Everything inside the club seemed to stop. The noise fell to a low hum and the lights seemed to dim. Dev didn't know what he wanted to do or say as he looked at one of the few people who could have him hurt the most.

He'd known from the start putting any kind of trust in Castigo would be a gamble, one that would probably blow up in his face. It was a risk he'd been willing to take and one he still stood by. Shit, even his dealings with Sy could eventually come back to haunt him. But, again, he'd gone into that with his eyes wide open. He'd known what may or may not happen, and had chosen to go with it anyway. But this woman... He hadn't seen her coming. He wasn't prepared for what their meeting the previous night might mean for his future.

God, what was he going to do?

Everything he'd worked so hard to accomplish, all the hopes he had of getting out of here and being free, he saw dying in her eyes.

Dev could only pray that, for one reason or another, Maria wouldn't tell Andras about their encounter. But why wouldn't she? He was nothing to her but a pawn. Something he was very used to being. Hell, she could tell Andras what he had done as a sign of how much help she could be to him. His pain could help her cement her place at Andras' side.

Devlin.

His name whispered through his mind as he watched a seductive smile spread across her lips.

Hello, Devlin.

Why had he given her his full name? Why had he approached her in the first place?

Chills raced down his spine as he continued to stare back at her. Then, just as suddenly as everything had quieted, the noise level raised and the club once again came to life around him. The music's bass drummed through his head as he tightened his grip on the rail, his knuckles white from the strain.

Maria's smile turned into a knowing smirk right before she sent a playful wink his away and disappeared into the halls below.

What do I do? Shit. What do I do?

His mind worked on overdrive. Before he knew he was even moving, Dev was on the steps leading down toward his office. He was through the crowd and almost around the corner in the hallway before he forced himself to slow. Leaning against the wall, he heard his office door close with a soft click. Dev knew nobody would be standing in the hallway guarding the door because, well, who would be stupid enough to try and listen in on one of Andras' meetings? He smirked. Yeah, what he was about to do was really, *really* stupid.

Walking quietly toward the closed door, Dev pulled in all his power, tethering it into his center and erecting a cement wall around it. He wasn't sure how powerful Maria was, but since she had him believing she was an innocent with white light residing within her, he could only assume she was stronger than any he'd come up against to date.

How had he been so blinded to what she truly was?

How didn't he see?

Well, he would have time to go over how much of an idiot he was later. Right now, he needed to concentrate. Silently, Dev stopped next to the door and leaned against the wall. Taking a deep breath, he closed his eyes and focused on the voices in his office.

If Maria did rat him out to Andras, at least he might have a chance to run before the demon's power ripped through his mind.

Maybe.

Andras stared at the female sitting across from him. She wasn't what he'd expected, but then again, nothing lately had turned out how he had expected. So why should this be any different?

Leaning back in his chair, he watched her look around the room, her lithe body seeming relaxed as she curled her legs beneath her. If he weren't already so attuned to the wildness of her power curling throughout the space, he may have actually believed the casualness in her pose.

She wasn't fooling him, though. His own senses were on high alert in response to her proximity, and he felt his skin crawling.

Sending a nod to Agalon, he watched as his second made sure the door was securely locked. The demon had made his concerns known on more than one occasion. Andras had put a stop to his growling, but he couldn't help but agree with what he said.

He hated dealing with witches, regardless of how much of a benefit they were. And she was definitely going to be a benefit. He had gone too long having only a portion of his power. Narrowing his eyes, Andras mentally chastised himself for the millionth time. Had he known when he'd shoved some of his power into Ella that it would end up being such a fight to get it back, he may have decided to go about it differently. Or maybe thought up a contingency plan. He wasn't sure. All Andras did know was he needed to get to her...now.

Hell, every time Ella allowed her own power to emerge, he could feel his humming in the air, calling to him. Yet he couldn't find her. She was hidden from him, cloaked, and his patience was running out.

That was where the witch sitting before him came into play. He'd use her to find Ella. Not only so he could finally claim her as his own, but to get his power back. He needed to be complete again, preferably before those who would rise up against him found out he'd been weakened. If he were able to get his hands on those damn angels' witches while he was at it, all the better.

"So, shall we get started on the reason I'm here?"

The sound of the witch's voice pulled Andras from his thoughts. With a roll of his shoulders, he sent one last glance at Agalon before pinning her with a glare. "Yes, let us get this over with." At her nod, his eyes narrowed. "I didn't get your name."

"I didn't offer it," she said simply. "There is a certain familiarity that comes with knowing a person's name. We aren't going to have that kind of relationship."

He smirked, acknowledging her response with a click of his tongue. "Of course. Let's get down to business then. What I need is simple. I need you to find this woman and deliver her to me." Sliding a picture of Ella across the desk, he watched the witch pick it up and study it. "Her name is Ella Roberts and she has something of mine. Something of great value. I need you to locate her so I can get it back."

She laid the picture back on the desk, her eyes flashing as she looked up at him. "What does she have?"

"That is none of your concern," he all but growled. "All you need to know is the sooner you locate and bring her to me, the sooner you get what you want."

"And how do I know you'll deliver once I get you this girl?" she asked, her tone light as she tapped one polished red nail against the arm of the chair.

"I would say trust me, but I assume that would mean very little to you."

She smirked. "You assume right. After all, you are a demon. You can't really blame me for not trusting you."

Andras stared at her for a moment. He thought about his part of this deal, what she wanted in return for finding and delivering Ella to him. It wasn't that what she wanted was unreasonable. And it was definitely something he could do. The problem was if he did what she wanted, delivered who she wanted, he would not only be losing a possible asset, but would be giving her a link to power Andras wasn't sure he wanted her to have. So, until he decided, he'd just let her think this was a done deal.

Allowing his expression to take on a bored look, Andras smoothed his hands down his suit jacket. "Well, I guess you'll just have to do what I ask to find out."

She seemed to think that over. He figured she didn't have a choice, though. If she needed him to hold up his end of this deal, she was going to have to do her part. He watched her reach up, pushing her soft, blonde hair behind her ears, thinking how ironic it was that some of the most beautiful things were also the deadliest.

And, especially in this case, the craziest.

"Fine," she finally said. "I'll find your female and bring her to you so you can get...whatever it is she has of yours." She stared pointedly at him, leaning forward with a definite sense of eagerness in the air. "Then you will give me what I want."

"Out of curiosity," Andras said slowly, leaning toward her. "What exactly do you want with him?"

"As you so eloquently put it a few minutes ago, that is none of your concern."

"Well, seeing as you plan on taking someone who belongs to me," Andras said, steepling his fingers under his chin, "it very much *is* my concern." Before she could object, he went on. "After all, I'm asking you to give me someone who has no bearing on you at all. You are asking for much more. So, tell me, what do you want with him?"

They stared at each other quietly. Andras could practically see her mind spinning on what to say. Agalon shifted against the wall, the first sign of any kind of agitation from him since he'd locked the door moments ago. Andras knew his second was itching to get away from the witch. Hell, he was, too. But this meeting couldn't end until they were on the same page. At least as far as she was concerned.

Sending a glance Agalon's way, Andras looked back at the woman. "So?" he pushed, keeping his gaze level and unblinking.

"I need a Being to syphon power from. One who won't be missed once they're gone."

"What do you need the power for?" Agalon asked, glaring at her.

"That is definitely none of your business," she snapped. "I just need someone to use." She nodded toward Andras. "You happen to have someone at your disposal."

"How do you know I'd be willing to part with him?" Andras inquired. He thought about the pros and cons of what she offered.

"With his brothers sniffing around, probably closing in on his location as we speak, do you really plan on holding onto your little toy much longer?" At his silence, she smirked. "Let me replace the toy you have with a new one. You get who you want, allowing me to take a potential problem off of your hands. Win-win."

Andras returned her smirk with one of his own. The longer he thought about the witch's offer, the more he noticed how eager she was for him to agree. He knew she wouldn't bring him Ella until he did, so... "You get me Ella, unharmed, and in return, I'll give you Dev."

With a grin, he watched her lean back, her eyes lighting as she chuckled. "It's a deal then. I'll get started right away. You just make sure my...reward remains in one piece."

Shifting in his seat, Andras nodded. Soon, Ella would be back where she belonged. Once that happened, he'd deal with Dev and this little witch. Handing the angel over, possibly increasing the witch's power, was not something he cared to do. But, until her job was done, he'd let her think what she wanted. If he needed to offer up Dev to make sure she did what he needed her to, so be it.

Chapter 18

She and Nicholas had talked for hours. It had been the best time she ever had on the phone. Hell, she hated talking on the phone. The awkward silence, not knowing how the person on the other end was taking the conversation, the occasional instances where she had to listen to the other person chewing. That sound grated on her nerves more than she could ever put in to words.

So the fact she truly enjoyed being on it for the past couple hours said a lot. For as much as she hated talking on the phone, the conversation with Nicholas had been something else entirely. Scratching behind Charlie's ears, Amy couldn't help but smile. Everything about Nicholas just felt right.

She'd felt like she was right there in the room with him. In her mind, she saw his eyes light up every time he'd laughed, saw that sexy smile spread across his face as he'd teased her.

Damn, she missed his presence in her house. Even when he'd been unconscious on her couch, she'd been able to feel him in every room.

Staring at her laptop, she ran her fingers lightly over the keyboard, trying to focus on the blog she was writing. It was a piece on a new author, one whom she had instantly liked after just a short conversation via email. She really wanted to do this blog justice. Taking a deep breath, she thought over what she knew of the author, the book he'd released, what he was working on next. As her mind sifted through it all, her fingers began to move across the keys. Certain parts from the author's new book played over and over in her mind as she quickly filled up her screen. It was a romance story, of course, where the ridiculously perfect hero saved the sassy woman from a cruel and nasty warlock.

Yes, it was a paranormal romance. No, it wasn't the only genre she read. But, in her opinion, it was the best one out there.

It only took her about an hour to finish and polish the blog. Looking it over for what was probably the fourth time, Amy's mind started wandering back to Nicholas. Glancing at her phone, she'd hoped to see a message from him. Even though she was slightly disappointed, she really wasn't surprised when there wasn't one. He'd sounded exhausted when they talked on the phone. It made sense seeing that he claimed he'd been up late, then one of his brothers had woken him early this morning for breakfast.

She chuckled softly as she remembered hearing the smile in his voice, even as he complained about his brothers. She could tell his family was really important to him. Even the little bit he'd said about Cyrus, who scared her just a tad, was laced with emotion. It meant a lot to her. She had always been close to her family, so hearing that Nicholas was also close to his just made her feel all warm inside.

Not that she needed any help feeling warm inside. Just hearing his voice or catching a whiff of his scent would cause the inferno that had been growing within her ever since she'd first laid eyes on him to burn hotter. Even now, hours after she'd last seen him, kissed him, she felt that familiar warmth.

And that kiss... *Holy toe-curling lip-lock, Batman!* That had been one hell of a kiss. One that Amy was definitely hoping to experience again.

Soon.

Preferably without any interruptions and with less clothes on.

The sudden sound of Justin Timberlake's "Can't Stop the Feeling" brought her out of her musings. Looking over at her phone, Amy grinned when she saw her best friend's name flash across the screen.

Misty had been her best friend since freshman year of high school. She was crazy, loud, and the most loyal person Amy had ever known. Misty was as much her family as her parents were. She was also someone Amy never lied to, which left her in a weird position because she wasn't sure how to explain Nicholas. She would have to tell her something. After all, her friend would know something was up as soon as she answered the phone. Sighing, Amy's finger hovered over the screen before swiping and hitting the speaker so she could continue going over her blog entry.

"Hey, girl. What's up?" Amy asked.

"Woman, where have you been?" Misty immediately asked.

"Hmm?"

She stared blankly at the screen. Amy knew exactly what she was asking. She had purposely avoided her calls, texting her anything she could think of that would stop her friend from showing up at her house. The last thing Amy had wanted was to try and explain the hunky male lying unconscious on her couch. Hell, she had a hard time explaining it to herself. There was no way she would have been able to talk to anyone else about it. So she'd been distant, told her she was busy. Even blamed her need to be anti-social on her monthly visitor. Now that Nicholas was gone, Amy guessed it was time to tell her best friend...something.

"I've been here," she finally murmured. "I've just been busy." She knew it was a weak response, but whatever.

"Busy?" Misty asked, her tone clearly showing her disbelief. "Doing what? And don't feed me those flimsy excuses you've been sending my way."

"I was just...helping out a friend," Amy responded slowly, cringing more and more with each word. Absently running her hand over Charlie's head, Amy tried to slow her racing thoughts as she listened to her cat's loud purring increase in volume as he leaned into her. She realized there was no way her best friend wasn't going to push for more information. Sure, there were probably millions of other excuses she could have come up with that would have led to less questions, but "helping a friend" was the first one that came to mind.

"Who?"

"You don't know him."

"Him? Oh, now you *have* to tell me," Misty gushed. "Who's this *him*, and what exactly was the help he needed that kept you too busy to talk to your best friend?"

Blinking several times, Amy glanced toward the window. How did she explain Nicholas? How she found him lying on her back porch, shot, and doctored him back to health? How she watched over him until he woke up? Connected with him more in the first few seconds than she had with any person previously? How she hadn't been able to stop thinking of him since he left?

The answer was easy. She couldn't. At least not fully. Truly, it all came down to the simple fact that she didn't know what was going on herself.

"His name is Nicholas. I met him a few weeks ago." *Give or take*, she thought with a frown. "He was in need of some help." *Bleeding all over my porch*. "I don't know how to explain it, but I couldn't *not* help. You know?"

"Yeah, I know. We've had this discussion before."

Amy could practically see her friend frowning. "What discussion?"

"About you being too nice for your own good. Always willing to help someone out, whether you know them or not."

"This was different."

"How?"

Amy let out a loud sigh. "It just was. I don't know. From the second I found him-"

"*Found* him?"

"Met him... I meant met him. Anyway, as soon as I did, I could tell he was different."

"Uh-huh. And what was so different about this guy? Amy, you'd help a homeless man if he asked for it."

"And what's wrong with that?"

"Nothing," Misty was quick to say. "Absolutely nothing. You are one of the sweetest, most giving people I know. And I love you for that. You know this. It's just, well... I just worry that people take advantage of you."

"Hey, I've gotten better at saying no to people."

"Saying no to your elderly neighbor when she asks you to mow her lawn is a good thing, but that's just one time."

"It took a lot to say no to her."

"You had to say no because you were already on your way out."

"Yes, but-"

"You were heading out to get *her* groceries...pick up *her* laundry."

"Well, she's old and can't get around like she used to."

Amy heard Misty sigh. She knew her best friend worried about her, but Amy just had to help someone if she was able to. Sure, maybe there were times she'd put off doing something she wanted to do so she could be there for someone else. Well, maybe more than a few times.

There was nothing wrong with wanting to help people, was there? Amy thought, chewing on her bottom lip.

"You know what you need?" Misty asked, her suddenly chipper voice breaking through her thoughts.

"What?" Amy asked, leery about where this sudden change of topic was going.

"You need a night out with the girls."

That statement usually consisted of traveling into the city, dancing, drinking, and fending off guys Amy wouldn't touch if they were the last guys on the planet. And that was only the start. The icing on top was having to limp from one club to the other as she tried to figure out how she'd let Misty convince her to wear some ridiculously high heels, all the while trying to corral their two other friends who always drank way more than they should. Yeah, that sounded exactly like what she needed right now.

"I don't know, Misty..."

"Come on. It'll be fun. We'll just go out for a few drinks and you can fill us all in on Nicholas."

"There really isn't much to tell."

"The tone in your voice says otherwise."

"What tone?"

Misty chuckled. "Just say you'll come out."

"I really don't feel like going into the city," Amy said honestly, submitting her blog entry and closing down the site.

"Me, either. I thought we could check out that new local club that just opened up."

"Local club?" Amy questioned, frowning as she tried to think of what club her friend was talking about.

"Yeah. The, um... Shit, what's it called? I know I have the flyer here somewhere." Amy heard rustling. "Oh, here it is... The 9th Circle. I don't think it's been open very long."

"Oh, I think I remember hearing about that place."

"It's supposed to be a wicked place to go dancing."

"Isn't it, like, a gothic club?" Amy asked, frowning. Goth wasn't exactly her scene, but if that was where her friend wanted to go, she'd give it a try.

"I actually heard it was more of a pop dance club."

"Hmm... Do you know anyone who's been there?"

"No, but every night since it opened, there's been a line a block long to get into it. So it must be awesome."

"Must be," Amy hummed absently, pulling up Google on her laptop. "What was the name of it again?"

"The 9th Circle."

Amy quickly pulled up the club's website. The page was filled with pictures of beautiful people dancing, drinking, and laughing. It looked like every other club website she'd been to. With eye-catching drink specials and over-the-top graphics, it promised a night to remember. But as she stared at the site, scrolled through the various quotes, Amy started to feel a sense of uncertainty bloom in her chest. There was something bothering her. She couldn't put her finger on it, but something didn't feel right. It all just seemed too...appealing.

"I don't know," Amy said slowly.

"Come on. It'll be fun. Please," her friend begged. "Listen. How about we go check it out. If it turns out to be place we don't want to stay, we'll leave."

Chewing her bottom lip, Amy glanced from the laptop to the window. She really did want to get out of the house for a bit. The more she thought about staying in, surrounded by nothing but her own thoughts, the lonelier she felt. God, she was tired of being by herself. But did she really want to go to this club? If the feeling in her gut told her anything, then no, she really didn't.

"Come on, Amy. It's been ages since we've hung out." Misty's voice drifted through the phone, pulling her from her thoughts. "Just for a couple hours... I'll pick you up."

"Maybe we should just chill tonight. Go to the café and gossip over some coffee."

"But we've done that the last few times we've all met up. I want to go dancing... Have some shots... Flirt with some hot guys I normally wouldn't even talk to. You've been a social recluse for far too long, my friend. You owe it to yourself to drink some overly priced alcohol and flirt with overly eager men."

"Misty-"

"Amy," her friend cut in.

Amy sighed as she stared blankly at the club's website. It was just a club. She could go, hang out for a bit, then call it a night. Just because she'd ride with Misty didn't mean she couldn't grab a cab home. It would be good to get out. Maybe after she got a little tipsy, she could use the alcohol as an excuse to text Nicholas for a ride home instead of taking a cab. The possibility of seeing him made the idea of dealing with a club that she didn't want to go to bearable. Hell, she even felt a little giddy about it.

"Okay, Misty."

"Yay! Oh, this is going to be so much fun. Start getting ready. I'll be over to grab you in a few hours."

"Great. See you then," Amy said, hanging up after Misty said her goodbye.

Charlie's loud purring brought her gaze down to where he lay sprawled along her side. His green eyes watched her intently as she set her phone down. "Looks like I'm heading out for a girls' night. Well, at least it'll only start as a girls' night. Hopefully." Blinking slowly, he continued to stare at her, tilting his head until she obliged and resumed petting him. "Okay. A little more Charlie time, then I'll start getting ready."

And then, if she were lucky, she could maybe get a little Nicholas time tonight.

A girl could hope.

Chapter 19

"Are you sure this is going to work?" Nicholas asked from the middle seat in the Hummer.

Manuel's glare that he sent over his shoulder told Nicholas he was getting on his nerves.

That was maybe the third or fourth time he'd asked. But he wasn't as tech savvy as his brother. The gadget he'd given Hayley was supposed to allow them to hear what was going on around her inside the club. It was very *James Bond.*

He'd even said as much back at the house, earning a soft laugh from Ella as she'd given his arm a squeeze.

When he'd first seen the little hair clip, he'd asked Manuel how it worked. After listening to his brother spout a bunch of technical terms and impressively long, complicated sentences, Nicholas had quickly realized he shouldn't have asked. But he could now say with confidence he knew a lengthy way to say it was a tiny microphone.

You know, should the topic ever come up.

Yet he still continued to ask if it was going to work. Not because he didn't think Manuel knew what he was doing, but because he was nervous. There were so many things that could go wrong, which he voiced while they'd been running around the house, getting ready.

One of his biggest was that the demons would find out who Hayley was. They were all aware of how fast a situation could go to shit. Though he had no doubt Manuel could get to wherever she was in the blink of an eye, a lot could happen in a blink. Not only had Manuel been adamant that their plan would work, Hayley had also promised to play things safe. She swore she wouldn't linger. She'd just get in there, find Dev, and bring him up to the roof. Plus, as Manuel pointed out, Andras and his crew would be looking for any sort of power play or magical interference. Not someone with any sort of listening device on them. Hell, the possibility of someone coming into their club with something like that probably hadn't even crossed their minds.

That was the hope anyway.

Now here they sat, an hour after he'd watched Hayley chant a few lines and transform herself into a rather pretty, albeit plain, twenty-something-year-old woman. She still sounded like her, but Hayley thought it highly unlikely they knew her voice.

Though he agreed, he still worried. They all did.

Glancing around the Hummer, he saw his brothers sitting tensely as they listened to Hayley's footsteps and steady breathing through the speakers. Ella had been convinced, by a very pouty Christian, to stay home. Of course, she had fought him on it, swearing she could help. She'd been working on controlling her ever-growing power and, with the help of Hayley, had become rather good at keeping her warring forces from tearing her apart. Until they figured out what to do about that extra power residing within her, which still threw him for a loop, they needed her to stay as calm as possible. After they had rescued Ella and Manuel had dropped that little bomb about her extra power, Nicholas had thought the house would implode. Everyone talked over everyone else as they all tried to come to terms with the fact that part of Andras had not only been stowed away within Ella, but was attempting to reach out to him, slowly destroying her light.

Ever since, Hayley had been working on drawing the darkness out of Ella...to no avail so far.

Nicholas' head still hurt thinking about it all. It was just one freakin' mind-fucking event after another.

"*Here we go,*" they heard Hayley softly say, bringing Nicholas out of his wandering thoughts. Everyone seemed to sit up straighter as they watched the club from down the block.

Cyrus had wanted to park right out front. Like that wouldn't be suspicious. His request had not come as a surprise, though, seeing that he just wanted to walk right in the front door and demanded the demons hand Dev over. An idea Nicholas couldn't exactly argue with.

In the end, Darren did what he did best and they all agreed that parking a block away would be the better choice. It would keep them out of sight, yet have them close enough that they could get into the club quickly if they needed to.

The goal right now was to keep under Andras' radar and wait for Hayley to make contact with Dev.

Yeah, right.

Nicholas had a feeling one of those goals was going to end up being easier to do than the other.

Loud music suddenly boomed through the Hummer. They heard multiple voices mixed in with the bass as they listened to Hayley make her way farther into the club.

"*This place is intense,*" she whispered.

Nicholas watched his brother shift in his seat. The need to get to her rolled off Manuel in waves. Reaching up, he gave his brother's shoulder a light squeeze.

"She's got this," Nicholas said, scooting over so he could lean in between Manuel and Darren in the front.

"I know. It just gets me that she's in there and I have to wait out here," Manuel said, fiddling with the dials on some devise he'd brought with him. Nicholas glanced up at Darren to find him watching Manuel intently. A look of both understanding and concern flashed across his face.

"Nicky's right," Darren said calmly. "Hayley will be fine. We all went over every detail of what she should do, what she should expect. Hell, you even pulled up the blueprints for the club so she would know exactly where everything is. With her charms in place, she'll be in and out in no time."

"You're right," Manuel sighed. "I just wish I could be in there with her."

"We all do," Nicholas agreed.

Grumbles from the back seat told them Christian and Cyrus felt the same. There was just no way any of them could get inside without setting off the demons. Hell, he'd be surprised if they could get up to the roof without being discovered. Yet they had to. This whole mission came down to meeting Dev on the roof in the hopes of bringing him home with them. He knew Darren wanted to keep Dev on the inside, having him be their eyes and ears so they could remain one step ahead of Andras.

And Nicholas understood the pros of that, could see exactly where Darren was coming from. He just couldn't agree with it.

For decades, Nicholas had wondered what had happened to their long-lost brother. He'd hoped they would see Dev again, be able to hear his laugh, enjoy his carefree banter. But after Nicholas and his other brothers found themselves sent to Earth and the years had flown by, that hope had dwindled.

Until Hayley and Ella spoke of the man who had rescued them in the Indigo parking lot. The man who had materialized out of nowhere and taken on the demons who had been attacking them. Once they had gotten to the part of the fight where his wings unfurled around him as he pulled the evil essence right out of demons, Nicholas' gut had clenched. Even before Hayley had said the color of their savior's wings, he'd known it was Dev. Now that they had found him, were just mere feet away from the building he was in, Nicholas couldn't even entertain the idea of leaving without him.

"*I think I see him*," they heard Hayley whisper. Everyone in the vehicle tensed as they leaned even closer to the front.

The tricky part for Hayley was getting close to Dev. None of them had any way of knowing where he would be or who would be around him. Therefore, they couldn't plan for this part. Hayley just said she would get close to him. As soon as she was able to get him away from everyone, she'd grab his hand, which would allow him to see who she really was. Cyrus had asked her why she didn't just do that right away. She'd stated that, without knowing how he'd react to her being there, she felt it safer to do her little reveal away from prying eyes. Once she exposed who she was, she'd take him up to the roof. That made sense to Nicholas. He just hoped it worked out the way she planned.

"Okay, I'm going to head his way."

They listened intently to the music coming through the speakers. All of them held their breath as they waited.

"Excuse me?" they heard Hayley ask. Her voice sounded louder as she had to yell over the music. *"Sir, can I talk to you for a moment?"*

"Look, I don't really have time," Dev's voice sounded strained, but it was definitely him. At the sound of it, the first time he'd heard it in more years than he cared to count, Nicholas released a sharp gasp.

"All I need is a second," Hayley pushed.

"What is this about?" His caution was evident.

Nicholas bit his bottom lip as he imagined all his brother had been through to make him this careful. Damn it, they needed to get him out of there.

"*I'm a writer for the* Daily Paper. *I just wanted to ask you a few questions. Please. This won't take long at all.*"

"She's good," Christian murmured. Nicholas nodded as he silently willed Dev to agree. If his brother said no, blew her off, this little mission of theirs was over. They couldn't risk not getting in touch with him tonight, especially when there was no promise there'd be another opportunity.

"*I really can't-*"

"*This won't take long,*" Hayley cut in. "*And you* really *want to hear what I have to say.*"

A deafening silence followed her statement as they all waited for Dev to respond. The music in the background grated on Nicholas' nerves. It wasn't what he wanted to hear, and there was nothing he could do about it. Shifting in his seat, he stifled the growl threatening to rise within him. There was no sense in getting upset about anything right now. He just had to trust Hayley was able to get their brother to go with her. She hadn't let them down yet, so there was no reason for him to think she would now.

After some time, they noticed the music getting quieter.

"They're moving away from the dance floor," Darren stated. "Dev must have agreed to talk to her."

"Thank fuck," Cyrus growled.

"*Okay*," they heard Dev say as the music completely disappeared. "*You have my attention.*"

"*Good*," Hayley chuckled. A heartbeat later, they all heard Dev let out a hiss. "*Hello, Dev.*"

"*Holy shit, Red. What the hell are you doing here? Wow, did you pick a bad night to show up.*"

"Red?" Manuel asked, his eyes showing his amusement. They all just shrugged and shook their heads.

"*Nice to see you, too.*" Hayley laughed. "*Is there ever a good time to be here? Anyway, we don't have much time. We need to get up to the roof.*"

"*Ha, isn't that the truth. And it's nice to see you, as well. Now, what are you doing here and why do we need to get up to the roof?*"

"*I just need you to go with me-*"

"*Not until you tell me what's going on.*"

"*Dev, it took a lot of planning to get me in here, and-*"

"*What the hell do you think you're doing here anyway? This is the last place you should be. Don't you remember what I*" *told you and Ella? You need to stay as far away from-"*

"*Your brothers are here,*" they heard Hayley say softly, interrupting Dev's rant. Her voice was a mere whisper compared to the beating of Nicholas' heart. At this point, it was so loud in his ears, he was sure his brothers could hear it, too.

"*My...,*" Dev started, his voice trailing off. They heard him clear his throat, his emotions so strong, Nicholas didn't need to be by him to know the feelings he had running though him. The tremor in his voice as he spoke again caused Nicholas' jaw to clench. "*Why are they...? What are they doing here?*"

"*They're here for you,*" Hayley said simply. "*Don't look so shocked, Dev. You really think they would find out you were here and* not *want to see you?*"

"*Listen, Red, I'm having a really bad day, and as much as I want to believe my brothers have come for me, I just...*"

His pause caused Nicholas' stomach to turn.

"We need to get to him," Cyrus said from the back seat. "He doesn't think we're really here for him."

"What if he doesn't go up to the roof?" Christian asked, his voice low.

"He'll go up to the roof," Manuel insisted. "Hayley will get him up there."

Nicholas nodded as he glanced around at them. This had to work. Looking out the window as his brothers continued to quietly chatter back and forth, he waited eagerly for the next words to come across the speakers, hoping they were the ones he wanted to hear.

"*Dev, your brothers really want to see you...talk to you. So just go with me to the roof. It'll be okay. Trust me.*"

"*Shit, Red,*" they heard Dev say, followed by a soft sigh. "*Okay. Let's head to the roof.*"

"*Yay. The boys will meet us up there.*"

"That's our cue," Darren said, opening his door. They all followed, piling out of the Hummer.

"Let's duck into this alley," Nicholas suggested, nodding toward the alley beside them. "It'll be a lot easier to get up to the roof without being seen if we dematerialize rather than fly up the side of the building."

Darren nodded. "Yeah, okay. Let's do that."

Moving into the dark alley, Nicholas began to pull his power around him. Visualizing the roof of The 9th Circle, he felt himself slip into the shadows, walking onto the club's roof seconds later. His brothers all materialized next to him as he felt the cool night air shiver across his skin. Glancing over at Cyrus, who had stopped beside him, he opened his mouth to ask where they should wait when the harsh scrapping sound of the metal door opening caught his attention. A stillness settled over them as they watched the door on the opposite side of the roof open, Hayley stepping through. Her green eyes lit up when she spotted them, her smile almost blinding.

Looking past Hayley, Nicholas held his breath as he watched Dev step out into the night. He moved away from the door, allowing it to close behind him. Their brother looked the same, yet different. His body had a tenseness to it that it never had before. Where there had once been nothing but light in his bright blue eyes, Nicholas now saw darkness. But even as he met his brother's lost gaze, he saw a flicker of warmth run through them. That alone let him know there was hope to get Dev back.

Without waiting for anyone else to say anything, Nicholas began to move forward. This was his brother, someone who had been a part of them all, who had been lost to them for longer than anybody truly cared to think about. And now, after all this time, he stood in front of them. Nicholas knew he wasn't into any kind of hugging or whatnot, but it was going to happen.

"I'm going to hug you now, so deal," he said in warning right before he wrapped his arms around Dev.

He felt his brother stiffen. After a moment, a soft chuckle escaped as he returned the hug. Pulling back, Nicholas smiled as Dev glanced at him, then looked at the others hovering close by. They didn't stay there for long. As soon as Nicholas stepped to the side, they swarmed Dev. Hugs were shared, questions were asked, and apologies were given for not getting to him sooner. Those were brushed off as he gave them a soft, yet forced smile and said there was nothing for them to be sorry for. The look that flashed through his eyes screamed otherwise, but it seemed this topic was going to be dropped. For now.

"You seem more strung out than you were earlier," Cyrus all but growled at their brother. "What happened between then and now?"

Dev looked uncertain as he glanced around at everyone. Almost as if he wasn't sure whether he could tell them what had happened, like he wasn't sure they really wanted to know. Whatever he saw on their faces must have reassured him because he took a deep breath and began to speak. Nicholas felt his pulse speed up as he listened to Dev talk about the woman he'd recently helped out of the club, how she'd shown back up today to meet with Andras.

Once he'd gotten to what he'd overheard through the door to his office, Nicholas physically felt the tension from everyone on the roof.

"What does this Maria look like?" Darren asked, his eyes blazing as he stared at their brother.

"Beautiful." Dev shook his head. "And completely out of place in the club. I guess that was her plan all along. Just so she could get me to come to her. I'm not blind to her now, though. After that sneer she sent me and what she said she wanted me for..." He visibly shuddered. "I was just about to try and get away from here when I ran into Red."

"And you said she's a witch?" Hayley asked, her eyes on Dev as she leaned back into Manuel. His brother wrapped his arms around her waist, comforting her.

Dev nodded. "Yes. And she wants to syphon my power. I don't know what she wants it for, but Andras said he'd give me to her in exchange for her finding Ella."

Nicholas watched Dev turn toward Darren. They stared at each other in silence. He knew Darren was weighing what he'd just heard against what he'd wanted to ask Dev to do. After a short time, it seemed he'd made up his mind.

"Then I'm glad we got to you. It's time for you to come home, Dev," Darren said. "We aren't going to leave you here."

Just those few words seemed to visibly take a weight off Dev as his shoulders sagged forward. He looked down at his feet before glancing back up at them, his gaze landing on Nicholas. "I can't... I..." He cleared his throat. Straightening his shoulders, Dev gave them a brilliant smile. "Thank you for...for wanting me."

"Of course we want you," Nicholas said, blinking rapidly to hold back tears. "You're family."

"Not that I don't love this family reunion," Cyrus suddenly snapped out, "but do you think we could continue this at home? Away from the demons right below us?"

"Yes," Dev said, nodding. "I would very much like to leave."

"I agree," Nicholas glanced around him. "Let's get the hell out-"

He was cut off as a muffled yell reached his ears. Turning his head toward the edge of the roof, he frowned. Ignoring the warnings coming from his brothers, Nicholas made his way closer to the ledge. He didn't know why, but he felt his stomach clench as the voices in the alley below became clearer. As he got closer, he could just make out a sleazy looking guy leaning against the wall of the opposite building.

"Don't be like that, darling," Sleaze-Ball said. "We all know that when a woman says *let go* and acts like she's not interested, she's really just playing hard to get. What you women really mean is that you're looking to find a guy to fuck."

"Yeah," came another male voice out of Nicholas' sight. If he leaned over, he was sure to be seen by the people below, so until he knew what was going on, he needed to stay back. "And the way you were shaking this fine ass on the dance floor, damn, you were just begging for this. Shit, I love this ass."

"Nicholas?" Darren whispered from behind him.

Holding up his hand, he tilted his head, leaning just a tiny bit forward as he heard the shuffle of feet against concrete.

"Let go of me," he heard a female gasp out. Nicholas' power flared around him as the familiarity of that voice seeped into his skin.

Amy... Those bastards down there have my Amy.

"Shit," he heard Darren snarl beside him. "Christian, Manuel, you guys get Dev and Hayley out of here. Cyrus-"

"I'm helping," Cyrus growled from behind him.

Nicholas didn't hear what else his brothers said. He had now leaned far enough over the edge that he saw Sleaze-Ball's buddy shove Amy forward. Her foot caught and she fell to the ground, landing hard on her hands and knees. She tried to push herself up, only to cry out from a sudden kick to her side.

At that, Nicholas' vision went black.

He straightened, his power shivering around him as his wings blasted out from his back. With a quick step, he was over the edge, knocking one of the bastards against the wall as he landed next to Amy.

A gasp from her was all he heard as he turned toward the one who had pushed her to the ground.

"Fuck," the drunken man slurred.

Nicholas growled low as he lunged forward. His fist connected with the bastard's face, snapping his head back from the impact. The man crumpled to the ground in a heap, the faint heartbeat that reached Nicholas' ears the only sign he was still amongst the living.

Pity, Nicholas thought with a sneer as he turned toward the other drunk, his power shuddering as he sensed his brothers landing nearby.

One drunken piece of shit down, one more to go.

Nobody touched his Amy. Nobody.

The moment they stepped inside, Amy knew coming to this club was a bad idea. It wasn't the extremely loud music, the smell of booze and sex, or even the sneer from the bouncer that had her wishing she'd stayed home. It was the uneasy feeling that continued to build within her with each step she took. Looking around, she'd noted the crowd swarming around the bar, the scantily clad women grinding on the dance floor, and the drunken men drooling over them.

It was exactly what one would expect in a nightclub, but there was something else. Something darker lurking in the corners, causing the hair on her arms to stand up. Misty, Tina, and Daisy didn't seem to notice anything wrong as they pulled her out onto the dance floor. She'd tried to get lost in the music, the excitement building in the room as the songs changed from one chaotic beat to another.

She just couldn't.

She kept looking at the tables lining the dance floor, the seats hidden in the shadows. Every once in a while, the lights would move just right and she swore she would see what looked like glowing red orbs in the darkness. Red eyes glaring back at her. And as much as she wanted to blame it on an overactive imagination or trick of the lights, she just knew what she saw could not be explained away that easily.

They had only been three songs in when Amy decided enough was enough. Between the people bumping into her and some stranger splashing his drink down her back, she was ready to go.

Grabbing Misty's arm, she pulled her close to let her know she was going to head to the bathroom. Her friend had just started dancing with some guy, so she gave her a quick nod. Rolling her eyes, Amy chuckled and walked off in search of the restroom. Weaving between people, she spotted a restroom sign pointing down a hallway. The music started to fade the farther down the hall she walked. Reaching into her back pocket, Amy pulled out her cell. If she called Nicholas, she just knew he'd come get her.

At least that was the plan before two guys, who obviously invested way too much time moussing their hair, decided they were what she'd been looking for. She hadn't seen them come up behind her at first. Scrolling through her phone, she'd been just about to pull up Nicholas' number when her arm was suddenly grabbed and she was spun around into a man's sweaty chest. The act caused her to lose her grip on her phone. She heard it bounce against the floor, making a sound that Amy was positive meant it was now in pieces.

"Hey," she grunted, twisting around to try and get the guy's grip on her arm to loosen. "Let go."

"Well, aren't you just a pretty little thing," he slurred, spittle hitting her face. "Don't you think so, BJ?"

Her other arm was pulled behind her back as Amy suddenly found herself sandwiched between two bodies. She smelled the alcohol on their breath as they both laughed.

"You definitely spotted a cutie, Dale," BJ laughed, his hand tightening on her arm as she tried to pull away from them.

"I said let go," Amy yelled. Dale spun her around in his arms. Pulling her back against his chest, he reached up and slammed his hand over her mouth.

"Maybe we should take this outside." BJ grinned as Dale turned her toward the exit, maneuvering her as if she weighed nothing. She felt his fingers digging into her cheek as he held her snug against his shoulder. Wiggling as best as she could, she felt Dale's other arm suddenly wrap around her waist. "Follow me." BJ eyed her appreciatively right before he turned toward the exit door.

She tried to kick her feet behind her, but he was just too strong, lifting her up as he walked through the door. Tears ran down her face as she screamed behind his hand. The sound was muffled, even in the quiet of the alley that she suddenly found herself in.

"Don't be like that, darling," BJ said, leaning against the wall across from them. He nodded at Dale as he ran a hand over his chest. "We all know that when a woman says *let go* and acts like she's not interested, she's really just playing hard to get. What you women really mean is that you're looking to find a guy to fuck."

She tried to shake her head, but Dale's grip tightened. He leaned over, running his nose along her face, sniffing her.

"Yeah," he hissed by her ear. "And the way you were shaking this fine ass on the dance floor, damn, you were just begging for this. Shit, I love this ass." The hand that had been around her waist slid over her side, landing on her ass and giving it a painful squeeze.

Amy screamed, or tried to, before leaning into his hand and sinking her teeth into his palm. With a growl, Dale pulled his hand from her face.

"Let go of me," she screamed. She was about to yell again when she felt herself being shoved from behind. It happened so quickly, she didn't have enough time to get her feet beneath her before she felt herself falling forward. Pain shot through her knees and hands as she hit the ground.

Feeling the cold cement beneath her palms, Amy tried to push herself up. She didn't know what she was going to do, but she knew she wasn't going to just lay there and let these assholes win. She was so focused on straightening her arms beneath her that the kick to her ribs caught her completely off guard. With a grunt and a moan, she rolled to her side, hugging her legs up to her chest as she felt the pain spread through her.

She opened her eyes to slits as Dale shifted his feet. His eyes looked glazed over from the alcohol running through his veins, his smile lopsided. She screwed up her face and was about to yell out for help when something landed next to her. The force threw Dale against the wall.

A gasp escaped her lips as her eyes focused. A pair of black and red wings stretched out over her. She felt the air caress her face from their force. As her gaze flew over the impressive wings, she soon found herself in a state of shock. There was no way she was seeing this. Nope. She must have hit her head when she'd fallen. That was the only explanation. There was no way she was actually looking up at Nicholas, with wings, eye glowing red.

Yup, she hit her head. Giving it a little shake, she rolled onto her side.

"The fuck," she heard Dale slur as he pushed himself away from the wall.

She looked back up and saw Nicholas' eyes narrow dangerously. She opened her mouth to call his name when a sudden growl rumbled from his chest. The sound of it caused her pulse to quicken, but not from fear. Instead, the more she looked at him, standing above her, the safer she felt.

He suddenly moved so quickly, Amy realized that if she'd blinked, she would have missed it. She watched in awe as he lunged forward and drove his fist right into Dale's face. The bastard made a gurgling sound as his head snapped back. His body crumpled to the ground with an audible thump.

"Who the fuck are you? Fucking freak," BJ hissed. His eyes widened as he glanced from his unconscious friend to Nicholas.

Amy would have laughed if it hadn't been for the deep, feral growl rumbling from Nicholas or the sudden movement out of the corner of her eye. When her gaze shot to the side, her jaw dropped, seeing a very pissed Darren and Cyrus standing close by. Darren, his startling white wings engulfing the area around him, stood ramrod straight as he glared at BJ. While Cyrus, his equally stunning black wings barely visible against the darkened alley behind him, shifted from one foot to the other in what looked like a state of excitement. His lips twisted into a dark grin as he looked between Nicholas and the drunk still leaning against the wall.

"Now, now. Name calling is never a nice thing to do," Darren tisked, his blue eyes glowing dangerously.

"And I don't think you're asking the right questions," Cyrus snarled, his voice a steady growl as his black eyes landed on BJ.

"Oh really?" BJ sneered, the alcohol in his system obviously giving him a false sense of courage. "What the fuck should I be asking then?"

Personally, Amy didn't think she'd mouth off to any of these guys right now. Their presence alone was extremely intimidating. She'd noticed that when they'd been in her house...and they'd been in a good mood then. Well, except for Cyrus. But add in the fact that the three men standing here, all large wings and glowing eyes, were focusing their anger completely on BJ... Yeah, if she were him, she'd be running by now.

"The question you should be asking is how do you want to spend the rest of your miserable, pathetic life?" Cyrus said slowly, moving closer to Nicholas.

Amy felt a sudden breeze whip around her as Nicholas' body shifted forward, blocking her view from the now stuttering drunk. She watched as his wings flared out behind him, almost as if he were shielding her from the breeze that had begun to pick up.

"Wh-What do you mean?" BJ asked. Amy could hear a trickle of fear starting to leak into his voice.

"He means," Nicholas said, his voice low and threatening, "that you should be asking yourself if you want to spend the rest of your life eating your meals through a tube? Or do you want to be able to walk out of this alley? Come on. You really shouldn't have to think about this."

The breeze had increased to the point that Amy could hear it howling as it blew her hair around her face. Her knees throbbed as she edged closer to Nicholas, the energy rolling off him comforting her scattered nerves.

"P-Please," BJ stuttered. "Like you freaks, with your w-wings and holier-than-thou attitude, could do a-anything to me. Do you know who I am?"

"A dead man?" Cyrus snarled.

"A coward?" Darren offered.

"A worthless piece of shit," Nicholas growled.

"Fuck you guys!" BJ yelled. His demeanor changed completely, like a switch had been flipped. Amy couldn't see him, but she heard the difference in his voice, felt the transformation in Nicholas' stance in response. "My name is BJ. I suggest you remember that because I'm an important player, a natural soldier in the war that's coming."

"I don't know who's been lying to you, Blow Job, but-" Cyrus started, only to be cut off by Darren.

"Who are you a soldier for, BJ?" Darren asked, moving forward.

BJ sneered at him, his eyes glaring up at Darren as he moved closer. "I am a soldier. I will help fight all that is wrong in this world and get the power away from all you self-righteous assholes. We are growing in numbers, and-"

"Yeah, yeah," Darren growled. "We don't have time to listen to your whole campaign spiel. Now... Who. Do. You. Work. For?"

"He is more powerful than you will ever be," BJ ground out.

"A name, BJ. I need your boss' name."

He cackled. "Maybe *you* aren't asking the right questions."

Amy heard what sounded like a muffled *fuck this* right before shuffling feet and a strangled whimper. Peering around Nicholas' wings, her eyes widened when she spotted Darren holding BJ up against the wall, his hands grasped tightly to either side of his head as a blue glow began to build around them. BJ's unblinking eyes stared in shock, his lips thinning as the color drained from his face. In seconds,

Darren gave a tired sigh and dropped BJ to the ground, his body crumpling, unmoving.

"Is he...?" Amy began, only to stop with a shake of her head.

"No," Darren answered. "But I got the info we needed and wiped his memory. Once he wakes up, BJ shouldn't be a problem."

"What about this one?" Amy turned at Cyrus' voice behind her. She watched as he nudged Dale's still form with his foot.

"He was drunk. He won't remember anything," Nicholas answered. She glanced up to see he had turned around, his gaze softening as he looked down at her. "Are you okay?"

She felt a blush spread across her cheeks as she started up at him. "I think I skinned my knees pretty good, and my side hurts a bit where Dale kicked me." As soon as the words left her lips, her eyes widened at the growl that ripped from Nicholas' throat. "I'm just bruised, though," she hurried to say. "Nothing some aspirin won't take care of."

"We should get out of here before one of the pieces of shit demons wandering around this place decides to pop out here," Cyrus growled, giving Dale one last kick before turning around.

Amy frowned at the term *demon*. But after looking at Nicholas' wings again, which were still fanned out around him, did the fact there were demons in the club really surprise her? Nope. In fact, things made a lot more sense. Like the fact that Nicholas didn't want to go to the ER after being shot, the black lines spreading from his wound, which disappeared after she removed the bullet.

It was like her mind suddenly woke up, like she'd been staring at a puzzle for hours and suddenly looked at it from a different angle and had an *aha* moment. And what a moment this was. Nicholas' wings were beautiful, breathtaking, and she really wanted to reach up and run her fingers through the feathers. Her thoughts spun around in her mind, causing her to release a soft giggle.

"What's funny?" Nicholas asked, a small smile spreading across his lips.

Smiling up at him, she took a deep breath. "I was just admiring your wings."

His deep blush caught her off guard, causing her heart to skip a beat at how adorable he looked. She could sense his power rippling beneath the surface, but at the same time, he was an absolute sweetheart, someone she just knew she could trust with her life...and her heart.

She'd been so caught up in her thoughts, she hadn't realized Nicholas had leaned toward her until she felt his arms envelop her and pick her up. She released a startled gasp. His muscles bunched as he pulled her against his chest. Without a second thought, she reached up and wrapped her arms around his neck. A feeling of safety washed over her.

"I'll get you some aspirin as soon as we get back to my house," he said softly, placing a gentle kiss on the top of her head.

"Your house?" she whispered.

"Well, my brothers' and mine." She felt him smile against her head. "Are you okay with going there?"

"Yes." Being with Nicholas was all she'd wanted since he'd left her house. Being at his house, getting to spend time with him in his space, was even better.

"Good," he responded with a sigh, like he had been holding his breath. "I, um... I hope you're not afraid of heights."

"I get a little nervous on planes, but I think I do all right," she chuckled. "Why?"

She leaned back to look at him, her eyes widening. The huge smile gracing his face left her breathless. Glancing at his wings, she knew he intended on flying her to their house. Did the thought of that scare her? Absolutely. Would she stop him? No. If holding her in his arms and flying her around brought on that smile, she would let him do this whenever he wanted.

"Just hold on tight, sweetheart," he whispered, his wings spreading out behind them.

A chill of excitement ran through her as she rested her head under his chin. She felt a gentle caress slide across her skin from the power rolling off him and his brothers as they got ready. Their power made her feel safe and relaxed, like being engulfed in a warm blanket. Amy watched from the comfort of Nicholas' arms as they all flexed their wings, the light reflecting off the feathers. With a flick of those large wings, they lifted into the night. The warmth from his body seeped into her, keeping the chilly breeze at bay.

Her mind took advantage of the sudden silence and began to wander back to the club, to being dragged into the alley. If Nicholas hadn't shown up when he did... She didn't even want to imagine what might have happened. It may take some time for her to come to grips with what may have taken place, but the only thing that mattered was she was safe. Amy sighed softly when she felt another light kiss on her head as they soared above the buildings.

"I won't ever let anything happen to you," Nicholas said. "I promise."

Chapter 20

Nicholas didn't know what he'd expected to see when he finally turned around to look at Amy in the alley. He'd been prepared for shock, disbelief, maybe fear. But the look of acceptance in her eyes when she'd looked up at him... He hadn't been prepared for that. And then when she'd smiled at him, complemented his wings, he had to remind himself to breathe.

Even now, with her cradled tightly against him as they flew toward his home, he had to focus on every intoxicating inhale, each heart-pounding exhale. Her scent surrounded them as they soared high above the ground. In a way, he was thankful it would not take them long to reach the house. Then again, a part of him wished this were a longer trip...if for no other reason than to give him an excuse to continue holding her in his arms.

Yet, before he knew it, their yard came into view. The chill in the air helped cool Nicholas as he attempted to shake off the rest of his anger. Images of those two men standing over Amy, hurting her, were still fresh in his mind. As was the adrenaline flooding his system. He had a feeling that no matter how much he tried to calm himself, he wouldn't be successful until he had Amy inside the house. Even then, he just wasn't sure. At this point, Nicholas just hoped Amy couldn't sense how upset he still was. He could feel her emotions spiking, fluctuating drastically from one extreme to the next, and he really didn't want his own tension to add to it.

He wanted her safe, happy, calm.

Landing softly on the ground, he shuddered slightly as he pulled his wings back in, a flash of light causing them to disappear. Two separate flashes followed as Darren and Cyrus landed nearby, their power rolling over him as they began to walk toward the house. Shifting Amy in his arms, he felt her body tense as she sucked in a sharp hiss of air. Her ribs and knees had to be hurting, and he was sure the cool air didn't help, though he was happy his own body heat seemed to be keeping her somewhat warm.

"Let's get you inside," he murmured against her head, falling into step behind Cyrus. He needed to get her injuries looked at, find out what information Darren was able to pull from BJ's head, and see Dev.

Stepping through the back door, he immediately heard voices, a mixture of excitement and worry rolling through the air. Feeling Amy's body shudder, he began to move toward the couch.

"Nicky?" He heard the concern in Ella's voice as he leaned down, easing Amy onto the soft cushion.

"Amy was hurt," he said simply.

"I'm f-fine. Really," she stuttered.

"You're not." Nicholas knelt and ran a hand gently over her left calf. "I think you may be going into shock."

"What happened?"

Looking over his shoulder, Nicholas saw Dev standing behind him. His blue eyes flashed with concern as he looked between him and Amy.

"S-some assholes got a little rough at the c-club," Amy said shakily, her body shivering under Nicholas' hands. She grimaced as she shifted, her hand pressing down on her side.

"May I?"

Nicholas glanced back at Dev to see him nod at Amy. Making just enough room for him to kneel in front of the couch, Nicholas watched as his brother smiled softly at her.

"I can help," he said calmly, his hand hovering over Amy's leg.

"How-," she started, only to pause as her eyes widened.

Nicholas felt everyone in the room shift as Dev's power began to build around him. Its warmth pushed against Nicholas' skin, curling through the air as Dev's eyes began to take on a brilliant glow.

"Deep breath," Dev whispered. At his request, Amy did as he asked, her eyes sliding closed as Nicholas felt his brother push his power into her. Everyone in the room seemed to take a deep breath at the same time, none of them taking their eyes off what was happening before them.

Nicholas watched in awe as the torn skin on her knees, skin that was visible through the rip in her jeans, began to mend before his eyes, a white light closing around her, seeming to coat her body as his brother's power flowed through her. Just as quickly as it grew, Dev's power faded. Amy blinked rapidly as she stared at her knees, then back at him. Dev rocked back on his heels and released a soft sigh.

"How did you... What did you... Who are you?" Amy asked.

Dev just chuckled. "Um... It's complicated... I healed you... And I'm one of Nicholas' brothers," he finally said, answering her questions in the order they were asked.

At Amy's confused look, Nicholas reached over and gave Dev's arm a light squeeze. "He was just recently brought back home...where he belongs."

Dev smiled. Though it didn't quite reach his eyes, Nicholas felt it was a start. He had his brother back. Soon, they'd bring the light back into his eyes.

"My name is Dev," he heard his brother say.

"Well, Dev, it is very nice to meet you," she said, smiling at him. "My name is Amy."

Dev nodded. "It's nice to meet you, and I'm sorry to hear what happened. It's really none of my business, but may I ask why you were at that club?" The tightness in his voice made his brothers look at him in worry.

"Oh, my friends thought it would be fun to go out dancing. Since it just opened, they thought we should go check it out. It wasn't really my scene, though."

"I wouldn't think so," he murmured. His eyes seemed troubled as he briefly glanced toward Nicholas. "Do me a favor and don't go back there. Okay? It's just not someplace you should be."

"Oh, trust me. I won't be going back there," Amy responded with a grimace. "I had actually pulled out my phone to call Nicholas to see if he could come get me before Tweedledee and Tweedledum grabbed me," Amy responded, rolling her eyes. "My phone was broken in the struggle. Guess I know what I'm shopping for tomorrow... Crap!" she suddenly exclaimed.

"What?" Nicholas and Dev asked at the same time, their bodies tensing in response to her sudden cry.

"Misty and my other friends...
They're still at the club."

"Here." Dev reached into his pocket,
pulling out his phone. "Give her a call and
tell her something came up. Maybe suggest
they start heading home."

Reaching for the phone, Amy shot
him an appreciative smile before she
rapidly dialed her friend's number. They all
listened as several rings went by before
music and a loud voice came through the
phone.

"Hello!"

"Misty? It's Amy. Can you hear me?"

"Amy? Whose phone are you calling
from? Oh hell... Hold on." There was a
slight pause as they heard the music fade.
"Okay, now that I can freaking hear myself
think... Where the hell did you go and
who's phone are you using?" The woman's
voice made Nicholas cringe slightly, though
he couldn't help but notice the smirk on
Dev's face as he watched Amy wave her
hand through the air.

"I was heading back to the
bathroom–"

"Which was forfuckingever ago."

"Yes, well, I ended up getting
grabbed by these two drunk guys and–"

"What? Are you serious? Are you
okay?"

"Misty, I'm fine. They took me out a
side door and, well... I was lucky because

Nicholas was there. He and his brothers helped—"

"Oh... Nicholas? Are you guys still here? I want to meet him. And you said he was with his brothers? Are they hot?"

Amy's cheeks flamed as she heard all of the guys chuckle around her. "No... I mean, yes. I mean... No, I'm not... We're back at his place and—"

"You're at his place? What the hell are you still doing on the phone with me, woman? Go jump that man."

Amy ran a hand over her face and sent an embarrassed glance around the room, seeing everyone trying to muffle their laughs. "Misty. Just... Would you listen to me for a minute?"

"Is this Nicholas' phone you're calling from?"

"No. It's Dev's. My phone was broken when the drunks grabbed me. But listen—"

"Oh, Dev... Just by the name, I bet he's hot. Is he single?"

Looking over and seeing the red tinge that moved across Dev's cheeks had Amy's own face heating up. "Oh, my god... Would you focus? I think you need to grab the girls and get out of that club."

"What? Why?" Misty's voice dropped its playfulness.

"It's just... I got a real bad vibe there. Even before those drunks grabbed me, I saw...drugs. Yes. Lots of people dealing drugs in the back." Amy looked at Nicholas, giving him a slight shrug. "And with Tina's brother being a cop, you know how much shit you guys would be in if he caught you there."

"Shit. Drugs? Are you sure?"

"Yup. For all we know, the cops could be looking at that place right now."

"Crap," Misty hissed through the phone. "Fine. It kinda smells funny in here anyway. I'll grab the girls and head home."

Before Amy could respond, Dev reached over and tapped her on the arm, whispering, "Tell your friend to text this number when she gets home. So we know they got out okay."

Amy nodded. After passing on the message, a quick goodbye, and a promise to give Misty a call the next day, she got off the phone. Releasing a soft laugh, Amy shook her head. "My best friend is a nut." Her laugh quickly turned into a yawn as she found herself leaning into Nicholas' side.

"How about this. After a good night's sleep...I don't know about you, but I think we can all use one...I take you to get a new phone," Nicholas said with a soft smile.

She nodded and smiled shyly up at him before looking back at Dev. "Thank you," she murmured, handing back his phone. "And not just for the use of your cell. I'm not exactly sure how you made the pain go away, but thank you."

"You're welcome." Dev responded. He glanced away from her, almost as if the gratitude in her eyes made him uneasy. "I'm just glad I was here to help."

"We're all glad you're here," Darren voiced from behind them.

Nicholas felt a sense of rightness settle over him. Meeting Amy's eyes, seeing the warmth in them, he smiled. For all the uncertainty today had shown, he wouldn't have had it end any other way.

Amy glanced around Nicholas' room, smiling at the multiple movie posters covering his walls.

After Dev had healed her, something she still had trouble wrapping her brain around, the conversation had quickly moved into territory she knew nothing about. There had been talk about someone named Andras and a witch named Maria. Amy had felt like her head was going to come off with all the shaking it was doing. In the blink of an eye, she'd gone from reading and blogging about the paranormal to living it.

She knew she should be freaking out right now. And, to a certain degree, she supposed she was, just not enough to make her run for the hills.

There was just something about Nicholas, about how sweet he was and the honesty in his eyes, that had her wanting to stick around. She wanted to find out everything about him, ask him all the questions currently swirling around inside her mind.

And boy, did she have a lot of questions.

Walking over to his bookcase, she ran her fingers along the shelves, eyeing the titles. She smiled at several biographies and autobiographies on the first shelf. Her smile grew when she noticed most of them were about comedians. Given his sense of humor, it didn't really surprise her. There was also something about the shadows that crossed his eyes from time to time that led her to believe he appreciated the lighter side of life.

Amy's eyes drifted to the next shelf that held several leather-bound books, a few of which looked like they'd been read several times. One in particular, Bram Stoker's *Dracula*, looked like it'd been read the most. Running a finger over the soft leather, she had to laugh. This was one of her favorite books.

"Find anything you like?"

Nicholas' deep voice rumbled through the room, pulling her attention away from the books. "You have quite the collection." She watched a smile spread across his face as he glanced toward his bookcase. "I couldn't help but notice you have one of my favorite books."

"Which one?"

"Bram Stoker's *Dracula*," she said, noting the brightness in his eyes. Looking back toward the book, Amy shook her head. "Is this a first edition?"

"Maybe."

"Maybe?"

Nicholas only shrugged as he stepped farther into his room and took a seat on his bed. "How are you doing?" His eyes searched hers as he leaned forward, resting his elbows against his thighs.

Amy continued her slow walk around his room as she considered his question. How did she feel? She definitely felt a little freaked out. Well, overwhelmed may be a better word. There was also a faint feeling of unease curling through her, but she decided to chalk that up to still trying to come to terms with everything that had happened over the last few hours.

The recent events also caused small shivers of excitement to run through her. How could it not? For as long as she could remember, she'd immersed herself in all things fantasy and paranormal. Her mom would just roll her eyes at Amy's obsession. Her dad, on the other hand, had fed it. He constantly brought home books and movies, each one filled with vampires, werewolves, ghosts, or demons.

Of course, imagining a world filled with beautiful, fantastic, and magical Beings was one thing. Finding yourself actually living it... That was something else entirely.

"Amy?"

She turned to find Nicholas watching her. His impossibly deep, red eyes were filled with concern as he gazed steadily into hers. They grounded her, calmed her thoughts. She quickly realized that no matter how crazy this all was, she didn't want to be anywhere else. Couldn't even think about forgetting everything that had happened, unseeing all she'd seen...even if it were possible.

"I'm just...," she started, pausing as words escaped her. How did she tell him everything she felt without him thinking she was a crazy woman?

With a laugh, Amy reached up and ran her fingers through her hair. Here she was, standing in front of not only the most gorgeous man she had ever seen, but quite possibly a creation of every fantasy she'd ever had. Any response to his question would have him running for the hills.

Sure, he would probably be sweet and polite as he escorted her out of his house. Hell, he'd probably muster up an awkward hug or brief kiss on the cheek before he started backing away her.

Which, if Amy were being honest with herself, might just happen if she couldn't get her thoughts under control.

She would either come off as being completely crazy and on the verge of a panic attack, or would sound like some crazed paranormal fan, making his ears bleed as she squealed about how she always knew there was more to the world than she'd been told.

Even though she could see herself falling down that particular rabbit hole, she knew neither of those would happen. It wouldn't be a good outcome for her.

But how did one play it cool when every cell in your body wanted to split and head in different directions?

The answer to that was easy. You stood in one spot and stared stupidly at the man invading your every thought, all the while hoping for a hole to open beneath your feet and swallow you.

She had a feeling there weren't going to be any cosmic holes coming to her rescue, but if his raised eyebrow was any indication, she definitely had the whole staring stupidly thing down.

Great... Just great.

"You're totally freaking the fuck out, aren't you?" His lips pulled up slightly as he watched her. She wanted to deny it, but even as she started to shake her head, he nodded. "Yeah, you are."

"I'm not completely freaking out," she huffed. Sure, she probably sounded slightly childish, but with everything twisting around in her mind, Amy grasped for any sense of control she could. Maybe even some denial that she'd spiraled so far, even if it was a lie.

"Please," Nicholas chuckled. "It looks like you're two steps away from pulling a Wile E. Coyote on me, leaving nothing but an Amy-shaped hole in my wall as you make a break for it."

An image of that flashed through her mind and Amy couldn't help the soft chuckle. The tension slightly easing from her shoulders, she slowly made her way toward him. "Okay, I *may* be freaking out a little." At his snort, she rolled her eyes. Easing down next to him on the bed, she twisted around to look at him. "Fine. Maybe I'm freaking out a lot." They both grinned as she scooted a little closer. "A lot happened the last few hours. A lot of things I never thought possible. I'm just trying to process it all."

"I'm sure. Honestly, sweetheart, I'm a little surprised you're still here." Nicholas shook his head, turning his body so he faced her. There was just enough space between them that she couldn't feel his heat...a heat she found her body yearning for. "I mean, I almost expected to come up here and find you'd snuck out the door when none of us were looking."

It was Amy's turn to raise an eyebrow. "I kinda find it hard to believe that anyone could sneak out without at least one of you knowing it."

"True," he conceded with a smirk. "It was still a worry I had."

She spread her arms out. "Well, as you can see, I'm still here." She was trying to lighten the mood, though she could still see the worry in his eyes, even as he smiled and nodded. Truthfully, even as her thoughts had spun out of control, she'd never once considered leaving. Walking away from this, from him, just didn't feel like something she could bring herself to do. Given the short amount of time they'd known each other, that in and of itself should scare the crap out of her. But it didn't. "You have to admit, this all seems a little crazy. And I have *a lot* of questions. Most of which will probably make me sound like a loon."

Nicholas laughed. "I don't think you could be any more of a loon than the rest of the knuckleheads in this house. I mean, you've seen my brothers. They're loud, grumpy, noisy weirdoes, and that's on a good day." He waved his hand through the air, shaking his head. "And that's not even considering all the other more, um, extraordinary attributes my family has. I'm surprised what happened back in that alley alone hasn't made you question what the hell you're still doing here."

Though she laughed, Amy saw through his humor. She saw the vulnerability he tried to hide with his jokes and smiles. It made her gut clench with a need to take his uncertainty away. "What happened back in that alley was crazy...and scary. Hell, my mind is still trying to make sense of it all," she said, scooting closer, her knee touching his. She felt his warmth caress her as she laid her hand on his. "But, no matter how crazy all of this seems, I'm not going to run. I was never going to run, Nicholas."

"Promise?" She heard the humor in his voice dim slightly as a small amount of doubt crept into it.

"I promise," she said with a smile. "Anyway, why would I want to run away from my hero?" Confusion came over her when she saw the light in his eyes dim. "What is it? Do you really think I want to run?"

"No," Nicholas said softly. "It's just... I may be a lot of things, Amy, but I'm nobody's hero."

"I'm sure that's not true."

"It actually is." He looked away from her. "I'm more like comic relief, the jokester who usually ends up getting into trouble. I fight with my family when I shouldn't, make sarcastic comments, and no matter how hard I try, I just can't seem to be what anyone needs." He looked back at her, his eyes filled with so much emotion, Amy felt her breath catch in her throat. "I like you a lot, Amy. Have since the first moment I saw you. I want nothing more than to keep you close, get to know everything about you. But I'm just being real here. I was lucky to be in the right place at the right time tonight. It wasn't heroics."

Amy reached up and placed a hand on either side of his face, pulling him close so all he could see was her. "I don't know why you've come to have such a low opinion of yourself, but just know that I don't agree. Just like I'm sure your family wouldn't agree, either. Don't worry, though. This is something we're going to work on."

When he opened his mouth to argue, Amy leaned in and kissed him. Her lips moved against his until she felt him relax beneath her touch. Pulling back, she looked into his eyes, holding his gaze.

"I'm not going anywhere, Nicholas. So you should start preparing yourself because I'm going to completely overwhelm you with how much I believe in you. That's right." She nodded with a small smile. "You just got your very own self-esteem cheerleader, and I'm not going to stop until you see what I do. Until then, I'll believe in you enough for the both of us. You are, without a doubt, the most complicated, kindest, wonderful man I've ever known. And you're my hero."

The smile he gave her was the most beautiful thing she had ever seen, and it wiped away any of the doubt still residing in her mind. Leaning in, she felt herself melt into his heat as he kissed her. His actions conveyed how her words affected him. At that moment, she knew this was where she wanted...needed to be.

Sure, her world may have just been turned upside down. She may not know what was going on around her, or what was to come, but as long as she could see Nicholas' smile, feel his warmth, everything else would work itself out.

For Amy, there was no other option.

Chapter 21

"What in the hell do you mean Dev is gone?" Andras' body vibrated as rage rushed through him. "How the *fuck* do you lose an angel? I thought I made myself clear that he was to remain on the club grounds, no matter what. I personally gave you two the job to make sure that happened. So how did you both fail me on this?" When he didn't get an answer, he roared, "Answer me!"

He watched the twins shift their feet, each glancing at the other before looking back toward the floor. They'd had one fucking job, and it was to keep an eye on Dev. Make sure he didn't try to reach out to his brothers or get in the way of their plans. Andras cracked his knuckles as he attempted to keep his power under control. Even though the thought of ripping their bodies apart until there was nothing left except a pile of unrecognizable flesh and blood was awfully appealing, he knew it wouldn't solve this sudden dilemma he found himself in.

Not only was the absence of that pain in the ass going to be a problem with the witch he just made a deal with, but if he made it to his brothers, that little fucker could throw an even bigger monkey wrench into his plans. Andras' usually calm demeanor quickly slipped as he snarled at the demons before him.

"I can see you may be having trouble with where to start," he growled. His eyes narrowed as he looked from them to Agalon, who leaned against the wall to his right. His second glared at the twins. He could practically feel Agalon's agitation rippling off him. Turning back toward Lakmi and Vhin, Andras took a deep breath. "Why don't we start with the last time either of you saw Dev. Maybe if you walk me through what you remember, we can find out exactly where you two fucked up." He saw them both flinch slightly as his power lashed out.

"We both saw him right before your meeting," Lakmi said, his voice a low growl as he rolled his head to the side. "We had just heard that the witch was in the building. When I looked up, I saw Dev on the second floor, like he usually is when he's not at the bar."

Vhin nodded, his eyes fixed on the floor. "Yeah. I thought he'd stayed up there. We didn't know he was missing until..." His voice trailed off as he glanced at his brother. The look they shared screamed uncertainty and nervousness. It was a look that immediately had Andras' eyes narrowing to dangerous slits.

"Until what?" he growled. His voice snapped the twins' attention back to him, their features tense. Out of the corner of his eye, Andras noticed Agalon move away from the wall he'd been leaning against.

"My guess," Agalon sneered, "is that they don't know where Dev went because they were no longer out on the main floor where they were supposed to be. I'd guess it wasn't until Kanibal pulled them away from their latest human toy that they even knew Dev was missing. Isn't that right, boys?"

"We weren't away from the floor that long," Vhin argued. His eyes snapped Agalon's way before looking back at his brother. "We'd just gotten into the room and started getting comfortable when K barged in."

"Yeah," Lakmi chimed in. "We've left the floor for short periods before and never had a problem. That fucking angel has always known his place, knew not to step out of line."

"Obviously, your scare tactics didn't mean shit," Agalon growled, coming up to stand right next to Vhin. Their significant height difference made it easy for him to glare down at the demon. "Let's move past the fact that you two fucked up, shall we? What did you find once K got you?"

"Nothing," Vhin growled. At the look from both Andras and Agalon, he shook his head. "Truly. We fucking looked everywhere for that little shit and there was no trace of him."

"Did either of you idiots check the security cameras?" Agalon asked.

Andras focused his glare on the twins as he waited. Surely, they had thought to check the cameras. He couldn't have managed to choose that poorly for the club's guards. The longer it took them to answer, the more he started to realize he had indeed chosen wrong. Shit. The look they shared was all the answer he needed.

"Dammit!" Andras yelled. He looked over at Agalon, barely acknowledging the twins as they took a tentative step back. "Go get Rave and Labrihn. Tell them to get their asses in here. Then get Anarki on those fucking cameras. I want to know what happened while we were dealing with that fucking witch, and I want to know now."

Without a word, Agalon nodded and strode out of the room.

Turning his glare back to the twins, Andras snarled. What the hell was he going to do with these two? With both of them keeping their eyes on the floor, he could tell they were trying to show him either remorse or submission. It didn't fool him, though. They didn't care one way or the other what happened to Dev. As long as they were able to have their fun, everyone else's plans could go to hell. He knew they were like this when he'd brought them on.

The thought of them fucking up this badly, though, hadn't crossed his mind. He figured as long as he dangled a big enough carrot in their faces, an unlimited supply of humans to play with, they would do what he asked of them. Andras had told them they could go after any of the humans who weren't already claimed, as long as they did it on their own time. Not when they needed to keep their eyes on Dev.

Running a hand through his hair, he let loose another growl. "Fuck. I don't even know what to do with you two." When he noticed Lakmi start to raise his head, Andras flicked his power at them. They visibly shuddered. "Not that I'm asking for suggestions. Actually, I don't want to hear a word from either of you. Hell, I don't even want to see either of you until I get this mess figured out."

He watched the two demons shift back and forth on their feet. Obviously, the twins had something on their minds. They probably wanted to try to justify why they hadn't been where they were supposed to be, why Dev disappearing on their watch wasn't their fault. While they may have been able to argue that last part, there was no way he was interested in listening to them.

Not now.

Not while his blood was still boiling.

"Get out of here," Andras growled.

The finality in his voice spurred Lakmi and Vhin into action. Both gasped as they quickly turned, rushing out of the office just as Rave and Labrihn walked in.

"You sent for us, Andras?" Rave asked, stopping next to Labrihn in front of the desk.

Andras gazed steadily at the two demons before answering. They couldn't be more different, at least in appearance. Whereas Rave was slender with gray eyes and brown hair, Labrihn was stockier with red eyes and no hair. Rave's eyes showed an almost scary intelligence, but Labrihn's gaze seemed bored, empty. They both were extremely dangerous, though. Even more, Labrihn was his best tracker. If anyone could find Dev, it was him. With him sending for Rave, too, Andras felt confident nothing would be left to chance. There was no way they wouldn't be able to bring Dev back.

"I'm sure you both heard what is going on?" Andras asked, leaning back against his desk.

"You mean the angel the twins lost?" Labrihn spit out.

"Yes," he answered easily. "I need you two to clean up their mess."

Rave nodded. "You want us to find Dev and bring him back?"

"Or get rid of him?" Labrihn asked, his eyes flashing with the briefest sign of eagerness before he could hide it.

Andras shook his head. "I need you to find that little shit and bring him back here. And I need him in one piece."

"When you say in one piece...," Labrihn said slowly, his voice trailing off.

"You do what you need to get him under control and back here. I don't care how bloody or bruised he is, as long as he's still breathing. He's been missing for at least a few hours. His power is weak, has been for some time, so he couldn't have gotten far. Find him. Now."

Both Rave and Labrihn nodded before they turned and left the office.

The door had barely closed behind them when Agalon marched back in, his face a mask of anger and irritation. "Anarki was able to track Dev's movements through the club until he went up to the roof with some pathetic female."

"He took a woman up to the roof? Human?"

"From the looks of it. It seems she approached him, and after they moved into the hall, they went up to the roof. We don't have cameras up there, but we didn't see them come back down."

"What the fuck?" Andras slammed his fist onto the desk, the wood splintering from the force. "Who was the female? Did that dumb fuck at the door remember her?"

"Anarki is talking to him right now, Andras. I doubt he'll be any help, though."

Andras growled as he began pacing back and forth in the room.

"There's something else," Agalon said slowly, causing Andras to stop mid-step. "The cameras by the side door caught a fight in the alley."

"And?" Andras asked, his patience slipping.

"It would seem that two of the humans who were recruited to run errands for you decided to have a little fun. They grabbed a girl, dragged her through the back door to the alley, and started to rough her up. Anarki spotted it on the tapes before I had even made it back there to tell him what you needed. In fact, he said he was just about to come and find me." Agalon shifted as his eyes narrowed. "From what he saw, their activity drew the attention of some of the Guardians who just so happened to be nearby." From the tone of his voice, Andres knew he had little belief this was a coincidence. He had to agree as his mind latched onto the fact that Dev disappeared the same night some of the Guardians happened to be by the club. "Three of them, to be exact. They flew down, slamming the two males around, before quickly taking off...carrying the female with them. Before you ask, the answer is no. Anarki had already talked to the dumb asses before I got into the room. Neither of the idiots remember a thing."

The knowledge that not only had there been Guardians that close to his fucking club without him knowing, but that Dev could already be with his brothers caused what little control Andras had to snap.

Spinning around, he yelled his frustration. His power lashed out around him, causing the paint on the walls to bubble and darken from its heat. The lights flickered, and a loud roaring began in his ears as his power vibrated along his skin. He heard Agalon stumble behind him, his second-in-command's own power seeping out as he tried to stave off the sudden onslaught of Andras' anger.

Within minutes, he felt a dark calm begin to ooze through his anger. Taking a deep breath, Andras pulled his power back. His skin tingled as the air in the room began to cool. Looking back at Agalon, he found the demon pushing himself away from the wall, his legs shaking from the effort to keep himself upright. If he had felt any pain from the power that had just beat against him, Andras couldn't tell. In fact, he looked perfectly calm as he pulled himself to his full height and looked back at Andras, awaiting his orders.

Andras smoothed his hand down the front of his suit. "Get Qual, then take those two humans into one of the back rooms. If those damn angels wiped their memories, they probably only did it for what happened in the alley. I want everything they can remember leading up to that moment, and I want it now. I don't care how you two get it out of them."

Agalon dipped his chin before slipping out of the office.

Leaning back against the now damaged desk, Andras tapped a finger along its edge. There must have been something about the female to make the Guardians show up. Sure, he knew they were too goody-goody to ignore some innocent in trouble. They had to stand up for the weak, keep the balance, blah...blah...blah. But they didn't only stop the males from hurting her. They took her with them. Protected her.

He needed to find out who this female was. And who the hell was the female who got Dev onto the roof? Did she know who, or what, he was? And where in the fuck were those Guardians hiding Ella?

Rolling his eyes, Andras felt a deep growl rumble through his chest.

For the hundredth time in the last few weeks, the idea that it may not be just the Guardians he needed to worry about rushed through his thoughts. While he'd scoffed at the thought when it first popped up, he couldn't help but feel the weight of it lately.

No, it wouldn't just be the angels. With his luck, if things kept going the way they were, it would end up being their women.

Chapter 22

Castigo materialized in the park several blocks from the club. The moonlight filtered through the trees, surrounding him with just enough shadows to feel hidden from the world. Which was exactly what he wanted to be right now...hidden.

He cursed under his breath. What in the fuck had he been thinking? Lingering outside of Andras' office, listening as he enlisted Rave and the dipshit, Labrihn, to help find Dev. Sure, seeing Agalon storm out of the room, the twins running out not long after, had piqued his curiosity. But leaning against the door and listening in on what Andras told Rave and Labrihn had to be about the dumbest thing he'd done in, well...in a long fucking time.

Reaching into his pocket for his smokes, he began to pace.

The knowledge Dev had managed to get away from the club hadn't really taken him by surprise. In fact, as far as Castigo was concerned, it was inevitable. It was almost funny how the thought of Dev fleeing never seemed to cross Andras' mind. Like the idea of the angel jumping at the chance to be free of him, of all the demons, was unimaginable.

Snorting at the thought, Castigo paused to light his cigarette before continuing to pace. His footsteps sounded heavy against the ground as he made his way from one tree and back to another.

He could only imagine what would have happened had he been spotted standing outside the office. Andras would have used him as his own personal punching bag, taking his frustrations out on him without a second thought. Did that stop him? Make him back away and leave his curiosity unsated? Nope. Not his style. Instead, he'd stood there listening as Andras demanded Rave and Labrihn locate Dev and bring him back.

Hearing the demons striding toward the door barely registered in time for him to make it around the corner before he heard the door open. He hadn't gotten away fast enough, though. Just as he was about to step out of the hall, the two demons had come up behind him. He'd stepped to the side and acted like he was looking for something, but he'd seen Rave's gray eyes flash with a knowing look before he'd followed Labrihn into the crowd.

Castigo wasn't sure how he knew, but he did. There had been no time to question it. As they disappeared, he'd sensed another power swirling through the air. His nerves already twitching, Castigo had just backed into the shadows when he'd spied Agalon heading his way.

It had to have been dumb luck that he'd made it out of there without being spotted by that asshole. Taking a deep drag of his cigarette, his mind began to worry over what Rave knew. Or at least what the demon thought he knew.

This whole night had just turned into one big clusterfuck. For the life of him, Castigo couldn't figure out how he'd gotten himself into this situation.

"Fucking Dev," he growled, flicking his cigarette to the ground and smashing it into the dirt with his boot.

If he hadn't agreed to help Dev, hadn't agreed to snoop around and see what he could find out about Andras' plans, he wouldn't even have been in the club tonight. Wouldn't have been hanging out in that fucking hallway, his ear plastered to a door, playing Russian Roulette with his life.

His agitation growing, Castigo quickly lit up another cigarette. His mind went over the fact that Rave *knew* he'd been in the hall. He'd bet his life on it. But would he say anything?

He didn't really consider Rave an enemy, but in the end, everybody was an enemy, right?

Castigo's feet shuffled across the ground as he slowed his pacing.

"What the fuck am I doing?" he whispered, running a hand through his hair.

"Excellent question," a deep voice rumbled behind him.

Spinning around, Castigo stiffened as he searched for the owner of the voice. His eyes narrowed as they landed on a shadowy figure standing amongst the trees. Feeling the tension in his back, he reached into his coat. His fingers running along the hilt of his knives, he eyed the stranger.

"Who the fuck are you?"

"Oh, come now, Castigo," the stranger drawled. "Surely it hasn't been so long that you've forgotten me." Stepping into the rays of moonlight, the flash of onyx eyes made Castigo take a step back.

"Syre," Castigo snarled, taking yet another step away from the demon. Holding his hands to his sides, he unconsciously flexed his fingers as he eyed the demon. "It has been a while."

"That is has, and these days, it's just Sy," he murmured, stopping a mere ten steps away from him. "I couldn't help but notice you seem pretty upset. I believe you have worn quite a trail in the ground with your pacing. Problems at the club?"

Castigo opened his mouth to make some smartass comment, but quickly closed it as he stared at the demon before him. Having not seen Sy in several years, he wasn't entirely sure what the demon did or didn't know about Andras' club. Tapping the fingers of his left hand against his thigh, Castigo debated on how to answer. Or whether he really needed to answer at all. He didn't owe this demon anything. He must have been quiet too long because Sy lifted an eyebrow in question before taking another step his way.

"Or are your problems more with your boss?"

His question grated on Castigo. The urge to lash out came over him with staggering force. "What business is it of yours?"

"I have my reasons for being interested in what is happening at that club," Sy responded calmly, completely ignoring the aggression in Castigo's tone.

"And what reasons would those be?" Castigo saw the determination in Sy's gaze as he gave his head a signal shake. *Well, that won't fucking do.* "You know what? You tell me what has you so interested in the club, and I'll tell you what my problem is with it."

"Now, why would I tell you anything? Last I checked, you were still one of Andras' lackeys."

"And you're not?" Castigo knew that was a flimsy remark the second it left his lips. Yet he couldn't have stopped himself from saying it even if he'd tried. His brain was so messed up with everything that had been going on, he was convinced everyone would turn against him and it was only a matter of time before Andras ripped his world apart.

"I don't have dealings with Andras," Sy said with a smirk. "I've never been very good at taking orders."

"Well, if your interest in the club doesn't have anything to do with Andras, then what is it?" As the demon stayed silent, Castigo let out a growl of frustration. "Look, I'm not exactly working for Andras anymore."

"And what does that mean? *Not exactly*?" Sy sniffed. "Sounds like you are not sure where you stand or what side of this fucked-up situation you're on."

"Oh, don't worry. I know exactly whose side I'm standing on. Mine. I'm always on my side, looking out for my best interests." Castigo smirked, then shook his head and looked away from Sy. "I've just grown tired of playing Andras' good little soldier." He shrugged. "I'm starting to think I may need to re-evaluate whose side I should be concentrating on."

He saw the moment the demon's thoughts shifted. "So... Andras' plans are no longer in your best interests?"

"Not sure they ever were."

With that, the two demons stared at each other in silence. Castigo shifted his weight as he watched Sy, his mind slowly going over all the ways this little impromptu meeting could backfire on him. When Sy had started insinuating that he may be against Andras, Castigo's first reaction was to deny it. Better to let the demon think he was still in Andras' pocket than risk giving him the power to destroy him with the truth. Even after Sy stated he himself had no dealings with Andras, he still had a moment of uncertainty, felt like he was walking into a trap. So, why did he tell him the truth? Why did he just open himself up to a possible future of nothing but pain and hopelessness?

Truthfully, he had no clue. Looking off, he shook his head. Guess his mind was even more screwed up than he thought. And it all led back to Dev. Well, maybe not all of it, but he had to place the blame somewhere, and that fucking angel was as good a person as any to point a finger at.

Fucking Dev!

"Dev?"

Castigo's head shot up. Shit, did he say that out loud? Great! Because this conversation couldn't possibly get any more frustrating. "What?"

"You said something about Dev," Sy responded, taking a step toward him. "What about him?"

"Wait. You know Dev?"

"We have had some...dealings recently."

"Dealings? What could you possibly have to do with him? It's not like Andras has left him off of his leash long enough to make friends."

Sy smirked. "Friends... I wouldn't go that far, but I would say we have an understanding. I scratch his back, he scratches mine."

Castigo's eyes narrowed. "What exactly have you done for each other?"

"Oh, a little help here, a little help there." Sy smiled slowly. "And you? What is your relationship with our dear Dev?"

"We don't have any kind of relationship," he spit out.

"Now, Castigo. How do you expect us to build a solid alliance here if we start it off with lies?"

"Is that what we're doing, Sy?"

The demon didn't answer. Castigo watched as he turned from him, staring off into the trees. His ankle-length trench coat curled slightly as the gentle breeze caught its edges. The moonlight had shifted, rising higher into the black sky as they'd stood there. Its soft glow was more prominent as it hovered above them, lighting the ground while making the darkness around them even more daunting, consuming.

The sudden feeling of unease that washed through Castigo caused him to physically shudder. He kept his growing angst to himself as he stared at the demon, who still looked off into the darkness, as if it spoke to him.

After some time, Sy turned back toward him, his black eyes seeming to glow as he met Castigo's silver gaze. "I feel a change coming."

"Change?"

"Don't you feel it?" Sy looked around before once again meeting his gaze. "Andras should have never messed with the veil." Before Castigo could respond, Sy shook his head. "What's done is done, but he has unknowingly set things into motion that I am not sure he is prepared for."

"So you don't agree with him shifting the balance in our favor?" Castigo asked, not hiding how absurd he thought that was.

"Is it truly in our favor, Castigo? Who will gain something out of this little venture of his?" Sy shook his head. "Do you know what I see? I see a demon trying to prove he is something he is not. I see one mistake after another, all in the name of *our side* gaining power. Let me ask you this. How do you see this ending?"

Castigo frowned. "Andras is going to grow his army, take out all the pureness in this world - the Guardians being at the top of his list. Afterward, we will finally be in charge, like we were meant to be." Even as he said this, Castigo knew it wasn't going to end that way. Somewhere along the way, these lines he'd been fed about how great this plan was had started to lose their appeal.

"That is quite an intriguing idea. Complete bullshit, but intriguing nonetheless. When this wonderful idea of his doesn't pan out, which we both know it won't, who do you think he is going to blame?" Sy asked. "Do you think he's going to admit he was wrong? That he made a mistake? Or do you think he's going to blame it on his good little soldiers? On you?"

A slight shiver ran through Castigo as he realized that no matter how things played out, he was fucked either way. It was only a matter of time before Andras completely turned on him. Whether it happened from Rave saying he saw him in the hallway or Andras just deciding to use him as his personal punching bag, it didn't matter. If what Sy said was true, this was all a waste of his time and it would be better to bail out now. The demon certainly seemed sure of himself when it came to this matter. The fact Sy had some kind of contact with Dev and had watched what was happening at the club right under Andras' nose was not only impressive, but a little unsettling.

Watching the demon unconsciously smooth a hand down the side of his coat, Castigo couldn't help the shiver that ran down his spine once again. There was definitely more to Sy than he was letting on.

"You seem awfully sure about how this is going to end," Castigo said.

Sy shrugged. "Because I am."

"How? What makes you so sure Andras can't pull this off?"

"Not everyone is happy with what Andras is trying to do. With the position he is trying to put himself in."

"You included?" At Sy's smirk, Castigo shook his head. "But how can you be so sure? Just because a couple demons are against his plans doesn't mean he won't still make them happen."

"While that may be true, I can assure you, I know what I am talking about. You see, unless something truly drastic happens, Andras won't be allowed to see this to the end."

"Then why was he allowed to get this far in the first place?"

"There are advantages to be taken in every occasion. You should know that, Castigo."

Castigo rocked back on his heels. "While I may agree with you, I don't see what you get out of this."

"Personally? Nothing. But there are those I report to who will gain much from the rise and fall of your boss."

"First off," Castigo growled, "Andras is *not* my boss. I may have been biding my time with his little venture, but my days spent being one of his lackies is quickly coming to an end. Secondly, I didn't see you as the type to report to anyone. After all, didn't you just say that you aren't good at taking orders? I highly doubt anyone with any level of power would appreciate a demon beneath him not taking orders."

Sy smirked. "Just because I said I don't like taking orders does not mean I won't, as long as I'm going to get something of worth in return."

"I still find it hard to believe."

"Well, we all have a boss to answer to, Castigo. Mine just happens to be higher up on the food chain."

Castigo could tell by the tone of Sy's voice that he wasn't going to get anything else out of him. The question of this high-level demon Sy mentioned was definitely front and center in his mind. He would figure it out in time. While being patient was maybe not one of his strongest characteristics, he would have to be. Sy didn't strike him as the type to offer up any information if he didn't feel it necessary.

By the look Sy gave him, he'd told Castigo all he planned to...for now.

Curling his lips, Castigo glanced at the darkness around them. There was still a part of him that wanted to tell Sy where he could shove all his feelings on this matter. That there was no reason to still be here, listening to anything he had to say. In reality, it would probably be in his best interests to walk away. It would be easier. Safer.

But when had Castigo ever done anything because it was safer?

Never.

So why should he start now?

Decision made, Castigo looked back at Sy and let out a huff. "Dev disappeared from the club earlier tonight. I don't know if he is with his brothers or not, but I overheard Andras talking and he's pissed. He sent Rave and Labrihn to hunt him down. I'm pretty sure they're supposed to bring him back alive, though besides breathing, I'm not sure what condition he'll truly be in when they're done. I got out of there before Andras and Agalon continued their meeting..." He sighed, "but not before Rave spotted me."

"And what were you planning to do with this knowledge?"

Sy's question made him pause. He spent the whole time after leaving the club wondering what the hell he'd gotten himself into, but he never stopped to think what he *should* do from there. Well, not beyond the need to get as far away from all this as possible. Telling Sy as much, he watched as the demon tilted his head. He wasn't sure what response he thought he'd get, but this silent staring wasn't it. If anything, he felt his defenses rising as the seconds ticked by.

"Hmm," Sy finally hummed.

"Hmm? What... What do you mean hmm?"

"Simply that I expected this from our little Dev. Just not so soon." He paused, seemingly deep in thought. His eyes narrowed slightly as he stared intently as Castigo. "Well... I guess we should find him before Andras' minions do. If he's not with his brothers, which I highly doubt, we will just have to find a way to get him to them."

"Well, of course we... Wait! What?" Castigo took a step back, shaking his head violently. "I'm not sure how much you've been paying attention to what's been happening the last few months, but the Guardians... We don't like each other. At all. So, this plan of yours isn't a good idea."

Sy smirked. "Come now, Castigo. We have an angel to find."

Castigo laughed dryly. "You must not have heard me-"

"Oh, I did. I just think you should move past this fear of yours and come with me."

"What? I'm... I'm not afraid of those fucking angels," Castigo sputtered.

"Well... Guess you won't have a problem then." Sy smirked, turning on his heels and walking off into the darkness.

Clenching his jaw, Castigo stared after the demon. There was no way Sy's plan was going to work. At least not for Castigo. His past run-ins with the Guardians had not been the most pleasant, to put it mildly. He honestly couldn't imagine them being very welcoming as far as he went, so why even go that route?

Castigo shook his head. He'd help Sy find Dev, then disappear. It would be best for everyone involved, especially him. Now, if only he could keep himself alive long enough.

"Are you coming?"

With a quick nod, Castigo began moving in Sy's direction. His last thought before following him into the dark was how truly fucked he was.

Chapter 23

Nicholas had been watching Amy sleep for some time. After her promise to stay with him, at least for now, they had lain down on his bed, facing each other, and talked about nothing in particular until she'd fallen asleep. With the events of the evening still fresh in his mind, Nicholas figured he wouldn't be falling asleep anytime soon, which suited him just fine. He could spend a lifetime staring at Amy and never get enough.

Sure, it was probably a little creepy to stare at someone while they slept. But with this being the first time in ages that he had anyone in his bed, he just couldn't seem to pull his eyes away from her. The last woman who had been in his bed, slept in his room, ended up being the one and only witch he'd ever dealt with.

Well, until Hayley entered the picture.

But Hayley's nothing like Armina.

Just thinking her name made his eye twitch. She had been everything he thought he'd wanted. Of course, her request he not tell his brothers about her or their relationship, if that was what you wanted to call it, should have been a red flag. Yet he'd agreed, put a pretty smile ahead of his family.

Images of bright green eyes and ruby red lips flashed through his mind as Nicholas tried to push the memories back. Nothing good would come out of going down that road. After all, focusing too much on the past almost caused an irreparable rift between him and Manuel. It would be better if he just left the past where it belonged.

Reaching up, he ran a hand through Amy's hair, loving the feel of her soft tresses as they curled around his fingers. Glancing down, he found himself staring into her gorgeous brown eyes. Drinking in the sight of the beautiful woman before him, he felt his body heat.

"Hey," she whispered, reaching out to touch his arm.

"Hey." Pulling back his hand, he rested it against the cool comforter between them, the skin on his arm tingling beneath her fingertips.

"What time is it?"

Nicholas glanced over his shoulder, then looked back at her with a smile. "About two in the morning. You've been sleeping a little over five hours." Reaching out, he moved a stray strand of hair from her face before resting his hand back on the bed.

"Did you get any sleep?"

"No."

"Don't you think you should?"

Nicholas smirked. "Probably. But I doubt I'm going to anytime soon." At Amy's raised eyebrow, he just shrugged. "Just have too much on my mind, I guess."

Amy made a humming sound as she grabbed his hand in hers, entwining their fingers. "Do you want to talk about it?"

He laughed. "Where to start?"

"How about... Where has Dev been?"

His eyes widened. "Wow." Licking his suddenly dry lips, he chuckled. "Um... That is a rather long story."

"Hmm... How about just the cliff notes for now then?"

"Cliff notes." He nodded. "Yeah. I can do that." Curling his right arm beneath his head, Nicholas gave her a soft smile. "You know how we're angels, right?" She nodded. "Well, Dev was lost to us a long time ago. Long before we were sent to Earth."

"Where did he go?"

"That's part of the longer story, but the shorter version is he's been kept from us by the very demons who own the club you were at. It took us a while to find him...hell, we didn't even know he was here until he saved Ella and Hayley...but once we did, we've spent every day since looking for him. Well, at least everyone else did."

"Cuz you were unconscious for ten days?" Amy said with a grin.

"Yeah." He smiled back before continuing. "As soon as we got confirmation Dev was at the club, we headed there to bring him home. Luckily for me, I got to bring you home the same night."

The smile Amy gave him reached her eyes, causing them to brighten to such a degree, he found himself completely captivated by them. "Luckily for *me*, you mean." Pulling her hand toward him, Nicholas placed a gentle kiss on her knuckles, grinning at the breathy gasp that escaped her lips. "What else has been keeping you up?"

"You... Us."

"Oh yeah? What about us?" Amy asked, scooting closer to him.

He stared at her for a while. No matter how much his heart told him this was it, that what he felt going on between them was the real deal, his mind still pulled up images from his past. Images of Armina and their time together. How he'd thought the feelings they had for each other where real. All the other women he'd tried to get close to who had denied him without a second thought. It had finally gotten to be too much and he'd just stopped trying long ago. It was easier to focus on his brothers and whatever battle they were fighting than the loneliness slowly consuming him. He'd lied to Darren all those months ago when he'd said Christian shouldn't feel lonely because he had them. He knew exactly what Christian had been feeling, the hole he'd been falling down. He had just been in denial about it. He couldn't ignore his feelings anymore. Everything in him screamed that Amy was different, that she would be the one to fill that void.

"I haven't had a lot of luck when it comes to relationships," he finally said.

"Me, either." Biting her bottom lip, she rested her head on the edge of his pillow. "I've actually never had a relationship."

His eyes widened. "Never?" At the slight shake of her head, Nicholas felt his chest tighten.

"I mean, I've gone on dates before, but none of them turned into anything."

"Why's that?"

"They didn't feel right."

"Really?" Nicholas asked, scooting even closer. He felt the heat of her skin, smelled the sweet scent that was purely Amy. Inhaling deeply, he looked from her soft lips to her warm eyes, longing to pull her to him. To rise above her and see her gorgeous body lying beneath him. He pushed down his sudden need to own her, all of her. If she'd truly never been in an actual relationship, he was going to have to slow this down. "And how do I feel?"

He watched as she pulled her hand from his grasp and reached toward him, her fingers skimming his face. "You feel pretty good to me."

"Yeah?"

"Yeah."

"Well..." He grasped her hand, kissing her palm. "You feel pretty good to me, too."

"I know this is crazy, because we barely know each other, but I already feel so connected to you. I think... I want to see where this goes." She leaned in, her lips just a breath away from his. "Do you? Do you want to see where this goes, Nicholas?"

The word yes had barely passed his lips before he found himself pushed to his back. Amy used her hand against his chest to keep him down as she moved close to him. "I've never been with anyone before," she whispered against his lips. "I've never felt that closeness."

His eyes gazed into hers, taking in the want and need, as well as the uncertainty. *A virgin? Amy is a virgin*? That was a heady thought. Nicholas couldn't tell what he was more blown away by. The fact he was going to be her first, or that she trusted him enough to give him this gift.

Her nervousness told him she may not be ready to go all the way, but her body needed its release. She needed to feel the pleasure that only a lover could give her. Nicholas would give her that pleasure, and when she was ready, he'd make her fly.

"I... I want that closeness with you," she whispered, just as her lips connected with his.

It started soft, tentative. If anything, her uncertainty should have slowed Nicholas down. He should have pulled back, put more of an effort into not rushing into anything. But who was he kidding? The second her lips touched his, he may as well have raised a white flag. As her kisses grew more confident, needy, he answered back with a neediness of his own.

The sudden feeling of her hand under his shirt, traveling greedily over his skin, brought a moan from deep within him. It had been too long. Arching into her touch, he growled as her nails bit into his side, pulling him closer. Maneuvering herself above him, he found their positions switched from where he originally imagined they would be...and he was loving every second of it.

"Off," Amy breathed against his lips as she tugged at his shirt.

Not even considering denying her, Nicholas sat up enough to reach behind him, yanking his shirt off with such force, he heard the fabric rip. Amy's mouth watered as she watched him discard his shirt over the side of the bed. Much to his delight, hers quickly followed.

Lying back down, he ran his hands over her hips, hungrily eyeing her gorgeous breasts still encased in a satin bra. Pulling Amy toward him, he ran his tongue along the curves of her breasts, eliciting a breathy groan from her as she tilted her head back.

"Need to see you," he murmured. His hands reached up to unhook her bra, watching in appreciation as the straps fell down her arms.

Amy sat back a bit, pulling her bra the rest of the way off. Her skin was flushed a gorgeous pink hue, and Nicholas couldn't stop himself from bringing one of his hands around to gently squeeze one of her firm breasts. "Gorgeous," he moaned before leaning up and taking a rose-colored nipple into his mouth. The sounds falling from Amy's lips spurred him on as he lavished one nipple, then the other. When she began to grind down onto his almost painfully hard cock, he thrust up to meet her. Their jeans caused an added friction as they moved against each other.

"Oh, Nicholas... Oh...," she rasped.

Nipping along any part of her warm flesh that he could reach, Nicholas slowly moved one of his hands down her back. His senses in overdrive, he felt the light sheen of sweat coating her skin. She grabbed his arm with one hand, reaching up with the other to latch onto the back of his neck, pulling his lips to hers.

Nicholas' mouth opened, welcoming her tongue, as his wandering hand made its way down. Slipping it between her jeans and underwear, he grasped onto her ass. A deep moan rushed from her as he used his hand to push her down against him.

They moved so quickly, he felt his orgasm building, and judging by the shudders racing through Amy's body, he knew she was getting close, as well. A sudden tingling in his arm was his only warning as his power flared to life. It flowed over him, reaching out to Amy as she pulled her lips away from his, her hair flying around her face as she arched her back.

"Oh, my god... Oh, Nicholas," she yelled, her movements against him becoming more erratic. "I... Oh yes...."

Running his tongue along her neck, Nicholas felt the warmth from his power wrap around them. The saltiness from her sweat and the scent of her arousal slammed into him as he tightened his grip on her smooth skin. He was sure he would leave a mark on her firm ass, but he was unable to help himself.

"That's it, beautiful," he breathed against her flushed skin, rolling one of her taut nipples between his fingers. "I've got you."

With a final tweak, he rolled his hips and felt her come apart in his arms. Her whole body tensed as he pushed her down onto him. The warmth seeping through her jeans, his name passing her lips as she gasped had him coming in his pants. Shockwaves raced through him as he felt his muscles tense from his own release.

"Shit, Amy...," he panted, falling back onto the bed.

Pulling her tightly against his chest, he could feel her heart pounding, matching his beat for beat, her breath coming in short gasps. They lay there for several long minutes, not saying a word, just basking in the wonderful afterglow that had them still feeling boneless and sated.

"I can't believe I just humped you like a horny teenager," Amy giggled softly, her hands curling where they rested against his chest. After another second she lifted her face to gaze happily at him. "I feel like I need to slip out your window now so we don't get caught."

Shaking his head, Nicholas grinned as he tightened his arms around her. "First off, you can hump me like a horny teenager whenever you want. Truly, I'm not complaining." Her laughter had his grin widening. "Secondly, you're not going to be slipping out of here. At least I hope you want to stay the rest of the night."

"Well, it is awfully late," she stated. Smirking, he nodded. "And I did sort of have my heart set on having breakfast with this guy I'm kinda fond of. If I left, I would just have to turn around and come back in a few hours. That just seems like a lot of extra driving around."

"That it does. Plus, I'm sure this guy would want you to be here when he wakes up."

"Oh, would he?"

"Uh-huh."

"Then it looks like I'll be staying the night." Amy smiled, wiggling forward so she could place a kiss on his chin. "I do need one thing first, though."

"Anything."

"A shower..." She gave him another quick kiss before maneuvering off of the bed and walking toward the bathroom.

Nicholas watched her hips sway as she made her way across the floor. The need to go with her was undeniable, but he didn't want to push. She was quickly becoming an addiction, and they hadn't even had sex yet. The thought of scaring her off made his stomach clench. Slowly sitting up, he decided he wouldn't pursue her any more tonight. No. He'd go into one of the spare rooms to shower so she could enjoy hers without him crowding her.

"You go enjoy your shower, beautiful. I'll grab you some clean clothes."

She turned at the door and smiled at him. A mixture of relief and disappointment flashed through her eyes, but he knew he'd made the right decision. If he had his way, there would be many more chances to shower together in the future.

"Thank you," she said softly before disappearing into the bathroom.

Not wasting a moment's time, Nicholas jumped out of bed and ran into his closet. After finding a pair of sweats, which he was certain would be huge on Amy, and a t-shirt, also huge, he laid them out on the bed. Wanting to get back to her as soon as possible, he was out of the room and dashing down the hall shortly after. Thoughts of cuddling and holding her against him as they slept forced his feet to move quickly. He may have made the right choice in not showering with her, but that didn't mean he wanted to be away from her longer than necessary. So this was sure to be the quickest shower of his life. Get in, get washed, and get back to his room. Nothing else mattered at that moment.

Chapter 24

The days seemed to fly by as they all fell into a more relaxed routine around the house.

Darren had never seen everyone so calm, but with finding Nicholas and getting Dev back in the same day, it seemed they were finally able to take a breath.

Not that the house wasn't still on high alert. There was just no way Andras or his followers would let Dev go without a fight. Everyone knew it, so whenever one of them left the house, they were never alone.

Even Amy traveled back and forth between their home and hers with Nicholas and at least one other person by her side. She had fought against it at first, but after Nicholas pulled her to the side and they talked it out, she finally accepted it. Not that she was happy about having a chaperone every time she wanted to go somewhere, but she understood it.

Risking a chance the demons could decide to target her in order to get to them was not even an option. So they could either keep her happy, putting her life at risk, or have her be annoyed with them but safe. They all agreed to go with the latter.

Tilting his chair back, Darren ran his fingers through his hair. His thoughts strayed to Dev, who was more quiet and withdrawn then he used to be. But that was to be expected. Actually, given where he'd been for over a hundred years, he was doing a lot better than they thought. Just thinking of the length of time their brother had been in Andras' grasp made his stomach churn. Dev hadn't talked about what happened to him, hadn't really talked about anything, but again, that was to be expected. After all this time, they were practically strangers to him. Sure, he probably remembered how they used to be, but things had changed. They'd changed.

Among them, Cyrus had changed the most. Yet over the past week, he and Dev had often been seen sitting quietly together, passing a bottle of Crown back and forth. Darren supposed it made sense. While Cyrus had only been in the hands of demons for two days, he had a way to connect with Dev that the rest of them didn't. Though he wished Dev would reach out to him, he'd have to push down his need to help his brother for now. Hopefully soon, he would open up to everyone so they could start to help him heal.

Until then, he was just thankful Dev had latched onto someone in the house.

As for Cyrus, he was still as irritable as he'd been before they'd brought Nicky and Dev home. He just wasn't snarling at everyone as much. Apart from Nicholas' first morning at the breakfast table, he'd been giving Nicky a wide berth. Darren knew things were still tense between them. He just hoped they'd figure it out sooner rather than later. The last thing they needed was to be at odds with each other, especially when they could come under attack at any time. Which was exactly why he'd tried talking Ella out of having Cindy over for dinner tonight.

"Ugh..." Darren rocked his chair, turning it toward the door. It wasn't that he didn't want to see Cindy, which was weird because when he first met her, he couldn't get away from her fast enough. But now, for some reason, he was looking forward to being in her company. Darren wasn't sure when his feelings had changed. He just couldn't help but feel that now wasn't a good time for a get-together.

There were so many things that could go wrong, not to mention they'd only had Dev back for a week and he hadn't yet ventured any farther than the back porch. Introducing him to Cindy didn't exactly seem like the right thing to do right now. Darren frowned at the thought of Cindy and Dev being around each other. It wasn't that he thought they wouldn't get along, but he was afraid they'd get along *too* well. That thought, along with the clenching in his stomach that came along with it, made no sense to him...but it was there.

Throw in the fact that demons could show up at their house at any time, and Darren had raised a stink when the dinner was first mentioned. Not his finest moment, but whatever. He argued and made his concerns known.

Ella, a smirk on her face the whole time, wouldn't hear it.

So, against his better judgment, tonight's family dinner was a go.

Making a mental note to ask Manuel to double check the security around the house, he slowly rose from his chair. Stretching his arms above his head, he felt his back crack in several places, the sound loud in the quiet room. Sitting in his office chair for hours on end always played havoc on his back. He'd say he was getting old, but, well... They were already old when they fell to Earth.

"You almost done hiding in here?"

Darren turned, rolling his eyes at Christian. "I'm not hiding."

His brother hummed, stepping farther into the room. His blue eyes seemed to brighten as he glanced around Darren's office. "So you were just down here... What? Doing research? Looking for demon activity or something?"

"Or something."

Darren watched as Christian walked over and sat in the chair he'd just vacated, turning it around a few times. Darren had to chuckle as he watched his brother spinning in the chair. It wasn't too long ago that Christian had started pulling away from them, getting reckless on hunts, and spiraling into a depression Darren had feared he'd never find his way out of. But with the constant support of his brothers and the love only Ella could provide, Christian was back to being the amazing, fun-loving brother Darren remembered. They owed Ella so much. The grin on his brother's face as he finally stopped spinning further showed Darren how far he'd come. Christian was finally happy again.

"Your hiding...I'm sorry...*researching* down here wouldn't have anything to do with a certain dinner guest who will be showing up tonight, would it?"

"Who?" At the look of exasperation on his brother's face, Darren released a loud sigh. "Okay, fine. I just don't think now is the right time to have someone outside the family, someone who has no idea what's going on, coming around the house. I know Ella wants to be around her friend. I get that. I just don't think now is a good time."

"Is there *ever* a good time?"

"You know what I mean, Christian."

"I do, but Cindy is part of this family, Darren. She has been since the day I brought Ella home."

"I know, but these demons are a lot different than what we're used to. What if they find out she's connected to us? What if they go after her because of it?"

Christian stood, walking over to stop in front of Darren. "Nothing will happen to Cindy. If these demons are dumb enough to go after her, we'll be there. Right?"

"Yeah," he agreed.

He knew he and his brothers would protect Cindy if the need arose, just as they defended everyone connected to their growing family. This knowledge didn't help ease the knot in his chest. The knot that had been growing ever since he'd realized the demons could get to her. Darren doubted anything would help, outside of getting rid of the threat altogether. Not that he saw that happening anytime soon. Each battle seemed to be getting them closer. To what, he wasn't sure. Whatever it was felt big, though. Maybe to the end of this mess they'd found themselves in. Then again, maybe this was all just wishful thinking on his part.

The sound of the doorbell jolted him from his thoughts.

"Come on. Sounds like Cindy's here." Christian gave Darren's arm a squeeze before walking out of the office.

After a moment, Darren began to follow. Knowing Cindy was in his house gave him a sudden need to hurry, to rush to her and assure himself that she was here, that she was safe. He held back, though. He still wasn't sure where all these feelings concerning her came from or what he should do about them...if anything.

There was just so much on his plate right now, so many questions that had gone unanswered for too long, he wasn't sure he could take on any more uncertainty. And that was what he felt when it came to Cindy. Uncertain. He needed to be strong for his family. He needed to be confident in his thoughts and the direction they were going.

Everyone needed him to concentrate on what was best for them right now. Everything else would have to wait. He just couldn't risk being distracted. He would make sure Cindy was protected, just as he did everyone else in his family. And that would be as close as he would allow himself to get to her.

No matter how much his heart yearned for more.

Chapter 25

Amy released a sigh as she fell back onto Nicholas' bed. His thick comforter fluffed up around her as her body sank into its softness. She felt a calmness settle around her. They'd just finished dinner, and she was not only full from all the yummy food, but mentally exhausted.

Conversation had been lively, to say the least. At one point, she'd felt like she was watching a tennis match with all the back and forth between the brothers. The way they all seemed to know what the others were thinking, feeling, spoke volumes of how close they were.

Then there was the sexual tension between Darren and Ella's friend, Cindy, which was an almost living, breathing thing. As soon as Cindy had walked through the door and made eye contact with Darren, it was like the temperature in the room had spiked. Sure, they had played it cool, a nod here and a *how are you doing* there, but it was obvious to everyone. Even Dev had looked between the two for a heartbeat before shaking his head and following Cyrus into the dining room.

Knowing what she did about Nicholas and his brothers, it was easy for her to pick out areas in their stories they altered, the pauses where they debated on how to continue. She was confused when she realized they were being careful, censoring their words. She'd thought Nicholas had filled her in on everything she needed to know concerning him and his family. At least she'd hoped he'd told her enough that his brothers would feel comfortable talking in front of her. So imagine how shocked she felt, albeit relieved, when Nicholas leaned over and whispered that they had to be careful because Cindy didn't know what they were.

That had floored Amy. She'd just figured anyone close enough to the brothers to be over for dinner was also close enough to know who they really were. On the other hand, it made her feel a little special.

To be trusted with the knowledge of something so huge, so amazing, so sensitive was humbling to her. Then to find out that she knew more than someone who'd been around Nicholas and his brothers for longer than she had, well... That had her mentally puffing out her chest. Then she quickly realized the reason Cindy was probably not *in the know* was for her own safety. That thought really sobered her to the seriousness of what was going on.

Sure, it was mind blowing to find out that Nicholas was an angel. But she hadn't truly appreciated what she was seeing, what she was a witness to, when everything went down in the alley about a week ago. Everything had happened so quickly. From the moment those men cornered her in the hallway of the club to the moment Nicholas scooped her up and flew her to their house felt like a dream. Then there was Dev, and Hayley, and Ella.

The days that followed hadn't done a lot as far as helping her make sense of what was going on. She'd found herself spending her days traveling between her house and here. She'd sat and talked with Ella and Hayley about all of the confusing, amazing, terrifying moments they'd experienced since they'd met their men. Both their stories were so different, yet so similar, it made Amy's face hurt from smiling so much. The love they felt for their men was beautiful, something Amy longed to have.

Images of Nicholas swam through her mind. She felt the warmth spread across her face as she thought of the last couple nights. They hadn't gone all the way yet, something she hoped to rectify soon, but she felt like they were getting closer each night. In a short period of time, Amy had come to really care about Nicholas, more than she'd cared about anyone else. She craved his smile, his touch, the warmth she felt in the pit of her stomach every time he said her name.

In the last week, she'd gone to sleep every night with his warm, hard body curled around her, had woken snuggled up atop his chest. She couldn't remember the last time she'd slept so well. Whether or not it was too soon to feel this way, she couldn't imagine not having him by her side. Nicholas was it. Her one. She just had to hope and pray he felt the same.

The sound of her phone ringing pulled her from her musings. Reaching over, Amy grabbed it up off the nightstand and instantly grinned when she saw her dad's face smiling back at her from the screen. She swiped to answer.

"Hey, Dad."

"Hey, sweetie. Where are you?" her dad asked. "I just stopped by your place to get you for dinner."

Her mind froze as she remembered the plans she'd made with her dad several weeks ago. Pre-Nicholas. Pre-angels. *Crap.* "Oh... I'm sorry, Dad. I completely forgot."

"Ha. Just forget about your old man. I see how it is." Amy shook her head, hearing the laughter in his voice. "Well, are you somewhere that we could meet up for a quick bite?"

"I, uh... Well... I'm with some friends right now." Amy's mind warred with itself on what to say. Should she mention Nicholas? If she did, how would she explain how they met? Damn, this could get tricky.

"Who? Misty?"

"Oh, um... No. I actually met someone the other day. We've been spending a lot of time together."

"And who is this mysterious someone?"

"Nicholas," Amy said with a smile. She figured it was best to stick as close to the truth as possible. That would keep the brothers' secrets, just as she promised, but there was no way she couldn't tell her dad about him.

His voice hardened slightly. "Nicholas, huh? What does he do? Where did you meet him?"

She rolled her eyes. "Dad..."

"What? Okay, fine. When do I get to meet him?"

Amy ran a hand through her hair as she rolled onto her back and stared up at the ceiling. "I'm not sure, Dad. He's pretty busy."

"Too busy to meet your father? Don't you think he should make time to meet me, you know, since you guys are obviously serious?"

"What? Why would you assume that?"

"Well, you're blowing off our dinner date-"

"Dad..."

He laughed. "I'm just kidding. Seriously, though. I'm glad you've met someone. I just hope you'll get to the point where you want him to meet me."

"It's not that I don't want him to meet you, Dad. I mean, I hope we get to that point."

"So you really like this Nicholas?"

"Yeah, I really do." She smiled. "There's just something about him, Dad. I mean, I realize I haven't known him long, but I just..."

"Does he treat you right?"

Movement by the bedroom door caught her eye. Looking over, Amy felt her cheeks heat up as she saw Nicholas leaning against the door frame. He gazed intently at her, a slow grin spreading across his handsome face. Amy's stomach fluttered as she returned his smile.

"Yeah, Dad. He treats me right."

"Well, good. I really hope I get to meet him someday."

"I hope so, too, Dad."

Amy rolled onto her side so she could watch Nicholas comfortably. His muscular arms were crossed loosely across his chest, his right hip resting against the frame. She bit her bottom lip as her eyes traveled over him. But it wasn't just his body that called to her. It was all of him. Hidden beneath his layers of humor and tough skin, he had a sweetness about him. Each day, she learned more and more about Nicholas and yearned, with every fiber in her being, to be able to be around him for many years to come. She wasn't going to lie, though, His sexiness was definitely a plus. Releasing a soft sigh of contentment, she felt her lips pull into a soft smile.

"How about we make a plan for dinner in a few days?" her father asked.

"That sounds great. I'll call you tomorrow and we can figure out an afternoon to meet up."

"Sounds like a date, sweetheart. You tell that man of yours he'd better be good to you."

Amy giggled. "I will, Dad. I'll call you soon."

"Okay, hon. Love you."

"Love you, too."

Hanging up, Amy kept her eyes on Nicholas as she rested the phone beside her. "He would like to meet you."

"I heard," Nicholas purred. "I would like to meet him someday, as well." He pushed away from the door frame and closed the door softly behind him before making his way toward the bed.

"Oh, you would?" she asked softly, feeling a wave of excitement run through her as she watched him rest one of his knees on the mattress, moving closer.

"I want to meet everyone who's special to you, Amy." Moving slowly, he stretched his body out, gently forcing her to roll to her back as he braced himself above her.

"Well, there aren't many," she whispered, gazing up into his ruby-colored eyes. Being this close, she could make out gold flecks sprinkled within the red. It was mesmerizing. Damn, his whole body, all hard and tempting, made her want to roll him over and feast on him until neither of them could take it anymore. The heat coming off him, soaking into her sensitive flesh, caused her mind to cloud over. God, just the thought of him running his hands over her made her want to arch up into him. She wanted to pull him against her and never let go.

She was so lost in the images of what she wanted him to do to her, it took her a moment to realize he'd asked her a question.

"Huh?"

He smirked. "I asked why you'd say that."

"Oh, um...," she said slowly, trying to pull her mind out of the sexual haze it had started swimming in. "My mom... My mom passed away a few years back. Besides my dad, the only other person I'm truly close to is my best friend, Misty."

"I'm sorry about your mom."

"She'd been sick for a while. Lung cancer," Amy said with a sad smile. "It was time."

He blinked down at her, his eyes swimming with concern and something else she thought she recognized but was afraid to put a name to.

Her heart swelled as she looked up at him, even as her stomach dropped at the thought of her mom. Sure, she said it had been her time, and on a certain level, she was happy her mother wasn't in pain anymore, was finally at peace. It still hurt, though, even after all these years. It had gotten better, but she still missed her. Missed being able to call her whenever she wanted, knowing her mom was there for her when she had something exciting to share or she had a bad day and just needed to talk. She would probably always miss her, and that was okay. It was in missing her, in finding her smile and hearing her laughter in everything Amy did, that would keep her alive. Even though she was sad when she thought of or talked about her, it was better than never thinking of her again and forgetting.

Reaching up, she ran her fingers lightly along Nicholas' jaw. She wanted the sudden sorrow in her thoughts to go away, needed to have her mind pulled back into this moment once again. Sliding her hand to the back of his neck and into his hair, she gently pulled him toward her. Her movements were met with no resistance as he lowered his mouth. His lips brushed gently across hers once, twice, then landed firmly against them as his own need seemed to grow. Just the simple act of his tongue tracing the length of her mouth caused her body to vibrate with want.

Skimming one of her hands down his back, she pushed down on his ass as her hips raised up to meet him. Even through the jeans they both had on, wiggling against him had her yearning for more. Her stomach quivered as she latched onto the soft sounds passing his lips. Sucking his tongue into her mouth, she groaned at the overwhelming feeling of him surrounding her. Of how right he felt. She needed more.

So what started out as a slow grind quickly built until the friction between them became too much. She was vaguely aware of her clothes disappearing. Almost as aware as she was about ripping his shirt over his head and yanking down the zipper on his jeans.

She was a mess of emotions, needs, and wants...and she absolutely loved it.

With a mental sigh of relief, she felt his warm, naked flesh rub against hers for the first time. Every inch of her ached to touch him as she devoured his mouth. She wrapped her legs around his waist, pulling him closer to her until she felt his dick slide deliciously over her damp center. He was long and thick. Perfection. She had the pleasure of feeling his length slide between her lips several times over the past week, but the thought of finally having him between her legs was all-consuming. Her stomach clenched with the sudden need for him to fill her, to own her completely.

It was like her very soul knew that once he pushed into her, there would be no one else but him. That, while he would be her first, he would also be the last man she would ever want this way. Her heart whispered words of love and forever with each beat, and as much as she felt it was too soon to put her feelings into words, she couldn't deny them.

"Please," she moaned against his lips. Her voice shook as she felt her nails bite into his arms.

"Are you sure?" His voice sounded deeper than usual as he turned his head, running the tip of his nose along her cheek. She felt his dick pulse against her, slightly sliding between her folds as he swiveled his hips. Nicholas' need to continue what they'd started was almost visual as she felt his muscles strain above her. However, she knew that if she were to say she wasn't ready, if she were to show even the slightest bit of uncertainty, he'd stop.

Looking into his eyes, there wasn't even a second thought to his question. Being with him was something she wanted. Something she needed.

"I want this, want you, need to feel you in me," Amy breathed, tightening her hold on his arms. His pupils widened with lust, the air around them seeming to become electrically charged as his tongue shot out, licking across his bottom lip.

He grabbed her hands and pulled them up to his lips, placing a soft kiss on them before raising them above her head. "Grasp the headboard, baby. I'm going to make this so good for you."

She had no doubt about that.

Wrapping her fingers around the wooden edge, she felt her excitement thrum through her. Amy watched as he braced himself above her with one arm, his other hand traveling over her face, down her neck, to the taut peak of her right nipple. He only lingered a moment, gently tweaking it before moving over to give her other one the same treatment. By the time he moved farther south, she was a panting, moaning mess. She didn't think her body had ever felt this warm, this responsive, to someone's touch before.

The rough pads of his fingers connected with her clit at the same time he ran his tongue over her right nipple. The combined feelings had Amy crying out as she tightened her grip on the headboard. Every swipe of his tongue, every pass of his finger, had her gasping for breath. By the time she felt him slide his finger deep into her wetness, Amy was practically vibrating. One finger was quickly followed by a second, then a third, driving her crazy with every thrust.

Just as Amy felt her orgasm rising, he pulled his fingers out, leaving her feeling empty. A whine escaped her lips.

"Shh... I got you, baby," Nicholas whispered, shifting. Her legs automatically tightened around his waist in her attempt to pull him closer. His chuckle warmed her as he rested his left hand on her hip. "Are you ready for me?"

"Yes, Nicky," she panted, arching her hips up to him. He gently pressed her back into the mattress. Holding her steady with one hand, he reached down to grip the base of his cock.

She reached up, tightly gripping his shoulders. She felt his muscles bunch as she tugged his body toward her, feeling the delicious pressure of his cock entering her. Groaning, Nicholas allowed her to pull him down. His lips greedily latched onto hers as he devoured her gasps.

Only the slightest twinge of discomfort snaked through her body as he pushed into her. He paused for a moment, allowing her to get used to the feeling of him. His eyes, filled with both concern and need, searched hers. Feeling her body relax, Amy tightened her inner muscles around his length, marveling at the moan that was ripped from his lips and the flash of heat that brightened his eyes.

Sending her a wicked grin, Nicholas moved his hips back, almost pulling the whole way out before sliding back in. The feeling of him moving inside her was better than she could have ever imagined. With a satisfied groan, she gasped for more.

It didn't take long for them to find a steady, toe-curling rhythm. He rocked into her with such wildness, it was hard for her to pull in any air between thrusts. Not that she would ask him to slow down. She just clung to him tighter, moaned louder as the sound of skin slapping against skin filled the room.

Feeling a warmth begin to grow beneath her hands, she pulled back slightly, gasping when she saw his skin had taken on a faint glow. The lightning tattoo running down his arm seemed to come to life, pulsing with every thrust of his hips. Her mind tried to make sense of what she was seeing, but the sudden shift of Nicholas' hips tore away what little concentration she had. Throwing her head back, she reached above her to grip the headboard.

The lights within the room flickered before going out, casting the room into almost complete darkness. They didn't need any light, though. The soft glow spreading around them, the feeling of his skin against hers, and the almost animalistic growls leaving his lips were more than enough.

"So close," he gasped. Her eyes latched onto his as he reared back. His fingers gripped onto her soft flesh as he lifted her up, making him sink into her even deeper.

"Please. Oh... Nicky," she rasped, grasping the headboard with both hands. Her whole body vibrated beneath his punishing pace.

"Keep your eyes on me," Nicholas demanded. "I want to see those gorgeous eyes as you fall apart."

Her eyes widened as a sudden flash of lightning lit up the night beyond the window. Nicholas' features in the soft light made her heart clench from the beauty of him. His mouth slightly open, eyes wild with an auburn glow as he moved. A rumble of thunder shook through the room as Nicholas pulled her legs up to rest over his arms.

Amy knew that within a few strokes, she would be done. The warmth pooling in the pit of her stomach started growing fast and she feared the strength of her release. Never had she felt like this before. "I... I need..."

"Let go," Nicholas panted, once again shifting and leaning over her. "I got you."

Before she even realized what was happening, her vision blurred. She screamed his name as every one of her muscles tensed. She was only faintly aware of Nicholas pulling her against him as he growled her name. Another bolt of lightning crackled though the air, followed by a boom of thunder so strong, it shook the house.

Her lungs practically hurt from the air she dragged into them. Her hands shook as she slowly moved them to rest on the pillow by her head. As her vision began to clear, she realized Nicholas now rested his head on her chest, his breath warm against her cooling flesh. Amy felt his dick twitching inside her as he released her legs, slowly lowering them to the bed.

With a soft groan, he pulled out and eased himself down beside her, lying on his back. She turned her head and smiled. His own grin was wide as he gazed back at her. "Wow... That was..."

"Perfect?"

He chuckled, wrapping one of his arms under her and pulling her to his side. "Yeah. Definitely perfect."

She laid her head on his chest, listening to his heart. The storm outside seemed to be calming. Humming softly, she closed her eyes as he ran his hand in slow circles along her back.

"Get some rest," he whispered, placing a kiss against her hair.

Snuggling closer, Amy's body begin to relax. She wanted to tell him how much he'd come to mean to her. That she wanted him in her life for as long as he'd have her. That she needed him, was quickly falling for him. But she was just so comfortable, so happy, so tired.

Giving in, she slowly drifted off to sleep. Her last thought was that if she were being honest with herself, she wasn't falling for this strong, sweet, amazing man beneath her. Amy had to admit that sometime over the past few weeks, she had already fallen.

Chapter 26

Nicholas smiled as he felt Amy cuddle closer to his side. His arm tightened around her as he listened to her steady breathing. She'd been sleeping for a little while now, and though he felt the need to sleep himself, his mind just wouldn't stop. Their lovemaking had been just that. He couldn't stop the tumble of emotions racing through him. She already meant so much to him. And the way she'd opened herself up to him tonight, given him everything, had only cemented the fact that he needed her. Now he just had to figure out a way to convince her to be his.

His problem was that he knew she deserved so much better than him and all the fucked-up baggage he'd bring into her life. But he was selfish in the fact that he wanted her with him anyway. He'd find a way to keep as much of his and his brothers' shit off her plate as he could. Christian did what he could for Ella, Manuel for Hayley. There had to be a way.

Running his hand absentmindedly along her spine, he sighed. There was no way Amy would be put into his life just to be pulled back out of it. He didn't think he would make it if she left him now. Wasn't that a crazy thought. They were just getting to know each other, but he could already feel how special she was to him.

Christian had told him that it was the same when he'd first seen Ella, first talked to her and saw her smile. Manuel had said it was unlike anything else he would ever experience and to just go with it. Not that Nicholas had any intention of fighting his attraction to Amy, but there was something reassuring about knowing his brothers had felt the same way about their women.

At dinner, he'd watched the other two couples at the table interact, finally understanding the long glances and soft touches. He couldn't seem to go very long without touching Amy as she sat next to him. Even just a brush of his knee against hers was enough to make him feel secure in the fact that she was there. He just wished his other three brothers could feel this level of emotion, too.

Darren seemed closer to it than the other two. He'd spotted his brother's gaze straying to Cindy on more than one occasion when he thought nobody was looking. Just as she would do the same to him when he'd look away. It was cute in an *I just wish they'd hook up and be together* kind of way. But Nicholas figured that whatever was going on between them would work itself out.

Cyrus and Dev, on the other hand, were quiet. While this unsociable quietness was the norm for Cyrus, Nicholas couldn't help but frown as Dev shied away from any conversation. He knew Dev needed time to become accustomed to not having to constantly look over his shoulder and watch what he said, but it still hurt to see him that way. The past week had flown by so quickly, what with being busy with Amy and helping Darren do his research, he hadn't really had time to sit down with Dev. Which he now regretted.

His mind too full, he decided that sleep was just not going to come to him. At least for a while.

So, gently rolling Amy off his arm, he slid out of bed. The cool air chilled him as he leaned over to grab some sweatpants off the floor. Though he didn't get cold very easily, the house definitely seemed a tad chilly, even for him. He leaned down and pulled the comforter, which had slid to the foot of the bed, over Amy. Smiling down at her, he chuckled softly as she rolled to the warm spot he'd just vacated.

After another few seconds, making sure she was sleeping soundly, he walked toward the door, flipping off the light switch on his way out.

He wasn't sure how, but it seemed his powers had gone a little crazy, causing a storm that quite possibly knocked out the house's power. Either that, or he blew the light in his room. Deciding it would be best to check the fuse box while he was up, Nicholas made his way through the silent house.

The darkness surrounding him as he moved quietly down the stairs led him to believe he had, in fact, shorted out the whole house. His hope that everyone else had already been in bed when it happened was probably long shot. If even one of his brothers had been awake when the storm blew a fuse, he would never hear the end of it. Especially from Cyrus. Rolling his eyes at the thought, Nicholas headed past the kitchen and down the flight of stairs leading to the basement.

Skirting around the dumbbells and workout pad at the bottom of the stairs, he felt grateful for the excellent night vision he had. Shaking his head at the mess, he walked down the hall. He could only guess which one of his brothers had begun to set up their workout stuff, only to abandon the project, leaving a mess at the foot of the stairs.

Seconds later, he stood in front of the fuse box. Flipping the main switch, he released a breath when he heard the soft hum of the power starting back up. Though the downstairs still remained dark, he could just make out a soft glow filtering in from the top of the stairs. Making his way back up and around the second floor, Nicholas switched off various lights as he went.

There were enough lights on before his power shut everything down that he believed someone had been up. The question was who, and how much shit was he going to get from them. Not that he would begrudge them their chance to toss some jokes his way. Hell, he'd dished out his fair share. Thoughts of the first few nights after Ella came to live with them came to mind. Laughing softly as he remembered all the good-natured ribbing he'd given Christian, Nicholas turned toward the stairs to head back to his room when he noticed the sliding back door was slightly open.

His first thought was that someone had forgotten to lock it up earlier. He couldn't remember anyone going outside after dinner, but after he helped clean up, he'd headed upstairs to see Amy. With everything going on, he didn't think anyone would have gone out, come back in, then forgotten to close and lock the door. Especially with Andras and his gang of undesirables breathing down their necks.

Letting his power roll out around him, he didn't sense anyone milling around the house. At least nobody who shouldn't be there. He did, though, feel his power brush against someone outside. His curiosity piqued, Nicholas quietly opened the sliding door a little farther and slipped out onto the porch, softly closing the door behind him.

Within two steps, he found who his power had touched. Biting his lip, he silently debated on whether he should head back in or continue forward. It wasn't that he felt he'd be intruding, but he also understood that sometimes people just needed to be alone. To think through whatever was going on in their lives. Maybe if he just sat quietly on the bench, he'd be offering some much-needed support.

Releasing a soft sigh, Nicholas made his way over and eased down next to Dev. His brother didn't move as he settled on the cushion, which told him his sudden presence was not a surprise. Glancing at Dev briefly, Nicholas turned to look out over the back yard. Besides the rhythmic song of nearby crickets, the night was quiet. All signs from the sudden storm were gone, leaving a star-filled sky and full moon in its wake. The peacefulness was only broken up by the hum of uncertainty and sorrow hovering around his brother's still form next to him.

Nicholas wanted to help Dev feel safe and get him back to how he was, but he just wasn't sure how. Not knowing what had happened to him, Nicholas wasn't sure his brother could ever make it back to his old self. Then again, were any of them the same as they used to be? Nicholas knew he wasn't, and maybe that was okay. Dev was still his brother, no matter what had happened, and he would take him any way he could get him.

Leaning over a bit, Nicholas nudged his shoulder against his brother's. "Want to talk about it?" Even whispering, his voice sounded loud in the silence of the night.

Dev released a soft sigh. He remained quiet for so long, Nicholas thought he wasn't going to answer. A rush of sadness ran through him at the idea of his brother not being comfortable enough around him to discuss whatever was on his mind. Just as he was about to tell Dev it was okay if he didn't want to talk, his brother glanced his way.

"I just don't feel like this will last."

Nicholas frowned. "What do you mean? Being here with us?"

"Yeah. I mean, I know it doesn't make a lot of sense. It's just... I've been dreaming about being reunited with you all for so long, it just doesn't feel real." Dev shifted uncomfortably. "I guess a part of me keeps waiting to wake up and find this was all just a dream. Or have Andras show up and drag me back."

Nicholas turned so he could completely face his brother. "First off, this is very real. We *really* came for you, *really* got you out of that club, and we are *really* here with you now. None of us can apologize enough for not getting to you sooner, but you are where you're supposed to be. Here with us, your family."

He watched Dev lower his head. He was doing it to try and hide the storm of emotions flowing through his eyes, but Nicholas had seen it. He felt the hope and fear warring in his brother, pain being a constant in the background. What Nicholas wouldn't give to be able to heal him, but he knew it was up to Dev to realize he wasn't alone anymore.

"And secondly," Nicholas continued, his voice sounding strong and sure, "there is no way any of us are going to allow Andras to even get near you, let alone take you from us. It's just not going to happen, so I need you to stop worrying over that, okay? You're not going anywhere."

Dev gave a slight nod, still not meeting Nicholas' eyes.

"Okay?" Nicholas pushed again.

"Okay," Dev said, finally looking up. "In my heart, I believe you. It's just... It's hard to get my mind to move past everything that's happened."

"Do you...," Nicholas started, pausing when he saw the tightness in Dev's face. "Do you want to talk about it?"

Dev's eyes took on a haunted look as he turned away and gazed out across the yard. Whatever he had been through, Nicholas knew it still affected him and was the reason behind all the pain he held right below the surface. As the silence stretched on, he became more aware of the tightness in his brother's shoulders, the heaviness in the air around them.

"It's okay." Nicholas looked from his brother to the moonlight shining on the landscape before them. "Just know that whenever you're ready, I'm here. No pressure, no judgment. Okay?"

"Thanks, Nicky," Dev whispered.

"Hey, what are brothers for? Besides, you know, picking on and pushing around."

Dev laughed quietly. "True." Pulling his phone from his pocket, Nicholas watched his brother frown at the screen.

"What's up?" Nicholas asked.

"Nothing. Just figured Cyrus would be back by now."

"He's not here?"

Dev shook his head. "No. He left about thirty minutes or so ago. Said he was just going to run to the store."

Looking at his own phone, Nicholas shook his head. "Why would he run out to the store this late?"

Dev smirked. "I think he was out of Crown."

With a snicker, Nicholas stood and slid his phone back into his pocket. "I'm sure he'll be back soon. Him and his Crown Royal. I think if he could hook that up to an IV, he'd do it."

"Yeah. He definitely drinks a lot. But everyone has their own way of dealing with their inner demons."

Nicholas stilled, blinking at Dev. "He talked to you about what happened to him?"

"Not in detail." Dev stood slowly, stretching his arms above his head. "He just mentioned some shit had happened a few years back that he was still dealing with. Guess he didn't want me to feel alone, ya know?"

"Yeah." Nicholas nodded, thoughts of those few dark days filtering through his mind. When they'd discovered Cyrus missing, he'd never felt as helpless...or as guilty. Maybe that was why no matter how much he tried to get close to Cyrus, tease him in the hopes he'd crack a smile, his brother always kept him at arm's length. It made sense. This was karma, his punishment for not being there when he should have been. And Cyrus, just like everyone else, knew it was his fault he had been taken. Well, he wouldn't let that happen again. Not to any of them. He'd be there for Dev and make sure those pieces of shit never laid a hand on him again.

"I thought I noticed some hot chocolate in the kitchen. Do you want to have some while we wait for him to get home?" Dev's uncertainty was clear in his tone.

Nicholas smiled, leading his brother back inside. "That sounds great, Dev."

Making their way into the kitchen, Nicholas watched Dev walk over to the mugs. He might not be able to change what happened to Cyrus or his guilt in the issue. And he may not be able to right the wrongs that had been done to Dev. But he could be here for them now. If having hot chocolate with Dev made his brother feel some security, and if being awake when Cyrus got home tonight gave his other brother a sense of being wanted, that was what Nicholas would do.

Well, it was a start at least. Better late than never, right? With any luck, this would get all of them on the right road to reconnecting. Becoming the family they'd always been meant to be. He hoped.

Chapter 27

"Do you even know where we're going?" Rave questioned for what felt like the hundredth time. Not that he was really complaining. The longer he followed Andras' supposed *best tracker* around the back alleys of downtown Fhallon Heights, the more time he had to figure out what in the hell he was going to do.

He knew what he was supposed to be doing, what was expected of him, but he was getting tired of playing Andras' game. It was interesting at first, something to help with his boredom as he made his way from day to day. He'd decided a long time ago to let other demons take the lead. Not because he couldn't or didn't have the power to make others do as he wanted. It was mainly because he'd never wanted to oversee anyone other than himself. Normally dealing with these *I got more power than you* demon shitheads wasn't a hardship, but times were changing. Everything was changing.

No, that was wrong. *He* was the one changing, not the demons around him. Little by little over the past few decades, he'd noticed a change in how he felt about what was going on around him. How he reacted to what he'd been asked to do.

Tracking down Dev was just one in a long list of demands that had been placed on him since coming topside. And just like all the others, he found it harder and harder to follow through. This time, though, he wasn't sure just how he could change the outcome Andras demanded. Rave really had no interest in taking Dev back to that club.

He couldn't necessarily pinpoint when his views on the angel had changed, or what brought on this strange sense of concern for him, but there it was.

Maybe it's the fact I'm only half-demon, he mused.

With most of the demons he knew being grade-A assholes and him only being a half-blood, therefore only half an ass, this could mean the other half of him could be the reason he kind of gave a shit.

Chuckling softly, he gave a mental shrug. Maybe it all boiled down to his growing dislike for Andras and that two-bit thug, Agalon, who was never too far from his side.

Either way, he needed to make a decision on how to handle the impending fight with the angels without getting his ass sent straight to the Nether Realms. He knew that would be easier said than done.

As Rave emerged from yet another alley, he glanced at the store window to his right. A flower shop. Even if the window wasn't filled with artfully designed bouquets, he would have known it by the heavy floral scent hanging in the air around it. The shit he would get if any of the demons he dealt with knew he liked that smell.

Taking a deep breath, he savored the aroma in the air as he waited for Labrihn to get done sniffing, well...whatever it was he was sniffing. Actually, Rave had no idea how Labrihn went about his *tracking*. With how long they'd been wandering around aimlessly, he figured either the demon really didn't know what he was doing or the angels were better at hiding their tracks than anyone thought.

Rave could make an argument either way.

What he did know was the longer they went without finding Dev or his brothers, the better. Not because he didn't think he could beat them in a fight. It was that he didn't *want* to fight them. He knew he wouldn't have a choice, but one could hope.

This thought brought him right back to his earlier concerns. Damn, this whole mess was giving him a headache. Rolling his eyes, he shook his head.

Gazing into the flower shop, he blew out a steady breath. *One step at a time.* Right now, he just needed to concentrate on not killing Labrihn. Andras would probably frown on it, and even though he'd never tried to take on Rave, there was a first time for everything. He felt his demon side smirk at the thought of going head to head with Andras. Thankfully, he had his other half to balance everything out. Otherwise, he'd be as impulsive as all the other idiots in the club.

"I think one of the angels went this way."

Repressing another eye roll, Rave glanced over at Labrihn. He watched the demon slide a hand over his bald head. His sickly, pale skin glowed in the harsh streetlights. The guy made his skin crawl. Maybe he should be hoping to run into the angels sooner rather than later, if for no other reason than to get him away from Labrihn.

"What makes you say that?" he finally asked.

"Why do you think?" Labrihn asked smugly. "That's what I do, and I'm good at it. I won't bother taking the time to explain what makes me a good tracker cuz I know you won't understand. Just trust me when I tell you we're close."

Like he'd been so sure the last ten times he said we were close, Rave thought as he took a steadying breath.

There was so much wrong with what Labrihn just said, it made Rave want to scream. It hadn't taken long for him to realize he was a much better tracker than Labrihn was. If he'd been on his own, he probably would have located Dev by now. This conclusion had come to him within the first ten minutes, and he'd wanted nothing more than to shake the shit out of the demon ever since. Right now, he just really wanted to toss him through the closest wall and be done with it. But he knew there was no point. No matter how good it would feel to toss him around like a ragdoll, it would ultimately do no good in the grand scheme of things.

Sighing, Rave waved his hands out before him to signal Labrihn to carry on. He barely held back his disgust as the demon shot him another smirk before moving down the street.

"There is definitely a feeling of power coming from this area," Labrihn hissed.

Yeah, probably ours, Rave thought.

Following the demon, he looked around the empty street. Normally, even on a weeknight, Rave would still be able to find at least a couple humans milling around the darkened streets. But he'd only ever really been on the streets around the various bars and clubs. There had never been any need to venture out this far.

"We are close," Labrihn whispered, breaking through Rave's thoughts.

Rave gave him a soft grunt of acknowledgment. He really didn't see them running into any of the angels here. Looking around, he saw they were coming closer to a practically empty parking lot beside what could possibly be the only open liquor store in town. *Must have a late customer*, he mused. They may not find any angels here, but he could definitely go for a drink. Something to take the edge off and help him get through the rest of this ridiculously long night.

He contemplated leaving Labrihn to head into the parking lot when movement caught his eye. Pausing, he stared toward the darkened street and empty buildings across the way. Rave was certain he'd seen something, someone, over there.

Not voicing his concerns, he felt Labrihn move farther down the street. Glancing over to see the demon was far enough ahead not to hear him, Rave looked back across the street. Murmuring a soft Latin chant, he felt his power soar out ahead of him. It curled through the air as it searched. If there was someone hiding in the dark, he'd soon know.

He felt the coolness of the cement, the heavy metal of a streetlight... *There.* His senses slammed into a wall of magic so much stronger than his own, Rave physically recoiled. Yanking his power back, his eyes widened as a demon stepped out of the shadows. No, there wasn't just one. There were two.

Great, he thought with a growl. *What the fuck is going on? Did Andras send these guys to check up on us?*

Even as the thought crossed his mind, he knew that wasn't the case. What made this situation potentially more dangerous, though, was the fact he recognized one of the demons.

Castigo...

What was he doing here? The last time Rave had seen him was in the hallway at the club. He knew the demon had eavesdropped on the conversation in the office. Why? Rave had yet to figure that out, but at the time, he'd decided he had too many other things to worry about. Even now, his attention was drawn away from Castigo as he recognized the massive amount of power the other demon gave off.

That must have been what my power ran into, he thought. He knew Castigo's power too well to get it confused with the brick wall he felt his own slam up against. Eyeing the other demon, Rave opened his mouth to say something. He didn't know what. He just felt the need to figure out who this demon was.

Whatever was about to leave his mouth stopped as he slammed his jaw shut. The demon in question had stepped out a little farther from the shadow and held a finger to his lips.

He wants me to be quiet? Okay. Why? What are they doing here? And who in the hell is with Castigo?

Too many questions, all of which made his stomach churn. He watched as Castigo and the mystery demon glanced off to the side, their eyes narrowing. Following their gaze, Rave spotted Labrihn hurrying back his way.

A quick glance across the street showed that they were alone. At least to the naked eye.

"I was right." Labrihn grinned as he came to stop right beside him.

"About?" Rave asked absentmindedly. He hoped his frayed nerves didn't show in his voice.

"There's an angel in the liquor store."

"There's a what?" Rave looked at the demon. "Really?"

"Yes, really. He's standing inside, waiting to buy some alcohol. We should go get him."

"Now? While he's inside with who knows how many humans?"

Rave's mind worked furiously as he tried to figure out what to do. What if Castigo and that other demon were looking for the angel, too? What if they were here for them? Or maybe he was just being paranoid. Nope. In his very long life, he'd discovered there was no such thing as a coincidence.

"Okay. We'll get him in the parking lot. It's secluded. Plus, there are two of us and only one of him. This should be a piece of cake." Labrihn's almost childlike glee made Rave's head spin.

"Which angel is it?"

"What's that matter? We have him outnumbered."

"Yeah, but... We're supposed to be looking for Dev. Not his brothers."

Labrihn gave him a strange look as he shook his head. "I don't really think Andras will be upset if we bring him one of Dev's brothers, do you?"

No, he didn't. With another look around, Rave made up his mind. "Right. Let's get him in the parking lot. We'll grab him and get him back to the club. Should be easy." Except he knew it wasn't going to be easy at all. But Rave didn't have any intention of grabbing this angel anyway. His only thought at this point was getting through the next fifteen minutes unscathed. Between the demons across the way, his idiot companion, and the unknown angel inside, he wasn't very confident right now.

Maybe he could use this as an opportunity. He just needed to get close enough to the angel, preferably without dying, and tell him Andras was looking for Dev. If he could do all of this and lose Labrihn along the way, even better.

"Good. Let's go hide behind some of the cars," Labrihn said, rubbing his hands together. "This will be over before you know it."

Following the demon into the shadows, Rave couldn't help but pray he was right. The sooner this was over, the better. If all went according to plan, he'd walk away from this very much alive...and one demon short.

"Castigo, I need you to stay here."

Castigo, eyes narrowing, glanced at Sy. "And do what?"

"Keep that idiot with Rave from getting to Dev's brother."

He started to nod, stopping suddenly. "Wait... What? Which brother? And how do you know Labrihn is going to come up against one?"

Sy shot him a smirk as he began to move away from him. "Cyrus is inside that liquor store, and if I'm reading this situation correctly, Labrihn wants to overpower him and take him back to Andras."

"Overpower... That's... I really don't..."

"Just keep anything from happening until I get back. Kill Labrihn, if need be, then hold Rave for me to talk to."

"And what about Cyrus? If you're right and he's here, he isn't exactly going to just nod at me and head home."

"You'll be fine. Just try to stay out of his way."

"Stay out of his way? Sure. Yeah. No problem." Castigo watched Labrihn make his way toward the parking lot, a rather reluctant Rave following close behind. "And where are you going while I try to figure out a way to keep this clusterfuck from getting out of hand?"

"I need to reach out to an old friend," Sy said cryptically. "I won't be long."

"An old friend. Who?" As Castigo turned toward his travel companion, he found the street around him empty. He sighed. "Great."

He watched as the demons across the way ducked down behind some vehicles near the back of the lot just as the door to the liquor store opened. Watching as Cyrus stepped out and glanced around, Castigo pressed closer to the wall behind him. His mind immediately warred between the need to get the heck out of there and the understanding that he had to get across the street to keep the big idiot from getting caught. Not that he really thought Cyrus was in any danger from Labrihn, but he wasn't too sure about Rave. With not knowing what side Rave was truly on, he couldn't just leave the outcome to chance.

Well, I could...

Shaking his head, he continued to watch Cyrus make his way toward the parking lot where Rave and Labrihn hid. At any moment, all hell would break loose. He needed to make a decision on what part he wanted to play in it. What choice did he have? He could back an angel, who would probably try to kill him for his trouble, not do a damn thing and perhaps get taken out by Sy, or head back to the club and possibly be killed, or at least severally maimed, by Andras.

Fuck, fuck, fuck!

He took a step forward, then took one back. Anger began to bubble up with each passing second. He was angry at Andras for pulling him into this foolish plan. He was angry at Sy for throwing all the issues with said plan into his face, even though he was already preparing to distance himself from it. And he was angry with himself. Castigo knew better than most that you couldn't hinge your future on the outcome of a single option. But that was exactly what he'd done. There had been no plan B, no backup option for him to fall back on if Andras' ideas didn't pan out. For that, he could only kick one ass. His own.

Then again, he could just let Cyrus do it for him. He was sure the angel would be more than happy to do the job. Knowing he was indeed going to head across the street, Castigo also concluded that getting his ass handed to him was probably exactly what was going to happen.

"Well, shit. Looks like Sy's plan just became my backup," he growled, looking around. "Hope his endgame is better than Andras'."

Looking around one last time, Castigo darted into the street. Moving at an angle, he silently ran up to the front of the liquor store. Standing flush against the building, he took a moment to figure out what his next move should be. He heard Cyrus' steps echo against the silence of the street. This was about to go really bad, really quickly. But maybe...

Reaching into his pocket, he pulled out his cell. If he could let someone know what was about to go down, give the proper individuals a heads-up, maybe he could stop this without actually having to get involved. Well, without having to be in a position to be pummeled by a pissed-off angel anyway.

Scrolling down, he stopped on the name he'd been looking for and hit call. After three rings, Castigo was just about to hang up when someone answered.

"Hello?" a man said hesitantly over the phone.

Suppressing a smirk, Castigo leaned around the side of the building and glanced into the lot. Seeing Cyrus standing quietly by a dumpster, with no sign of the demons, Castigo pulled back and rested his head against the brick wall. "Don't hang up, Dev," he began quickly. "I know you probably want to since you're in hiding and all, but-"

"I must not be hiding so well if I'm on the phone with you."

"Well, you did keep your phone with you. So..." He heard Dev release a harsh laugh at the same time a sudden crashing sound echoed from the lot. "Shit," Castigo hissed out.

"What's going on, Castigo? Why did you call me?"

"Listen, I don't have time to talk. I just wanted to let you know that I'm at the liquor store on McHenry. Your brother's here. And so are a couple demons who are waiting for him in the parking lot."

"What the fuck? What-"

"I know you're with your brothers. So you need to get down here or send them or something. Whatever you're going to do, you need to do it fast. I'm sure Cyrus can take these two, but...." His voice trailed off as movement down the street caught his eye. Castigo heard Dev calling his name as he slowly took the phone from his ear.

There was no way this was happening. His day really couldn't have gone this badly. It just couldn't have. But there it was. At least a dozen of Andras' foot soldiers waltzed their way toward him like it was a damn demon parade.

Fucking Andras! Fucking hell!

Bringing the phone back up to his ear, he growled, "Just get down here."

Hanging up, Castigo slid the phone back into his pocket. Looked like he was going to be in this fight whether he wanted to or not.

Dammit!

Chapter 28

The second Dev's phone started ringing, Nicholas knew something was up.

That phone, which had been a big focal point in a lot of arguments over the past week, had remained with Dev since he'd arrived. A part of Nicholas couldn't quite figure out why his brother insisted on keeping it, but he also didn't want to argue with him. Plus, with how much of a fight he put up to keep it, Nicholas was sure Dev had a good reason.

Watching his brother's hands shake as he answered the phone, Nicholas thought maybe he should have pushed the issue and found out why Dev insisted on keeping it.

After taking a couple deep breaths, Dev answered. "Hello?"

Nicholas knew if he wanted to, he could hear what was being said on the other end, but he still held out hope that his brother would eventually let him in. He frowned slightly as he watched Dev's eyes narrow.

"I must not be hiding so well if I'm on the phone with you," Dev said slowly.

Nicholas watched as his brother ran his free hand over the table, his fingers seeming to brush away some invisible lint.

The nervousness flying off him was undeniable. Looking past Dev, he noticed Darren and Christian leaning against the kitchen counter. He hadn't seen them come in, but was sure if he could feel the sudden emotions swirling around their brother, so could they. Especially Darren, who had made a point of being there for Dev, even when their brother said he didn't need it.

Hearing a forced laugh leave Dev's lips, Nichols turned his focus back on him. He watched Dev's eyebrows furrow and he started shaking his head, his movements jerky. He reached up and thrust a shaky hand through his hair.

"What's going on, Castigo? Why did you call me?" he growled.

As soon as that name left his lips, Nicholas heard a growl behind him. Nicholas didn't have to look up to know that it was Christian throwing his aggression out, and he had good reason. They all did. Castigo was one of the few demons they had ever gone up against who had walked away from the fight. Not once, not twice, but three times. Nicholas wasn't sure if it was a testament to the demon's strength, or just his ability to get the hell out of trouble in the nick of time.

It was probably a little bit of both. Not that he would ever give the demon any kind of credit out loud, but he still had to acknowledge that he had some skills.

Right now, none of that mattered. The only thing that did was finding out why the demon was calling his brother and what needed to be done about it.

Shaking his head, Nicholas glanced up and caught Darren's eyes. His brother's irises were glowing as he nodded at him. Darren obviously thought the same thing.

"What the fuck? What-" Dev's voice was strained as he jumped up from his seat. Nicholas rose, too, as he watched his brother pace back and forth. Christian, who was deathly silent, moved up next to Darren as they came closer to the table. They never took their eyes off Dev as he began to visibly shake. "Castigo?! Castigo?! Dammit, what the hell's going on?"

They watched him continue to pace. His aggravation and worry seemed to grow wildly with each step, then he came to a sudden stop and yanked the phone from his ear. He stared at it in confusion for several long seconds before glancing up and meeting Nicholas' eyes.

"What exactly did he say?" Darren's voice rang out in the silence.

"He said he's at liquor store on McHenry. Cyrus is in trouble," Dev said quietly. He seemed to be warring with what he'd just been told. His eyes flashed angrily, like he wanted to storm out of the house that second, while his body gave off obvious signs of uncertainty and mistrust at what he'd been told. "Castigo said to get down there."

"This is a trap," Christian bit out with an aggressive certainty. His eyes glowed dangerously as he stared at Dev, almost daring him to say otherwise.

Castigo had been one of the leading players in all their recent problems. Nicholas had fought him the first time they'd met. The demon was arrogant, uncaring, and cruel... All things that pointed to this being nothing but a ploy to get them into a position to be harmed. Or away from the house so the demons could try to grab the girls again. Thoughts of Amy still sleeping soundly in his bed upstairs flashed through his mind. He couldn't leave her here unprotected.

A miniscule part of him whispered in the back of his mind. What if Cyrus really were in trouble? What if Castigo were indeed calling to warn them about someone attacking their brother? Could they risk not going only to have something happen to him? Images of the last time Cyrus was taken flew into his mind, causing a chill to crawl up his spine. Pushing them down, he looked over to see Darren shoving his phone back into his pocket.

"Cyrus isn't answering his phone," he said harshly.

"That doesn't mean anything," Christian immediately argued. "He probably just forgot it in his car when he ran into the store. Or maybe he's just ignoring your call. You know? Like he's been ignoring them the past few months. This isn't anything new. Hell, he's probably on his way home right now. If he were in trouble, we'd know."

"Like we did the last time?" Nicholas quietly asked. Standing straighter, he met his brothers' eyes.

"Nicholas-" Christian started.

"Hey, I'm not saying this isn't some kind of a trap. I'm sure it is. But what if he really *is* in danger? Do we really want to just sit here on our asses when there's even a tiny chance Cyrus could be taken from us again?"

The silence stretched out between them as they stood there. Nicholas couldn't explain it, but the more time that passed, the more confident he was that they needed to get to Cyrus.

"I understand why you guys don't trust Castigo. Shit, I don't trust the bastard either. But..." Dev paused, shaking his head. "The past couple weeks or so, I've noticed things have been changing amongst the demons. A few weeks ago, I heard Andras practically attacking Castigo. I don't know exactly what the issue was, but once Andras and Agalon, his second, left the room, I had a chance to talk to the demon."

E.F. Rose

"And?" Darren pushed when Dev seemed to fall into deep thought.

"I don't think he's going to be Andras' puppet much longer, if he even still is." At the mixture of disbelief and trepidation on everyone's faces, Dev raised his hands. "Look, I'm not saying he suddenly woke up and decided to switch to our side. Whatever the reason for his call, I'm sure there is something in it for him. Some agenda he has a stake in. But I did ask him to keep an eye out for anything having to do with Andras and you guys. Actually, I'd asked him to find out if Andras has any other weapons he could use against us. Now, I know you guys must think I'm an idiot for asking a demon to help, but-"

"We don't think you're an idiot," Nicholas jumped in. "If any of us had been in the situation you were, we'd probably reach out to whomever we could, too. I just..." He blew out a breath. "We've had a lot of run-ins with this particular demon. He isn't someone any of us are too eager to trust."

"I get that. I do." Dev looked around the group. "It's just..." He sighed. "Something has felt off to me ever since Cyrus left."

"You didn't mention anything," Nicholas said, moving closer to his brother.

Not meeting any of their gazes, Dev moved off to lean against the counter. His shoulders looked tense as he fidgeted with the bottom of the t-shirt he'd borrowed from Darren. "I figured it was just me being paranoid, worrying about something I had no reason to. I was going to mention it, but..." He looked back up at them, blinking rapidly, eyes shining with unshed tears. "If everything turned out to be okay, I didn't want you looking at me like there was something wrong, like I was broken."

At a loss for words, Nicholas moved over and placed a hand on Dev's arm. "Hey," he said gently, giving his brother's arm a squeeze until he met his eyes. "At no point did I or anyone else in this house think you were broken. Okay? Not once." At Dev's nod, Nicholas looked over at Darren. "I think at least two of us should go to McHenry Street and make sure Cyrus is okay."

"And if we get there and it's a trap?" Christian asked.

"Then we deal with it and get our asses home."

"I think Nicky's right. If Dev has had a bad feeling since Cyrus left, that's even more of a reason to give this info from Castigo some weight," Darren said, raising his hand when Christian opened his mouth. "Even if this is a trap...which is probably the case, considering whom the information came from...there is a huge possibility the demons do, in fact, have

Cyrus. We go, see what's going on, get Cyrus, and come home. I'm sick and tired of these demons, and I'll be damned if we're going to lose another brother because of them."

"So, we go then," Dev said with a nod.

Darren shook his head. "*You* will be staying here with the girls."

"But-"

"No. If this is a trap, it might be just to get you out in the open so they can grab you. You'll stay here, where it's safe. Anyway, we need someone to keep an eye on the girls."

"And why does someone need to keep an eye on us?"

Turning, the guys frowned as they saw Ella, Hayley, and Amy standing in the kitchen doorway next to a very quiet Manuel. The anger in his eyes told Nicholas he'd heard enough to know what was going on. Castigo's involvement in this was meaningless when running the risk of one of their brothers being taken. At least that was how Nicholas felt, and it looked like Manuel was on the same page.

"Because Christian, Manuel, and I-" Darren started.

"And me! I'm going," Nicholas cut in. There was no way he was getting left behind on this. He owed Cyrus a lot, and standing by his side while they fought off demons seemed like a great way to start mending their relationship.

Darren eyed him for a minute, then sighed before turning back toward the girls. "And Nicholas... The four of us need to go downtown for a bit and we'd all feel better if Dev stayed and kept an eye on things."

"Where's Cyrus?" Ella asked as she walked through the room and into Christian's waiting arms.

"He ran to the store," Darren mumbled lamely.

"And you guys need to go downtown to... What?" Hayley narrowed her eyes. "Lend him a hand at almost one o'clock in the morning?" She turned to look squarely at her man, her hands resting firmly on her hips. "Manuel? What's really going on?"

Seeing Amy standing there looking uncertain, Nicholas reached out for her. He was sure she could feel the rising tension in the room, practically see it in the way she held herself. Arms wrapped protectively around her waist, eyes wide as they took in everything going on around her. Grabbing her arm, Nicholas pulled her against him. One hand rubbed circles on her back until he felt her relax in his arms.

"They got a call. I don't know exactly what was said, but it sounds like Cyrus might be in trouble," he heard Manuel tell Hayley.

"So Cyrus called?" Hayley asked him.

"No, um..."

"He texted?"

"Well, no. It wasn't Cyrus who called," Manuel said, waving a hand through the air. "He probably doesn't even know he's in trouble."

"Unless they tried to take him already," Christian murmured.

"If they did, we definitely would have felt it," Nicholas chimed in.

"Because he would have leveled the whole block," Darren said with a shake of his head.

"Probably half the town," Manuel smirked.

"Okay, okay," Hayley said, smothering a laugh at their antics. "If you didn't hear from Cyrus himself, who called? How do you guys know he's in trouble?"

As Nicholas and his brothers glanced at each other, the women all pulled back and gave them *the look*. The look that said you'd better tell the truth or else. And you couldn't even think about lying because they would know if you did. Even Amy had a beautiful eyebrow raised as she looked up at him. Knowing the reaction they would get when the women discovered they planned on listening to what a demon said caused him to pause in his response.

We obviously all feel the same way.

"It was Castigo. He called to tell me Cyrus was in trouble," Dev said, causing his brothers to groan.

Okay, maybe not.

"What?" Ella gasped.

"Are you guys out of your mind?!" Hayley demanded.

"Who's Castigo?" Amy asked, gripping his arm.

Nicholas glanced at her, tuning out the rising voices around him as he rubbed his hands up and down her arms. "He's a demon we've had run-ins with before."

"Obviously not very positive run-ins, if the way everyone's acting says anything." She smirked and tilted her head to the side.

"No, not very positive at all."

"But he called to tell you Cyrus is in trouble?"

"Yeah," Nicholas said with a frown. "Not too sure why, though."

"Do you think it's a trap?"

"Probably."

Amy seemed to think on that as she looked at him, her eyes searching his face. He wasn't sure for what, but she must have found whatever it was because she gave him a small smile. "You should go check it out."

"You think so?"

"Yes," she said with confidence, drawing everyone else's attention. "Regardless of your past with this demon, you believe him. I can see it in your eyes." She reached up and ran her right hand over his cheek and around his neck, pulling him toward her until their foreheads touched. "Go, bring your brother back."

He pulled back and looked at her before turning to see his brothers watching them. "You heard her," he said with a smirk. "Let's go get him."

Darren nodded. "Dev will stay here with you girls." He looked at everybody, especially Hayley, who opened her mouth. "No arguing. This is as much for him to be here for you three as it is for you to be here for him. We don't know what we're going to find once we get there, so we need to keep our heads on straight. We can't do that if we're worried about you. You four will watch over each other until we get back. There shouldn't be any people around, so we'll materialize in a nearby alley, then get in and grab Cyrus before those demons even know we're there. With any luck, we shouldn't be gone long."

Nicholas ran upstairs to grab his compound bow and arrows, Amy following close behind.

"We'll be back soon," he murmured, strapping his harness across his chest. "Just stay by Dev until I get back."

Amy nodded, watching him closely as he clipped his bow to his back. "I will. Just... Be careful."

Walking up to her, he leaned down, giving her a soft kiss. "Hey, this is nothing we haven't faced before." Running his fingers along her cheek, he smiled. "Like Darren said, we'll be in and out in a matter of minutes. Everything's going to be okay."

"Promise?"

"Promise."

With a last kiss, they headed downstairs and out the back door. Nicholas stepped up next to Christian, Manuel, and Darren as he glanced back at Amy. She stood with Dev and the girls, her arms crossed over her chest, her bottom lip pulled between her teeth. He wanted to go to her, tell her again that everything would work out, even though they both knew it may not. He was sure going to try his damnedest to make it so.

The air around him hummed as he and his brothers allowed their power to grow. His skin tingled as he readied himself, picturing the street surrounding the liquor store.

With one last breath and an exaggerated wink, which made Amy smile, he felt the world around him dim to nothing. When his surroundings came back into focus, he stood next to his brothers right down the street from the liquor store...and into the midst of utter chaos.

What the fuck!

Chapter 29
Thirty Minutes Earlier

A mixture of lemon, disinfectant, and stale air assaulted Cyrus' nose as he stepped into the empty liquor store. The sound of the door closing behind him made him pause for a second before turning toward the isle where he knew the Crown Royal was stocked. The past few months, he'd almost become more familiar with this isle than he was with his own closet.

He had to admit that his drinking had become a problem. What started out as just a way to get his mind to relax after his time with the Shadow Demons had quickly become a necessity for him to be able to get through each day.

The amount he needed had increased, too.

At one time, it would only take a drink or two to drown out the nightmares and dull the pain. Now he was lucky if a bottle of Crown got him through the night. And, contrary to what his brothers thought, a bottle was the only company he had in his bed in a long, long time.

The stories that had helped give his brothers this false idea of his many conquests was nothing but a fabricated, sometimes detailed and outlandish, lie on his part.

It was just easier if they believed he was a player who enjoyed an occasional drink rather than the truth.

Running his fingers over the bottle's cool glass, he felt a shiver race over his skin at the thought of taking in that amber liquid. He wished he didn't need this, but even now, he felt the haziness in his mind receding as the last bit of alcohol in his system started to wear off.

With a sudden sense of urgency, he grabbed the bottle off the shelf and made his way to the counter.

No words were spoken as the cashier rang him up and took his cash. At almost one in the morning, what was there really to say? He managed to hold back a sigh as he listened to the computer spit out his receipt.

Another night, another bottle, he mused as he watched the guy put his bottle into a brown paper bag. Always a brown paper bag. *Like nobody knows what's in there.*

Cyrus gave the man a nod before picking up his bag and heading out into the cold.

Silence greeted him as he began to make his way toward the parking lot. The sound of his shoes hitting the damp sidewalk echoed through the street. He couldn't remember it being this quiet when he'd pulled up. Looking around the empty street, he immediately noted the lack of...anything. Even at night, he could count on there being at least one or two people driving down the main road. He couldn't even hear the crickets that were normally around, and the air had an eerie stillness to it, as if the world itself was holding its breath.

Yet he couldn't sense anything. If he were to just go by his senses alone, he'd swear it was just a normal night, nothing dark and menacing lurking in the shadows. But he'd learned that senses could be mistaken, messed with, and every cell in his body told him something was wrong.

At the opening of the parking lot, he paused. Cyrus' mind screamed at him to get the hell out of there. To just step back into the shadows and get his ass home. If he were smart, he'd do just that. But smart, or practical, or insightful, or any of the other words Darren liked to throw around didn't seem to play a role in his line of thinking at that exact second. There was just something, some physical force holding him there, an inner voice whispering that he needed to stay.

Scanning the practically empty lot, Cyrus' eyes hovered on the three vehicles parked there. He'd parked his Dodge Ram near the back of the lot. More out of habit than anything else. He supposed if they'd been born and raised here, not chucked down from the Heavens, he would have probably been the kid who always sat in the back of the class. Unlike Nicky, who would probably be smack dab in the front, making everyone laugh with his smart-ass remarks.

Barely suppressing a chuckle, Cyrus looked toward the other two vehicles. The one closest to him and near the parking lot entrance was a beat-up Toyota, its paint visibly chipping. It was old, worn, and if he concentrated hard enough, he could just catch the essence of the store's clerk around it.

The third car, what he assumed had been a rather nice Camaro at one time, was so rusted and covered with weeds, he doubted its owner even remembered the car was still there. It had been backed into the spot, the dumpster on one side and the worn, brick wall surrounding the lot on the other side. It was the darkness around the weathered car that Cyrus found his gaze lingering on.

There was something there, something in the corner. A presence hiding in plain sight, causing his skin to crawl.

A soft noise suddenly reached his ears, drawing his attention away from the corner. It sounded like shoes scraping against the ground. Narrowing his eyes, he could just make out a small movement in the shadows underneath the Toyota. Taking a deep breath, Cyrus set his bag on the ground and began to move toward the car, keeping the darkened parts of the lot in sight.

The closer he got to the clerk's car, the more he began to make out the sound of someone breathing. With a frustrated shake of his head, he realized his other senses seemed to be slightly off. Try as he might, Cyrus couldn't tell if he was about to come upon a human, demon, or something else.

Not like anything can go easy for me, he thought with a mental snarl. *Just one more fucked-up day after another*.

He didn't get time to put too much thought into it, though. The sound of shoes once again reached his ears and pulled him from his musings. This quickly led him to realize that whatever was on the other side of the car may be planning to run. Quickening his steps, Cyrus dove around the car. In one smooth move, he had his fingers curled in the shirt of the Being and lifted him into the air, harshly pushing the figure into the wall. A sudden gasp and the smell of fear stopped Cyrus cold. He became aware of three things.

One, he was holding a very human male up against the wall.

Two, this human couldn't be more than fourteen.

Three, the kid was scared out of his mind. Wide brown eyes blinked rapidly as the kid's hands gripped Cyrus' wrists.

"What the hell, kid?" Cyrus whispered. His head whipped around as he looked at the empty parking lot. Looking toward the broken-down car in the corner, he noticed it seemed to have become even darker there.

Demon.

The word whispered through his mind as he narrowed his eyes. It made sense. There were demons out there who could cloak themselves, hiding in plain sight. If one of those were hiding in the parking lot, as seemed to be the case, the shit was about to hit the fan.

"Let me go," the kid's voice suddenly reminded Cyrus of what he was doing.

"Shh," he hissed.

"Dude, j-just put me down. I didn't do nothin'."

Looking down, Cyrus saw that he held the kid so high, his feet weren't touching the ground. Instead, the soles scrapped along the bricks as the kid struggled. With a grunt, Cyrus lowered him to the ground. He still gripped his shirt, though. Not only to steady the kid as he found his footing, but to make sure he didn't do something stupid, like run right into the demons Cyrus was sure waited in the shadows.

"Let go," the kid growled, twisting in Cyrus' grasp.

"Would you just...," Cyrus whispered, giving the kid a little shake and pushing his back against the wall. "Hey. Just stop. Shit, be quiet."

"Dude, get off me," the kid said, pushing against Cyrus' chest.

"For the love of... Just stop already. I swear-" Cyrus stopped when he heard a chuckle from behind him. Spinning around, he gripped the kid's arm as he pushed him behind his back. His eyes latched onto the demon's red gaze. "Great," he growled.

"Having trouble managing that kid, Feathers? Damn. It's a wonder you and your brothers have been able to accomplish anything when you can't even keep a kid in line," the demon laughed.

Cyrus' eyes shifted to the side as another demon came out of the shadows. A sharp gasp from behind him gave away the fact that the kid had just noticed their new companions. Taking a closer look at them, he could only guess at the nightmarish images these two would bring to the kid's dreams. While the one running his mouth was bald with red eyes, the newcomer had a mess of brown hair and light gray eyes. He also had a slight smirk on his face as he looked between Cyrus and the other demon. It wasn't until his gaze moved past Cyrus that the smirk slipped away.

Obviously, the demon wasn't happy about having a human in the mix, though Cyrus had no idea why. After all, the rule of thumb with demons was the more bodies to draw blood from, the better. This boy should barely be a blip on the demon's radar, especially given the shitstorm that was about to go down. Yet the look on his face said he was definitely not happy with the kid's presence.

Meeting his stormy gray eyes, Cyrus felt his own narrow. "The only trouble I see is the sudden arrival of you dipshits."

"Now, now," the red-eyed demon drawled as the other remained silent. "There's no reason to be like that. We just happened to be waltzing by and noticed you having some problems corralling this...child."

"I'm not a child," came a disgruntled voice from behind him.

Sparing only the briefest glance over his shoulder, Cyrus turned back toward the demons. "Waltzing by, huh? Last I heard, Andras had all his dogs on a tight leash. I didn't think you were allowed to walk around unsupervised."

"What the fuck do you know, angel?" Red Eyes growled, taking a step closer. "I'll tell you what. Nothing. You know nothing."

"Fine. Enlighten me," Cyrus said, pushing the kid farther behind him.

If it were just him, he'd lash out at the demons and get his ass home, like he should have before walking into the lot. However, he couldn't leave the kid. He was actually glad he ended up in the lot because there was no way this kid should be left out in the cold. Something he would need to talk to him about as soon as he figured out a way to get them both out of here, preferably alive. Maybe he could get the demons to argue amongst themselves, or get them distracted so he could get the kid out of there. Cyrus' mind jumped from one idea to another as he stared the demons down. Anything that came to mind was quickly discarded because the outcome ended up the same. If he could only get a message to his brothers...

Feeling the weight of his phone in his back pocket, Cyrus shifted his feet. If he could slip his hand from the kid's arm to his back without the demons noticing, get his phone out, and hit the right button, maybe he would luck out by reaching one of his brothers and both of them would make it out of this okay. Cyrus could practically count all the ways this could go wrong. But he was quickly running out of options, and if the tension radiating off Red Eye told him anything, he was also running out of time. Decision made, he slowly began to move his hand. He soon had it in his pocket, sliding his phone free. If he could just-

A sharp pain radiated through his arm, making him gasp and drop his phone to the ground.

The red-eyed demon tisked. "I don't think we need to get your family involved in this. Not just yet anyway."

Glancing at the singed material on his coat sleeve, Cyrus growled. The fucking demon had somehow thrown a bolt of power right at him and he hadn't even seen it coming. "That's just fine with me. I don't need them here to kick both your asses."

"I highly doubt that," Red Eyes sneered. "But why don't we just put it to the test. Then, once we've beaten you down, you can watch as we do the same to that pansy ass brother of yours. You really should have left Andras' pet where he belonged."

As flashes of Dev ran through his mind, Cyrus felt his jaw clench. "So that's your endgame here? You want to use me so you can get my brother back into your hands? Well, I hate to burst your bubble, since you've obviously put a lot of thought into this little plan of yours, but it's not going to work."

"Oh yeah? And why is that?" the demon growled.

"Isn't it obvious?" Cyrus asked, angling his body as he prepared for a fight.

He felt his power building as he reached out to the shadows around them. A small part of him worried about what the kid behind him was about to witness, but it just couldn't be helped. Cyrus highly doubted these two demons would allow him to call a timeout in order to get the boy out of there.

Smirking, Cyrus let out a soft chuckle as he saw the barest flash of unease in the demon's red eyes. "There's no way you can take me. It just won't happen. Hell, I'm not even sure *both* of you could take me."

"Well then," the red-eyed demon smirked. "It's a good thing we aren't alone." As the last word left his lips, Cyrus heard growls and shouts coming from the street.

Reaching beneath his shirt to grab his crescent moon knives, expecting to find the solid metal handle of his intertwined curved blades, Cyrus growled when he realized they weren't there. Since this was only supposed to have been a quick trip to the liquor store, he'd opted to leave his blades at home. Which, in hindsight, was dumb since he knew the chances of running into a demon had risen drastically in the last few months.

Idiot.

Seeing the knowing smirk on the demon before him, Cyrus just snarled. "Missing something?" the demon asked with a laugh.

Deciding he was done talking, Cyrus felt his power swell within him. It called to the darkness, to the shadows that curled around the edge of the parking lot, which were normally kept at bay by the lone light flickering nearby. The red-eyed demon seemed to guess that the time to talk was over because Cyrus watched his body tense. The other demon, still sporting a faint look of uncertainty, took a couple steps to the side. Whether to distance himself from his companion or get himself into a better position to attack, Cyrus wasn't sure.

Hearing a soft gasp behind him, Cyrus suddenly remembered the boy at his back. *Shit!* His mind whirled with different ways to get the kid out of there. Unfortunately, each idea was quickly discarded at the knowledge that his window of opportunity had closed. If the two demons before him didn't scream that, the increasing growls and yells from the street definitely did.

Reaching behind him, he gave the boy a gentle push. "Get down and stay against the wall," he hissed over his shoulder. Cyrus didn't have time to see if the kid did what he said because the red-eyed demon suddenly rushed him.

Moving quickly, Cyrus pushed his power out, slamming the shadows into the demon and shoving him back, knocking him off his feet. He watched him bounce against the ground. A loud grunt was heard before the demon jumped back up. He sent a shot of power toward him, but Cyrus was ready. Batting the glowing ball away, he decided it was time to go on the offensive and lunged toward the demon before he could get off another shot. The sound of yelling reached his ears, telling him the other demons where getting closer. He'd soon be surrounded by them. Having no idea how to get out of this, he felt his stomach clench.

The air seemed to crackle as he collided with the demon. Their powers slammed into each other with such force, he was surprised either of them was still in once piece. As it was, the momentum of the demon sent Cyrus flying backwards, hitting the ground with a grunt as he felt like a truck had landed on him. The demon was a lot heavier than he'd expected, so the physical impact rocked him to his core.

Damn heavy ass demon!

Grunting, Cyrus batted away a weak attempt at a punch from the demon above him. *Obviously, this idiot never thought he'd need any hand-to-hand training.* With a quick jab of his elbow, Cyrus landed a solid hit against cold flesh. Reveling in the curses gasped by Red Eye, he thanked whomever was listening that he was only up against one of the two demons. Dodging another sad attempt at a hit, he rammed his elbow into the demon's side once more, hearing a grunt.

Take that, you piece of shit.

Cyrus had lost track of the other demon as the fighting began. But he couldn't really worry about that now. Not when the red-eyed demon was breathing in his face...literally.

Twisting his body, Cyrus used his power to try and get out of the demon's grasp. He didn't know how long he'd been on the ground, but he knew he couldn't remain there. Any chance he had of getting himself and the kid out of this alive would disappear if he couldn't get back on his feet.

Concentrating on the shadows around them, Cyrus willed them to move. He felt the darkness, as if it was an extension of himself. Just like the weather was to Nicholas and the atmosphere was to Manuel. Visualizing the shadows doing what his hands couldn't, Cyrus saw the demon above him jerk backwards. A ribbon of darkness had wrapped itself around the demon's neck. Red Eye tried to rip at the shadowy binds, having no luck as he was pulled away.

When Cyrus started to climb to his feet, he felt a rush of power slam into him. Spinning, he spotted several demons running into the parking lot. Two in particular had separated from the rest and headed in his direction. Their red eyes blazed as if they'd just won a prize, and if they got their hands on him, Cyrus supposed he would be. He was sure Andras had offered up quite the reward to any of his demons who managed to bag themselves one of the Guardians. He could only imagine what that prick had in store for them. Not that he was going to allow himself to get caught so he could find out.

Fighting to get his feet under him, he staggered to the side, dodging another ball of power flying toward his head.

Damn, that was close.

Hearing a yelp from his right, he turned to see a demon lunging for the kid. The boy's eyes looked wild as he scrambled back, tripping over his own feet in an attempt to get away from the nightmare that was almost upon him.

Cyrus growled as he fought against the demonic power pushing against him. The two headed his way sneered as they moved closer, their power attempting to keep him down, hold him there until they could get to him. Yeah, that wasn't going to happen.

As he pushed his power at them, all the while keeping the shadows gripped around Red Eye's neck and listening to what was happening with the kid, Cyrus knew he would soon start losing strength. So if he was going to do anything to make a dent in the fucking chaos around him, he was going to need to do it now.

Fighting against the power the two demons threw at him, he lashed out with some of his own, relishing in the small sense of joy he felt when he watched them stumble from the hit.

Taking advantage of the small reprieve, Cyrus looked at the boy just in time to see the demon lurch forward, grabbing onto his arm and yanking him off the ground with a powerful jerk.

"No!" the kid yelled, trying to pull his arm out of the demon's grasp...unsuccessfully. Panic made his body shake uncontrollably, the vibration in his demeanor clear even from where Cyrus stood.

"Let him go," Cyrus ground out, putting as much force behind his words as he could muster. He felt his power slip a bit, accompanied by a growl from the demon that seemed to echo around him. "You don't want him."

"Don't worry, Guardian. We didn't come here looking for some little human to play with," the demon smirked, yanking the boy up against him. He curled his hand around the kid's throat, effectively putting a stop to any further struggle. "After all, we're here for you."

"Well then, if you're only here for me, there's no reason to hold the boy."

"We did come for you, but now that I have this kid in my arms, as well..." Cyrus cringed as he watched the demon lean down to run his nose along the side of the boy's head. "Well, I can't very well just let him go now, can I?"

Cyrus met the boy's eyes. He tried to convey to him that even though it may not seem like it, everything would be fine. Hell, if Cyrus had his way, these demons wouldn't make it out of this lot at all. He couldn't tell if his message had been received, but the boy visibly relaxed as they stared at each other. The demon, possibly frustrated at his lack of response, gave the boy a not so gentle shake. At the slight flinch in the kid's eyes, Cyrus felt the anger within him erupt. He lunged toward them.

His forward motion was halted as the two demons he'd momentarily forgotten took hold of his arms and pulled him back. This mistake cost Cyrus the tentative hold he had on his power. His body was flooded with a rush of demonic power, the two holding him digging their nails into his arms as he fought against them.

Cyrus felt a scorch of heat hit his back, causing him to gasp and look behind him.

Red Eye was now on his feet. His eyes blazed as he threw another ball of power into him.

"That looked like it hurt," the demon holding the boy said, drawing Cyrus' attention. His grin widened now that Cyrus was looking at him, a grin that grew larger as he shook another whimper from the kid. "Guess you pissed off Labrihn, huh? Not a smart idea."

He didn't answer the demon as the others chuckled at the comment. Too much of what was happening pulled at his memory. Chills began to race down his spine as Cyrus attempted to remind himself to keep breathing.

"Well, I don't think Andras will fault me if I choose to rough up his newest pet," the demon, Labrihn, laughed from behind him. Cyrus felt another burst of pain spread across his back, making him cry out. He felt his knees buckle, only the hold of the two demons at his side keeping him from falling as his mind fought the need to give up. Flashes from his time with the Shadow Demons clouded his mind, images of that horrific nightmare he'd thought long buried.

"Wonder if the boss will let me keep the human," the one holding the kid asked.

"I don't see why not, Etch," Labrihn said, moving closer to Cyrus. "After we get this one to Andras, I'm sure he'll be more than happy to reward our hard work."

"You leave him alone," Cyrus gritted out, still fighting, even as the growing fear from his own past threatened to consume him.

"Why would I do that?" Etch hissed. "It's been too long since I've been allowed to have any fun. Plus, this little toy is my reward for all the shit I've had to deal with." The demon twisted his upper body, raising his arms just enough to lift the kid's feet off of the ground.

The sense of fear and look of pain on the kid's face pulled Cyrus from the darkness his subconscious started falling into. Grinding his teeth, he pulled against the demons holding him, his back bowing. In a flash of light, his black wings spread out behind him. A loud curse and the sound of something hitting the ground behind him told him the force of his wings had hit Labrihn hard enough to drop his ass.

That was one demon off his back.

Thank fuck!

The other two were a lot luckier. While they'd definitely felt the power from him releasing his wings, their grip on his arms hadn't loosened.

Dammit!

Flapping his wings, he lifted off the ground slightly, only to be yanked back down. "Fuck," he growled, his knees giving under the sudden pressure the demons pushed on him.

He knew his eyes blazed as he stared at the demon, Etch, who still had a tight grasp on the kid's throat. He was about to yell, scream, let his power roll through him like an atom bomb and pray for the best when the silver-eyed demon suddenly appeared in his peripheral vision. In all the chaos, he'd completely forgotten about that one. Cyrus watched him now, though. His eyes narrowed, the demon made his way toward Etch and the kid.

"I can't allow you to harm the child," the demon said, his voice low and threatening.

"Good thing it's not up to you," Etch growled. "This kid is mine. Get your own toy, Rave."

"No," Rave responded simply. Cyrus watched in stunned silence as the demon walked up to Etch with such confidence, anyone would wonder if he were in charge. Reaching out, Rave grasped Etch's wrist. Cyrus saw his wince of pain at the contact. His grasp on the kid instantly loosened as he attempted to pull back from Rave.

Rave used his other hand to pull the boy away from the demon, instantly pushing him to the side as he stepped into Etch's face. "You take things too far, brother."

"In your eyes maybe," Etch gasped.

It was obvious he was trying to hold onto his anger, even as his lips thinned and his eyes widened. The two demons stared at each other, neither blinking. All the while, angry yells came from the street, the demons on either side of him seeming to tense further.

"What is your game here, Rave?" one of demons holding Cyrus asked.

"Game?" Rave echoed, slowly turning from Etch. His eyes met Cyrus' briefly before narrowing to look between the two demons. The silver in his gaze flashed, the light from them visible to Cyrus.

This guy is intense.

"This isn't a game," Rave continued, holding the demons' gaze. "This is a war."

"You say that as if you are not with us," the demon to Cyrus' left sneered.

"Yeah," the demon to his right bit out. "If you're not with us, we have a serious problem."

"Oh, I'm not the one with the problem." Rave chuckled darkly. Cyrus barely repressed a shudder from the power threading through the demon's obvious threat. Keeping his gaze on Rave, Cyrus' eyes just about popped out of his head when, in a millisecond, the demon had gone from Etch's side to now standing in front of the demon who'd last spoken. "And to address the question I see swimming in your eyes... No, I'm *not* with you."

In a move that happened so quickly Cyrus almost missed it, Rave snapped one of his hands out, twisting it into the demon's shirt as he pulled the demon away from him. The demon's grasp on his arm disappeared as he reached up to clutch at Rave's hands, which were now gripped tightly around his throat.

The sudden cries of pain that left the demon's lips echoed around them as Rave lifted him into the air. The power thrumming around them made Cyrus take several steps back, pushing at the other demon who, even though he still gripped his arm, had now become nothing more than a frightened statue.

Cyrus watched as a light began to blaze from the screaming demon's mouth and eyes. The brighter the light got, the louder the demon's screams became until it finally seemed like he couldn't scream anymore. Whatever power Rave pushed into him seemed to be burning him from the inside out. The smell of sulfur and ash burned Cyrus' nose as he blinked against the now blinding light. He physically felt the light pouring from within the now silent demon getting brighter until, suddenly, everything went dark.

Blinking rapidly, Cyrus watched as the demon's body, now nothing more than a husk, hit the ground with a resounding thud.

Cyrus had never seen a demon do that to another before. Never. It almost looked like what Christian did to a demon when he removed their blackness. But instead of sucking it out, it looked like Rave had just burned it.

"What the f-" he began, cut off by the cursing from the demon next to him.

"What the fuck, Rave? You've really done it now. Wait until Andras hears about this, you piece of shit. He'll have you locked in his dungeon before you even know what hit you. He'll-"

"Oh, shut up," Rave hissed, stepping over the lifeless body at his feet. "If I were you, I'd start seriously thinking about whether or not you should finish that thought."

"Fuck you, Rave," the demon snarled, moving away from Cyrus. "Etch, grab this fucker so we can take him, the angel, and your new pet back to Andras."

At the mention of the boy, Cyrus glanced over to find him curled into a ball by the fence, his eyes huge as they flickered around him. A need to get to the boy, to get him out of there, came over Cyrus. He shifted quietly on his feet and began moving in the kid's direction. He kept his steps light so as not to draw the attention from the still snarling demon. A quick glance in Rave's direction showed the demon looking back at him, his eyes blank while his stance gave off the impression he was no threat. Though he would never trust a demon to not be a threat, Cyrus figured he needed to go with his gut on this one. It told him to leave the other demons to Rave and get to the kid.

His eyes landing back on the boy, he quickly caught his gaze and lifted a finger to his lips.

A nod was his only response, the only one Cyrus needed, before he tucked his wings to his back and continued moving in his direction.

"What the hell, Etch?" a loud growl rang out, causing Cyrus to pause and look toward the demons.

The one called Etch had moved closer to the other two, but not to grab Rave. Instead, Etch stood close to Rave's side, staring down at the demon who had been holding onto Cyrus only moments ago.

"You know how it is, Trao." Etch shrugged. "Whether I agree with Rave or not, he's still my brother. From the looks of it, I guess I'm switching sides."

"You fucking traitor," Trao snarled. "Then I guess you'll being joining your brother in Andras' cell, won't you?"

"Not likely. But you don't need to worry your little head over that. It's not like you're going to be around to find out."

"Oh, I'll be around all right. And I'll be laughing at every ounce of pain the boss inflicts on you. Cuz it's not just me you're going up against," Trao crowed as he glanced toward the street.

Following his gaze, Cyrus spotted several more demons heading their way, each with a glint of rage in their eyes. If that wasn't bad enough, a grunt from his left showed Labrihn pushing himself to his feet.

Fuck.

Rave and Etch spread out, both getting ready to take on the demons quickly surrounding them.

"Glad I didn't miss out on all the fun," Labrihn snarled, drawing Cyrus' attention.

"Oh, good," Cyrus growled back as he turned toward the demons, positioning himself between them and the kid. "Here I thought your weak little demon mind was out for the count."

"I'll show you who's fucking weak."

Spreading his wings, Cyrus felt the power within him begin to build once again. "Bring it, you red-eyed piece of shit."

As Labrihn and the other demons snarled and surrounded them, Cyrus mentally shook his head as he realized he was about to be fighting alongside demons. If anyone had ever asked him if he'd willingly work with a demon, let alone two, he would have punched them right in the face for even suggesting something so ridiculous. It looked like that was exactly what was about to happen, though. His brothers would have a field day with this whole mess.

Cyrus felt a pang run through him. He hoped he'd make it out of this. Even with the odds against him, he had to hold onto the belief that he'd get home to his family. He just couldn't leave them, not now that they had Nicky and Dev back where they belonged.

A sudden shift of the ground beneath their feet caused everyone to quiet, glancing around. Looking up, Cyrus couldn't stop the grin from spreading across his face when he noticed the heavy clouds that had gathered above them. A second later, a flash of lightning hitting the street was followed by a shriek of what Cyrus could only assume was an injured demon. He laughed hysterically.

Still chuckling, he glanced at the demons, who now stared at him in anger and hatred. "Sure hope you guys brought out the big guns tonight," he cackled, sending a quick nod toward a smirking Rave and confused Etch. Looking at Labrihn, he tilted his head and watched in amusement as uncertainty flew across his face. "It seems my brothers have joined the party and things are about to get real interesting."

Chapter 30

Dodging yet another demon who had been sent flying through the air by one of his brothers, Nicholas couldn't help but chuckle. As much as he was pissed these assholes thought they'd take his brother away from them, he had to admit, he was enjoying himself.

Judging by the taunts and laughing coming from his brothers, he wasn't the only one.

Calling upon the storm he'd conjured up, Nicholas sent a lightning bolt onto an approaching demon. His scream was music to his ears as he felt the lightning strike vibrate across his skin.

The demons appeared to be multiplying by the second. Every time he blinked, it seemed like more of them came out of the shadows. There was a feeling of unease in the back of his mind about the fact that Andras had this many demons at his beck and call, but he just didn't have much time to put any real thought into it.

Shelving his concern for later, Nicholas faced off with another demon. This one just as angry and ugly as the rest. His red-black eyes glinted in the dim light as he shifted on his feet.

Flipping his crossbow in his hands, Nicholas angled it so the razor-sharp metal edges faced the incoming demon. He'd created his bow in such a way that he could not just send one arrow flying after another, but if the need arose, he could use the metal edges along the back as a knife. With this many demons around, he'd never been happier about the added option.

Nicholas watched the demon's face twist into a snarl as his body tensed. It didn't take long before the demon let out a growl and lunged, his clawed fingers splayed before him in preparation of ripping into Nicholas' flesh. Though he would give the demon kudos for looking to inflict a shitload of damage, he would never know if his plan would have panned out. As soon as the demon was within striking distance, Nicholas flicked his wrist away from him, slashing the edge of his bow across the front of the demon...opening him up from stomach to collarbone. As he howled in pain, Nicholas finished him by dragging his bow across his throat, silencing his cries and dropping him to the ground.

Turning, he watched Christian slice his dagger through the air, dropping another demon who tried to attack him. *Wow*, Nicholas thought as he twisted to the left, sending an arrow into the chest of an oncoming demon. *We're going to have quite the mess to clean up once this is all said and done.*

The ground shook beneath his feet, causing him to teeter a bit. An angry shout drew his attention toward Manuel. He watched his brother open a hole beneath a group of demons. His hands flung out before him, he pushed his power into the Earth, causing the ground to swallow the demons.

"Holy shit," Nicholas hissed, watching the ground close over them. He'd seen his brother in action before, but the power residing within Manuel still never ceased to amaze him.

"Right?" Christian said from beside him. Nicholas didn't know when his brother had made his way to his side, but he chuckled at the look of awe spreading across his face. It didn't falter as Christian shifted his weight and plunged one of his black daggers into the side of a demon's head. "Where are all these fuckers coming from?" he grunted, yanking his knife back and letting the demon drop to the ground.

"I was just wondering the same thing," Nicholas responded, reaching for one of his arrows and letting it fly straight into an approaching demon's sternum. "We need to figure out how to deal with them all, though. I can sense Cyrus in that parking lot and he needs us."

"Your brother is ours," a guttural voice said from beside them.

"Yeah, I don't think so," Nicholas snapped, pulling another arrow from his case. He felt Christian next to him, saw the glint of his blades out of the corner of his eye, sensed his power swirling through the air. Watching another five demons come up beside the one who spoke, Nicholas tightened his grip on his bow.

Glancing around, he spotted Manuel battling it out with two other demons. His sica sliced through the air in a smooth, sure arc as he went on the offensive. Its curved edge glowed softly from the power flowing through it, the air around it practically singing as it twisted and turned in moves so practiced and beautiful.

Not far from him, Darren also took on his own group of demons. His broadsword clashed with theirs, the sound ringing in the air as he swung the powerful blade over his head and across his center. Nicholas saw his brother pull his sword back with one hand while thrusting his other out before him, sending his power into two of the demons, causing them to drop to their knees and grasp their heads, wailing in pain.

The area was chaotic, demons attacking them at every turn. The thought there may be no end in sight to the number of demons crawling out of the shadows brought on a very real, very dark feeling in the center of Nicholas' chest.

Feeling Christian's presence next to him, he brought his focus back to the six demons fanning out before them. Each one held a blade of some sort, their eyes narrowed and glowing. In response, Nicholas pushed his own power into the night. The wind picked up around them as he fed into it, even reaching so far as to cause a deep rumble of thunder from above them.

"You can't possibly believe you'll win against us." Nicholas smirked.

"Of course not," one of the demons hissed. "We're just here to keep you all busy."

"Busy?" Christian shook his head. "I'd hardly say you're keeping us busy. That would infer this is work for us, that you think we couldn't just end this little fiasco right now if we wanted to. But, for the sake of argument, let's say this *is* a hardship for us. What exactly is it you're trying to keep us from?"

"Thought that would be pretty obvious," another demon chuckled. "Guess you guys are not as smart as Andras thought. Pity, I was really hoping for more of an intellectual challenge over, well...this." His snarkiness caused the other demons to snicker as they shifted on their feet.

"I think you should watch your mouth," Manuel sneered. "I may start to take offense."

The banter continued as Nicholas felt his stomach drop. Looking past the sarcasm in the demon's comment, he came to the sudden realization who these demons where working to keep them from. "You'll never take Cyrus," he spat, giving voice to what he suspected was their main goal. He felt Christian tense next to him.

"Please," a demon laughed. "He may be powerful, but he's no match for a group of demons, let alone Labrihn and Rave. He'll never take them all. Shit, I'd love to see him try. I mean, he may be able to take out a few, but all of them?" He shook his head. "No. He'll be taken from you before this night is out."

"Yeah," another demon piped up. "And after Andras has him in his cell, we'll be sent out to retrieve Dev next. Andras wasn't too happy when his little toy disappeared. Not that you guys would know anything about where he could have gone, right? No? No worries. I'm sure once he hears that we have one of his brothers, the pathetic piece of shit will come to us."

By now, all the demons seemed to have stopped their advance and surrounded them. They'd spread out, causing the angels to stand back to back so they could protect themselves. Nicholas felt

Manuel bump up against his arm at the same time he sensed Darren moving up closer to Christian. The four of them stood there, staring down the demons. Nicholas felt their powers growing as the seconds ticked by. His own hovered just above him, mixing with his brothers' powers as they shifted their stance, preparing for when the demons attacked.

The more time that passed with them all just looking at each other, the more irritated Nicholas became. Seriously, if they took any longer, he'd run over to the liquor store for a snack. Smirking at the thought, he glanced that way, chuckling when he saw the open sign still on. As soon as they got there, the Guardians threw up the Shade, but there had to have been some yelling before then. Guess the business owner figured he should stay open in case someone needed a drink after the fighting. Maybe he was right. Nicholas could sure use a drink, and he wasn't even done beating on these idiots.

"What are you laughing at?" one of the demons in front of him snarled. His red eyes glowed as he glared his way.

"You," Nicholas said simply, grinning as he shifted his weight from foot to foot. "I find this little show of force rather funny."

"Yeah? Well, we'll see who's laughing once we're done here," the demon growled.

"Right. And what exactly do you think is going to happen?" Nicholas glanced around. "Do you think you're actually going to get out of here in one piece? Taking one of our brothers with you, no less? I can tell you if that's the case, you'd be wrong on both counts."

"As we pointed out, we only need to keep you idiots busy while the others grab your brother."

"We're not worried about Cyrus. If you think he'll just go quietly with those shitheads you're boasting about, you obviously haven't done your homework on us. Once we're done sending you all down to the Nether Realm, we're going to help Cyrus do the same to them." Darren smirked.

Nicholas saw the glint in Darren's eyes as his power began to build. He just knew he was about to send it into these demon's minds, bringing them to their knees and taking them out.

He'd seen it time and time again.

Darren would get into their heads. Depending on what he felt, he'd extract information, if the mind were weak enough, alter their memories...kind of like how they could wipe a human's memories of them, only Darren was able to do this in more depth...or fry their brain. This would lead to skin melting, eyes rolling back, and a smell that just seemed to stick with you days later. This was probably the foulest thing he'd ever witnessed one of his brothers do. Unfortunately for these demons, he had a horrible feeling he was about to witness that right now...but on a much grander scale.

Not that Nicholas wasn't more than ready to get on with getting to Cyrus and heading the hell home, but with his imagination suddenly running wild with ideas of what he was most likely about to witness....

Well, he'd like to skip that visual because, yeah. Eww!

"No, no, no," the demon closest to Darren suddenly said. Nicholas looked toward the demon. His eyes widened when he saw him pointing a gun at Darren's head.

Nicholas was transported back to when a similar gun had been aimed at him. Images of the street he'd been on flashed behind his eyes as the sound of a gunshot echoed through his mind. Even his body shivered as a phantom pain sliced through his side from the memory of the bullet that had slammed into him. He relived the fear, the anger, the despair.

All these feelings curled through him within the few seconds it took for his brain to comprehend that these demons, these fucking pieces of shit had another of those fucking guns.

Dammit!

He couldn't let his brother get shot. Nicholas knew that he'd been lucky. Logically, with the rate that poison had started spreading through his body, he shouldn't have made it. He also knew the next bullet that met its mark, be it in him or one of his brothers, would probably end much differently. Even just considering losing one of them caused a darkness to creep around the edges of his vision.

It wasn't until he realized the demon was talking that Nicholas even noticed he'd stopped breathing. Pulling in a gulp of air, he forced his mind to remain in the present, to try and figure out what needed to be done.

"If I even feel a tickle of you in *my* head," the demon with the gun said, "I'll put a bullet in yours. In response to your earlier comment, I *did* do my homework, on all you, and I know what you can and can't do, like heal from a bullet to your head. Even if this bullet wasn't made to take you out, which it was, it would still do the trick." The demon smirked, cocking the gun with an audible click. His black eyes focused on Darren, who stared back unblinkingly. "Some things you just can't come back from. If I shoot you, Darren, the unspoken leader of your little family, what do you think would come of your brothers? Hmm? Sure, they would probably retaliate, fight back with all the rage that comes with the brutal loss of a loved one. But once the reality of what happened set in...once they no longer had their leader to turn to, to count on...how long do you think they'd last? How long until their anger and pain over your death caused them to turn on each other?"

Darren remained silent, an unmoving statue in the face of this threat, as the rest of them held their breath. The only outward sign of the stress flooding his system was the slight tic in the corner of his left eye. Nicholas glanced between the gun and his brother. The fear that any type of movement, no matter how small, could cause the demon to pull the trigger was almost paralyzing.

"Get that gun off my brother," Manuel snarled. Nicholas saw his grip tighten on the hilt of his sword. His anger reflected noticeably in the power rolling off him. In fact, it was so strong, it pulsed in the air. Nicholas shivered as his brothers growled. "Do it now, you piece of shit demon, or I'll-"

"You'll what?" the demon cut in, his finger hovering over the trigger. "You'll do nothing. None of you will be doing a damn thing. Actually, I want you all to place your weapons on the ground. Now!" He took a step closer to Darren. Nicholas felt the uneasiness run through his brothers as they all slowly leaned down, placing their weapons by their feet. Christian growled at a demon who made a move to grab his daggers, causing the demon to jump back. "Now, kick them away." Reluctantly, they did. The demon nodded.

"I think it's time to teach you all a lesson on what it means to lose everything. I don't think any of you truly appreciate the levels of pain a person can feel as they watch their world crumble right before their eyes. Personally, I have never been through it, for obvious reasons, but I've seen the look in a human's eyes as I took away someone they loved. Someone they knew they could never live without. Such a sentimental group these humans are, just as bad as you guys. As I said, I've studied you over the years. The pain I'm about to cause you, the torment, will be...my greatest masterpiece," the demon said with a sigh, his eyes so cold, it caused Nicholas' gut to clench. "I really feel like I should savor this moment, you know? How many can say they were able to bring the infamous Guardians down to their knees with a single bullet? Hmm..."

He waved his hand through the air. "Well, let's get started, shall we? I have places to go, lives to destroy, and you guys, well... You have a brother to morn." A grin spread across his pasty face. "Say goodbye, Darren. I hope you told your brothers you love them."

Nicholas felt a rush of panic sweep through him at the demon's words. In his mind's eye, he saw his brother fall to the ground, blood pooling beneath him as the crack of the gunshot still echoed through the streets. The light fading from his blue eyes as he stared unseeingly at the darkness above him. Flashes of pain followed these images. A despair Nicholas had never known curled like a sickness within him as a scream of agony quickly lodged within his throat. He couldn't lose his brother. He couldn't lose Darren.

What happened next was like watching a movie in slow motion. Darren's eyes narrowed as he slowly raised his hands toward the demon. Even as he began to pull his power around him like a shield, Nicholas' own body twitched as he took a step forward, Christian and Manuel doing the same as yells of outrage left their lips. Their attempts at getting in front of Darren, at putting themselves between him and the bullet, were suddenly halted.

Staring in shock, Nicholas and his brothers watched as a black mass reached out from the shadows behind the demon and curled around him. His sudden screams of surprise and fear rang through the air with such intensity, Nicholas felt it in his soul. As quickly as it started, the demon's screams were lost as the darkness engulfed his body, cutting off their view of him and the gun in his hands.

Darren stepped back as all four of them stared into the dark mass, watching with a mixture of awe and fear as it began to quickly spread toward the rest of the demons. The ones who seemed to have stiffened in shock were quickly overcome with the black shadow, their bodies hidden from view as their screams filled the air. The other demons, seemingly regaining their senses, quickly turned and ran, disappearing into the night.

Within a matter of seconds, the brothers found themselves surrounded by a living, breathing black wall. Quickly picking up their weapons, they scanned their surroundings, looking for a way out. However, just as quickly as the darkness appeared, it vanished.

Nicholas blinked rapidly as he looked around. Not only was there no black wall blocking his view, but there were no demons, either. Nothing left of the ones who had stood around them only seconds before.

"Holy shit," he whispered, eyeing the empty street.

"What the fuck?" Christian growled from beside him. His question was quickly echoed by Manuel and Darren.

Turning, Nicholas felt himself tense back up as he spotted someone standing there. "Castigo," he said, practically spitting his name out. His brothers spun around.

"Boys," Castigo smirked, leaning back against a streetlight.

"The fuck are you doing?" Nicholas bit out.

"Besides saving your brother's ass?" Castigo looked at all of them, letting his eyes linger on Christian, who was still growling, before coming back to Nicholas. "I don't know. Maybe I got bored sitting on the sidelines, watching you have all the fun. Or maybe I saw you getting your asses handed to you by some of Andras' peons and thought I'd jump in. After all, it's been a long time since I've had some excitement."

"So you just happened to be walking past earlier and found some demons going after Cyrus? Then, after you called with your warning, you thought you'd hang around to help out? I find that hard to believe," Christian growled, continuing when Castigo opened his mouth. "And even if you did want to do all this just for some shits and giggles, why in the hell did you stop to help us?"

"Who said I was helping you? Maybe I'd been planning on taking out those demons for some time now. Realizing they were the ones who were going to be out here fighting you guys gave me the opportunity I needed."

"And why were you planning on taking those demons out? Like you said, they're some of your boss' minions. Kinda like you, right?" Nicholas asked, glaring at the demon.

"First off, I'm not anyone's *fucking* minion. Just because I aligned myself with Andras at the beginning, following his lead, doesn't mean he owns me. Secondly, and the most important point you need to understand, I don't need to explain shit to you guys. I saw Cyrus in trouble, I made a phone call. I saw you all fighting, I took out the demons. Now, I got other shit to do. That's all you need to know."

"What other shit?" Manuel asked.

"And why does it sound like you may not be siding with Andras anymore? Dev had mentioned there may be some issues going on within Andras' fucked-up army. Is that what this is about? Trouble at the club?" Nicholas raised an eyebrow. "Or maybe... Maybe you've lost one too many demons to us. Failed one to many times. I mean, I'm sure Andras can't be too happy with how your last few run-ins with us ended. I'd feel the same. With all the hype surrounding your name, I'd expected more. Then again, he may have realized you're only good for menial labor, like being used as his personal punching bag. Or did he find himself another chew toy?"

Something flashed behind Castigo's eyes. An emotion so out of place and unexpected, Nicholas wasn't sure he'd seen anything at all. As quick as the look was there, it was gone. Angry silver eyes glared back at him as Castigo seemed to try to collect himself. Then, with nothing more than a shake of his head, the demon pushed off of the streetlight and started to walk across the street.

"Where the hell are you going?" Christian yelled.

Nicholas saw him heading toward the parking lot and quickly followed. He wasn't sure why Castigo was there, why he had called in the warning, or why it seemed like he was helping them. The demon surely had an agenda, some reason for doing what he did. There was no way he saved Darren out of the kindness of his heart. Maybe he did it because he was switching sides and wanted to try to get in good with them. That didn't feel right, though. Why would he want to? Even if he were turning on Andras, why would he want to switch to their side? Why not just get out of there completely? Shit, maybe he really did just want to wipe those demons out and used the fight as his opening to do so.

That didn't feel right, either.

There were just too many questions. If Castigo were helping them, regardless of his reasoning, that led Nicholas to the conclusion that he could no longer fit Castigo into the category he'd put all the other demons in. He'd always believed there was no such thing as a good, or even decent, demon. Now he'd have to rethink everything. If Castigo, who had been a prick every time he'd seen him, could be a help to them, then what other demons could be? Maybe he'd have a chat with Dev when they got back.

Nicholas felt his brothers following close behind him. Darren had been pretty quiet since Castigo had made his grand entrance, though it didn't really surprise him. Even without having a gun aimed at him, Darren had always been more of a silent observer. Especially compared to the rest of them. That was probably why he was the one they all turned to when they had a problem. The demon had been right. He had always been their leader, the one to make the plans and figure out who needed to do what. So Nicholas wasn't surprised when he passed him and led the way into the parking lot.

They all followed him to a parked car, stopping when Darren raised a hand.

Stepping up beside his brother, Nicholas could only stare at Cyrus facing off with four demons. Another two demons stood at his back, facing off with five of their own.

Cyrus' eyes seemed to glow as the shadows built up around him. His wings stretched out wide behind him, the silver streaks within the black feathers glinting in the dim light around them. It really was an awesome sight, and if it weren't for the demons surrounding him, Nicholas would have been content to just stand there and watch him work.

Letting his gaze drift toward the other demons, Nicholas watched as two of them threw out snarky comments and made aggressive movements toward the others...like they were trying to get their attention off his brother. If Castigo hadn't just saved Darren, the sight before him may have struck him as odd. As it was, all he felt was a sense of wariness and confusion so strong, it was suffocating. It was just too much to think about and examine, and right then was definitely not the time to be having a Dr. Phil moment.

Feeling his brothers tense around him only proved that point. He figured it was only a matter of time before they all jumped into the fight. Nicholas was all for that, but who should he run at first? The obvious answer would be to go to his brother, even though he was pretty sure

Cyrus didn't need any help. His eyes kept straying to the two demons who seemed to be covering Cyrus' back. He knew nothing about them. They may be excellent when it came to fighting, or they could last about just as long as it took him to decide what to do.

Hmm...

Normally, the thought of two less demons brought a smile to his face. After all, fighting against them was pretty much their whole purpose...at least in the past. Now, though, he wasn't sure how he felt about it.

One of the demons at Cyrus' back, one with brown hair and gray eyes, stared intently at the demons before him, while the one at his side was actually grinning. A shiver ran through Nicholas. This whole thing was just a clusterfuck, and all he wanted to do was get his brother and go home.

"Well, I feel like I should be hurt," Castigo's voice suddenly rang out above the growls, causing everyone to look his way.

Shit, almost forgot he was there.

"It looks like you boys are throwing a right fine party here. My poor heart's hurting that you all didn't think to invite me," Castigo continued. His toothy smile flashed at them as he looked around.

"Castigo," the demon with the gray eyes said.

"Rave." Castigo nodded. "Looks like you and your brother have your hands full."

"Nothing Etch and I can't handle." Rave smirked.

"What the fuck are you doing here, Castigo?" a demon uncomfortably close to Cyrus asked.

"I'm trying to put together the very first demon baseball team. You interested? I'm figuring you'd make a good benchwarmer. All the best teams usually have at least one," Castigo snarked.

Nicholas had to bite the inside of his cheek to keep from laughing because, well... That was pretty funny. He continued to listen to insults fly as he reached back and slowly unhooked his crossbow. The demon glaring at Castigo seemed to be especially pissed about their arrival. One would think it was a given that if you got into a fight with one of the brothers, the rest of them would eventually show up to join in. By the look on that demon's face, along with the others attempting to take on Cyrus, they hadn't gotten the memo. Shame, really. It was never much of a fight when only one side was prepared.

Oh well, Nicholas thought, removing an arrow from his case. *Looks like I'm just going to have to make do with a half-assed showdown.*

The demon glaring at Castigo snarled, his red eyes flashing as he took a step forward. "You need to watch your mouth, Castigo, before it digs a hole you can't crawl out of."

"Oh, Labrihn. Always with the clichés," Castigo tisked. "And here I thought you'd eventually grow out of using those."

"You know what? Why don't you kiss my ass?"

"First off, you're not my type. Second off, as far as comebacks go, I'd give that a five."

"Fuck you, you sorry piece of-"

"Now, now. Not in front of the kids." Castigo shook his head.

"Enough," the demon standing in front of Rave hissed.

"Eager to get your ass kicked, Trao?" Etch smirked.

"Like that could ever happen."

"You know what I noticed?" Christian suddenly asked, drawing the demons' attention. "You guys talk too fucking much."

That was all of the warning anyone had before the shit really hit the fan. Manuel released his power into the ground, causing it to shudder beneath them. The Earth growled and shifted under their feet until a couple of the demons lost their footing. Nicholas saw them stumble, quickly shooting an arrow into the closest one, belatedly noticing the ball of power flying past his head.

"Shit," he exclaimed, diving behind a car parked nearby, Christian and Castigo following.

"Fuck off," Nicholas heard Christian growl right before shoving Castigo away from them.

"Now really isn't the time," Castigo growled back, ducking lower as another ball of power slammed into the car's hood.

"I don't think there'd ever be a good time to deal with you. I don't even know why you're fucking here, other than to be a tremendous pain in my ass."

"Tremendous... Is that one of those nifty three-syllable words they teach you in Fallen Angel school to help you fit in? Or is your little girlfriend teaching you some new tricks?"

"What in the fuck is that supposed to mean?"

"Well-" Castigo started, pausing when the car got blasted again, shards of metal falling on them.

"Listen, can we hash this out later?" Nicholas shouted before quickly standing and letting another arrow fly over the trunk. Screams and curses echoed all around them as the ground once again shook beneath their feet. He couldn't see what was happening on the other side of the car, but from the sound of things, it was a rather fine battle going on. And here he was, stuck behind a car, listening to Christian and Castigo bicker. Turning to Castigo, Nicholas glared into his silver eyes. "Can't you just do that foggy thing again, the one you did just a minute ago, and finish these fuckers off?"

Castigo rolled his eyes. "That *foggy thing*, as you so nicely put it, doesn't work on higher-level demons. Those little shits out there on the street were lower level. Even the one holding the gun. He was no more than a little peon with a severe superiority complex."

"*Now* who's using large words?" Christian grumbled, earning himself a sideways glance from both Nicholas and Castigo. "What?"

"So these guys are more powerful?" Nicholas asked.

"Than the ones I got rid of for you? Yes. Than me?" Castigo shrugged. "I just know I can't wipe them out as easily as the others. Doesn't mean I can't take them out another way."

Nicholas glanced over just in time to see Darren take a demon to the ground. He wrapped his hands around the demon's head, slamming it into the ground as he started glowing, making the demon scream out in pain. Manuel ran up behind them, his wings spread wide as he watched Darren's back. One demon down.

Shaking his head in frustration, Nicholas let out a snarl. "And how do you plan on taking them out?" When Castigo didn't answer, Nicholas looked his way, finding the demon gone. Christian was looking the other direction and turned at the same time. "The fuck?" Nicholas growled. "Where'd he go?"

"Who fucking knows. Let's just get out there and end this. I'm tired of these fucking demons and just want to get home."

That sounded excellent to Nicholas. For once, he had someone other than his brothers waiting for him at home. With a nod to Christian, they both got to their feet and vaulted over the car. A raw source of power immediately slammed into his chest, pushing him back. The pain was instant, but not strong enough to put him down. Rolling his shoulders, Nicholas looked up, feeling his power race through the air. Storm clouds rolled in response to the pulsing of his tattoo as it came to life along his arm and back. He knew his eyes had changed to black just as thunder crashed above them.

It was time to end this. Amy was waiting for him.

Chapter 31

Amy rocked back and forth on the couch, her knees drawn up as she watched Hayley and Ella pace around the room. Nicholas and the others had been gone well over an hour with no word as to what was happening.

She had a sick feeling in her stomach that had grown since they left. Being new to this, she didn't know how these fights usually went. Did Nicholas fight demons often? Had they lost anyone before? She knew he'd been shot and almost died, so the possibility of death was real. What if he got shot again? What if he never made it back to her?

Amy shook her head. She couldn't think like that. Of course Nicholas would be coming back. All of the guys would be. Glancing over, she watched Dev enter the room. He looked around, his eyes sad. He always seemed sad, even when he was smiling. It was like a part of him didn't feel he deserved to be happy. Amy didn't really know him, but from what she'd heard, he hadn't had a lot to smile about. She just hoped he'd start to see what he had now - a family, people he could truly count on to have his back.

Ella turned toward Dev standing in the entrance. "Anything?"

"No," he said slowly. Licking his lips, it looked like he was about to say more, but the ringing of his phone stopped him. Amy watched his blue eyes dart down as he pulled it from his front pocket. He released a heavy sigh before tapping the screen and lifting it to his ear. "Yes."

Hayley and Ella stopped pacing, both watching Dev intently. Like Amy, they were probably hoping to hear word. To hear that all was well and they were on their way home. The more she watched Dev's expression, though, the more she was sure it was either bad news or it was someone he hadn't really wanted to talk to.

"Hey," she heard Dev say, his voice sounding gruffer than what she was used to. "I'm not at the club any-... Oh, I didn't know you-... Yes. Of course, Sy."

A quick glance showed both Hayley and Ella seemed as confused by this name as she was. Amy mirrored Ella's slight shrug before looking back toward Dev.

He frowned as he glanced at them before focusing back on the person still talking. "Yes, I plan on staying here. I doubt my brothers will want me to go far... No. Just my phone... Well, I kind of left in a hurry..." Dev gave Hayley a small smile. "Yeah, they got me out, but I was planning on leaving anyway... Well, I overheard

Andras talking to this witch... How did you... Never mind," he said with a dry chuckle. "No, it's just... I should have realized you already knew about her... Okay... All right... Goodbye, Sy."

She watched Dev slowly slide the phone back into his front pocket. His eyes looked somewhat glazed as he stared off, probably caught up in whatever memories the phone call had provoked. Whether they were good or bad memories, Amy wasn't sure. Though from the slight tightness around Dev's eyes, she would have to go with the latter.

"Who's Sy?" Amy asked after some time, breaking the silence.

"A demon I know," Dev answered absently. "He has helped me out of a few jams in the past."

"A demon?" Ella hissed. "Should you really be talking to any of those, especially now that you're pretty much in hiding?"

"Sy's different," he said, glancing her way. His eyes were wary, as though waiting for them to call him a liar, maybe pass some kind of judgment on him.

Ella let out a sound of disbelief as she shook her head. Amy was sure the woman would have something to say, but before she could, Hayley cleared her throat. The look that passed between the two women seemed to convey a whole conversation before Ella begrudgingly nodded, returning to her pacing.

Hayley, on the other hand, offered a gentle smile to Dev. "Maybe he is, Dev. We just want you to be careful. Yeah?"

"Yeah. Even though I wouldn't go as far as to say I completely trust Sy, he's never done anything to make me believe I couldn't." Dev raised his hand as Ella turned at his words. "I'm not saying he hasn't had his own reasons for helping me. Shit, I'm sure he gets just as much, if not more, out of everything he does. But..." He sighed. "With everything I went through, I had to latch onto what little lifelines were sent my way. Sy was just one of those lifelines, and he's been a surprising ally ever since."

"What did he say?" Amy asked. "Did he say anything about what's going on right now?"

Dev nodded. "Yeah, actually. He said he got some backup for my brothers." His features seemed more tense than relieved at this news.

"Backup? As in, other demons?" Hayley frowned.

"I guess. He didn't really get into specifics. Sy just said he knew about the witch who was trying to get her hands on me and knew Andras had sent his demons out tonight in the hopes of either bringing me back or grabbing one of my brothers.

I'm not sure how Sy found out all of this, but he told me to stay here and not worry because he has someone downtown helping make sure Andras' demons are taken care of." Dev shrugged, looking about as uncertain as Amy felt. "I don't really like it, but he's right. I must stay here... *We* must stay here. So, I guess in this instance, we need to believe Sy is on our side."

"I don't like it," Ella murmured.

"Neither do I," Hayley said, sitting down beside Amy. "But there's nothing we can do. Right?"

They all looked at each other as the gravity of the situation set in. They could either go crazy worrying that the worst-case scenario had truly happened and Andras' demons had won, or they would have to trust in Sy and believe that whoever he sent to help the brothers would actually do just that. There was just too much up in the air, too many unknowns.

Amy felt a dull headache beginning to form behind her eyes as she ran through the different possibilities, the various outcomes. Throughout it all, the main thing that kept repeating was that there was absolutely nothing she could do to help. She'd never felt as helpless as she did right then, waiting to see if Nicholas would come home. It was enough to make her sick.

"You're right," Ella finally said, sitting on Hayley's other side. "As much as

I want to just say forget it and head straight to wherever they are, I know we can't. One, I am nowhere near ready to go up against a demon. Not with my powers still all wonky. And two, we all seem to have a target on our backs. If we went out there and got caught, all the fighting Christian and the rest of them have been doing to protect us will have been for nothing."

"I don't think I would be able to help even if we did go find them," Amy said sadly. Glancing down, she absently picked lint off her jeans as she gave voice to her inner fears. "You guys are so strong, so powerful, and I'm what? A blogger with a taste for action movies and strong coffee. Hell, I'm more of a distraction and a liability than anything."

"Now you just stop that," Hayley snapped, turning on the couch so she could face Amy. Her green eyes seemed to flash as they stared at her. "You may not be a witch or a psychic, but you are strong. Don't doubt that for one second. Your strength comes from in here." She reached out and tapped the center of Amy's chest. "And here." She tapped her head. "I bet you're stronger than even I can imagine. Hell, I'm sure of it. You know how I know that?"

Amy gave her head a quick shake. Unable to pull her eyes away from Hayley's, she held her breath, waiting to hear what the woman had to say. A part of her understood that while she didn't truly see herself as weak, it was going to be nice to hear someone say it out loud. Especially someone she viewed as a superwoman in her own right.

"I know because not only can I see the strength in your eyes, I see the love in Nicky's when he looks at you. Something led him to your door when he was in trouble that morning. Call it fate, call it destiny, call it whatever you want. Whatever it was gave you the courage to do what you did. Because of that, you saved his life. You brought him back from the brink of death so he could return to his family. A weaker person couldn't have done what you did. Wouldn't have put aside their uncertainty and saved him. Then, at the club, he was there to save you. You two are meant for each other." Raising her hand to stop any possible argument, Hayley smiled. "I know it's only been a few days, but trust me." She glanced over at Ella, who wore an equally soft smile. Hayley turned back toward her. "A couple days is sometimes all you need for your soul to recognize your other half. Right?"

She thought about Nicholas, how his smile made her feel loved, how being held in his arms made her feel like she was safe...like she was home. There was no doubt in Amy's mind that Nicholas was it for her. Their lives had been entangled from the second his eyes met hers. Hell, maybe farther back than that. Nodding at Hayley, she felt herself returning the woman's grin.

"Then you should know that you can't possibly be anything but a strong, spirited, passionate woman. Fate wouldn't link your soul to Nicky's if you were anything less. Who else will be able to keep him in line?"

At that, they all broke out in laughter. Even Dev, who'd been quiet during their talk, chuckled where he leaned against the wall. It was not only exactly what Amy needed to hear in her moment of doubt, but it also brought a smile to all of their faces. Gave them a break from the stress and worry. She felt closer to them then she had before, more accepted, stronger.

Now she just needed to keep her newfound faith alive until Nicholas came home. Before she left, she hadn't properly expressed how she felt about him. Something she planned on rectifying as soon as she got him alone.

Hopefully over the course of many uninterrupted hours.

Chapter 32

Nicholas' last arrow plunged into the demon before him. He watched as his head flew backwards, his body crumpling to the ground. Releasing a steady breath between his teeth, he glanced around to see if any of the demons where left.

He spotted Manuel sliding his short sword back into its sheath. His left arm was covered in blood, but he didn't even wince as he moved it around. Nicholas figured either it had healed already or his brother was just trying to play it off like he was fine. Most likely, it was the latter. *Idiot.* He'd leave the yelling about taking better care of himself to Hayley.

Smirking, he glanced over and spotted Darren and Christian standing next to a very irritated Cyrus. That wasn't new. Given the three demons still hovering around like they were waiting for an audience with them, he couldn't really blame his brother for being irritated.

When Nicholas began moving toward his brothers, he noticed a kid curled up against the fence. Slowing, he took advantage of the boy not seeing him yet to look him over. By Nicholas' guess, he was probably in his early teens. His olive skin was flushed, his brown eyes wide beneath a mess of dark brown hair as they stared toward his brothers. All in all, he looked like any other teenager. However, it was what the kid wore that lead Nicholas to believe that wasn't the case here. His jean jacket was a couple sizes too big, but it added to the already thick layers of several t-shirts he wore beneath it. His jeans were also baggier than they should be, coming all the way down to cover the tops of his shoes, the holes in them more from wear than style. A pang of sadness squeezed his chest as Nicholas realized this kid had probably been living on the streets for some time.

With all the hate and pain humans spread, it was what some did to the young that really made his skin crawl. Sure, he didn't know this kid's story, but he knew of hundreds that had been in his place.

Finally making his way to the group, he watched the kid's eyes grow even larger when they landed on him. Deciding to give him some time to adjust to yet another stranger, Nicholas looked at Cyrus. Given everything he'd been through tonight, his brother looked like he was holding up nicely. At least he seemed to be. What he actually felt was anybody's guess. Ever since his time with the Shadows, none of them had been privy to anything but his anger.

"Did we get everyone?" Nicholas asked, coming to a stop next to Darren. His eyes hovered over his brothers before meeting Darren's cobalt gaze.

"Looks like it," he said, running a hand absentmindedly over the hilt of his broadsword.

"Yeah. Etch and Rave had taken care of the demons they faced before joining up with Castigo to go after some of the others," Christian mumbled. His tone conveyed he was less than pleased with the demons' help, regardless of the outcome. Nicholas could definitely second that.

"Rave showed up with Labrihn, then turned on him as soon as those other goons surrounded me." Cyrus' voice rumbled through the quiet parking lot.

Glancing over at the demon in question, Nicholas watched as he leaned forward, obviously in some kind of aggravated conversation with Castigo, who seemed bored. Etch, the third demon in that little group, kept glancing around like he didn't have a care in the world. There was something off about that one, even more so then any of the other demons Nicholas had ever come across. He had a feeling they were going to need to be extra vigilant where that one was concerned.

"What's Castigo doing here?"

Cyrus' question drew Nicholas from his thoughts, bringing on images of a gun and a memory of the fear that had coursed through him at the thought of losing

Darren. He opened his mouth to tell him what happened, but Darren interrupted.

"It's a long story," he said.

Nicholas and Christian shared a brief frown at that. Deciding that maybe Darren just wanted to wait until they got home to tell Cyrus what had happened, Nicholas gave Christian a shrug. Probably better to not go into the horrors of what could have taken place in front of the demons.

Speaking of...

"What are we going to do about those three?" Nicholas asked, tilting his head in the demons' direction.

"If by *those three* you mean us," they heard Castigo say as he sauntered up to them, the other two not far behind, "you don't need to do anything. Actually, we're done here."

"Really?" Christian glared at him. "Then why are you still here?"

"Waiting for someone," the demon answered. "Why else would we be standing around this..." He waved his hand at all the demon bodies littering the ground, "this graveyard?"

"This *is* quite the mess," Rave drawled, coming to a stop between Etch and Castigo.

Cyrus nodded at Rave. "You could do your thing."

"What thing?" Nicholas asked.

"That thing he did where he literally burned a demon from the inside out."

His eyes widened as he looked between Cyrus and Rave. "That's..." Nicholas' voice trailed off as he tried to decide what word would best describe how that sudden image made him feel. Horrified? Sick? Somewhat intrigued? All three seemed to describe how he felt while not really describing it at all. So, with no idea what to add to his sentence, Nicholas just left it like that, looking toward Darren to see how he reacted to this news. His brother's gaze gave nothing away.

"That *thing* is just something I can do," Rave said. "But it only works when the demon is moving about. These husks are just that. There's nothing I can do to help with their remaining presence."

"Yeah," Etch chimed in, causing everyone to look his way. "I only make things dead. I don't do anything with them once they're cold."

Frowning at Etch, Nicholas just shook his head. *Okay then.*

"We could take care of them," Darren finally said. "It'll take some time, but-"

"I'll take care of this mess for you," a deep voice came from behind them, cutting off anything else Darren was going to say. They all turned to see a tall figure slowly walking their way. The way he moved spoke of power. His black eyes glinted at them as he got closer, stepping over a demon's body without even batting an eye.

As the male...Nicholas could now tell he was a demon based on the considerable amount of power flowing over him...got closer, Nicholas noticed how Castigo stood up a little straighter. Rave had his head tilted, like he was trying to figure out how to react to the demon, and Etch, who had seemed bored with everything, now looked somewhat curious. Taking a really good look at the demon as he stopped before them, Nicholas had to admit he felt the same.

"I know you Guardians can take care of these bodies yourselves, but if you allow me to, I can get this done a lot quicker," the demon said, looking around the group. His black eyes lingered on the demons before his gaze seemed to lock on Castigo. "Well done, Castigo. I see you did as I asked and you're still in one piece. Bravo."

Castigo's answering grunt caused the strange demon to chuckle before turning his black eyes toward Nicholas and his brothers. "I'm sorry. I didn't introduce myself," he said with a smile. "My name is Syre, but you can call me Sy."

It didn't take long for everyone to recognize his name as the one Dev had mentioned.

Nicholas' eyes went wide as he took a second to look at the demon who had, in one way or another, helped their brother out when he was in Andras' grasp. That didn't mean any of them would trust him anytime soon, but they wouldn't immediately discount his advice or turn their nose up at his help, either.

"I see you've heard of me," Sy smirked. "Wonderful. Well, as much as I'd like to sit here and chat, I have some bodies to clean up."

Before any of them could say a word, the demon turned from them. Sy took several steps away until he was able to kneel without a body under his feet. Nicholas watched him brace his hands against the ground, his head bent as if praying.

Which, given the fact he was a demon, made Nicholas chuckle.

Seeing Christian shoot him a glance out of the corner of his eye, Nicholas just smirked and shook his head. He'd share his little inside joke later.

At first, it really didn't look like Sy was doing anything except kneeling on the ground, but after a matter of moments, a soft humming filled the air. The sound continued to grow until it was so loud, Nicholas literally felt the vibration on his skin.

Looking around, he noticed everyone had a confused, almost alarmed look on their face. Each of them, even the demons, rubbed their arms as they glanced around. It was a sudden burst of light that brought their attention back to Sy. The demon was glowing, like a black light, in the center of the lot. The light began to spread out from him. Like ivy, it moved across the ground in every direction. The angst that had started building in Nicholas began to turn to shock as he watched each line of light gravitate toward a body.

In seconds, each of the dead demons were lit up. Not just by a glow, though. They actually looked like they were on fire. Black and purple flames licked across the bodies and the ground surrounding them. And then, just as quickly as it had started, the flames flashed, then went out completely.

Releasing a breath he hadn't even been aware of holding, Nicholas looked around, astonished to see that no evidence remained of the fight that had just gone down. Not even the scorch marks from the balls of power the demons had thrown around. Shit, it looked like nothing had happened at all.

"Damn," Christian muttered. Nicholas couldn't agree more.

"That's some power you got there," Darren spoke up. His voice seemed to hold some curiosity while still sounding guarded.

Standing in one smooth motion, Sy turned to them and grinned. "It gets the job done."

"I bet," Darren said, moving a few steps in front of their group. Though he was holding himself in a relaxed pose, Nicholas could still read the tension running through his brother. It was obvious Darren wasn't entirely sold on the demon's *I'm just here to help* demeanor.

Sy and Darren stared at each other for a bit before Sy looked off and nodded toward the other demons. "Well, not that I don't love chatting it up with you, but we have someplace to be."

"We do? And where are we-" Etch began, only to be stopped by Rave's growl.

"Yes," Sy answered without looking toward the demon. "We have a lot to discuss, plans to make."

"Plans? For what? Us?" Cyrus snarled, speaking up for the first time since Sy showed up.

"For you? No," he said, shaking his head and smiling. "We have...other issues to consider besides what our local Guardians are up to. For now. Oh, and do pass on my well-wishes to Dev. I am glad he is finally away from Andras. Him being in that demon's grasp was...troubling. I'm sure you agree."

Without another word, Sy gave them a quick wink and turned to walk toward the back of the lot, Rave and Etch right on his heels. Castigo, on the other hand, held back and glanced around at them.

"Well, boys, this has been fun," he smirked. "May have to do this again sometime, huh?"

"Don't hold your breath," Christian responded in a tight voice, making Castigo laugh.

"Right." Castigo tilted his head and gave Christian a mock salute. "I'll be seeing you."

Watching him disappear into the darkness behind the others, Nicholas shook his head. *What a fucked-up, crazy night.* He suddenly felt a tiredness seep into his bones, a need to get back to Amy and his...their bed.

"Wow," a small voice came from behind them. Turning, Nicholas saw a young face peeking around Cyrus' back.

Shit. Forgot about him.

"You guys are like... And they were... Then all of the..." The kid's eyes were wide as he threw his hands up, making an explosion sound. His cheeks were red from his excitement, the grin on his face growing by the second as he looked around at them. "I'm mean, that was all just.... Who are you guys?"

Nicholas and his brothers looked at each other before looking back at the boy.

"Who are *you*?" Manuel asked.

"Nope," he shot back. "You guys first."

"Oh, for fuck-" Cyrus started, only to be cut off when Christian coughed, loudly, behind his hand. With a roll of his eyes, Cyrus glared back at the kid. "I'm Cyrus. That's Nicholas, Darren, Christian and Manuel. Now, who are you, and why were you hiding in a deserted parking lot in the first place?"

"I'm, um... I'm Miles," he said, suddenly looking nervous. "And, well..." He straightened his back and raised his head, staring at Cyrus, eyes narrowed. "I wasn't hiding. It...It's really none of your business why I'm here."

"Why aren't you at home? Isn't it a school night or some shit?"

"What do you care?"

"Listen, kid-" Cyrus growled.

"I'm not a kid," Miles interrupted, taking a tiny step toward Cyrus. "I'm... I'm old enough to take care of myself."

Nicholas looked over and saw a brief flicker in Cyrus' eyes. Something that looked a lot like compassion...concern. Whatever it was, the emotion was quickly hidden behind his brother's mask of indifference.

"So... What? Does being an adult include sleeping out in the cold and huddling next to a liquor store?" Cyrus asked. "Because I highly doubt that would be considered taking care of yourself. Also, you don't look old enough to be loitering around a liquor store. So, don't be a little shit. Tell us where you live."

Miles winced. His eyes seemed more red then they had been only moments ago, but he kept himself standing tall. Nicholas was impressed. He also knew enough to see that no matter what, this kid was not going to admit to the fact that he'd been living on the street. None of them needed him to say it, and he didn't understand why Cyrus was pushing so much. Maybe he needed to hear the kid say it. Or maybe all the stress from the demons and everything else that had been going on had finally gotten to him.

Whatever the reason, he could figure it out later. Preferably at home. Because they needed to get out of here. Saying as much just brought five sets of eyes flying his way. Nicholas shrugged. "Unless Miles has somewhere pressing he needs to be at..." He sighed, making a show of digging out his phone to look at the time, "two in the morning, he should just come with us. We have a spare room he can crash in. After everyone gets some rest, we can figure everything out in the morning. Well, maybe in the afternoon. Whenever we get up."

"You, um..." Miles' voice cracked a bit before he paused to clear his throat. "You want me to come with you?"

Nicholas just nodded before glancing at his brothers. Christian and Manuel both smiled and shot a glance of approval Nicholas' way before looking at Cyrus, who still stared at the kid. Even with his *I don't give a shit* expression firmly in place, he gave a sharp nod of his own. Then, as one, they all looked toward Darren.

His brother stood there silently, looking at Miles. He had a strange look in his eyes, his lips thin as he seemed to be trying to figure something out. Miles shifted his feet as he stared back at Darren, his nervousness evident as he twisted his hands in front of him.

"I think you need to come back with us," Darren murmured. "It isn't safe for you out here."

Miles looked around, his eyes filled with uncertainty. "Okay..."

It seemed like that was all Cyrus needed to hear because he walked to Miles and began pulling the youngster toward his SUV.

"I'll ride with them," Darren commented. "You three get yourselves back to the house and make sure the girls and Dev are okay. Also, get a room ready for Miles, since he'll be staying with us."

"Permanently?" Christian asked. Darren ignored him and climbed into the passenger side of the car. "Well, shit."

"Yeah. It's a good thing I found us a house with so many rooms," Manuel smirked.

"No shit."

Nicholas just shook his head as he rolled his shoulders and allowed his mind to pull up images of their front room, materializing in it within seconds. His gaze immediately locked on Amy. Warmth spread through him as she jumped up, a sparkle in her eyes. Opening his arms, he felt all the frustration and anger from the night's events drain out of his body as she burrowed into him.

Inhaling her delicious scent, Nicholas tightened his arms around her protectively. He wished he could just stay in this moment, forget about the demons wandering around town, the gun that had been pointed at Darren, the endless possibilities of how all of this was going to play out. Nicholas was certain this was just the beginning. The club, Andras, the demons suddenly popping up everywhere they turned. Even Sy's and Castigo's sudden willingness to help was a sure sign everything was changing and leading up to some unforeseen endgame. Nicholas pushed back a shudder as he pulled Amy into him even tighter.

The soft murmurs from his brothers and their women told Nicholas Christian and Manuel had shown up. He felt their presence behind him.

"I'm so glad you're home," Amy sighed, her arms wrapping tightly around his waist.

Home.

The word never sounded so good, and as the sound of tires crunching over the gravel driveway reached his ears, Nicholas finally felt that last bit of stress leave his body. The rest of his family was here. New additions and all.

Looking over her head, Nicholas noticed Dev leaning against the wall. His blue eyes scanned the room, his shoulders tense. The small lift to his lips spoke volumes, though. As anxious as their brother still was, Nicholas could tell he was happy to be here. Happy to be with the family. Safe.

Everything was so up in the air right now, so unbalanced, Nicholas wasn't sure what to expect, what to prepare for. But with Amy in his arms and his family by his side, he knew they'd figure it out. Make it through the storm he felt heading their way.

They had to.

There wasn't another choice.

Chapter 33
Two Months Later

Cyrus walked down the hall from his room. The sound of laughter filled the house, causing a warmth to spread through his chest. Not that he'd let his brothers know, but he actually felt...happy.

Well, as happy as he could be.

His nights were still filled with horrific dreams, reminders of pain and the feeling of hopelessness. They had started getting worse as he'd begun consciously making an effort to drink less and less. After his need for alcohol had led to the battle a few months back, he finally acknowledged that his habit had become dangerous. At least to himself. If the demons could find him once, they could find him again.

The sleepless nights wore on him, and he expected them to get worse. So now, without the alcohol that would help him fall into dreamless unconsciousness, he'd just have to get used to spending his days in an exhausted fog. Part of him felt pathetic, weak, for allowing what the Shadow Demons had done to him to have such an effect. But he couldn't help it. And it wasn't something he felt he could fight.

Passing by the room that had been given to Miles, he paused. The walls within the room where still bare, the shelves still holding the smallest proof that the room was occupied. For whatever reason, the kid didn't seem to want anything. Sure, he laughed with the others, entered into conversation with them, acted like he was happy. But, for someone who knew all about putting on a show, Cyrus could see right through the kid's bullshit.

He was hiding something. Cyrus just knew it. The kid not wanting to put down roots, make this his home, even though everyone had told him it was, only seemed to be part of it.

It was like Miles was just waiting to be kicked out, to get hurt.

Something pulled at his heart as his eyes wandered over the made bed and folded clothes. He wasn't sure who Miles was trying to be perfect for, but he wished the kid would just be himself. Trust them to help him with whatever he was dealing with, instead of hiding behind a forced smile and tense laugh.

Do I really have room to talk?

Shaking his head, Cyrus moved away from Miles' door and continued down the hall. His heart clenched with every door he passed.

So many of his brothers had found their other half, their soul mate. While he was happy for them and acted like he never wanted the same for himself, he secretly did. He wondered what it would be like to have someone who understood him, who was there for him to lean on when his memories became too much. Someone who would accept who he was, moodiness and all.

Well, those were definitely questions he didn't need to think about too much. It may have happened for his brothers, but he didn't see it happening for him anytime soon. His hand unconsciously traced the scar that ran down the side of his face. Who would ever want him?

Making his way down the steps, he passed the kitchen with only a nod to everyone standing within it. Nobody asked him where he was going. And that was okay. He'd put up walls between him and his family a long time ago. Ones they'd eventually stopped trying to tear down.

Suppressing a sudden pang of loneliness, he gritted his teeth and gave himself a mental shake. He had other things on his mind, other things to worry about than trying to dodge conversation with his family and thoughts of the lonely, loveless life that was stretched out before him.

He had bigger problems to look into. Such as the phone calls Dev had been receiving, ones he had tried to keep from them, and whatever it was Miles was hiding.

Thoughts of Miles forced his mind to wander back to what happened in the parking lot in front of the liquor store. The demons who had tried to grab him, the ones who had stood by his side. He still couldn't figure that out. As if that wasn't enough to ponder, there was the look in Darren's eyes when he had all but insisted Miles come stay with them. Cyrus had been all for it when Nicholas had suggested the kid come back to their house, but the extra push from Darren had given him pause.

Maybe whatever was going on with the kid, whatever he was running from, had somehow been clear to his brother that night.

It wouldn't really surprise him if that were the case. Out of all the brothers, it seemed like Darren was the one who always knew what was going on. Or at least knew how to find out.

Too much shit was up in the air. Too many *what ifs*. A growl ripped from his chest as he rolled his shoulders. He needed answers, and he needed them now.

It wasn't until he stopped in front of Darren's office that he realized he'd walked through the whole house without really seeing it. Damn, he needed to keep his thoughts in check. Now wasn't the time to be unaware of his surroundings. He could never drop his guard, not even at home where he should feel the safest.

That was something he had learned the hard way.

Hovering his hand over the doorknob, Cyrus pushed back the cascade of memories attempting to push themselves on him. Taking a deep breath, he opened the door and stepped into his brother's office.

"Cyrus," Darren said, without looking up from his computer. "I was wondering how long it would take you to come see me."

Cyrus just nodded as he walked over and sat down on the couch at the side of his desk. He watched Darren's fingers fly over the keyboard as pictures and articles flew across the screen. After a few moments, he finally stopped typing and, with a deep sigh, turned to Cyrus.

"You have questions?" Darren asked with a raised eyebrow.

"What do you think?" Cyrus snarked. "We have demons after us at every turn. But now, some of those demons want to... What? Be on our side? And what about the phone calls Dev has been receiving? Yeah, you can say I have a few questions."

Darren nodded, staring unblinkingly at him as he tapped a finger against his desk. "True, but that's not what you came here to ask me about, is it?"

"Could be," he shot back defensively.

Darren just stared at him. "But it's not."

"Fine. Maybe the demons and Dev's mysterious phone calls aren't all I wanted to talk about. There's also the fact that we seem to have adopted a child. It's raised a few eyebrows. Mainly mine."

"I thought you wanted him here."

Sitting back, Cyrus attempted to school his face as shock rippled through him at his brother's words. "I... Whatever. It doesn't matter to me if the kid's here or not." The lie was obvious, even to his own ears. "But he's clearly hiding something."

"And you want to know what that something is?"

"Shouldn't I? Don't you think we have a right to know what trouble we're bring into our house? I mean, what if he's dangerous?" At the smirk on Darren's face, Cyrus rolled his eyes. "You know what I mean. Anyway, maybe someone is looking for him."

"Someone is," Darren said simply, pulling his notepad toward him and grabbing a pen.

Cyrus jumped up from the couch. "What? Who? Why haven't you said anything?"

"I didn't say anything because I wanted to make sure the person looking for him was actually doing it because they wanted to help him, not hurt him."

"Why would someone be out to hurt the kid?" Cyrus asked, a wave of protectiveness washing through him. "Is he in trouble?"

"Miles is...special. He needs to be here where he is safe, protected. As I said, I needed to research the one looking for him. After some digging, it would seem he is not the only kid in danger." Darren tore off a corner of the paper he'd been writing on and handed it to Cyrus. "I need you to locate this woman and the child who's with her and bring them here."

Cyrus glanced down at the paper in his hands. "What's so special about them?"

"I'll explain everything once you get back. I was actually just about to call you down here before you showed up. We need to locate these two...immediately."

"What do I look like? A bloodhound?" Cyrus shook his head. "Why don't you send one of the others? You know they're a lot better at tracking than I am."

"Cyrus, this is something I need you to do. Do you trust me?"

He gazed at his brother. In his heart, he knew he could trust him, even as his mind pushed for him to be leery. "Of course, Darren."

"Then do this for me. I wrote down the last few places these two have been seen. I know they're looking for Miles and are searching everywhere downtown, trying to find anyone who may have seen him. They'll be scared, possibly even trying to get away from you once you locate them, but we need them here. These two aren't safe out there, especially not once Andras finds out about them."

Cyrus' muscles tensed. "Fine," he snarled, pointing at his brother. "I'll find them and bring them here, but then I want some answers."

"You have my word," Darren said.

Cyrus tilted his head at his brother, then left the office. Glancing down at the paper in his hand, his ran his finger over the names.

Sasha McDaniel.
Benjamin Trest.

Repeating Sasha's name in his mind sent a shudder through his body, a tingle in his chest he didn't care to really investigate.

Whoever these two were, he knew he needed to find them. And fast. Scanning the first address Darren had listed, he smirked. It had been a while since he'd been on a good hunt. It was usually for demons, and those hunts had always been exhausting and dangerous. He had a feeling this was going to prove easier.

Thinking about downtown, he allowed himself to be pulled into the shadows. He pictured the coffee shop they'd last been to.

God, they aren't even trying to be sly.

Before Darren could even shut down his computer, this little trip was going to be over and he'd be back home. Hell, he'd probably be back before dinner.

After all, what trouble could a woman and some kid be?

E.F. Rose

Want to know what trouble the boys get themselves into next? Be sure to keep on the lookout for the next book in The Fallen Guardians Series....

Twisted Mercy

The Fallen Guardians Series, Book 4

Coming Soon

E.F. Rose

Author's Notes

Wow, I can't believe Nicky's book is finally finished. I absolutely love Nicholas and hope I did his story justice. I have a feeling there is more to come for Nicholas and Amy. She's talking wedding, and he's giving me nervous looks. For now, though, it's time to start concentrating on one of the other brothers. I have a few people who have been asking me about Cyrus. He's let me know it's his turn... Bossy man!

Before I go, though, I just want to say that I wouldn't be where I am without the amazing group of people I have backing me up. These individuals are not only my family, my friends, but also my lifeline that I can count on, my rock in a sea of uncertainty. I don't really feel saying thank you is truly enough for the support some of them have given me, but here goes...

To my mom, dad, sister, fiancé, and soon-to-be mother-in-law – Thank you for being my cheerleaders, for forgiving me my disappearing act when I hit the writing cave, and for always being there when I need you. Love you guys!

To my amazing editor, Kim – You help give my words life and my characters a voice. Thank you so much for all you do!

To Diana at Diana M. Photography – Thank you for yet another gorgeous cover. It is exactly what I wanted to see for Nicholas. It's just beautiful. You're the best, girl, and I love you to pieces.

To Lacey, my soul sister – Thank you for helping me work through some of my ideas and for the long nights just chatting about where to take my boys from here.

To my author sisters and book besties, Karen and Brittany – Thanks to you two, I was able to stay somewhat sane during this crazy journey. I know you guys have been itching to get Nicky's book. I hope I did you proud!

To my beta readers, Julie, Riann and Jenny – You three are absolutely amazing and helped me make Nicky's book what it is today. I can't thank you enough for all your help and invaluable suggestions. Hugs!!

To the best fan group in the whole world, the Sinful Smutters – You guys just rock my world and I love you all!

Above all, thank you, the person who picked up my book and decided to give me a chance. With all the amazing authors and stories out there, the fact you chose my book means more to me than you will ever know.

Well, dolls... I'm going to head off now, back to my writing cave to start working on more from the characters who you love. I hope you have enjoyed Nicky's story as much as I have. I know for a fact that he and his brothers love taking you along with them as they continue to mess up Andras' plans and find their happily ever after.

So, until next time, my loves...

Dance like nobody can see you... Laugh like you can't get enough... And never, ever stop reaching for your dreams!

E.F. Rose

About the Author

E.F. Rose lives in the Central Valley of California, surrounded by her family, friends and fiancé. She has always enjoyed writing and considers herself to be a multi-genre author, urban fantasy and dark romance being her main focus. If she isn't writing up a storm, Emily can probably be found chatting with friends online, reading a good book or out enjoying life.

"You are my drive, my inspiration, the life behind my words." ~ E.F. Rose

E.F. Rose

My Work

Echoes (A Book of Poetry)

The Fallen Guardians Series

Divinely Entwined (Book 1) – Christian & Ella
Bound in Fate (Book 2) – Manuel & Hayley
Faithfully Entangled (Book 3) - Nicholas & Amy *you just read it*
Twisted Mercy (Book 4) – Cyrus' Story *coming soon*

Contact Information

You can email me at...
emilyfrose13@gmail.com

or follow me on....

Facebook @
www.facebook.com/DarkestRose13
https://www.facebook.com/groups/sinfuls
mutters/

Twitter @
www.twitter.com/Emily_F_Rose

E.F. Rose